Sons of Thunder

www.rbooks.co.uk

Also by Giles Kristian

Raven: Blood Eye

For more information on Giles Kristian and his books,
see his website at www.gileskristian.com

SONS OF THUNDER

The Second RAVEN Adventure

Giles Kristian

BANTAM PRESS

LONDON · TORONTO · SYDNEY · AUCKLAND · JOHANNESBURG

TRANSWORLD PUBLISHERS
61–63 Uxbridge Road, London W5 5SA
A Random House Group Company
www.rbooks.co.uk

First published in Great Britain
in 2010 by Bantam Press
an imprint of Transworld Publishers

A CIP catalogue record for this book
is available from the British Library.

ISBNs 9780593061640 (cased)
9780593061657 (tpb)

Addresses for Random House Group Ltd companies outside the UK
can be found at: www.randomhouse.co.uk
The Random House Group Ltd Reg. No. 954009

The Random House Group Limited supports The Forest Stewardship Council (FSC),
the leading international forest-certification organization. All our titles that are
printed on Greenpeace-approved FSC-certified paper carry the FSC logo.
Our paper procurement policy can be found at www.rbooks.co.uk/environment

Typeset in 11½/14½pt Sabon by
Kestrel Data, Exeter, Devon.
Printed and bound in Great Britain by
Clays Ltd, Bungay, Suffolk.

2 4 6 8 10 9 7 5 3 1

Mixed Sources
Product group from well-managed
forests and other controlled sources
www.fsc.org Cert no. TT-COC-2139
FSC   © 1996 Forest Stewardship Council

Sons of Thunder is for my parents,
who sent the wind and turned the tide

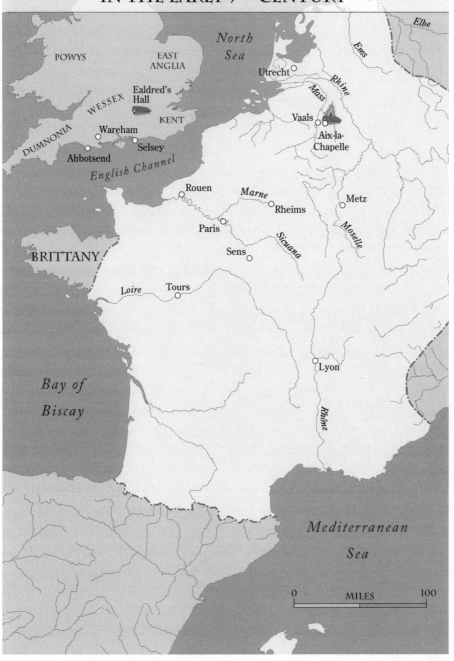

CHARLEMAGNE'S EMPIRE
IN THE EARLY 9TH CENTURY

POWYS

EAST
ANGLIA

North
Sea

Utrecht

Elbe

Ems

Rhine

Maas

WESSEX

Ealdred's
Hall

KENT

Vaals

Aix-la-
Chapelle

DUMNONIA

Wareham

Selsey

Abbotsend

English Channel

Rouen

Marne

Rheims

Metz

Moselle

Paris

Sequana

BRITTANY

Sens

Loire

Tours

Lyon

Bay of

Biscay

Rhône

Mediterranean

Sea

0   MILES   100

LIST OF CHARACTERS

NORSEMEN

Osric (Raven)
Sigurd the Lucky, a jarl
Olaf (Uncle), shipmaster of *Serpent*
Knut, steersman of *Serpent*
Bragi the Egg, shipmaster of *Fjord-Elk*
Kjar, steersman of *Fjord-Elk*
Asgot, a godi
Svein the Red
Black Floki
Bjarni, brother of Bjorn
Bjorn, brother of Bjarni
Bram the Bear
Bothvar
Arnvid
Aslak
Gunnar
Halfdan
Halldor, cousin of Floki
Hastein

Hedin
Gap-toothed Ingolf
Kalf
Orm
Osk
Osten
Ulf
Yrsa Pig-nose

WESSEXMEN

Ealdred, an ealdorman
Cynethryth, his daughter
Father Egfrith, a monk
Penda
Mauger
Baldred
Cynric
Gytha
Ulfbert
Wiglaf

FRANKS

King/Emperor Karolus (Charlemagne)
Alcuin, his adviser
Fulcarius, commander of the shore guard
Radulf, a reeve
Bernart, a soldier
Arthmael, a soldier
Winigis, a fisherman
Borgon, bishop of Aix-la-Chapelle
Arno, a priest
Abbess Berta

DANES

Steinn, son of Inge
Rolf

GODS

Óðin, the All-Father. God of warriors and war, wisdom and
   poetry
Frigg, wife of Óðin
Thór, slayer of giants and god of thunder. Son of Óðin
Baldr, the beautiful. Son of Óðin
Týr, Lord of Battle
Loki, the Mischiefmonger. Father of lies
Rán, Mother of the Waves
Njörd, Lord of the Sea and god of wind and flame
Frey, god of fertility, marriage and growing things
Freyja, goddess of love and sex
Hel, both the goddess of the underworld and the place of the
   dead, specifically those who perish of sickness or old age
Völund, god of the forge and of experience
Eir, a healing goddess and handmaiden of Frigg
Heimdall, Warden of the gods

MYTHOLOGY

Aesir, the Norse gods
Midgard, the place where men live. The world
Asgard, home of the gods
Valhöll, Óðin's hall of the slain
Yggdrasil, the World-Tree. A holy place for the gods
Bifröst, the Rainbow-Bridge connecting the worlds of the
   gods and men
Ragnarök, Doom of the gods

Valkyries, Choosers of the slain
Norns, the three weavers who determine the fates of men
Fenrir, the mighty Wolf
Jörmungand, the Midgard-Serpent
Hugin (Thought), one of the two ravens belonging to Óðin
Munin (Memory), one of the two ravens belonging to Óðin
Mjöllnir, the magic hammer of Thór
Gjallarbrú, the bridge to the Underworld
Módgud, Giantess who guards the bridge over the river Gjöll
Gjallarhorn, 'Yelling horn' which Heimdall sounds to mark
    the beginning of Ragnarök
Urd, one of the Norns
Fimbulvetr, 'Terrible winter', heralding the beginning of
    Ragnarök
Bilskírnir, 'Lightning Crack', Thór's own hall
Fáfnir, 'Embracer', a dragon that guards a great treasure
    hoard
Sleipnir, the eight-legged grey horse of Óðin
Tanngnjóst (Gnash-tooth) and Tanngrísnir (Snarl-tooth), the
    goats who pull Thór's chariot
Gleipnir, the magic fetter forged of a mountain's roots and
    bird's spittle, which restrained the wolf Fenrir

Men with arms of iron
Drove the tired spruce oars
Through the snaking Frankish river.
Brothers now in slaughter,
Saxon, Dane and Sword-Norse,
Fled the Emperor's anger.
Far from fjord and mountain,
Across the storm-tossed sea,
A hoard of fame was waiting.

Raven's Saga

PROLOGUE

HAVE YOU EVER SAILED IN A LONGSHIP? NOT A STUBBY, ROBUST knörr laden with trade goods and wallowing like a packhorse across the sea, but a sleek, deathly quick, terror-stirring thing – a dragon ship. Have you ever stood at the bow with the salt wind whipping your hair as Rán's white-haired daughters cream beneath the beast's strong, curving chest? Have you travelled the whale road with wind-burnt warriors whose rare skill with axe and sword is a gift from mighty Óðin, Lord of War? Men whose death work feeds the wolf and the eagle and the raven? I have done all this. It has been my life and though it would make those skirt-wearing White Christ followers sick with disgust (and fear, I shouldn't wonder) I have been happy with my lot. For some men are born closer to the gods than others. By the well of Urd, beneath one of the roots of the great life tree Yggdrasil, the Norns, those sisters of fate, of present and future, take the threads of men's lives and weave them into patterns full of pain and suffering, glory and riches, and death. And their ancient fingers must have tired at the spinning of my life. Ah, but wait. The ale has greased my tongue and it slides ahead of itself. Come in, Arnor! Come flatten some straw,

Gunnkel, we have all night ahead of us and very far to go. That is if my old head has not leaked memories like a rotten pail. Last night you heard just the beginning, slurped merely the froth from the mead horn. Now, together, we shall drink more. That's it, Hallfred, stir some life back into the embers. Make the flames dance. Make them leap like the fires of Völund's own forge. Yes, yes, there you go. Ingvar, give that threadbare hound of yours something to eat, for the love of Thór! He's been chewing some poor clod's shoe for the last hour! Is young Runa not here? That is a shame. There's nothing like a plump pair of tits to make an old man add a little more gilt to his tale. I'm no skald, I admit. My only song has been the sword song, the whisper of the great bearded axe as I made it dance before my enemy's shieldwall. But skalds venture so far up their own arseholes that a man cannot smell the flowers amongst the farts. In their tales they paint Sigurd as one of the Aesir, the gods of Asgard, his sword the slayer of mountain giants. Their Raven is a red-eyed monster, an ugly death-sowing beast. Pah! What do they know? Did they ride the whale road with Sigurd the Lucky? Whoresons. Sigurd was a man. His sword was like any other sword, a thing forged of iron and steel by another man who knew his business. As for myself, am I a monster? I was handsome . . . after a fashion. I was young, anyway, and that is good enough. I had grown from carpenter's apprentice, from a boy skulking on the toe end of his village, to a wolf amongst a pack of wolves. I was part of a fellowship of warriors. I had become a rider of the waves and a killer of men.

So, haul up the anchor. Raise the old battered sail. Tomorrow's labour is far away and the night stretches before us like the starlit ocean on a spring night. So . . . we are away . . .

CHAPTER ONE

YOU DO NOT BETRAY A FELLOWSHIP AND LIVE TO SEE YOUR HAIR turn white. For a fellowship is an honour- and oath-forged thing, as strong as a bear, as fast as a dragon ship, and as vengeful as the sea. If you betray a fellowship you are a dead man, and Ealdorman Ealdred of Wessex had betrayed us.

With the sail up and the spruce oars stowed, the men looked to their gear. They took whetstones to sword edges, patiently working out the notches carved in battle, and the rhythmic scraping was to me a soothing sound above their murmured conversations and the wet whisper of *Serpent*'s bow through the sea. Men laid mail brynjas across their knees, checking for damaged rings which they replaced with ones taken from brynjas stripped from the dead. Two of the Norsemen were throwing a heavy-looking sack back and forth, grunting with the effort. The sack was filled with coarse sand and if you put your mail in it and threw it around the sand would clean the rust from the mail and make it as new again. Other men were smearing their brynjas with sheep grease, winding new leather and fine copper wire around sword grips, mending shield straps and stretching new hides across the limewood planks. Dents were hammered out of helmets, spear blades were honed to wicked points slender enough to skewer a snail from its shell, and axe heads were checked to make sure they would not fly off at the first swing. Silver was weighed, furs were examined and men argued or grumbled or boasted about the booty they had piled in their journey chests. We combed fleas from our beards and hair, relived fights, exaggerating our deeds and prowess, played tafl, checked *Serpent*'s caulking, laid leather strips in boots to fix holes. We nursed wounds, exchanged stories about friends now sitting at Óðin's mead bench in Valhöll, watched gulls soaring high above, and revelled in the creak of the ship and the low thrum of the rigging. And all the while we believed Njörd, god of the sea, who is kind to those who honour him, filled our sail and that we would soon spy our quarry, *Fjord-Elk*, as a speck on the sunlit horizon.

For we were blessed with a lusty following wind and were making good progress so that the land of the West Saxons was soon little more than a green ribbon on the horizon to the north. If Njörd's favour held, Sigurd would sail *Serpent* through the night to try to shorten the distance between us and *Fjord-Elk*, and when we came across her and the treacherous men who sailed her, our swords and our axes would run red.

Asgot the godi produced a hare from an oiled sack. It was a mangy thing that must have been kicking and scratching furiously ever since we set off, for its fur was sweat-soaked, its mouth was bloodied and its eyes were wild with fear. The godi took its head in one old fist, drew his wicked knife and jabbed it into the animal's chest. Its long feet ran hopelessly in the air. Then Asgot dragged the blade along the hare's belly. Some of its guts fell across *Serpent*'s sheer strake and still it kicked as though it hoped to dash across a summer meadow. Then he wiped the bloody knife on the hare's fur, sheathed it, and ripped out the rest of the guts, the throbbing heart and the dark twine of the creature's intestines, and threw them into the sea, followed by the carcass itself. We watched for a while as the waves bore the tiny offering away, and then *Serpent* carried us on and the hare was lost amongst Rán's daughters. All the while Asgot spoke to the gods, asking them to bless us with fair seas and good weather. Father Egfrith made the sign of the cross to ward off Asgot's old magic and I believed he was muttering counter-spells, though I stayed away, not wanting those Christ words to maggot into my ears.

It would be a blood-drenched fight, this one. A real gut-ripper. For Ealdorman Ealdred of Wessex and his champion Mauger were feckless, snot-swilling whoresons who had betrayed us all. Ealdred had the holy gospel book of Saint Jerome, which we had stolen from the king of Mercia, and the toad's arsehole raced now to sell that Christian treasure to the emperor of the Franks, Charlemagne, or King Karolus as some called him then. The worm would become as rich as a king, having betrayed us and left us for dead. But Ealdred's god and that god's peace-loving son were not strong enough to make all this happen. They could not save him from us who held to the true gods, the old gods who still shake the sky with thunder and curse the ocean with waves as high as cliffs. And I believed that we would catch the half-cocked maggot the next day or the day after that, because the English did not know *Fjord-Elk*, did not know her ways. For ships are like women – you cannot touch one in the same places as another and hope to get the same ride. But Sigurd knew every inch of *Serpent*, and his steersman Knut knew every grain of salt in every rolling wave. We would catch the English and then we would kill them.

'These Christians know how to puke, Raven!' Bjorn called, the sunlight gleaming across his teeth. 'The fish will eat well today, I think.'

'And we shall eat the fish and therefore be eating Christian puke,' I said in Norse so that Cynethryth would not understand.

She and Penda leant side by side over the sheer strake, emptying their guts into a sea so calm that Bjorn's brother Bjarni was bailing *Serpent*'s bilge with all the urgency of a cow on its way to the slaughter. I had seen *Serpent* flex and writhe like a supple sea creature, so that water continuously seeped in through the seams of her clinkered hull. But not that day. On that day the sea was calm as a breeze-stirred lake, yet it was enough to curdle the Saxons' stomachs. The Norsemen were grinning and laughing at the two new crewmen, and whilst I pitied Cynethryth I was happy it was not me they were laughing at this time, because I had done my share of puking in the early days.

As for Penda, the Wessexman was as vicious a man as I have ever known, and I had seen him slaughter the Welsh outside Caer Dyffryn so that the green pasture turned blood-slick. But Penda did not look vicious now, with his spew splashing on to the glass-like surface of the sea.

'It's not fucking natural to float across the sea on a piece of kindling,' Penda said, turning from the ship's side and dragging the back of his hand across his mouth. 'It's not civilized,' he growled, and I smiled because Penda was as civilized as a pail full of thunder.

Sigurd grinned knowingly at me because he knew I had stood in Penda's shoes not so long ago, but though this was true I would never have referred to *Serpent* as 'kindling'. I had always appreciated her workmanship, because I had been apprenticed to old Ealhstan the carpenter and so I knew woodcraft when I saw it. *Serpent* was a beauty. Seventy-six feet in length, seventeen feet in the beam and made from more than two hundred oak trees, she could originally accommodate sixteen oarsmen on either side, but Sigurd had built raised fighting platforms at bow and stern, meaning now there was only space for thirteen rowers on each side. With our crew of thirty-two men and one woman it was to my mind a little cramped, but not uncomfortable. Olaf told me that on one of Sigurd's expeditions, when *Serpent* was newly built and before he had *Fjord-Elk*, she had carried a double crew of seventy warriors, one crew resting whilst the other rowed. This must surely have been a useful thing when it came to a fight, but I could not imagine sharing sleeping space with so many fart-stinking men. The ship had a small open hold for trade goods and supplies and a sturdy mast step and keel. She was fourteen strakes high, had a great square sail of wool which had been dyed red, and at her bow stood the head of Jörmungand, the Midgard-Serpent that encircles the earth. That beast's faded red eyes stared out across the grey sea, into our futures. Every Norseman aboard, every warrior sitting on the sea chest containing his possessions, respected *Serpent* as they respected their mothers, loved her as they loved their wives, and relished her as they relished their whores.

Cynethryth turned round, palming sweat from her forehead, and I swear her face was as green as a new fern. She caught my eye and seemed embarrassed so I looked away, pointing out to Black Floki a length of tarred rope caulking which was working itself free of two of the strakes beside him. The Norseman grunted and with a gnarled thumb began to press the thin rope back in. Once I had thought Floki hated me, but we had since grown close, as sword-brothers do. Today though it seemed he was back to his miserable, brooding self.

Father Egfrith, as far as I could tell, suffered no ill-effects from *Serpent*'s motion and maybe that had something to do with Glum's having cracked open his head with a sword blow. Somehow, the little monk had survived. Worse than that, he had chosen to come aboard – an odd path for a monk to board a ship full of heathens – and maybe that had something to do with the sword blow too. He was a sniffling little mörd, a weasel, but in a strange way I admired him because he must

F/2215204

have known that any of us could squash him like a louse if he gave us reason, or merely for want of something to do. Truly, the Christ slave believed he would turn *Serpent* into a ship full of Christians, just as he boasted his god had turned water into wine. Though if you ask me, turning Norsemen into Christians would be more like changing wine into piss. Perhaps he even hoped to change *Serpent*'s name to *Holy Spirit* or *The Jerusalem* or *Christ's Hairy Left Ball* or who knows what? Egfrith was a fool.

By the time the day's heat had been chased away by a cold breeze whipping off the sea and the gold disc of the sun had rolled into the west, we had yet to set eyes on *Fjord-Elk*. At *Serpent*'s prow Jörmungand nodded gently, its faded red eyes staring seaward, tirelessly searching for her sister ship. I almost believed the snarling figurehead would give a roar of triumph if *Fjord-Elk* came into sight.

'I am thinking that the crawling piece of pig's dung might have set a more easterly course than our own,' Olaf said, dipping a cup into the rain barrel and slurping. He stood by Knut, who gripped the tiller with the familiarity of a man holding his wife's hand. Sigurd was behind and above them, standing on the fighting platform, looking out as the sun which plunged towards the world's rim washed his long fair hair with golden light.

'You think he's that shrewd?' Knut asked, hawking and spitting a gob of phlegm over *Serpent*'s side. Olaf shrugged.

'I think he's got the sense,' Sigurd said, 'to take the shortest crossing and then head south within spitting distance of the coast rather than crossing the open sea as we have done. Then he will enter the mouth of the Sicauna, that great river that eats into the heart of Frankia.' Olaf raised one bushy eyebrow sceptically, but I thought Sigurd was probably right. As a Christian lord, Ealdorman Ealdred would have less to fear from Frankish ships patrolling the coast than we as pagans

22

would. He would also have more to fear from open water than us, for even though the sailing conditions were perfect now, a sudden change in the weather or an irreparable leak could make a man wish he had stayed in sight of land. And Ealdred did not know *Fjord-Elk*.

A quizzical look nestled itself amongst Olaf's bushy beard, like a dog settling in a pile of straw. 'So, that English arse leaf is sucking the coast like it's his mother's tit,' he said, 'and that's why we've not had so much as a sniff of him.'

Sigurd pursed his lips, scratched his own golden beard, but did not reply. He looked up at the square sail, studying the way the wind moved across it, rippling the cloth. He watched the dance of the thick sheet ropes and the direction of the waves and then he looked towards the sun. It was low, so gave him a reliable east–west bearing. His thick lips curled like a wolf's just before the teeth are bared, because if he was right and Ealdred had crossed the shortest stretch of sea, putting him further north along the Frankish coastline, then all we had to do when we came to the coast was choose a mooring with a good view of the open channel. And wait.

With dusk came land. Frankia. I knew nothing of Frankia then, but even so the word was a heavy one. It was a word that meant power, a word that carried with it, at least to pagan ears, the threat of sharpened steel and hateful warriors and the new, ravenously hungry magic – the magic of the White Christ. For the king of the Franks was Karolus, lord of Christendom. Emperor they called him, as the Romans had named their kings who ruled lands as far and wide as the skies above. And despite his fealty to the nailed god, men said this Emperor Karolus was the greatest warrior in the entire world.

'Can you smell that?' Father Egfrith called. He was standing at *Serpent*'s prow, being careful not to touch the carved beast-head of Jörmungand. Perhaps he feared it had a taste for

23

Christians. 'You can smell the piety!' he called, sniffing eagerly, crinkling his weasel-like face in pleasure. The coast loomed ahead, a low, green line broken by grey rock. 'The Franks are a God-fearing people and their king is a light in the darkness. He is the cleansing fire that guides men from iniquity, like a beacon, a great, wind-whipped flame which saves ships from splintering against the rocks,' he said, taking altogether too much pleasure in the comparison. 'If we are lucky, Raven, we will meet the great king, and because God loves him, and because Karolus is said to be a generous and gracious king, maybe you will be given the chance to wash your black soul. Scrape the sin from it like fat from a calf's skin. Christ the Almighty will drag Satan out of your blood-filled eye by his gnarly ankle.' The mörd was grinning and I wondered what it would feel like to put that grin through the back of his head. But then I smiled, because although Egfrith thought I was the spawn of Satan, worthless as snail slime, there was something about him that I had come to like. No, not like. Rather the little man amused me.

'Your god had better have strong arms, monk,' I said, encompassing *Serpent*'s Norse crew with a sweep of my own arm, 'if he is to yank the devil from us all. Perhaps he will find Satan hiding in Bram's armpit, or skulking up Svein's arse.'

'Sin has no refuge, young man,' Egfrith chided, as *Serpent* reared a rogue wave, causing him to unbalance and stumble, though he somehow kept his feet without reaching for Jörmungand. 'For the wages of sin is death; but the gift of God is eternal life through Jesus Christ our Lord!'

'What's the little man creaking on about, Raven?' Svein the Red asked, turning to me, his massive head cocked to one side. He was tugging a new ivory comb though his thick red hair and I guessed he had already forgotten about his old one with the missing teeth. Svein was the biggest man I had ever seen, a fearsome warrior of few words, and he was watching Father Egfrith the way a battle-scarred hound watches a playful pup.

'He says his god wants to look for Satan up your arse,' I said in Norse. 'I told him you might enjoy that.' The others laughed but Svein frowned, his hairy red brows meeting above his bulbous nose.

'Tell him that he and his god are welcome to anything that comes out of my arse,' he said, rousing more 'hey's. Then he lifted his right buttock and farted and Rán must have heard it at the bottom of the sea. 'There you go, Christ slave,' he said, 'come and get it while it's warm.'

The smile was still on my face when I caught Cynethryth's eye. I clenched my teeth and cursed myself for an insensitive fool. Cynethryth's eyes, the colour of ivy, were distant and heavy, as though she saw in mine the terrible events that had ripped her life apart. Her soul was singed by those memories like silk left too near a flame. Her face was pale and drawn from the seasickness and yet she was still beautiful. She blinked slowly, as though in nothingness there was freedom, then she turned away to watch the distant shore as *Serpent* slithered through the sea. The girl, thin as a birch sapling, had all but carried me away from a fight with the Welsh when I was too weak to carry myself. Together we had hidden in a hollow oak and she had stitched my shoulder and fed me berries from the forest and kept watch for our enemies. But her father had betrayed us and now, with the Frankish coast looming, Cynethryth must have known it would not be long until we faced Ealdred. She knew also that we had nothing for that treacherous worm but cold, ripping steel. Every man aboard was a better warrior than I, except for Father Egfrith I dare say, and so now, despite what I had hoped earlier, it seemed unlikely that I would be the one to kill Ealdred. Yet for his betrayal of my jarl and for the hurt he had caused Cynethryth, but most of all because I was young and ruled by pride, I wished Ealdred to die by my blade. Maybe with the ealdorman dead and cold Cynethryth would gain some peace. But maybe she would hate me.

CHAPTER TWO

'REEF THE SAIL, LADS. WE'D BETTER REIN HER IN A LITTLE, UNLESS any of you whoresons can swear on your mother's milk that these Franks don't have rocks in their sea,' Olaf called from the tiller, stirring a flurry of movement from six Norsemen who seemed relieved to have something to do. Two of them released the halyard, lowering the sail some way down the mast, and this itself was enough to slow *Serpent*. The other four rolled the bottom surplus of the sail tightly and evenly, then lashed it with the short lanyards. The men on the halyard hauled rhythmically, stretching *Serpent*'s faded red sail up again so that the wind caught it with a loud snap. The whole manoeuvre took the time it takes a man to empty his bowels, and Olaf's indifference suggested he expected no less efficiency from his crew. Olaf was Jarl Sigurd's second, his most trusted captain and his friend. He had been the first of Sigurd's wolves, the first to swear his life and his sword to the jarl, and the other men affectionately called him uncle because he was older and more experienced than any of them except old Asgot, Sigurd's godi.

Olaf, Sigurd and Knut had been deep in conversation at

Serpent's stern since before the yellow sun touched the western sea. Now, somewhere beyond our senses, the hiss of fire in water declared the day's end and so we had to make landfall before we risked running *Serpent* on to submerged rocks. According to the steersman Knut, the land towards which the dragon ship's prow pointed was a place called Bayeux. We would have to turn into the wind now and point east or else risk being blown past the Sicauna's estuary, which would then mean a slow and dull tack north against the wind. This could ruin our chances of catching *Fjord-Elk* before she entered the river's mouth.

'Now, Raven, we have to make a choice,' Sigurd said. 'Do we want to frighten these Frankish spirits away? Or do we come in peace?' I knew he referred to *Serpent*'s carved prow, Jörmungand, which was either left in place or stowed depending on the Norsemen's intentions. We could leave it staring balefully at this new land, but perhaps the land spirits, who were unknown to us, would be provoked rather than scared away and maybe those spirits were powerful.

'I would stow her,' I said, nodding at the figurehead, 'until we know more about this land.'

He nodded. 'Bjorn! Bjarni! We are traders today!' he called, and the brothers grinned as they stood from their journey chests and weaved their way to the ship's bow. They would detach Jörmungand and place her in *Serpent*'s hold. There the beast would wait patiently in the dark beneath a layer of skins, red eyes always staring, tooth-filled maw ever hungry.

I knew, despite his orders, that Sigurd had not made his decision on my counsel. Sigurd was an awe-inspiring warrior, but even he would not come as a blood-crazed bear to an unknown land. He had been testing me, for Sigurd always believed that a jarl should possess both the low cunning of Óðin and the brute strength of Thór. He owned both qualities in equal measure and that was why his men would follow him to the ocean's end.

But even though we would come in peace, we must prepare for a fight. There was a flurry of activity as the men readied for landfall. We helped each other into our mail, never an easy thing on a moving boat – one man holding the brynja up so his pal could wriggle into it. Bram Bear helped me with mine and as always I was surprised by the sudden weight of the thing. It had belonged to Sigurd's oathman Glum, but Glum had been a greedy lump of goat shit. He had betrayed Sigurd and now he was dead.

I twice thanked the Welsh blades that killed him, first because he deserved to die and secondly because his fine brynja was now mine. Few men owned mail, but every warrior in Sigurd's Wolfpack did, and good mail will turn a blade aside, which meant that one of Sigurd's wolves was worth four men in leather armour. And in those days I was young and eager to prove that I deserved that brynja and was worthy to wear what cost a fat hoard to buy.

'We want a quiet mooring,' Sigurd said to his steersman.

Knut pulled his long thin beard through his fist and nodded. 'Somewhere sheltered but with a nice view of the sea, hey,' he said.

'A wolf must have his lair,' Sigurd agreed, throwing his green cloak around his shoulders and pinning it at the neck with a silver wolf's head brooch. All the men were putting on cloaks so that their mail brynjas would be mostly concealed, at least from any distance, and I made sure my own brown cloak hid the sword at my hip. That sword too had belonged to Glum and it was a fine thing. It had a five-lobed pommel with silver inlay and twisted silver wire. On the crossguard the smith had traced eight tiny Thór's hammers, four on each side, and each was perfect, showing that the smith knew his work and was skilled. Glum must have paid much silver for the weapon or

29

else killed a rich lord in battle and taken it. Perhaps he had even stolen it, though I doubted it, for even though in the end Glum had broken his oath and betrayed his jarl, he had once been an honourable man. But he was a simple man too, and Sigurd's ways had befogged him. Where Glum would have made blood sacrifice, slaughtering a man for no better reason than because Glum feared the Norns and the gods, Sigurd would trust his own judgement. Where Glum would strike first and think later, Sigurd would weigh possible outcomes like hack silver on the scales, choosing the course that he could most easily read. Not that Sigurd was necessarily more cautious. I believed he would wrestle the Midgard-Serpent if he knew the skalds were watching, so that they could sing of it and their descendants' lips would still be wet with it a hundred years after his death.

As I looked at Sigurd then, in his fine mail and with his great sword, the sword of his father, I thought of the hero Beowulf who slew the monster Grendal, whose stories had filled my head on cold nights around the hearth. I thought of brave Týr, god of battle, of mighty Thór the Lord of Thunder, and of Óðin god of war, Father of the Slain and Master of the Fray. For Jarl Sigurd was the marrow of our ambitions. He was the legends and the tales and the fireside whispers. But the ledge he walked was a narrow one and I think he knew it, too. Either the gods would love him and favour him because he was a great warrior and wise, or they would be jealous of him and seek his destruction. These were the thoughts that filled my head as we came to the Frankish coast, a stone's throw from rocks and small islands, seeking a bay in which to plunge *Serpent*'s anchor.

My mouth was as dry as a herring hung in the wind, but I was not the only one on edge. I saw other Norsemen licking salt-cracked lips, clenching and unclenching their fists, and plaiting their hair to keep their hands busy. The coast we had come to, as dusk filled the world, looked windswept and empty, but that was not to say there were not warriors waiting in the long grass, crouching behind boulders and lurking in the shady marshes. A lookout on a high bluff would have seen *Serpent*'s red sail long before we could have seen him, and by now there might be a hundred warriors waiting to cut us down when we waded through the surf. We rounded a bluff where the water broke, sucked and plunged, and beyond it we came to a bay carved out by an eternity of wind and waves. As we drew closer the air filled with a keening noise, which at first I took to be an effect of the wind, perhaps made louder by the surrounding rocks. Then I noticed that the sounds were slightly different in pitch and suddenly I understood. Seals! The black and brown 'rocks' were not rocks at all. Dozens of seals were hauled up on every kelp-slick skerry and crag, moaning and crying without seeming to, the way bees or flies hum.

'Get the sail down, lads,' Olaf called, gesturing for two men to ready the anchor, which was a boulder wedged into a wooden frame tied to a length of thick rope. 'Oars out. Easy now.' He moved to *Serpent*'s bow so that he could watch out for submerged rocks. Hastein, a squat man with a round face, red cheeks and yellow hair, was already there, leaning over *Serpent*'s sheer strake, taking depth measurements. He used a line on the end of which was tied a lead weight. Every time the weight reached the ocean bottom, Hastein hauled it back in and measured the line against the distance between his outstretched arms. He tapped the lead weight's hollow bottom against his palm, depositing a dollop of wet sand there and holding it up for Olaf and Knut to see. Olaf nodded.

'It's a nice sandy bottom!' he called to Sigurd. 'And a rising tide.'

Sigurd nodded because these conditions favoured us. We could, if we wished to, ride *Serpent* right in, beaching her above the high water mark. I plunged my oar's blade into the swelling surf with short chops, thinking that we were lucky and that the omens were good. But Sigurd had other ideas. He strode down from the stern fighting platform and marched along the deck, past us all, towards Hastein.

'How tall are you, Hastein?' he asked.

The man frowned. 'Five and a half feet, lord.' I suspected he was shorter and so did Sigurd by the smile that touched his lips.

'Then you had better shout when we come to five feet of water, Hastein, otherwise you'll hope you're here because your mother fucked a fish.' He turned to face us all. 'Hitch up your skirts, ladies. I have heard the water in Frankia is especially wet.'

There were a few groans because no one liked to get seawater in his mail. There was also the very real possibility of a man's drowning if he jumped off a boat wearing his brynja.

'Stop your whining, you farts,' Olaf bellowed, tying his helmet's leather chin strap. 'You'll be lucky if Karolus himself isn't somewhere up there waiting to send the White Christ's legions against us with swords of fire and pagan-gutting spears!'

'I'd rather jump into the middle of a hundred Christians than paddle to shore like a dog,' Svein the Red grumbled, thumping his helmet down as the anchor was lowered over *Serpent*'s stern with a splosh. Two bow ropes would be taken ashore and tied to trees or rocks, making the ship fast in the bay where it would be safe from rocks and enemies alike. I wondered what Svein had to complain about, as he was so tall that the water would only come up to his chest whilst it leaked into other's mouths.

'Bjorn and Bjarni, you'll stay aboard with Knut and the girl,' Olaf said as we dipped the oars in the darkening water, carefully manoeuvring *Serpent* so that her prow remained facing the beach, whilst Hastein and a man named Yrsa slipped over the side with the thick mooring ropes. When *Serpent* was leashed, we stowed the oars and plugged the ports. Then we dropped into the cold sea, each of us holding his sword above his head so that the fleece-lined scabbards would not fill with salt water and take an age to dry. I gripped *Serpent*'s sheer strake whilst my feet sought something solid and I knew that the shield slung across my back would prove a terrible encumbrance in the waves and currents.

'I want to come, Raven,' Cynethryth said suddenly, leaning over to me as I hung there afraid I would lose my footing and that the mail would drag me spluttering to the seabed. I tried to hide the panic in my face but must have only succeeded in looking angry. 'Why should I stay aboard? My head has been churning all day and my stomach hurts from being sick. I just want some time away from you stinking men! I want some privacy. Can you understand that?'

I clung to *Serpent*, up to my chest in cold water, dreading letting go of the ship. The sea is a killer of men, and the Franks were killers of heathens. A wave rolled over me and the salt water went down my throat, making me retch horribly. 'Besides,' Cynethryth said, the hint of a smile playing at the corners of her lips, 'you look as though you need some help. The others are halfway to the beach already.'

'Do what you want, woman,' I said, then let go, splashing into the sea. I was relieved when my toes stirred the soft seabed. I turned to the shore. There was another splash and suddenly Cynethryth was beside me. Then she was swimming ahead, as assuredly as an otter, whilst I lumbered and tiptoed along, looking up at the purple and black rimmed sky and holding my mouth tight against the swells.

'Wait for me, Cynethryth!' Father Egfrith called. It seemed he had finally summoned the courage to go ashore. 'By all the saints, girl, wait for me!' Another splash followed and I gritted my teeth and sprang forward, careless of the sea and Rán's white-haired daughters, because I would rather take on every one of those greedy bitches than let a Christ monk beat me to the shore.

We squeezed the water from our sodden cloaks, jumped up and down in our clinking mail, and squelched about in our boots, all of which made the nearest seals waddle away or slip into the sea. The ones further away paid us no attention at all and I guessed that some of them would wish they had soon enough, for we were hungry. I could see from the high water mark further up the beach, where the sand gave way to rocks and jagged ledges, that the tide was more extreme here in Frankia than it was on the Wessex coast. I hoped Knut had noticed this too and had moored *Serpent* far enough out to prevent her becoming grounded at low tide.

Black Floki was already loping ahead up the beach, spear in hand, his black plaits and shield bouncing as he ran up a narrow trail, heading for a high point from which he could keep watch and gain some idea of where we had landed. Egfrith looked like a drowned rat, his sodden habit clinging to the puny body beneath. I noticed that Cynethryth's dress was clinging too, in an altogether more pleasing way, and after a moment I looked away, feeling a stab of anger when other men did not. Freyja, goddess of beauty, makes men lustful and even shivering from cold, her sopping hair stuck to her white skin, Cynethryth drew men's eyes like a silver torc.

Sigurd pulled his wet yellow hair back, tying it at the nape of his neck, and looked back to *Serpent*, which was nodding gently in the sheltered bay.

'She is so beautiful, hey, Raven.' Low evening light spread pink and orange across the calm water, broken only where the surf rolled in with white hissing foam.

'She is magnificent, lord,' I said, still thinking of Cynethryth.

'There is still a chance the worm Ealdred will pass by this place before dark. But I think it more likely he will have moored somewhere by now and will pass at dawn. So, we stay on this beach until *Fjord-Elk* comes.'

'If we are lucky Njörd will blow her into this very bay,' I said, watching two shrieking gulls high above tumble and plunge in the cooling air. Men said that Njörd loved sunlit coves and creeks because they were home to his sacred sea birds, and so he must have loved this place. Beyond the sand, pink sea thrift grew in low clumps, its bright blossom vibrating in the breeze so that it seemed in that twilight that the ground itself was shivering. Further up, dense sandthorn bushes sat stiff and steadfast, their pale silvery green leaves bearing thousands of bitter berries that would be orange by September.

'Do you still think I deserve my name?' Sigurd said, catching me off guard with the question. I knew he referred to 'the Lucky'. He turned to me, his eyes temperate and unjudging.

'*Serpent*'s hold could not take another brooch pin,' I said, nodding towards the ship. 'You have made your men rich with silver and all kinds of treasures.' I smiled. 'Svein is happy as a hog in shit and all it took was a new comb! And Floki . . . he's content so long as he has something to brood about. Before I saw those seals I thought the noise was just Floki moaning because he was hungry.'

Sigurd dragged his teeth across his lip and made a low hum in his throat. He held my eye a while longer and then blinked slowly, giving the slightest nod. Then he turned on his heel and marched up the beach, his left hand clasping his sword's pommel, barking orders for men to find their own bit of high ground and keep a lookout for *Fjord-Elk*. For a moment I watched him go, taking a deep breath and filling my nose with the oniony smell wafting off the sea thrift's crisp flowers. Then I turned to see Cynethryth appear from behind three sea-smoothed rocks in the surf. I wondered if she was already regretting her decision to leave Wessex and come with us, for she could not hope to enjoy such privacy often amongst the Fellowship. The sun had gone completely now, leaving only gashes of orange light in the grey clouds to the west. On a rock out at sea a cormorant, which had been drying its great black wings, took to the sky, its croak loud and hollow across the water. I sensed Cynethryth beside me.

'He is troubled, your jarl,' she said, her eyes following the bird skyward as it stretched its long neck and flapped away into the gathering night.

'He thinks his luck is falling through his fingers. Like sand,' I said, toeing a wet-looking tangle that looked like a worm. They were everywhere, as were the tiny holes from which they had been excavated. 'He worries that the gods have turned against him and that he cannot give his men that which they desire above all else, above silver and furs and new ivory combs.'

'And what *do* they want, Raven?' Cynethryth asked and I knew she was really asking what did I want. Her eyes searched mine and I felt conscious of my blood-eye, the eye which had caused most men to hate and fear me but for which Sigurd had spared me, thinking I was touched by the gods, by Óðin himself. Before I could answer, something jabbed me in the back and I turned to old Asgot, Sigurd's godi, who seemed about to poke me again with the butt of his spear.

'I've swallowed it now, boy, so you might as well,' he said in his ancient, cracked voice. I was upwind of the man but I still caught his stink and so did Cynethryth, because she put her knuckles to her nose.

'Swallow what?' I asked, as always wary of this man and his strange magic that fed on blood sacrifice.

'You are Óðin's brat.' He screwed up his wind-ravaged face. 'Or, at the least, your life thread is woven into the All-Father's cloak.' His brown teeth built a smile that sent a shudder through me. I wondered by what seidr he had known what I was thinking.

'Sigurd was right about you, for all the good it has done us.' He nodded, planting the spear's butt in the sand. 'You are marked. How else are you still breathing? Half of the warriors who set out with Sigurd are gone. You have stood in the shieldwall with men four times your measure, some of the finest blood-loving wolves our land has weaned. Yet here you are alive and spitting.' He shared that horrible grin with Cynethryth, who frowned back, ill at ease around the godi. 'This one's wyrd is safely hidden beneath the Far-Wanderer's hat, girl,' he said in Norse, which Cynethryth could not understand, 'or the worms would have been sucking his guts by now.' He screwed up his face, adding, 'Isn't that right, Raven?'

'I have been lucky, Asgot,' I said, aware that my hand rested instinctively on the sword hilt at my hip. We touch our weapons for luck and the Christians scorn us for it, but why should we not? Our weapons keep us alive. I have seen the Christians sign crosses over their chests with their fingers. Perhaps that brings them luck. I would like to see them try it in the clash of shieldwalls.

'Lucky, you say?' Again Asgot glanced at Cynethryth, the bones plaited in his hair rattling. His faded blue eyes widened, stretching the old wind-burnt skin at their corners. 'Then perhaps that explains why our jarl's luck is dripping away like snot from a troll's nose. You have stolen Sigurd's luck, Raven. It has jumped,' he suddenly hopped from one foot to the other, 'from him to you, boy, like a louse.' He grinned sourly at Cynethryth, pointing a bony finger at her. 'You should stay . . . away from him,' he said clumsily in English. 'Death follows him. Like a stink.'

'It is your own fetid stench that taints the air, old man,' Cynethryth said, turning her back on the godi. 'Walk with me, Raven. My legs are happy to be on solid ground and itch to move.' We left Asgot cackling with a sound like breaking finger bones.

Further along the beach I saw Bram and Svein bent low, spears in hand, creeping up on a group of five or more slumberous seals, several of which had fox-red fur. I could not imagine two more conspicuous men, and yet by the grin in Bram's beard they seemed confident enough.

'We'll gather some wood for the cookfire,' I told Cynethryth, nodding towards the high ground beyond the beach. 'There should be some at the top of that bluff.' Of course, the higher we went the more chance I would have of catching sight of *Fjord-Elk* riding the dusk waves, though I knew she was more likely to be moored up somewhere for the night, just like us. Still, I stepped ahead of Cynethryth and she followed me, and though I was relieved that Asgot no longer seemed to want to introduce my throat to his sacrificial knife, his talk of my stealing Sigurd's luck froze my chest like January rain in a barrel.

CHAPTER THREE

TWO GREAT IRON COOKING POTS WERE FETCHED FROM *SERPENT* and into them we put the meat and some of the blubber from four seals. Now that the tide was high, the creatures were sleeping in the water, floating upright with just their heads breaking the surface, and we were relieved that they had stopped their strange singing. To the broth we added handfuls of whatever shellfish we had managed to scrounge in the bay, including cockles, mussels and winkles. Arnvid found a clump of fennel and another man, Bothvar, pulled up three large roots of horseradish, which he chopped up and tossed into the bubbling stew, so that our mouths burnt no matter how much water we drank. Bram insisted that ale was the cure, so long as you were prepared to drink enough of it, and we followed his advice wholeheartedly. We soaked this tasty stew up with stale bread taken from the tents on the Wessex shore spread with the remaining seal blubber, which had been melted with a palmful of salt.

'It was a shame to kill that red seal, hey Svein,' Bram said, his bird's-nest beard glistening with grease by the cookfire's stuttering light.

'I am still sad about it,' Svein replied, slurping the broth from a deep spoon. 'She had such pretty eyes.'

'Aye, reminded me of your sister,' Bram dared, winking at Arnvid, who chuckled.

Sigurd had sent men inland to search for any settlements or houses, warning them to make sure they were not seen. The last thing we wanted was a Frankish levy waking us up in the middle of the night, for Father Egfrith had it in his mind that the holy spirit, so strong in this land, would warn the good Christians of the presence of heathens and they would march as one to kill us, brandishing flaming crosses and swords dipped in holy water.

'Then let them come, monk,' Sigurd had said, 'for I've yet to see a wooden cross fare well against a Norse axe, and whether these Franks keep their blades in holy water or barrels of virgins' piss means nothing to me. Such blades will be rusty and not worth fearing.' The Norsemen had laughed at this, but we kept one eye open, just in case.

There was no sign of *Fjord-Elk*. At any one time there were at least six men with their eyes turned to the channel beyond the bay. Even after dark Sigurd set three watches of two men each and these men stared out by the light of the moon and stars in case Ealdred had been daring or stupid enough to follow the coast at night. So we waited, lulled by the ceaseless sighs of the ocean.

I slept next to Cynethryth, which meant I was also close enough to Father Egfrith to hear his constant sniffing and fidgeting. I suspected that being a follower of the White Christ did not protect you from fleas and his habit must have crawled with the biting bastards. I would have wagered the thing would shuffle along the ground of its own accord if the monk ever took it off. But Cynethryth seemed to find some comfort in the man and for this, at least, I was grateful.

As Cynethryth was never far from Egfrith, so the Wessexman

Penda was never far from me. Penda wanted his ealdorman dead as much as any of us did, maybe more so. He no doubt imagined himself swinging the deathblow as payment for Ealdred's treachery, for the ealdorman had as good as killed every Wessexman who had marched into the lands of the Welsh with us. But Penda's bloodlust made him no less wary of the men he now travelled with. For all his wild battle fury and death-skill, the spiky-haired warrior was still a Christian, and as such it was no easy thing for him to find himself in the company of those who kept to the old ways. Yet Penda and I had fought and bled together. We two had survived when death had claimed so many and no matter what our differences, we had a bond as strong as Gleipnir, the magic fetter forged of a mountain's roots and bird's spittle which restrained the wolf Fenrir. Penda also kept one eye on Cynethryth, though I judged it protective rather than Freyja-stirred. Certainly it was not the same way I had seen him look at a red-haired beauty in Wessex. To my eyes the redhead had looked a loose woman, perhaps even a whore, but Penda had talked of marrying her and so I reckoned he was merely soft for Cynethryth because she was from his own land, or because she was a woman amongst brutal men, or because he had loved her brother Weohstan. Nevertheless, none of this would be enough to save her father when the time came. In this regard also, he and I were joined.

Dawn broke late because of a skein of low grey cloud through which the sun was hard pressed to burn. A drizzle had filled the air since the early hours and we woke damp and irritable, not least because the local inhabitants, the seals, were keening again as though they had forgotten all about our spears. The men of the last watch returned yawning, their eyes red and heavy as they stoked up the fire and hunkered under their blankets and oiled skins. Egfrith handed me a cup of rainwater and I grunted thanks before drinking and passing the cup to Penda. Cynethryth's blankets were empty and Penda must have read the lines on my brow because he grinned and nodded over towards the rocks, of which there were many more now that the tide was out. Cynethryth's gown lay on one of them whilst she bathed out of sight and for a moment I imagined her washing in the cold, plunging surf, but the image was as tormenting as it was beguiling and I shifted uncomfortably, steering my mind to something else.

Penda nodded up to the high ground above the beach where sea thrift and white stars of chickweed fought for their place amongst prickly sea holly and coarse grass.

'Sigurd has been up there since before first light,' he said.

'He wants his ship back,' I said, choosing not to mention Sigurd's fear that his luck was on the wane, for death had followed the Fellowship like a hungry shadow and the man who had betrayed us had escaped. 'If *Fjord-Elk* were mine I'd want her back, too.'

Penda nodded. The cormorant had returned, barking somewhere in the grey morning, as miserable about the drizzle as we were.

'What will he do when he gets her?' Penda asked. 'Are we enough to crew two ships?' Somehow his thick hair was still standing in spikes despite the damp. We should have gathered sticks and stuck them in the sand to make tents of our oiled skins, but the night had been fine and dry when we had turned in. It was too late now. We were already soaking.

'Sigurd will know what to do,' I said, scratching my beard. In truth it was still not much of a beard. A good breeze would have blown it off, but I was proud of it, though it itched like Father Egfrith's fleas. To make matters worse, the biting flies that love summer drizzle were gathering in faint brown clouds and beginning to test our patience. 'That hoard we got from Ealdred must be fat enough to buy another dragon the equal of *Serpent* or *Fjord-Elk*,' I said. 'We are rich men, Penda.'

He shook his head. 'It shines well enough, that trove,' he

said, gesturing to *Serpent*, which sat serene, gently dipping in the low tide, 'but for me it's like looking at another man's wife.' Two Norsemen had swum out to replace Bjorn and Bjarni, who were now wading ashore, their swords and shields held above their heads. 'I will earn my own silver, lad,' Penda said gruffly, touching the spear beside him. He stretched out a leg, kicking a burning stick back into the fire. It hissed angrily. Other Norsemen sat around more fires, waking slowly, drinking and talking in hushed voices. The day was foul but the air smelled green and fresh.

'Sigurd knows your worth,' I said, recalling the slaughter I had seen Penda make. The Wessexman was a rarity, a warrior worthy to join Sigurd's wolves. He must have known it too, yet he still ached to prove himself as all warriors do.

He shrugged. 'When we run into that treacherous bastard Ealdred, your Jarl Sigurd will see me for what I am. My sword will talk for me. It will sing, Raven, like a good scop.' He grinned, snatching some invisible thing from the air. 'Then I will take what I am owed.'

And so we spent the day complaining about the weather, playing tafl, looking to our war gear again – a constant job in wet weather – and being bored. Other than the scouting parties, we dared not venture far from the bay for risk of running into any Franks or in case we had to put to sea quickly because *Fjord-Elk* was seen in the channel beyond. But *Fjord-Elk* did not come. We ate seal again that night because the creatures were too stupid to get away from us, and the sky continued to spit on us, and this time there were few jokes around the fires.

Sigurd brooded. The jarl kept his own company and Olaf was the only one who dared talk to him, though even he said little, wrapped in his own thoughts. Perhaps he thought of his son, white-haired Eric who had died full of arrows outside Ealdred's hall. He had been Olaf's only son and now there was no one to carry Olaf's bloodline forward. I wondered if the man would ever return to the dead boy's mother or whether he had set his course by another wind; a wind that would whip his own name into a story to be sung in future years in the stead of a living heir. For I had seen Olaf offer war against unbeatable odds on the English shore and this had made me believe that his heart was broken.

The watches were set again and this time I was part of them. I was pleased to climb the wet hill, clutching tall saltbush stems and pulling myself up, the shield on my back, the sword at my hip and a spear in my hand. Penda went with me, though I guessed he was as reluctant to leave Cynethryth as I was.

'The monk will watch over her,' I said, breaking the silence as we climbed. We were about a hundred paces from a narrow ledge that wound steeply up and to the right above the northern end of the bay. This sheep path would take us to a headland crag of limestone, one of the lookout places from which a man named Osk from the previous watch said he had seen the Wessex coast, though the others said it was just low cloud on the horizon.

'That old goat Asgot irritates me,' Penda said eventually, hawking and spitting. 'I've seen his eyes slithering all over Cynethryth and I like it about as much as I like wiping my arse with nettles.'

'I'd take a burning arse over Asgot,' I said, coming to a cluster of terns on their nests, which were shallow scrapes in the soft ground. I carefully stepped around the birds and they kept their black-capped heads low, watching me intently with blinking yellow eyes. 'Asgot is a blood-crazed old fool,' I said, admiring the birds' courage, for not one of them fled to the darkening sky. 'He's probably not seen a woman like Cynethryth for thirty years or more, that's likely all it is.'

Penda grunted. 'There are eggs here,' he said, coming to the nests I had passed. 'We could add them to tomorrow's pot. It can't make Arnvid's stew any worse.'

'Those beaks look sharp as arrows, Penda,' I said. 'Let the birds keep their eggs. As for Asgot, if he's hatching some mischief, we'll know. Though I'd wager Cynethryth can take care of herself.' In truth I was annoyed with myself for not seeing what Penda had. Asgot was dangerous. I did not doubt it. Along with Glum and Glum's kinsmen, the godi had killed my old friend and foster-father Ealhstan. They had hung the old man in an oak tree and strung the purple rope of his innards round the trunk. They had sacrificed my friend and one of them had died on my sword for it, but not Asgot. His old dusty lungs still creaked well enough and his bloodthirsty knife was sharp as ever.

'Aye, we'll watch him, lad,' Penda said, 'and the old bastard had better not try anything shady.'

When we reached the white rocks it was dusk. It was still raining and even the marrow in my bones was sopping. We leant on our spears and looked east into Frankia. Grassland stretched across rolling hills as far as I could see. Scattered throughout this green landscape were darker copses of oak and beech and there were no human dwellings to be seen, though some of the scouting parties reported making out curling smoke against the sky from isolated farmsteads further inland towards the south. The bay we had moored in must have been less than a day's sailing from the mouth of the great Sicauna river which snaked into the town of Paris, the only Frankish town I had ever heard of. Olaf said there were other settlements along that river's banks, maybe even small towns, and I believed him, for if the river was as great as folk said, it must surely support many people.

We knew Ealdred would have to pass our bay some time, for he was no fool and would stay close to land for safety and to harness the offshore winds, though they would be less than a fart's worth in that dismal weather. But when he would pass was anyone's guess and so we would just have to wait.

Penda unrolled two oiled skins and unwound some slender rope from his waist and we laid one of the skins beside a large storm-crumbled rock. Using our two spears as supports and the ropes as guys, we made a passable shelter under which we sat looking out to sea as the incessant rain tapped against the leather, reminding us that we were about to spend a miserable night. For stealth's sake Sigurd had forbidden the sentry groups from lighting fires. He did not want any Franks, intrigued by flames or smoke, to come blundering into his camp. Neither did he want the crew of *Fjord-Elk* to fear making landfall, though the Norsemen all agreed that when Ealdred did come, caution would most likely carry him directly from the open sea into the Sicauna river, thus avoiding the rocks that can tear into a ship's belly, and the greed of men who would attack a ship for the treasures in her hold. But caution would not save Ealdred or his champion Mauger from us. Their wyrd was death and it waited for them on the Frankish coast.

I took a hunk of stale bread from my tunic and held it beyond the shelter, watching as the rain turned it into a foul-looking mush that would at least spare my teeth. Penda lifted a buttock and unleashed a fart that would have filled *Serpent*'s sail for a day, then shook his head and chuckled.

'I'll never forget your face, lad, when the Welsh were all over us like flies on cow dung. That blood-red eye of yours shone like the devil himself. And your teeth . . .' he gnashed his own like an angry hound, 'you looked ready to tear hell a new arsehole. I reckon you would have scythed my head off if I had got too close.'

'I'll relieve you of it now if you fart like that again,' I said, screwing up my face at the awful smell. He grinned contentedly, altering the course of the livid scar someone had carved from his left cheek to beneath his chin.

'The Welsh must have thought some demon from their

children's nightmares had come for them,' he said. 'Poor bastards.'

'The way I remember it *they* mauled *us*, Penda,' I said with a grimace. 'It's a miracle we're still alive to enjoy this pissing rain.'

Penda's gaze rested on me, his eyes dulling like standing water growing a skin of ice. He had lost countrymen and friends that day. He nodded, his eyes sharpening again. 'You never know, we might make a decent fighter of you one day. Give you some craft to go with that black temper of yours. You really don't take it well when someone tries to kill you, eh, lad?' He smiled. 'Lucky you've got that over there,' he added, pointing towards a rock half hidden in a tuft of grass.

'Got what?' I asked.

'That invisible shield, you clod,' he said. 'I've got to get my hands on one of those.'

I shook my head. 'Very rare those invisible shields,' I said, 'you hardly come across them these days. But if I find another one I'll let you know.'

'Good lad,' he said. But it was a thin joke, for Penda was not the only one who thought it some strange wyrd that I had survived this far when other war-skilled men had not. Perhaps there was some seidr shield raised before me. And perhaps that shield belonged to Óðin.

I swallowed the wet bread as my mind swam back to that bloody day and the hillside where we had made our stand. Men had turned that grass greasy with gore and afterwards the pale dead had lain like a litter of bones. In truth Penda had saved my life, dragging me to my feet when my limbs had given up. I owed him. But then, I owed Sigurd too and all the Norsemen. They had stood with me, killed for me as men do for those in the shieldwall beside them, but more than this, they had taken me into their Fellowship. I was young and arrogant and wrapped up in the blind lust of young life, and yet, in the quiet times, I sometimes considered all I had been given: a row bench, a sword, a place amongst men who were weaving a rare saga tale. Whenever I thought about these things I became dizzy. I would shake my head and puff my cheeks. My chest would fill with warm pride and my heart would thump like an axe head on a shield. I wanted to repay the debt somehow. So on that pissing night I stared out across the bay, over the channel towards the north-west and the last glow of the fallen sun, hoping that I should spy *Fjord-Elk* and be the one to give Sigurd the news.

The moon had bobbed and sunk again by the time Svein the Red and Bram Bear came to relieve us of our watch. Their figures loomed on the crunching ledge beside us, black shapes against a dawn the colour of dragon's fire. At last the rain had stopped and in the pure morning air I could smell the mead on the two Norsemen as they approached.

'I hope you two didn't get too scared up here on your own,' Bram said, winking at Svein. One hand gripped his ash spear, the other a bulging skin of mead.

'With that Englishman's hideous hair and Raven's blood-eye, it would be a brave draugr that tried to spook these two,' Svein said, resting the butt of his spear beside a thicket of sea thrift which rustled in the breeze. Just then a screech ripped the air behind us. Bram ducked and spun, extending his spear ready as a peregrine streaked like an arrow down into the long grass.

'Don't be afraid, Bram,' I said, laughing with the others, 'Svein's got your back. You wouldn't let that mean old bird peck the Bear's beard off, would you, Svein?'

'I might,' Svein replied with a grin. 'Something should be done about that beard. Bram's face is hairier than Thór's ball sack.'

Bram growled something about us pissing off back to the beach, and I was sure his cheeks were red beneath his bushy brown beard. We stood and stretched our limbs, which were stiff as wind-hung cod, and Penda yawned and smacked his lips together drily, nodding at the skin in Bram's hand and winking. I understood.

'It's thirsty work keeping watch all night,' I said in Norse. 'A man deserves to wet his tongue.' Bram offered me the mead skin, though it clearly pained him.

'Don't know why I should give you any,' he grumbled. 'My old father would have skinned me alive if I'd spoken to my betters the way you do.'

'He should have,' I said, taking a step backwards and handing the skin to Penda. 'A pelt like that could have made him rich,' and with that Bram came for me and I scrambled out of his reach, leaving him cursing Svein for laughing.

'I'll deal with you later, whelp!' he rumbled, picking up a stone and hurling it after me.

We made our way back down to the beach, past the burrows of the terns and shearwaters, along the ledge of wind-moulded grass and through the field of sea thrift. Below, the seals had begun their keening again, the noise somehow too lusty for the still summer's morning. The smell of onions and melted fat and sweet woodsmoke wafted up to me, making my mouth slippery and my stomach ache to be filled. It was a strong enough spell to dull the edge of my need to spy *Fjord-Elk* ploughing the channel, and as we drew closer it blended with the delicious sound of sizzling food and the foggy hum of low voices. Usually we left the cook to his work, only falling on him like wolves when the shout went up that the meal was ready. Now such a pack had gathered that only the rising smoke betrayed the cauldron's exact whereabouts.

Olaf turned to greet us, scratching his backside. 'No sign of the goat dropping, then?' he called.

'Not so much as a ripple, Uncle,' I replied, shaking my head and wondering if Sigurd had been wrong in thinking that

Ealdred was clinging to the coast. Perhaps the ealdorman had taken the straight crossing as we had done and was already drinking wine with the emperor of the Franks. The jarl was sitting alone on a rock, running a whetstone the length of his long sword.

'He'll come, Uncle,' Sigurd called without looking up from his work. Olaf shrugged and turned back to the pot and as he moved I saw what was holding the Norsemen's interest. Cynethryth. She was standing there stirring the broth with a smooth stick. She wore a gown of woad blue, the hem sandy above bare feet. Her hair, gold as ripe barley, hung in two long braids, shining in the dawn light, and her skin, white as milk curds, gave her eyes an acute sense of life and intelligence. Amongst those travel-worn warriors she was impossibly beautiful. Just looking at her tore out my guts.

'Have you told her, lad?' Penda asked. I stopped suddenly and gripped his arms, turning him to face me before we got close enough for the others to overhear. I felt the blood rushing to my face. You could have cooked an egg on my cheek.

'Told her what?' I asked. It was a pathetic attempt at ignorance. Penda dipped his chin and raised his eyebrows. I sighed. 'No, I have not told her,' I said, 'and neither will you, Penda, unless you want to feel my boot up your arse.' He grinned and shook his head, scratching his long scar and running a hand through his thick hair, raising it into spikes.

'You are a strange one, Raven,' he said. 'You'll take on a horde of Welshmen for something to do, but your young knees buckle at the sight of a skinny-arsed girl.'

'Don't open that mead hole of yours, Penda,' I warned him, aware of what a sorry sight I must have made, half threatening, half begging the man not to speak of my feelings. But I could not help myself. 'Please,' I added, the crown on my shame.

Penda looked over to Cynethryth and then back to me, like

a man standing at a fork in the road deciding which way to go.

'I'll keep your secret, lad,' he said eventually, 'so long as you keep my tongue wet with Bram's mead. The sneaky whoreson keeps his own supply hidden away and if that last gulp is anything to go by it's a damned good drop. My father used to say a jug of good mead can convince a man he can do anything. Told me he once walked three miles home on his eyebrows after a particularly tasty splash, so keeping your little secret shouldn't be too hard.'

I extended my arm and we gripped each other's wrists. 'I'll get you your mead,' I said. Bram was drunk as often as he was sober so stealing mead from his store could not prove too hard. Even a bloody nose or a black eye would be a price worth paying for Penda's silence.

'Keep stirring it but take it off the flame as soon as it begins to bubble,' Cynethryth announced, handing the stick to Arnvid as Olaf translated into Norse. From Arnvid's face you would have thought he had hung nine days and nights starving and spear-pierced on the World-Tree and now grasped the secret runes of knowledge. 'If you let it boil, you'll ruin the taste.' Arnvid nodded gravely. Then she sniffed the stew one last time before turning from it. The others watched Arnvid hungrily, their hopes hanging on him, and Cynethryth looked at me and smiled and the spirit of a peregrine flapped its wings in my belly.

'You are filthy, Raven,' she chided, running her eyes over me. My tongue was stuck to the roof of my mouth, so I nodded and smiled dumbly. 'Well, you've no good reason to be, unless, of course, you haven't noticed that drop of water over there.' She nodded at the ocean, as flat as beaten gold beneath the dawn, except for the languid waves frothing on to the beach. 'Let's just hope there is enough to wash this grime off.' She dragged a finger across my cheek. 'Some of it looks older than Olaf.'

51

Then she linked her arm through mine and some of the Norsemen winked and nudged each other, but Cynethryth ignored them, leading me to the water.

'You still wear the feather,' she said. I was pulling off my boots so I could wade into the surf with her. 'I did not expect you to wear it for ever, Raven.' She frowned. 'It was meant in fun, that's all.'

I shrugged. 'I like it,' I said defensively. The hint of a smile touched her lips, honing her cheeks into sharp edges. I stepped into the waves.

'And the rest,' she said, nodding at my tunic and breeks, 'if they're not stuck to your skin. We can't have you befouling the ocean for the rest of us.' I took off my tunic and dropped it next to my boots and brynja, giving Cynethryth a smile which she answered with the stone-face mothers give their whelps before letting the hazel switch say the rest.

'Everything?' I asked.

'Oh, of course, Norsemen bathe fully clothed,' she mocked, 'in case the water is cold.'

'Norsemen don't bathe at all,' I said, which was not true. We washed our faces and combed our hair in the mornings and liked to clean our hands before eating. We bathed too, when young English girls were not standing there with their eyes set like a pair of scales to weigh the goods. Cynethryth's eyes rolled.

'Don't rush me, woman,' I said. Under those eyes my fingers fumbled awkwardly and might as well have belonged to someone else for all the control I had over them. 'Now look the other way,' I said.

'I will if you will,' she replied, one eyebrow arching mischievously, and suddenly my breath snagged in my chest like a fish in a withy trap.

Because Cynethryth was getting undressed.

CHAPTER FOUR

I PRETENDED NOT TO HEAR THE WHISTLES AND WHOOPS AS I LEFT my clothes and brynja in a crumpled heap on the sand and walked naked as a bairn to the water's edge. I knew the whistles were not aimed at me, for Cynethryth was naked too, or near enough. The short linen under the kirtle she wore lost its colour when touched by water, revealing the dark patch of hair at her groin. Her nipples were sharpened points pushing against the linen and I dared one last lingering look before ditching into the water. I came up quickly, shaking my long hair like a hound and blowing snot from my nose.

'It's colder than it looks,' I said. Cynethryth swam easily, rolling on to her back and floating as I had seen the seals do in play.

'When I was a girl my father told me that the Romans built great stone pools and filled them with water that always stayed hot. They bathed in hot water every day. Can you imagine that?'

'How did they keep the water hot?' I asked sceptically.

'They built chambers beneath the pools and lit fires and the hot air from the fires travelled through these chambers,

53

heating the water above.' For a moment I thought Cynethryth was teasing me, but the tight line of her lips told me she was not.

'Then it's no wonder the Romans lost their empire and that their city was burnt to ash,' I said, 'if they were too busy washing their skins to save them.' I imagined crowds of men lazing in huge stone baths in some hot land, scrubbing each other's backs whilst wild-eyed warriors pillaged and burnt their homes and raped their women. 'Fools,' I muttered, scooping a handful of sand from the seabed to scrub beneath my arms. 'Warm water makes a man soft,' I said with a shiver, then dived under again. When I surfaced and looked round all I could see of Cynethryth were her feet sploshing and churning the sea in her wake. I called out but she could not hear me above the surf and the seals' keening and her own splashing, so I kicked my legs and clawed the water and followed her.

When we stopped I was exhausted. I had not known that swimming could leak a man's strength like a cut vein, and whilst I had lost my respect for the Romans, my admiration for fish had grown. We were not very far out, but we had swum past *Serpent*, raising jeers from Bjorn and Bjarni, back on board, and around a small outcrop where the water sucked and plunged. Just beyond it a small, sheltered cove looked a good place to catch our breath.

'You . . . should . . . rest,' I managed to call, timing the words so that I only swallowed half the ocean's water and not enough to sink myself, for I was always a poor swimmer. I was relieved to see Cynethryth already swimming for the cove with long, lithesome strokes. I confess I quickened my own flailing, hoping to catch another glimpse of that secret hoard hidden beneath her kirtle. Then I remembered my own nakedness.

She sat on the sand hugging her knees and shaking her hair free as I reached the beach, which was less than a spear's throw from end to end. I lay in the surf with my face turned towards the dawn sun, feigning contentment when in truth I was too embarrassed to stand up. The sand beneath my hand shuddered suddenly and I flinched, catching sight of a flat fish as it darted away in a cloudy swirl. White gulls tumbled and shrieked in the pale blue above, reminding us that we were intruders in this quiet cove.

'Even you must be clean by now,' Cynethryth called.

'You were right,' I shouted over my shoulder. 'Some of this dirt has been with me a long time. It's as stubborn as Bram Bear.' I began to scrub, startled a moment later by hands on my shoulders. I looked up into Cynethryth's eyes, swallowing hard, then took the hand she offered and stood to face her. Neither of us spoke. The gulls called and the waves supped at the shore. Then she led me to a patch of grass and sea aster on whose fleshy leaves and flowers a hundred black and orange butterflies rested. They muddled into the air like wind-whipped blossom. Cynethryth's eyes, emerald green, endless and unbound in the first blush of the day, roved across my body like a dragon ship on the whale road. Her fingers brushed my cheek and beard as though her skin and mine had never touched and I trembled. We closed our eyes then, letting other senses rise, and my soul began to drift like a boat cut free of its mooring. Then Cynethryth's fingers wrapped the crown of my head and I leant towards her and our mouths touched. A shiver licked my spine and I realized my excitement was blatant, but there was nothing I could do about it now. Her lips parted and our tongues touched and I tasted her and some deep part of me cursed because it knew that sweet taste had Gleipnir-bound me to this woman.

I felt ridiculous standing there with my stiffness pointing at Cynethryth's belly and so I pushed her down to the sand and she did not complain but lifted off her kirtle, exposing her small breasts. Her nipples were dark and hard-looking as acorns. Then she lay back and I entered her and because she was wet it was easy and she gasped, pushing her hips up hungrily. My hunger ruled me then. Cynethryth scarcely made a sound other than her breath, which was hot against my neck as I pushed deeper into her, our tongues ravenous. I knew I would be embarrassed afterwards, but I did not care. My heart hammered and every sinew strained to entwine with Cynethryth. With a shout of pleasure twisted with pain I shot inside her, my body quivering wildly, and she cried out, throwing back her head, and I bit her white throat.

Afterwards, I rolled over on to the sand and Cynethryth lay on her side, running her hand across my chest through the sweat that had churned white with salt. I stared up at the sky, grinning like a witless fool, aware once more of the gulls and the bees and the seals in the next bay. I assumed Cynethryth was as content as I was to lie in the wash of that new dawn, but eventually I turned to look at her and saw a tear dart into her hair.

'What is it?' I asked, suddenly afraid that I had done something wrong. Had she not pulled me into her? My memory conjured the face of a Welsh girl amongst the ruins of Caer Dyffryn, and my stomach twisted painfully. 'What's wrong, Cynethryth? Did I mistake you?' Hot blood flooded my cheeks.

She sat up and reached for her kirtle, slipping it over her head as she stood. I stood too, feeling as coarse as a beast and yet vulnerable with my manhood still heavy and my clothes back in the next bay. I held her shoulders and asked again what was the matter. She chewed her bottom lip and looked about to speak, but then her eyes widened, the black holes in them swelling wildly at something over my shoulder.

'What . . . ?' I turned towards the sea and my chest thundered like two shieldwalls crashing together. *Fjord-Elk* had come.

CHAPTER FIVE

FOR SEVERAL HEARTBEATS WE STOOD SILENT, WATCHING THE dragon ship plough the smooth sea, a good arrow shot from the shore. Though you could hardly call it a dragon ship now. The snarling figurehead was gone and in its place sat a cross, showing that those aboard were in thrall to the White Christ. Her graceful clinkered hull creamed the ocean effortlessly. The long spruce oars dipped raggedly by Norseman standards but well enough in this sleeping sea to bring her on. My fists were knots, my teeth clenched against the rising fury of hard memories. When I had last seen that ship I had been trussed like a boar by Ealdred's men on the Wessex shore, and as *Fjord-Elk* sailed away Ealdred's champion Mauger had signalled to my captors to slit my throat. Those feckless goat suckers would have killed Cynethryth too for standing by me.

'*Meinfretr*,' I muttered. That rocky outcrop which separated us from the others might also prevent them seeing *Fjord-Elk* in time to spring the trap. There was the chance that when she did come into view the Norsemen would not recognize her, because her sail was not up and there was a cross at her prow. For a moment I agonized. I've always swum like a stone. It would take me too long to claw my way back round to the beach. But I had no boots either and so running over the jagged prominence would not be easy.

'Can you swim back, Cynethryth?' I asked. She blinked slowly, spilling a tear which settled on her lip, shivering. She nodded and I cursed the luck that had brought *Fjord-Elk* now when all I wanted was standing before me. I searched Cynethryth's face for one lingering moment, then turned and ran to the rocks and began to climb. The lower rocks, which were submerged at high tide, were treacherous with slick brown leaves and I fell more than once, cutting my knees and hands. I ran and jumped and scrambled over skin-tearing barnacles and crunching mussels. I splashed through sun-warmed pools where things that looked like blood clots lurked, and I must have looked like a wild animal, naked, my dark hair and its raven's wing trailing. And as I ran I felt the grin spread on my face and that grin became a snarl, a wolf's snarl, because the worm Ealdred had come and we would be unleashed to the kill. I jumped the last cleft, landing heavily on a smooth rock, then leapt down to the sand to see the Norsemen in a great, seething knot. They were fully armed with shields and mail and standing before Sigurd who, with his shining helmet and huge spear, could have been mighty Týr himself.

The men turned to me and more than a few of them laughed at my nakedness, but Sigurd did not laugh. 'You look like a mountain troll, Raven,' he growled, his top lip hitched, baring his white teeth.

'I came as fast as I could, lord,' I panted, wincing because my feet felt as though they were on fire. I glanced down to see that they were torn and bloody. Then Floki's cousin Halldor winked at me and I instinctively glanced back at the rocks and saw a narrow high-up ledge from which Halldor must have spied *Fjord-Elk* in time to warn the others. I grimaced because from there there was every chance he would have had a good view of the cove, too.

'Now we repay the ormstunga!' Sigurd bawled, and I thought calling Ealdred a serpent tongue was an insult to snakes, as the knot of men broke apart and I ran down to the shoreline where my clothes lay a spear's length from being stolen by the rising tide. But the water would be too deep to wade out to *Serpent*. In mail and helmets we would sink like rocks. Then the Norsemen were running past me, crashing into the surf.

'Here, lad,' Penda said, handing me my shield and helmet, which I had left further up the beach. 'I'd wager you don't want to miss this.'

'That wager would not make you rich,' I said, hopping as I pulled on my breeks. Penda bent and picked up my brynja and I wriggled into it like an eel. I glanced across to see that Sigurd had thrown one end of a shorter rope over one of *Serpent*'s mooring ropes and yanked it down, enabling his men to pull themselves along it without fear of drowning. Out they went, hungry for blood, and I could see Bjorn and Bjarni standing at *Serpent*'s bow yawping for them to move faster. Father Egfrith stood a few feet away in the surf, hurling prayers to the White Christ between imploring Sigurd to resist his bloodlust and seek peace terms.

'But for the love of God get the book, Sigurd! You must get the book!' the monk shrieked, his eyes wide and a strange look on his weasel face that could have been terror or elation.

Svein the Red stopped at the waterline and turned to me, a savage grin breaking his huge red beard. 'Hurry, Raven,' he said, then turned and lumbered splashing into the sea.

'So what happened?' Penda said, looking me in the eye and scratching the scar on his face. He was mailed and battle-ready and I could not believe he was asking me such a thing at such a time. 'Did you plough the girl?'

I looked out past the breakers but could not yet see

Cynethryth this side of the rocky outcrop. Penda and I were the last. Even old Asgot was halfway along *Serpent*'s mooring rope, moving as quickly as any of the younger men.

'Time to go, Penda,' I said. He batted a hand at me and plunged into the sea and in a heartbeat I was behind him, half wading, half hauling myself along. Sigurd's Wolfpack readied *Serpent*, fixing the beast Jörmungand at her prow and shields along her sheer strake, and slotting the spruce oars through their ports.

'A screw and a fight all in one day!' Bjarni called, hauling me up and over the sheer strake with the use of a short boarding rope. 'Sounds like Valhöll, hey, Raven.'

'I missed breakfast,' I gnarled, making him laugh, then took to my row bench, the chest in which I kept all I owned, and gripped my oar, which Svein had readied for me. I turned to look for Cynethryth but could not see her as Olaf gave one sharp 'Hey!' for us to pull the first stroke.

Then we rowed. We knew we were counting on surprise and surprise meant silence. So we watched Olaf, who had set himself at *Serpent*'s stern, plunging his fist over and over rather than calling out the time. Knut moved the tiller, turning the ship so that we hugged the coast and would emerge from the bay at the last possible moment, like a hawk out of the sun.

It always feels good to row. We would complain eventually of course, but for the first hour or two, when your strength is up and the rhythm is set, rowing is a joy, at least for me. Two oars may look the same to a man's eyes, but they are not the same. You come to know your own oar as you know your own arms and legs. By touch alone your calloused hands know your oar from a hundred others, just as they would know your lover's tits or arse. There is always comfort in familiarity.

Sigurd and Black Floki readied the grappling hooks and gathered together thirty or more spears, which we had taken from our enemies in the last weeks. I had never fought in a sea battle before, but I knew what would happen. We would throw spears and hand-axes into *Fjord-Elk* to clear her deck, then hurl the grappling hooks and heave on the ropes so that the hooks would bite into her sheer strake and the ships would crash together, making a floating fighting platform. A cautious jarl might continue to hurl missiles, spears, even stones, until the issue was settled. Not Sigurd. I watched him as the battle-trembling began in my legs and snaked upwards. The jarl's face was hard as stone, his eyes black as storm clouds below the helmet's rim. His left hand rested on his sword's pommel and his right gripped two great spears. If you'd told me that Óðin Spear-Shaker had come down from Asgard and entered the jarl's body, intent on making a slaughter to drown the world in blood, I would have believed you.

Yes, I knew what would happen in my first sea battle, just as I knew what Sigurd was seeing in his mind's eye. Ealdred's men had probably never fought at sea and they would not be ready for a fight now. We would board *Fjord-Elk* and then the real butchering would begin. And afterwards, when we had killed them all, Sigurd would claim three prizes, all equally valuable in their own way. First, Sigurd would have Ealdred's head on the end of his spear. Then he would take Ealdred's own personal treasure chest for himself, including the holy gospel book of Saint Jerome. Last, Sigurd would win back *Fjord-Elk*, which was as fine a ship as was ever made to cross the grey sea.

'The gods are smiling on us, Raven,' Svein growled behind me.

I was nervous now. Edgy enough to fear that I might piss my breeks. We had almost reached the end of the out-jutting rocks and would come into Ealdred's view at any moment. I hoped Cynethryth was sticking close to the submerged rocks so that we would not ride over her.

'How do you know, Svein?' I asked. 'That the gods are with us?' Our oars dipped and rose as one, the drops barely having time to fall from the blades before those blades fell again into the sun-gilded sea.

'There's no wind, lad. Even a fart's worth of wind makes it impossible to lash to another ship and fight. My uncle Bothvar was drowned when his jarl, Ragnvald, tried the same thing in a swell.' He sucked in a great breath. 'They grappled their enemy's boat and their enemy, a man named Moldof, even helped to lash them good and tight so that they could get on with the fighting. Perhaps Njörd was drunk that day and belched. Anyway, both dragons were swept off and wrecked on the lee shore. No man survived. Bothvar's father saw it all from the cliffs.' The oars sploshed and *Serpent* skimmed across the sea like a water snake. 'We have no wind and the sea is calm,' Svein said. 'Yes, the gods are with us.' I did not have to see Svein's face to know the smile that was on it. I whispered a prayer to Óðin asking him to lend me courage and stop the shivering that was deepening now, eating into my muscles, turning my bowels to water and filling my guts with ice.

I looked back at the beach and was relieved to see Cynethryth emerging from the low breakers. She stood in her sopping kirtle beside Father Egfrith and even at that distance I could see the short gown clinging to her breasts and I was glad that Egfrith was a Christ slave and, so far as I had seen, had no interest in women. I could not see her face but I remembered it well enough. Her scent was still on me like a spell, the only thing convincing me that we had just lain together and that it was not some dream sent by Freyja goddess of love, who weeps tears of red gold.

'There they are, the sheep piss drinking whoresons!' Sigurd bellowed, striding forward in sheer craving, like Fenrir straining at his chain. I could not look behind me easily but I could imagine the terror-struck faces of *Fjord-Elk*'s crew as they read the weave and weft of their doom. 'Kill them all!' Sigurd yelled, spittle lacing his beard in the red morning light.

'But leave the turd Ealdred for me. I'll take the head of any man who touches him.' I looked over to Penda. He stood at the mast step, feet apart, sword and shield ready, a thin smile on his scarred face. He was not trusted to row yet. Normally you could not take your place on a fine dragon ship such as *Serpent* unless you could row hard and well enough to carry a ship off the ocean's edge, and fight like a demon, too. It was unlikely that Penda could row well. He had spent the first day aboard puking his guts into the waves. But the man could fight and Sigurd knew it. Penda was a born killer, a warrior of rare skill, and to Sigurd's mind this made up for the rowing. Besides, even though we had lost many, with all who remained on one ship there were more men than row benches.

'You can't touch Ealdred, Penda,' I shouted in English to the Wessexman.

'Who says I can't?' he yelled above the clamour of men rousing themselves to violence with curses, prayers and howls.

'Sigurd says it,' I called, and Penda spat at his feet and growled something foul. Penda wanted his own revenge, but like the rest of us would have to wait. In the Fellowship Sigurd's word was law and that law was backed by his own right arm and his father's blade.

I leant back in the stroke, heaving, relishing the swell of the muscles across my shoulders, for I was broad now and proud of it. Sweat began to pour down my back beneath my leather gambeson and mail. I wondered how Penda could spit, for my own mouth was as dry as old pine needles, though I was not the only one whose nerves were dancing. Two of the men not at the oars were pissing over the side even as we sped to a battle. I could hear old Asgot shouting at *Serpent*'s prow, invoking Óðin Lord of War, Thór Slayer of Giants, brave Týr the battle god, and other gods too, gods whose names I had never heard, to help us kill our enemies, slaughter them for being followers of the White Christ who was a god of lepers and weaklings.

And whatever I thought of Asgot, there was comfort in his wild keening. We all put some stock in the godi's magic because he was old and skinny and had fought with Sigurd's father and yet was somehow still alive when stronger men were not.

'Oars in!' Sigurd yelled. We moved like a squall, pulling the oars back through the ports and stowing them with a thump and clatter before stuffing leather plugs into the holes. Now I got my chance to see what was happening. *Fjord-Elk* was all seething panic. Ealdred must have recognized Jörmungand and known then that Sigurd had come for him and if he had any sense at all he must have been terrified. His steersman had changed course, trying to take the ship out of our path and into the open channel. He might as well have been hoping for a boatload of young virgins to carry him away on a ship made of silver and gold. If they had seen us earlier they might have stood some chance, though not much of one. As it stood, our prow would strike *Fjord-Elk* amidships, and when that happened corpses would be made.

I gripped my spear tight enough for the knuckles to whiten, for I did not think that ramming the other ship would be a good thing for anyone. I could see faces now, perhaps even Ealdred standing at *Fjord-Elk*'s stern. I took a deep, stuttering breath and glanced at Sigurd, thinking that being amongst that clamour without clamouring myself was somehow like being underwater.

'Now, Knut!' Sigurd roared, dropping his arm, his eyes suddenly wild. Knut pushed the tiller and *Serpent* heeled violently so that some of us fell and I looked back just as our hull sent a wave crashing into *Fjord-Elk* with enough force to rock her like a child's cradle and send the crew reeling.

'Kill them!' Sigurd screamed, hurling his spear into the panicked press of the enemy who were desperately trying to arm themselves.

'Gut the leaking-arsed mares, you blood-loving wolves!'

Olaf bellowed, throwing his own spear, which took a huge, grey-haired man in the face. We all screamed and hurled our spears and it was devastating, for when a man with shoulders of iron from years of rowing launches a spear it is not always stopped by flesh; sometimes it tears right through the body. Our enemies had been under sail on a level sea with no reason to expect trouble, so were not wearing mail, and now there was a desperate press by *Fjord-Elk*'s shallow hold as they clamoured and brawled to get to the weapons stowed there. With the enemy packed so tightly it was hard for us to miss and blood-soaked screams rent the dawn. In the crush some of the Wessexmen tried to use each other as shields. Black Floki and Bram already had two grappling hooks biting into *Fjord-Elk*'s hull and they grimaced as they heaved on the ropes to pull the ships together. Osk and Arnvid threw two more hooks. Osk's did not catch but Arnvid's did and Bjarni gripped that rope with him and hauled. Once the grappling hooks were in the wood the only chance the enemy had was if they cut the ropes, which was no easy thing with spears streaking amongst them like lightning bolts. Three white-faced, wide-eyed Wessexmen stood at the stern, drawing bows and sending arrows into us, but the ships were rocking in the fray enough to spoil their aim. Still, one or two hammered into us, bouncing off shields or glancing off brynjas as the ships came together with a thump.

The Norsemen roared and that sound was thunder. Sigurd was the first to leap across, battering two Wessexmen with his shield and taking a third in the neck with his sword. All along *Serpent*'s length, Norsemen jumped, axes and swords swinging, carving into *Fjord-Elk*'s unprepared crew, and I jumped after Penda, slipping on *Fjord-Elk*'s deck which was already blood-slick. A man jabbed a spear at my chest but I met the blade with my shield and scythed my sword into his shoulder where it stuck like a knife in a tough joint of meat. He screamed and I rammed my left boot into his belly, doubling him over, and the blade came free so I whomped it down into his skull. It was easy killing. The English were not used to moving around *Fjord-Elk* and they tripped and fell as we hacked them to pieces, their torn flesh steaming in the morning air so that a dragon's breath fog hung over the deck.

'Ealdred! Ealdred! Where are you, worm?' Sigurd was yelling through the din. Men were begging for mercy, but when they saw they would find none some jumped over *Fjord-Elk*'s side and Norsemen ran across the deck to spear them like fish. A man dropped to his knees before Penda, wringing his hands and babbling as Penda swung his sword to send the man's head thumping across the oak deck, spraying blood as it bounced. Seeing this, another man who had thrown down his sword bent and clasped the leather grip again. If he knew Penda he must have known that begging would help about as much as fouling his breeks, so he chose a good death instead.

'Tell Satan that your bastard lord will suck his prick soon!' Penda snarled, knocking the man's sword aside. But the man was quick enough to parry Penda's next attack, which made Penda half smile and step back, holding his sword wide and inviting the man to try to kill him. The man suddenly screamed and swung his sword furiously and Penda leapt back and spun full circle on his heel, scything his blade into the Wessexman's neck, carving a splinter from his collarbone on the way, and that terrible white sliver pointed skyward as the man dropped to his knees. Bright blood spurted and stuttered from the wound and his jaw hung slack, a black hole in his black beard.

'Hungry?' Penda gnarled. 'Eat this.' He rammed his sword into the man's mouth and the blade burst out the back of his skull and still the Wessexman stared.

The bloodlust had barely taken a grip on me when I realized it was all but over. We had ploughed through the Wessexmen with sickening ease and now we stood amongst torn bodies and stinking open bowels and dead white faces that were twisted and frozen in shock and pain. Instinctively, we made a shieldwall, four lines deep across *Fjord-Elk*'s deck before the mast step. I looked back to *Serpent* and saw that Asgot and seven or eight Norsemen were still aboard her, as there had not been room for everyone to join the fight for risk of us getting in each other's way. These men stood ready with spears or bows, watching the English survivors who stood in a last desperate knot before their lord at the bow. They were big, grim-faced men, Ealdred's household warriors. Mauger, his bodyguard, was there and he must have known what lay in store for him, that the worms would soon be sucking his flesh. Though if he was afraid he showed no signs of it. There were five of them. All must have been putting on their mail whilst we were killing their countrymen and that had taken some nerve, meaning we would be fools to take such men lightly. They stood in a pitifully small but perfectly tight shieldwall before the dark wooden cross they had mounted in place of Sigurd's proud dragon's head. Ealdred's long moustaches were shiny with grease. His dark eyes stared out balefully.

Sigurd stepped from our shieldwall, his sword slick with dark gore. I could imagine all too well what he thought of the cross at *Fjord-Elk*'s bow.

'You are a man of no worth, Ealdred,' he said in English, 'and your word means less than the shit from a cow. You betrayed me. You even killed your own son.' Sigurd spat because this last was so disgusting to him. 'I have only steel for you, Ealdred. I have only the raven to peck the flesh from your bones, the wolf to chew the marrow and the worms to feed on the filth that remains until you are nothing but a stain in the mud.'

The Wessexmen held their shields firm, waiting for us to attack. They stood proudly even as they stared at their own deaths and I admit I did not want to kill them. They were fathers and husbands, but mostly they were warriors and they showed no fear, nor did they beg for their lives. It was their ill-wyrd that their lord was a milk-livered nothing and I hoped they could be saved even as I knew they could not.

Splashes at our rear told me that Norsemen were tipping the English corpses over *Fjord-Elk*'s side before their filth could seep into the oak deck. Even the sea breeze could not chase off the stench of shit and blood and I did not look forward to the hard scrubbing we would have to do when this was over.

Ealdred stepped up on to the bow's fighting platform so that he stood head and shoulders above his men, a tempting target to our bow- and spearmen.

'I am a lord of Wessex!' he said. 'What are you? You are heathen scum writhing in the shadows like maggots in a sheep's carcass. I do not deal with such as you. No Christian man should, unless he wants a spear in his back. Come, Sigurd, you son of a goat. Come and taste our English steel. Or do you only fight unarmed men?'

In truth it was well said, even if most of the Norsemen were none the wiser. We hefted our shields and moved forward, but Sigurd bawled that we should hold.

'Good, Ealdred,' the jarl said. 'I would have wagered that you would beg like the huglausi you are.' Coward was a heavy word to throw. 'But it pleases me to see you would rather die a man's death even though you have lived as a nothing. Wessex is fine land. A honeycomb like that will need men who are ready to die with a sword in their hands, or else it will swarm with Norsemen in twenty years. Norse bairns will tug your women's skirts and those bairns will grow into men who whisper to Óðin and Thór. Your White Christ will be a piss stain of a memory.' Ealdred eyeballed Sigurd fiercely, his long moustache trembling.

'I'll fight you, Sigurd!' Mauger bellowed, his broad face red and hateful. 'Fuck the gods! Let us see what men can do.'

Some of the Norsemen grumbled and murmured that we should just finish them all instead of talking. They could not understand most of what was said, but they knew a challenge when they saw one and it unsettled them. Mauger was Ealdred's best warrior; a granite-hard man who had lived through many battles. I had heard it said that Mauger was the greatest warrior that Wessex had so I did not want Sigurd to fight him. But Sigurd was a born warrior too and even a jarl can be in thrall to his honour. To Sigurd such a challenge shone brighter than a journey chest brimming with hack silver.

'Ealdred, first you will fight me yourself and if you do I will let your men go free after I have killed you. They are loyal men, it seems to me. They deserve better than to die for such as you.' He raised his sword and pointed it at the ealdorman. 'What do you say? Will you fight me?'

Ealdred's lip curled like old leather. 'I will not,' he sneered. 'But I will send Mauger in my stead, to fight you or any man.' Mauger nodded resolutely. The muscles in his bare arms squirmed beneath his many warrior rings and tattoos. He was a grim, grizzled, stone-faced thing and I shuddered for any man who had to fight him.

'I'll take the bastard!' Penda yelled, eyeing Mauger hungrily.

'What are they saying, Raven?' Bjorn hissed beside me. We were in the third line peering over other men's shoulders to see what was happening.

'Mauger has challenged Sigurd,' I said in Norse, raising a ragged hail of insults from Norse mouths.

'I'm going to shit on your heart!' one man yelled.

'Your own mothers will not be able to piece you together, you fucking farts!' another hollered. Black Floki and Svein the Red pleaded with Sigurd to let them fight Mauger instead, but Sigurd told them to hold their tongues.

'As jarl it is my right,' Sigurd said, sheathing his sword. 'Put down your weapons, men of Wessex, and I give you my word that you will not fatten the ravens this morning. I accept Mauger's challenge. If he wins you will all go free.'

'And if he does not win?' one of the Wessexmen asked, getting a sibilant rebuke from Ealdred for his trouble. I guessed that his situation had made the man bold enough to ask the question, for surely his fear of his ealdorman was shadowed now by his fear of us.

Sigurd shrugged. 'If I win I will weave your wyrds myself. Perhaps you will die. Perhaps not.'

The English warriors looked at each other then and their minds must have squirmed like snakes, for they had to balance the chance of Mauger winning against the certain but honourable death they would win by fighting us now rather than laying down their arms. A man's fate, his wyrd, is a fog-veiled thing. These Wessexmen could not have known just hours before, as they sailed the sleeping sea, what that dawn would bring. Heathens had appeared as if from their piss-soaked childhood nightmares. Those same heathens whom they had thought destroyed had come for vengeance. We had taken the threads of these Wessexmen's futures and we had severed them. But they were household men, proud warriors loyal even to the end, and at Ealdred's word they bent and laid their swords on *Fjord-Elk*'s deck.

'It'll be the hólmgang,' Bjorn said, the glint of excitement in his eyes, 'done in the old way.'

'But I am thinking it will take more than the first spilt blood to settle this one, brother,' Bjarni said with a grimace.

We split into two groups with Olaf taking charge of *Fjord-Elk*, and I found myself back on *Serpent* with Jarl Sigurd and our English captives. There were just enough men to row both ships, though both would lack for speed and this was a problem Sigurd would have to consider at some point. On the other hand, with smaller crews they were lighter, despite the packed holds, and under sail they would fly like winged dragons.

'Tie them up,' Sigurd commanded as we wriggled out of blood-slick mail and took off sweat-soaked helmets. They would stay filth-covered until the wind was enough to raise the sails and then we could clean them. It did not take long for the flies to come. They landed on mail, on our arms and on the deck, feeding on the congealing gore, and for a time we swiped at them but after a while we gave up. Men talk of the raven and the wolf as the eaters of the dead, the scavengers who come to every field of the slain. Rarely do they mention the damned flies.

Jarl Sigurd nodded, spitting over the ship's side. 'Cast us off, Uncle,' he called.

'Aye,' Olaf said, shaking his head and tutting as he yanked the grappling hooks out of *Fjord-Elk*'s sheer strake. The scars would be shameful reminders of how we had let the ship fall into the hands of our enemies.

'Ah, we can replace those sheer strakes easy enough, Uncle,' Bram said, slapping Olaf on the shoulder before moving to another hook. The ships rocked gently, bumping together in the still dawn sea. In no time we were free and Ealdred's men were bound and made to sit at *Serpent*'s bow beneath Jörmungand. Sigurd did not tie the ealdorman's wrists, which was an insult rather than a sign of respect for the man's rank. It was Sigurd's way of showing that he considered Ealdred no warrior and no more threat than a woman or a child.

The rising tide had carried both ships nearer to the shore and so we rowed out to sea, giving the rocky promontory a wide berth before re-entering the bay where Cynethryth and Father Egfrith waited on the beach. I was anxious to be with

71

Cynethryth and so I suggested that Penda take my oar and get some rowing practice whilst it was just a matter of countering the current and holding *Serpent* in one place. He was not what I would call an eager apprentice. I could tell this because he called me a dog's arse and told me to screw a mountain troll backwards.

'You have to learn some time, Penda,' I said, feeling the smile behind my eyes. 'Better now than out there in the teeth of a storm. Just watch Arnvid and do the same. I have faith in you.'

'You impudent whelp, how hard can it be?' he said. It's true my grin did not make him any keener to prove himself, but after a few more insults he sat on my journey chest and gripped the smooth spruce stave.

'An Englishman at our oars! You trying to sink us, Raven?' Bjorn called, stirring a smattering of laughter and a few prayers to Njörd.

'I hope the girl and the Christ slave can swim, Raven,' Sigurd said as we looked to the shore. 'This high tide will be hiding rocks I would rather avoid. They will have to come to us.'

'Cynethryth swims like a fish, lord,' I said, remembering my struggle to keep up with her that morning. Lying with her in the sheltered cove already felt like a lifetime ago. Now her father was our prisoner and I did not know what Cynethryth would think about that. 'As for the monk, lord, I don't know if he can swim that far. I hope he can't.' Sigurd chuckled. 'Or perhaps Asgot can ask Njörd to send a sea monster to swallow the weasel,' I said.

'Then I would pity the monster,' Sigurd said, 'for I am thinking that Egfrith would taste foul. Like rancid milk or rotten eggs . . . or worse.' He began to tie his thick golden beard into one plait. 'It was an easy fight, hey, Raven?'

'Too easy, lord,' I replied, slapping at a fly that would not give up some crusted blood on my arm. 'I almost felt sorry for them.'

He shook his head, tying off the plait with a strip of leather. The sound of chopping wood hammered across the water as *Fjord-Elk*'s crew dealt with the cross at her prow. 'Felt sorry for them? They would have cut off your balls and fed them to you if they could have. You are a strange one, Raven. Loving your enemies is better left to the Christ slaves. I took you into the Fellowship because you share Thór's love of a good fight, not so that you could *pity* the men who want to wind-dry your innards.'

'I said I *almost* felt sorry for them, lord,' I said. 'Then one of them pissed himself and soaked my boots and I thought to Hel with them.'

Sigurd laughed. 'That's better, lad. That's my Raven, my son of thunder.'

We gestured to Cynethryth and Egfrith that they would have to swim out to us and I could see Cynethryth encouraging the monk, even taking his hand and dragging him into the surf. In the event they swam easily, making me wonder if Egfrith was more otter than weasel. We lowered a rope which they clung to for a while, catching their breath whilst we backed oars to counter the current, then we hauled them in like fish and gave them blankets. Then Cynethryth saw her father below *Serpent*'s prow and her face, already pale from the cold water, turned death white.

'I want to talk to him,' she said, water dripping from her long hair and spotting the deck. I saw Ealdred's eyes fall on his daughter. He looked as though he had been struck in the face with an oar blade. He stood though, raising his chin, and gave the girl a strained smile whilst the Englishmen around him kept their eyes lowered. They had their own fates to think of now. I turned to ask Sigurd if Cynethryth could go to her father, but the jarl swung his eyes over my shoulder and I turned back to see that Cynethryth was already halfway along the deck, tying up her hair as she went, her wet blanket discarded.

'Make sure she doesn't kill him, Raven,' Sigurd said, scratching his bearded cheek.

I followed Cynethryth.

CHAPTER SIX

I STOOD AT CYNETHRYTH'S SHOULDER, STARING BALEFULLY at Ealdred who ignored me completely. His eyes were on his daughter's and they seemed to have wilted like his moustache.

'Have these devils harmed you?' Ealdred asked Cynethryth.

I wanted to tell Ealdred what I thought of him. Instead, I clutched the pommel of the sword at my side and bit my tongue.

'No, Father,' she said. 'Why should they harm me? I did not betray them.' The words sounded flat as barley bread but the accusation struck Ealdred for all that, for he clenched his sharp jaw, the muscles bouncing in his cheek as he stood swaying with *Serpent*'s gentle roll.

'Why are you here, daughter? Amongst these . . .' his eyes flicked to me, 'these savages? This scowling fiend has bewitched you, is that not so? Otherwise how could you stand to be near him, daughter? He is the spawn of the Dark One. You must know of the loathsome things they believe? Of their uncivilized ways?'

Cynethryth looked at me and I swear she seemed to be

weighing the truth in this. I folded my arms and raised my eyebrows, inviting her response, but she turned back to the ealdorman. 'My brother's death is on you,' she said. 'You might as well have killed him with your own hands.'

'Are you forgetting that it was the heathens that took him? Took you both in bonds from Coenwulf's land? If anyone killed my son it was them. You think I don't grieve for Weohstan? For my son? Now I have nothing. God has forsaken us, Cynethryth. I believe that now.' Ealdred was trembling and I hoped for his sake he would not cry like a meyla, a little girl. 'He has turned his back on our family. Look at us, girl.'

'Weohstan loved you,' Cynethryth said. Her voice was grief-hollow, wrung out like an old cloth. 'He was a better man than you.'

'Ah, Cynethryth,' Ealdred said, leaning towards her and forcing a grim half-grin, 'at least we agree on that.'

I touched Cynethryth's elbow. 'Come. Leave him to stew in his own grease,' I said. Two gulls screeched and tumbled above *Serpent*'s prow and one of them skimmed the sea, rising with nothing but a desolate cry. Cynethryth seemed about to speak again, then she gave a slight shake of her head and turned and walked with me to the stern.

'He'll be worm food before sunset,' Sigurd growled in Norse as we passed him at the mast step.

'The sooner the better, lord,' I muttered in the same language, bending to pull a dry blanket from the hold for Cynethryth. I gave it to her and she went to my row bench and sat by Penda with the blanket round her shoulders, hugging her knees and looking out to sea. I wanted to go to her, to try to recapture some morsel of what we had shared that dawn in the sandy cove. And yet I felt that whatever it was was already dissipating on the morning's breath of a breeze, like vapour from an open wound, and would be lost for ever. To my mind, Ealdred's presence poisoned the waters for Cynethryth and me. I would have been happy for Asgot to walk over to *Serpent*'s prow, slit the ealdorman's throat and dump him into the ocean as an offering to Njörd or any other lord of Asgard the godi was on talking terms with.

I took over from Penda at the oar, which the Norsemen were happy about. The Englishman was happy too, judging by the way he fled before I had even taken a grip of the oar so that the stave slipped through the port and we might have lost it if I had not leapt for it, smashing my knee against the hull for my trouble. Some of the men swore and I was embarrassed, but Penda did not seem in the least concerned. He sat on the deck, took a whetstone from his belt, spat on it and began to sharpen his sword.

Egfrith had found the gospel book in *Fjord-Elk*'s hold. None of the Norsemen had wanted anything to do with that White Christ thing and so Knut had had to bring *Serpent* alongside *Fjord-Elk* so that the monk could scramble aboard.

'Here it is! By the grace of the Almighty, here it is!' Egfrith had screeched after a while rummaging in *Fjord-Elk*'s hold, talking to himself or perhaps his god the whole time. He had clutched a silk bag against his chest and his little eyes had been wide and wild. 'I have found it! The book is safe again!' he yelled. 'Praise the merciful Lord, who has entrusted the precious words of Saint Jerome to His humble servant. *Calix meus inebrians*, hey Raven? My cup makes me drunk.'

'I have known little girls who can outdrink you, monk,' I had said, to which he had batted a hand as though I had not the wits to understand anything.

With our English prisoners, the gospel book of Saint Jerome, and *Fjord-Elk* riding our wake, we set an easy rhythm at the oars, heading south along the coast. We did not hug the land so closely now, as Sigurd did not want to run into any Frankish vessels that might be patrolling the shallow waters. Nor did he want any fishing skiffs returning to Frankish hearths with news of two surf dragons prowling offshore. But we were told to keep a lookout for an island, or the mouth of the Sicauna river, or a secluded monastery ripe as a windfall apple nestled along that green coast. For such a place, stuffed with silver and guarded by monks, was not a thing any good sword-Norse could ignore. If the river came first we would turn our bows and sail north again, for Karolus's kingdom was no place for heathens. As for a deserted island, that was what we needed, or rather what Jarl Sigurd needed to observe the age-old tradition of the hólmgang.

'Hólmgang?' Penda asked, tilting his sword in the sunlight, checking its length for notches. 'What heathen horseshit is a hólmgang?' Cynethryth's eyes were on me too as I pulled on the oar in perfect unison with Arnvid in front. Her face was pinched, her lips tight, and I guessed she was feeling seasick again.

'It's a fight, Penda,' I said, 'between two men. It must be on an island, I think.' But that was as much as I knew and so I asked Bjarni.

'It is a set-to over honour,' Bjarni said, his rowing fluid and effortless. 'A man's honour is like a set of scales evenly balanced, poised in harmony. A man must never let that balance be disturbed. If that happens, he is not on even terms with his people, and his family can be spoken of with scorn. Any man worth his skin will fight whoever has caused offence. He will win back the honour taken from him. But it is never a brawl. There are rules. The fight should be on land where no man lives. Or else at a place set aside for such things. My village has a place.' His blue eyes grew. 'The grass itself sprouts red now because of the blood spilled there since before any can remember.'

Behind me, Black Floki grunted. 'A man's honour can be a blood-hungry thing,' he mumbled.

As Bjarni explained the hólmgang to me, I explained it to

Penda and Cynethryth. It seemed there was no such thing as the hólmgang in Wessex or, as far as Penda knew, in any kingdom in England. There, blood feuds turn like cartwheels and revenge killings lie in corpses, one on the other, generation after generation until the original offence is long forgotten.

'The fight usually ends with a disabling wound to the leg,' Bjarni went on, 'but I have seen them end with both men corpses. The strangest one I ever saw was when I was a beardless boy. It happened four days' walk from my village but every man and his dog made the journey because of who the fighters were.' Bjarni's thick lips curled into a smile and from the neck up you would never have known he was rowing. 'One was a man named Gnupa, a hard son of a bitch from the north who had a reputation for ploughing any woman who so much as glanced in his direction and some who didn't, too. He was also a known killer, which was how he got away with getting his leg over other men's wives. Anyway, Gnupa often came to our village to sell his reindeer bones and bear skins and such. Made some good money too, then he'd drink himself stupid, cause a fuss, and leave before his shit got too big to be swept out of sight. The other man was Kraki, the son of our chief. A promising young man he was, strong and agile, and who knows why Kraki's young wife – I forget the whore's name – decided to part her legs for Gnupa's face, but she did. Least that's what folk said. Our chief tried to talk it off as nothing more than trade turned sour, hot words over Gnupa's prices. Tried to smooth over the crack in his son's pride. But Kraki demanded the hólmgang and I think the old man was proud of his son for it, for all he did not want it to happen.'

I stopped Bjarni so that I could translate his story to Penda and Cynethryth before I forgot too much of it, then nodded for the Norseman to continue.

'Well, they met at a place of Gnupa's choosing, which was miles from anywhere. I think he did not want too many to see him kill the chief's son. Bad for business. Still, as I said, we all turned out to watch. We liked Kraki and there were more than a few men there who hoped to see the lad do what they lacked the guts to do. Womenfolk turned out too.' Bjarni chuckled. 'Perhaps their private parts were slippery for Gnupa.' I left that last bit out. 'Both men spurned shields, which was unusual . . .'

'Fucking halfwits,' Black Floki put in.

'Aye, but brave,' Bjarni said. 'They started cautious, mind, circled each other like wolves, experience against youth, both right-handers.' He grinned. 'We thought we were in for a rare fight. We itched for it. Then both men yelled and stepped up swinging and each took the other's head clean off! Their neck stumps spewed gore over us and their heads bounced twice, finishing in the muck, eyes wide as the world and dirty. Gnupa fell sideways and shook like a fish but Kraki, he collapsed to his knees and there he stayed, headless and dead as a rock, his hand still gripping his sword. We were too thunderstruck to feel cheated of a good fight. We just looked at them, our mouths catching flies. And that was it. Over. Never seen anything like it since. By the next full moon our chief was dead. His heart cracked, so my grandmother said.'

I took a breath and finished the tale in English.

'That is a horrible story, Raven,' Cynethryth chided. I think she was gulping down vomit.

'It wasn't my story,' I said defensively.

'Well I liked it,' Penda said, scratching the scar on his face thoughtfully. 'Especially the ending. Saw an idiot hack his own leg half off with an axe once.' He shook his spiky head. 'But never anything queer as that. Ask the heathen if he has any more stories.'

I looked at Cynethryth who had shuffled nearer *Serpent*'s side as though she was about to spew. 'Maybe later, Penda,' I said.

'She's just seasick, Raven,' he protested. 'A good story will take her mind off it.' But the truth was that I did not want to hear any more such tales either. My thoughts were dark enough without more blood to stain them, for Sigurd was going to fight Mauger, the champion of Wessex, and there was every chance it would be his doom. And what would we do without Sigurd?

Three times that day men called out boats they had spotted nearer the shore and once a longboat sailing east on the northern horizon. There was little breeze and what there was was warm enough to let us row bare-chested, relishing the stir of the air as it dried the streams of sweat rolling down our bodies. The sky was still clear for the most part and we were beginning to make out palls of brown smoke hanging against the blue beyond the coastal hills and cliffs. If we did not come to the Sicauna that day we surely would the next, so Sigurd decided to make landfall one last time before turning the ships' prows to the north. There were matters to be settled and blood to be spilled and in a perfect world the hólmgang would take place on an island, some skerry where no man held dominion. But it was not a perfect world and we had come across no such places. Sigurd's fight with Mauger would have to happen on the Frankish shore.

'A hólmgang on Christian land?' Asgot spat, shaking his head so that the lank hair rattled the bones plaited in it. 'I warn you against it, Sigurd. The man you will fight is a Christian. His god will be powerful there.' He nodded to the coast. The rest of us kept to our rowing but our ears were catching what they could.

Sigurd pulled his golden beard through his fist. 'What do the bones say, godi?' he asked.

Asgot curled his lips. 'The bones are unclear,' he admitted. 'The future is hidden. We should wait.' He gestured to the English prisoners huddled beneath Jörmungand. They were talking amongst themselves now and seemed to be encouraging Mauger, their faces hard and fierce. 'Take them north, Sigurd. Kill the English and throw them into our cold waters. That will please the gods. Those worms are your enemies. You owe them nothing. Give them only death, my jarl. That is what they would give us.'

Sigurd seemed to consider this for a while, his brow heavy and his teeth worrying his thick bottom lip. Then he shook his head.

'The deal is made,' he said. 'I will fight the whoreson before the moon rises and the matter will be settled. When Mauger's blood dries on my sword I will give you Ealdred. Do with him what you want.' At this the godi's yellowing eyes flashed maliciously and his talon-like hand dropped to the knife hilt in his belt. He bowed to Sigurd, then turned with a flourish and made his way to the prow, where I heard him tormenting the Wessexmen in his bad English with promises of pain and death.

We stowed Jörmungand so as not to offend the land spirits, and *Serpent* and *Fjord-Elk* came safely to the shore, their hulls crunching on the gravel beach and us jumping off with ropes to pull their hulls clear of the surf. There were no boulders to tie up to, so we used eight sharpened stakes kept for the purpose and hammered them into the beach with the butts of our great axe heads. Then as usual Black Floki and several other Norsemen loped off to get an idea of the land, whilst others got on with the important task of gathering wood for the cookfire. When we knew it was safe, the iron cauldrons were brought from the ships and Olaf ordered a party of five to scrub the gore and filth from *Fjord-Elk*'s deck. He told me to watch the English, especially Ealdred, which I was happy to do because it involved no scrubbing. Blood soaks into oak and it takes a barrel's worth of elbow grease to get it out and even then it'll stain till Ragnarök.

Further up the beach were thousands of stones as smooth as hens' eggs and beyond them stood a wall of rowan, ash and elder, their green scent checked by the sea's slick tang but breaking through to waft down to us every now and then.

Asgot sent Bram and Svein the Red hunting for a fox or badger or hare or whatever creature this land had to offer, giving them strict orders that the animal should be alive when they brought it back. It did not hurt to make the gods a blood offering before your jarl fought a renowned warrior. By the time they returned we had eaten our night meal, a broth of seal meat and mushrooms, and by their faces and the late hour we knew they had not been successful. The big men slumped by the birchwood fires, taking the steaming bowls of food they were offered and eating in silence, and no man dared ask them about the hunt. Even Asgot held his tongue, though his face, sour as old milk, told me he saw in their failure some bad omen. We fed the prisoners too and Sigurd himself handed Mauger a bowl full to spilling so that the Englishman could not blame his coming defeat in the hólmgang on hunger weakness. Not that the loser would be in a state to blame anything, not in this life. Still, Mauger acknowledged the act with a curt nod and when he had finished slurping his second bowlful an ant could not have filled its belly with what was left. The fires cracked and popped as the birch split along its grain and the low murmur of the Norsemen hung above the flames like strands of some tale not yet told. What would become of the Fellowship if Mauger won? I presumed Olaf would lead us and I was sure the Norsemen would follow him, but where would we go? Would the men swear an oath to Olaf as they had to their jarl?

'It's time,' Sigurd said, standing and draining the mead horn he was clutching. He was the other side of the fire, whose light played over the sharp bones of his face so that he might have been carved from seasoned oak. 'Uncle, you will be my second.' Olaf nodded solemnly. I looked at Bjarni.

'In the hólmgang both men must have a second, a shield-bearer,' Bjarni explained, palming mead from his own lips. 'This man must be unarmed and cannot get involved in the fight. Oh, and . . .' he held up four fingers, frowned drunkenly, then folded one of them, 'both fighters are allowed three shields.' He sniffed. 'Shields don't last long in the hólmgang.'

'Raven,' Sigurd said, pointing off to where the prisoners sat, 'you will be Mauger's second.'

'Lord?' I said, half smiling because I thought he must be joking.

'Fetch three shields for the Englishman. Good shields with iron rims,' he said. 'And don't let him forget his sword,' he added, tying back his hair, which was a dull gold by the flamelight. 'Godi, prepare the ground. And stop fretting about your knife being dry. We'll make a sacrifice when it is over.' Asgot stood with a nod of his greasy head and enlisted the help of Bjarni and Bjorn before clacking off down the beach towards the lean silhouettes of the ships, their sterns glowing by the light coming off the white breakers at the water's edge. I stood still for a moment watching Black Floki hissing in his jarl's ear. Floki's hand was on his sword's hilt and I knew he was begging Sigurd to let him fight Mauger instead, but Sigurd put a hand on the warrior's shoulder and shook his head and Floki's shoulders slumped in defeat.

I turned towards *Fjord-Elk* to fetch three good shields.

CHAPTER SEVEN

BJORN AND BJARNI LAID TWELVE OLD CLOAKS ON THE GROUND IN A square measuring some nine feet across. We were up past the round stones, beyond the low murmur of the sea and the fire's crack and pop. The ground was more or less level here. Ahead, the stand of low trees shifted and swayed cumbersomely, their leaves rattling in the night breeze. Some of us had prepared the ground, hacking away clumps of honeysuckle and bindweed vines whose sweet smell drifted in currents as we disturbed them. With the cloaks laid out and pegged down, Asgot took the point of a spear and carved a series of three lines into the ground around the outside of the square, each a foot apart. At every corner he set a roughly hewn post of hazel and this boundary was made complete with four ropes. Then Olaf and Bram Bear lit the torches they had stuck in the ground. Their flames gave off a restless, stuttering light which twisted and pulled the arena, distorting it into some weird dreamscape. Resinous smoke tendrils meandered around us, gathering stealthily and curling upwards like black wraiths seeking the paler night sky.

When all was prepared, the old godi stood and considered

it and with a grunt of what I took to be satisfaction told me to fetch the putrid pig's bladders, by which he meant Mauger and Ealdred and the other Wessexmen.

I found Mauger on his back on the sand beside the longships. One knee was hugged tight against his broad chest, whilst the other leg pointed to the top of *Fjord-Elk*'s mast. He grabbed the calf of the raised leg and pulled it higher, stretching the hamstring, his arm muscles swollen and tight. The warrior rings, of which he was so proud, were already sitting amongst the treasures in *Fjord-Elk*'s hold, but there were still dents in his arms where they had sat. You can strip a warrior of his hard-won treasures, but some, men like Mauger, look no less impressive without them. You have to cut the pride out of these men with a good blade.

'Sigurd is waiting,' I said. Black Floki stood in the shadows keeping a hateful eye on the Wessexman, his spear's butt buried in the sand. Ealdred and his household warriors were still up by the fire, though like the remaining Norsemen they were stirring now with the whiff of the fight in the air.

'Let him wait,' Mauger rumbled, wincing at the self-inflicted pain of the stretch. Then he rolled over and stood in one fluid motion and my heartbeat quickened because I was within the man's reach. I knew Mauger's strength was enormous, that he could have snapped my neck or back as easily as I could have a dog's. He loosened his shoulders and neck, staring at me the whole time, and I could smell the sharp, violent stench of his sweat.

'I will be your shield-bearer,' I said sullenly.

He frowned, pulling his thick neck in. 'You?'

I shrugged. 'Me.'

'Why would you be my second?' he asked.

'I would not if it were up to me,' I said. 'If I had my way we would tie you up and use you for archery practice.' Black Floki stepped forward, sensing trouble. 'But Sigurd told me I must hold your shields. So I'll hold your shields.'

Mauger smiled and flexed his huge muscles, making the tattoos on his arms squirm. Then he turned towards the sea and took three deep breaths, his chest rising and falling like the slight swell beyond the breakers. He turned to me again, glanced at Black Floki, then back to me. 'All right, lad,' he said. He hawked and spat into the sand. 'Let's go and see your jarl.'

We gave Mauger his arms, his brynja, helmet, sword and shield, and I brought two more shields which were well made and undamaged, then we made our way up the beach. We passed the campfires, glowing piles of embers which pulsed red and black in the breeze, and the three surly Norsemen whose bad luck it was to remain with the longboats when they would have given anything to watch the fight. Then we stood for a while in the darkness, allowing our eyes to readjust, before Floki spotted the guttering flame of a torch and the dark shapes of the others disappearing amongst the scrub.

'You don't strike me as a Christ thrall, Mauger,' I said, 'but if you are a Christian now would be a good time to see to your soul.'

'You think your jarl can beat me, blood-eye?' he asked, seeming more surprised than affronted.

'Sigurd's veins carry the blood of the Aesir,' I said. 'He is descended from Týr, Lord of Battle. Maybe even from Óðin. You have a high reputation, Mauger, and I am sure you have put one or two warriors in the ground. But Sigurd is something different. He is a slayer of men.'

'We shall see what Sigurd is,' Mauger replied, clacking heavily over the rocks and barging his way through a tangle of thorns. I had merely been trying to scatter a few seeds of doubt in the warrior's mind, but of course I was wasting my breath. A man of Mauger's experience could no more be shaken by words than a mountain could be shaken by wind.

The crowd parted and the Wessex warrior strode through them, and I behind him, my palms slick with sweat and my breath short and ragged. The shadow-played, bearded faces were grim and tight-lipped and the press of warriors was heavy. Their smell – sweat, leather, grease and filth – filled the place, drowning the honeyed scent of flowers.

Mauger nodded to his ealdorman and Ealdred nodded back, and then the clearing was silent but for the hiss of the torches, the rustle of leaves and the woody snaps and cracks from the night-shrouded trees beyond. Somewhere a bird of prey screeched and was answered by the howl of a wolf claiming a fresh kill. Blood was already seeping out there in the dark.

Sigurd stood inside the ropes and I could not help but smile when I saw him. His steel helmet reflected the flamelight and below its rim was a line of shadow from which his unseen eyes stared out at Mauger. Beneath those eyes his cheekbones pressed like knife blades against the skin and his beard was full until beneath his chin where it hung plaited thick as a rope. The rings of his brynja glinted in the torchlight so that they looked to be made of gold, and his father's sword hung at his hip where it looked as much a part of the man as his limbs. He held a round shield against his chest, its boss polished and undented, and on that shield was painted a wolf's head. He was magnificent.

I knew Cynethryth was somewhere in that gathering but I resisted the urge to look for her. The Wessexmen stood with Ealdred and one of them cheered for Mauger, making the others bellow encouragement too, and then Sigurd's men clamoured for their jarl and for a moment all was chaos. I saw Penda. He stood, arms folded, and raised his chin at me and that one small gesture somehow embodied the gravity of what was about to happen. I wanted to ask Sigurd to get someone else to second Mauger, one of the Englishmen perhaps, or even Ealdred himself. Why must I hold the man's shields? I would sooner see him dead and I wanted to tell my jarl as much, but not a man alive would have interrupted Sigurd then. So I held my tongue and took my place behind Mauger who had ducked under the rope and now stood facing his opponent. Olaf stood behind Sigurd. The older man's face was hard as a cliff face.

Asgot shuffled into the middle of the skins and stood between the warriors, his yellowed eyes heavy with worry and his lips cracked and dry from prayers. With a raised hand the godi silenced every tongue.

'Mauger has accepted a challenge by the ancient rite of the hólmgang,' he crowed, nodding to me, meaning I was to translate for the Wessexmen, which I did. 'Each man must stand on this cloak and not draw a finger's length outside it. Normally, the fight is over when one man's blood shows on the cloak. Not tonight. This hólmgang will not end until one of these men is a corpse.' Now Olaf ducked under the rope and stood within the lines Asgot had etched in the earth. I wondered what he was doing as Asgot continued. 'Each warrior has his own shield-bearer who will defend him for as long as his shields hold.' I felt as if I had been struck in the face. Asgot pointed a bony finger skyward. 'But neither shield-bearer may strike his opponent or his opponent's man or take part in the fight other than to defend.'

I looked at Sigurd, my eyes boring into him for some explanation or reprieve. It was one thing to hold Mauger's shields, but defend him? How was I supposed to defend Mauger? Against Sigurd! I would sooner sink my knife into Mauger's rancid guts.

'As the representative of the man who has been challenged, Mauger may strike the first blow. After that the fight must rage unfettered and no man here may play a part.' Now Asgot turned to Mauger and his face was a twisted knot of ancient hatred. 'When my jarl has killed you,' he hissed, 'I will cut your limbs from your corpse. I will peel the skin from your flesh. Your soul will go screaming to the afterlife and for all eternity no other soul shall ever recognize you for a man.'

The words chilled my blood and I could not see Mauger's face, but I did see him spit at the godi's feet and I admired him for it. Olaf gestured to me to climb into the square and I did, my heart hammering like a banner in the wind. Silence reigned for three heartbeats, then Mauger drew his great sword and roared like the opening of Hel's gates. He leapt forward and smashed his sword into Sigurd's shield, hoping to split it, but it was a good shield, as was the arm behind it, and Sigurd took the blow, though it must have shaken the marrow from his arm. Now the jarl lifted his father's sword up and over his head and crashed it into Mauger's shield, but Mauger angled the shield well, catching the weight of the sword on the iron rim. The onlookers yelled with a storm's fury as the combatants swung their swords. The shields were battered and neither Olaf nor I could get close, not that I dared to even try.

Sigurd was taller but Mauger was broader and heavier. He slammed his right shoulder into Sigurd's shield, forcing the jarl back so that the heel of his right foot was over the edge of the cloak. Sigurd leant into his shield and heaved, the corded veins in his neck fit to burst as he drove Mauger back, growling like an animal. Then Mauger dropped his shoulder, rolling left and throwing Sigurd off balance. The Wessexman scythed his blade full circle and Sigurd raised his shield just in time but the limewood split with a loud crack. Both men jumped back, breathing heavily, their faces sweat-soaked. Sigurd did not have to look at his shield to know it was damaged and he must have known he was taking a risk by using it still. But it was too early in the fight to be down to two shields. I suddenly realized why each man got three. It was so they would exhaust themselves smashing each other's shields to kindling, and not have the strength left for a killing blow. But this was no ordinary hólmgang, and it would not end with the first spilled blood.

Sigurd dragged his forearm across his head and spat saliva thick as frogspawn. The two men circled, their eyes locked. Sigurd slashed high, fast as lightning, but Mauger was already moving and the sword's point passed a breath away from his face as he swung for Sigurd's shield, cutting the thing clean in half. Sigurd gripped the lower half, kicking the other part away. At least the iron boss still held, though he would not have long. So he attacked, launching a series of hammer blows which Mauger took on his own shield, and I cursed because I had chosen that shield and it was harder than a wheel from Thór's chariot.

Now Mauger attacked, no grace, just swinging his sword like a man hacking through brambles, battering what remained of Sigurd's shield and lopping another quarter from it, leaving the jarl with the iron boss, two mangled strips of metal and a sliver of wood. Blood dripped rhythmically from the inside of the shield boss.

'They said you were a great warrior, Mauger,' Sigurd said, giving his wolf's grin, 'but I can see that you are an old dog whose best days are long gone. Come. I will end your shame.'

'This dog still has teeth, heathen,' Mauger said, raising cheers from the Wessexmen. I glanced at Ealdred and saw that his eyes were gleaming with pride, or hope, or both.

Olaf handed Sigurd a new shield and Mauger waited until Sigurd had set himself, then the English warrior attacked again. Sigurd stood his ground and when Mauger stepped back to suck air into his belly, the jarl thrust for his neck. Mauger caught the point with his shield and drove it up and away, but Sigurd's lunge was a feint and he thumped his shield into Mauger's face, sending the big man reeling. Sigurd stepped up and slammed his foot into Mauger's thigh, almost taking him down. Mauger staggered and yelled and planted himself again, dipping his head and bringing his shield and sword up. Sigurd hacked at the man's shield. Splinters flew as he kept up the vicious assault and it was all Mauger could do to catch each blow, though each must have felt like Ragnarök, the end of the world. The Wessexman edged around the cloak, his shoulders bouncing with ragged breaths. He yelled and threw his right foot forward, swinging his sword from left to right, attacking Sigurd's unshielded side, but Sigurd hefted his sword. The blades bit and a shard of steel flew, slicing Sigurd's cheek. Sigurd punched his sword's pommel into Mauger's teeth, breaking them, and I heard Mauger's deep grunt as blood spilled from his chin like water down a mountain. The Wessexman was dazed. He stumbled, his thighs straining to keep his knees locked, and Sigurd sensed victory. He came on, his sword thundering down like a god's vengeance, and I threw myself forward, catching the sword on a shield, that one blow hammering me into the earth like a tent peg. Sigurd stepped back, wide eyes shining like silver coins. Around me the Norsemen clamoured. I cringed, expecting cold steel to tear my flesh.

Mauger had stumbled over to the far edge of the arena and was shaking some sense back into his head, spitting cracked teeth and great gobs of thick blood on to the cloaks. Sigurd had his back to the Wessexman. He was staring at me and I thought I had ruined everything. I had done my duty as a shield-bearer when I should have let Sigurd cleave Mauger in two. But then Sigurd's eyes flashed. He grimaced and turned back to Mauger, and the fight rolled on like a storm. The shields crashed, their bosses crumpling. Mauger swept his sword low and Sigurd blocked with his own blade but then the Wessexman slammed his shield's rim into Sigurd's temple, sending the jarl's helmet bouncing. Mauger frenzied like a bear stuck with arrows, chopping his opponent's second shield to a splintered mess. But Olaf was suddenly there, the last shield raised before his jarl, taking Mauger's blows. Olaf might have been older than the other Norsemen but he was an oak of a man. Try as Mauger might, there was no way through to Sigurd, though I did not know how a man could have such strength as to maintain an assault like that – or resist it. And this is how it went. Into the night. Each warrior taking his turn to attack, then defend, and breathing with an ocean's appetite at any moment in between. I have never known shields to take such punishment and yet hold so long, for all they could not possibly last.

Sigurd's golden hair had fallen loose and now hung soaking across his face, one half of which was sheeted in blood that glistened in the torchlight. He snatched the last shield from Olaf and banged his sword against it, beckoning Mauger to come again. Mauger's mouth was a gory, blood-filled hole. He was on his second shield now and he was limping. He was too exhausted to speak. He nodded at the Norseman, raised his shield and hitched across the space to the cheers of his countrymen. I moved too, staying behind and to Mauger's left, watching both men and hoping I would be quick enough to dodge or defend any wild sword swing from either of them. Olaf had no more shields for Sigurd and so he stood helpless now on the lines etched in the earth beyond the cloaks. His fists were balled like knotted rope, his brow was heavy, and he was growling under his breath, 'Finish it, Sigurd, finish it.'

The two warriors slammed shields, stepped back and swung their swords, Mauger high and Sigurd low. The Norseman was faster and his blade hacked into Mauger's hip, shattering the rings of his brynja, but Mauger's sword sliced through the mail on Sigurd's shoulder, carving a chunk of flesh from it. Sigurd yelled in pain and fury and slammed his sword against Mauger's shield and Mauger staggered backwards, cleaving Sigurd's shield in two with a mighty swing. Sigurd cast the broken remains aside and prepared for Mauger's attack. The Wessexman grinned savagely, limped forward and swung his sword to take off his enemy's head, but Sigurd dropped, spinning, and came round from the left, thumping his blade into Mauger's right thigh with a sound like a log being split. It must have broken the man's leg bone for he cried out and fell to his knees. The wound at Sigurd's shoulder was spilling blood, and the whole of his left side was drenched and shining slickly as he came at Mauger again. His father's sword hung for a moment, flamelight riding its length, then it fell, but Mauger caught it on his shield and Sigurd swung again. This time Mauger's shield split with an echoing crack. I ran forward with the last shield and Sigurd snarled but stepped back, allowing me to slip the leather straps over Mauger's forearm. Mauger grunted thanks and tried to stand but he could not. I jumped clear as he deflected another blow and then somehow Ealdred's man hacked into Sigurd's lower leg so that the jarl collapsed to his knees. The combatants stared at each other, their faces clenched in pain and their battered bodies heaving and shuddering with exhaustion. Norse and Englishmen hollered at their champions, willing them to rise and end the thing, but Mauger and Sigurd were in their own agony-filled worlds and seemed deaf to the noise.

Mauger laid down his sword, removed his helmet, shook off his shield, and threw out his arms, enticing Sigurd on with a bloody, hateful smile. Sigurd spat, then with a grunt thrust his father's sword through the cloaks into the earth. The crowd fell silent as the grave for a heartbeat, then Sigurd and Mauger slammed into each other like reindeer bulls and I cringed, hoping Olaf would stop the fight but knowing that he could not. They were punching and clawing wildly and then they were rolling, each straining to get the advantage, and then the air was rent by a blood-curdling scream. The sound was terrifying. It was Mauger. Sigurd had torn out his eye and it dangled on its bloody string, bouncing on the man's cheek. Mauger was screeching horribly but somehow he clubbed a fist into Sigurd's chin. His fingers found the slice in the jarl's cheek and those fingers dug and gouged, and a low moan came from the watching Norsemen. Sigurd slammed his forehead into Mauger's face, bursting his nose, then wrapped one of the warrior's brawny arms between his own and slammed himself down to the right, snapping Mauger's arm with a hollow crack. Then Sigurd roared, and taking the dangling eye in his fist he ripped the bloody strings out of the socket and threw it at Ealdred's feet.

Mauger's face and beard were all gore as he swung blindly with a fist, his left arm dangling uselessly. Sigurd grimaced and with awesome, unimaginable strength climbed back to his feet. Mauger was striking at him but the jarl took no heed as he stepped up and cradled the Wessexman's head in his arms.

'Óðin!' he cried, then he wrenched Mauger's head almost full circle. Another crack split the night. Mauger's right hand flapped like a bird's broken wing, then went still. Sigurd pushed his knee into the man's shoulder and the corpse pitched on to its side without a sound. It was over. And Sigurd had won.

CHAPTER EIGHT

OLAF AND BLACK FLOKI RAN TO THEIR JARL, WEDGING THEIR shoulders beneath his arms just as his knees buckled. Sigurd's face and brynja were blood-soaked and glistening. His beard and hair were dark, matted clumps, and he sagged between his men like an animal carcass. They bore him out of the arena as Ealdred and his Wessexmen crowded round Mauger, unable to accept that their champion was dead. Asgot barked at a knot of Norsemen, demanding that they prevent the English from disturbing Mauger's corpse, then he shuffled after Sigurd, wringing his hands and chanting to the gods as he went. I stood stunned. Despite all I had seen and done, the brutality of the fight both appalled and excited me. I was awestruck by the warriors who had fought, by their strength and skill and their refusal to yield, and yet it was a terrible thing to see a warrior of Mauger's stature ruined so, carved up like soulless meat. Before the fight both men had looked like gods of battle, lords of war. Now one was food for the worms and the other was a broken bloody mess. My lord and jarl was now so many splintered timbers from a storm-wrecked ship and we would have to wait and see whither the tides of his wyrd carried him.

Some of the Norsemen used their spear staves to push the Wessexmen back from Mauger's tortured corpse whilst others began to dismantle the stakes and ropes of the arena. Sigurd's sword still pinned the cloaks to the ground like some final judgement. Part of me, the part within which the blood yet bubbled, causing my muscles to tremble and twitch, wanted desperately to grip that sword's hilt, as though by touching the thing I could somehow imbibe more deeply of the event's terrible glory.

'You'd better pray that he lives, lad,' Bram Bear growled beside me. He gestured to the stained cloaks. Bjorn and Bjarni were pulling the wooden pegs from their edges. 'A skin full of that blood down there would still be warming Sigurd's innards if not for you. What in Óðin's hairy arse were you thinking? Mauger . . .' he spat, 'that treacherous dog was done for, lad. Sigurd had him beaten. But when you took that blow? You could have smacked my face with a fucking fish. I thought I was dreaming.' He stared at me, a deep crease across his brow, then shook his head and walked away. I saw that other Norsemen were looking at me too, their eyes questioning, and why wouldn't they? After all, Bram was right. I had played no small part in the hólmgang. The fight would have been over much sooner had I not thrown a shield between Mauger and Sigurd's blade. Because of that one inexplicable act, our jarl had taken several wounds, some serious enough to see him a corpse, and if he died from them there was every chance that I would be blamed. And yet it was not the vengeance of some Norsemen that chilled my heart. Rather I was terrified that by saving Mauger with that shield I had unpicked some thread from Sigurd's wyrd, undone what the Norns had woven. If I had done that, a blade in the gut would be a small thing, because those who dwelt in Asgard loved Sigurd – I still believed that, even if others had begun to doubt – and so I would have to face the wrath of the gods.

The camp that night was quiet and lead heavy. It was as though the air itself pressed down on us with the weight of issues and decisions being fought over in a realm unseen yet real enough. Asgot and Olaf were with Sigurd, though Olaf soon came to Cynethryth, asking if she had any experience of treating battle wounds. When she said she had some knowledge of healing herbs and of the binding of cuts, Olaf bade her help in any way she could, and so it was a strange party that fought for Sigurd's life that night. Asgot implored Eir, a healing goddess and handmaiden of Frigg, and of course Óðin himself, to save the jarl, to close his wounds and restore his strength. Every now and then I caught a whiff of some or other herb which the godi had taken from his stash to either apply directly to Sigurd's torn flesh or else burn to drown the jarl in bitter smoke. Olaf soothed him with soft words that I could not hear. He mopped his friend's brow with wet linen, washed the blood from his wounds and cut other cloth into strips for Cynethryth to use as bindings.

The rest of us left them to their work, though occasionally one of us would be called to bring more hot water and some- times mead, which they would force through Sigurd's grimac- ing lips to fog his agony.

More men than normal took up sentry duties on the high ground and I envied them being away from the gloomy mood of the beach. At first I wished someone would sing or wrestle or do anything so that we would not have to hear Sigurd's moans. But then I understood. The Norsemen, most of them anyway, wanted to know what road their jarl travelled now. By hearing each gasp of anguish, each miserable, suffering groan, we were in some small way sharing Sigurd's journey, and that was the least we could do and also the most.

The strange yellow smoke from Asgot's fire seemed intent on finding my eyes, which stung and watered, blurring my view of our Wessex prisoners, who sat in a wretched knot around their ealdorman. They were silent as the grave and perhaps they were practising, for their champion had lost, which meant Sigurd could do with them what he wanted. If he lived he was not likely to be in a generous mood. If he died his men might well tear the Englishmen limb from limb for the honey-sweet revenge of it. From where I sat Ealdred and his five men were lost souls. They were draugr, the walking dead.

'This should be good,' said a Norseman beside me. Hours had passed and the first glow of dawn was a fragile flush in the east. I looked up to see Asgot crossing the beach, leaving the huddled figures of Olaf and Cynethryth with Jarl Sigurd. The godi walked purposefully, though he must have been exhausted, towards the corpse of Mauger, which had been dragged from the hólmgang square, stripped of its brynja, and left face down in the sand. I could see that the body was stiff, for one arm bent backwards unnaturally, raised off the sand, the hand like an eagle's talon. Asgot raised his arms to the sky, then, without taking his eyes from the corpse, called for Svein to bring himself and his axe and be quick about it.

'And it had better be sharp as an old crone's tongue, you brain-addled, red-haired son of an ox,' the godi added for good measure. Without a word, Svein stood, grasped his great axe and made his way across the sand, a giant hulking shape against the weak dawn light.

I remembered the blood-chilling promise the godi had made to Mauger before the fight against Sigurd. The snake hiss of Asgot's voice, each word dripping venom, slithered through my mind.

I will cut your limbs from your corpse. I will peel the skin from your flesh . . . no other soul shall ever recognize you for a man.

A low moan came from the English with the first blow of Svein's axe, which took off Mauger's arm like a branch hacked from a tree. The red-haired giant's face was grim set as he swung again, taking the other arm off at the shoulder with a loud crack. It was too much for Father Egfrith, who stood shakily, crossed himself, then slunk off towards the shore. Asgot was grinning like a fiend as he bent and gathered up the limbs and I could tell that those limbs were heavy by the way the old godi leant back as he hefted them a short distance off. The legs were great hunks of meat, the sinew and muscle as tough as knotted oak, and even mighty Svein had to take several swings to sever them. When he had finished, Mauger's groin was a grotesque dark mess of flesh. I glanced at Ealdred but the ealdorman had his back to the butchering of his champion and I could tell nothing of his thoughts. We Norse watched it all. We murmured prayers to Óðin Lord of War, beseeching him not to take our jarl to his corpse hall in Valhöll but accept the offering of a great enemy instead. It was not a sacrifice as such, because Mauger was already dead, but we assumed Asgot still believed, or hoped, at least, that he could placate the god with the Wessexman's pared flesh. Now I think Asgot did what he did simply because he enjoyed it. The man's cruelty and contempt for his enemies ran deeper than the nethermost fjord. And yet we watched.

When Mauger's butchered corpse lay like joints of meat in the sand, Asgot set about spearing them, two spears thrust into each limb, and he and Svein hoisted the limbs above the fire to burn off the clothes that were stuck to the skin with clotted blood. When this was done, Asgot took his knife and began to strip the blackened skin from the arms and legs, his old face contorted in concentration, and that skin came off in crisp curls. Svein left him to it and came and sat by me, bringing with him the charcoal smell of burnt skin and the acrid stink of singed hair, which can stick in the nostrils for days.

'A bad end for a warrior,' he said, shaking his head.

'A bad end for anyone,' I muttered, and he pursed his lips and nodded, conceding the point.

Arnvid and Bothvar pressed a group into searching for mushrooms and roots amongst the trees beyond the beach, as well
as birds' eggs from the grassy bluffs, to complement the stew
they were nursing above the meal-fire. But what was gathered
would not feed a gaggle of old women, much less a fellowship
of warriors, and I guessed that the men's hearts were not in
the searching, just as our stomachs would not be in the eating.
Sure enough, men picked at their food so that you would have
thought it tasted bad. Neither Arnvid nor Bothvar fished for
compliments for their cooking, as they were wont to do, and
not one was tossed their way.

'Ah, he's the strongest of us all,' Bram rumbled after a silence
that had rolled itself out like a fur to smother the camp. 'He'll
be back on his feet and Loki-scheming before you know it.'

There were a few murmurs of agreement and several hands
touched amulets and sword hilts for luck. Black Floki suggested
we kill the prisoners, slowly, to steer our minds from the dark
thought of losing our jarl, and some of the men voiced their
ideas about how the Wessexmen should die and every one of
those methods was grisly enough to curl your spine. But Bjarni
argued that it was Sigurd's right and his alone to decide the
fates of Ealdred and his men. Our jarl had earned that right,
had he not? Earned it with the spilling of blood and the ripping
of flesh. And no man around that fire, not even Floki, could
argue with that.

*Óðin save him. Please do not take him yet. Give him strength.
Stop the blood. Thicken it, Óðin. Make it stiffen and clot like
cream in the churn. Close his wounds, mighty jarl of the gods.
We need him. I need him.*

What had I done? I looked at the silver ring on my arm,
which had been a gift from Sigurd. It felt heavy now, sitting
tight and constricting over the muscle, and I wanted to take it
off but I did not, for fear of others seeing me do it. A jarl must
be a ring-giver, a bestower of silver and other treasure, for this

is what you get in return for pledging your sword and your life to him and to the Fellowship. What had I done? I had hefted a good shield to protect my enemy and because of that my jarl's blood was spilling like water from a willow trap.

Cynethryth carried a bundle of red soaking rags and dropped them into the largest fire, where they hissed, hurting the flames and filling the morning air with the smell of iron. I looked down the beach at the robed figure of Father Egfrith staring out to sea, his bald white pate catching the first glow of the new day. We disgusted him, I knew, and his will must have been iron-strong to keep him here amongst us.

'You should ask him to put a word in for Sigurd,' Penda said, thumbing back towards Egfrith. 'Your jarl is going to need all the help he can get, lad.'

'You think I should ask that weasel-faced goat dropping to pray to the Christian god?' I asked, exaggerating my disgust.

Penda shrugged as though to ask what harm it could do.

'I'd sooner chew a handful of nails,' I said and Penda shrugged again, scratching the long scar down his face. In truth, I was half tempted to run down the beach, take the monk by his scrawny neck and wring a dozen good prayers from the ever-flapping hole in his face. And perhaps I might have done just that. But that might have angered Óðin even more and the way I saw it I was already walking on thin ice with him. My hopes hung with the All-Father like so many banners tied to a pole, and by beseeching the Christian god too I might stir enough wind to blow that pole over. So I left Egfrith and his nailed god alone and whispered and prayed and begged Óðin Far-Wanderer until my throat was as dry as an old weed-cracked well.

Sigurd's life thread twisted and stretched but it did not break. Olaf, Asgot and Cynethryth treated him with every care, using all their combined lore. They washed his wounds, applied poultices of rat's tail plantain and other leaves I did not recognize, then bound each gash tightly in clean dressings. They fed him meat for strength and herbs to smother his pain. They poured honeyed water and mead down his throat and all the while Asgot wafted a resinous smoke over him which had some strange power, for it made him sleep in spite of the pain. Even Egfrith helped, having disappeared and returned with fistfuls of fennel which, he said, the Emperor Karolus himself declared should be present in every imperial garden because of its healing properties. Asgot had curled his lip at this, but Olaf persuaded him that the medicine was worth a try, arguing that a man who worships a god said to have risen from death is likely to know something of restorative herbs.

We waited, unable amongst ourselves to decide what to do. Some were for taking the ships north. In other words, cutting our losses and going home. But still more would not hear of it, for to turn north now would be admitting defeat and a sword-Norse who does that is setting himself adrift, no longer deserving of the gods' attention, and as likely as not to sink unseen to the seabed. Better to spit in the Weavers' eyes, come what may, these men said.

Our prisoners grew wretched and stinking. We fed them next to nothing and every now and then a frustrated Norseman would punch or kick an English face. They just had to look at us wrong to earn a clout, because we blamed those men for all the trouble that had befallen us and for the empty row benches aboard *Serpent* and *Fjord-Elk*. No one touched Ealdred, though. Sigurd would deal with that son of a shit slithering snake. Still, Asgot itched to sacrifice at least one of the Wessexmen to Óðin and on several occasions the godi drew a crowd, convincing whoever would listen why he should soak his blade in English blood. The only good thing about his speeches was that whenever he talked of sacrifice, Cynethryth would come and sit by me. She did not understand his words, of course, but the godi's savage appetite fattened his eyes in a way that disgusted her. She would take my hand and say little and her eyes would settle on her father across the camp. Sometimes I would catch an exchange between those two, a questioning glance or heartsick look, which I would pretend not to have seen.

On the fourth day it seemed Asgot would get what he wanted. One of the Englishmen, a broad, strong-looking warrior with a dense black beard and long thinning hair, was dragged away from the rest and made to stand by a stake which Svein the Red had driven into the ground. I kept my distance, keeping the woodpile stocked and making a covering of skins to keep it dry though there was not a cloud in the sky. I had already had too big a hand in the weave of the last days and whatever the others decided was fine by me.

'The gods love the old ways.' Asgot's voice crackled like burning sticks as he pointed a lean, knotty finger at the stake. 'So we will do this the old way.' Some of the men nodded and murmured approval. Others frowned, less familiar with these old ways. Asgot drew an invisible blade across the man's abdomen. 'I will open this man's belly, take the end of his gut string and nail it to the stake. Then he will walk round the pole,' he said, drawing a circle in the air, 'like the serpent Jörmungand biting his own tail to girdle the world. Aye, he'll walk until the guts unwind and the meat pulls taut. He looks strong.' The godi grinned, considering Ealdred's warrior. The man's jaw was clenched but his eyes were terror-filled voids, for he did not need to know Norse to get the bones of what lay in store for him. 'He should manage it until the end,' Asgot went on. 'If not, I'll make him wish he had shrivelled and died in his whore mother's rancid womb.'

I almost smiled at that. What could be worse than unravelling your guts round a pole and watching yourself do it?

'Poor bastard,' Penda mumbled, needing no Norse to fathom what was coming.

'This was the way of our grandfathers,' the godi went on, gesturing to Black Floki to haul the prisoner to his feet; 'this will be our way.' The only men not gathered now were the six or seven posted as lookouts, and the air seemed to shiver with the anticipation of the blood rite. Floki shoved the Englishman against the stake and two more Norsemen took hold of the man's arms, for any man will wriggle like a mackerel when he sees a blade aimed at his stomach.

Asgot's knife hissed from the sheath. Cynethryth tensed beside me.

'Sheathe your blade, godi!' We turned. Sigurd. His face was ash grey and so gaunt that it seemed the cheekbones would split the skin. He stood unsteadily, dressed only in filthy breeks and wound dressings, which bore dark stains. 'There will be no sacrifice today.' The men turned to Asgot.

'But the All-Father is waiting, my jarl,' Asgot said, appealing with two hands, one of which still gripped the wicked blade. From the godi's expression I could tell he was as surprised as the rest of us to see Sigurd on his feet. I thought the jarl would fall on his face. He looked like a haugbui, a mound-dweller, some dead body just emerged from its tomb to torment the living.

'It was a good fight between me and Mauger,' he said. 'He was a tough old boar to kill.' A sickly smile touched Sigurd's green lips. 'And because of that these men of Wessex will live.' The Norsemen rumbled, their faces etched and dark.

'What is he saying?' Cynethryth asked, clutching my hand.

'He's saving them,' I replied, 'I think.'

Sigurd pointed at the pitiful clutch of Wessexmen who sat beside a sea-worn boulder half buried in the sand. 'The warriors will live, but Ealdred will die.'

Again Cynethryth asked what the jarl had said, but this time I lied, telling her that I had not understood some of the Norse.

The men grunted their approval. A heartbeat ago they would have happily watched their godi disembowel the prisoners one by one. Yet, as warriors, the Norsemen understood and shared Sigurd's respect for a worthy enemy. No one could deny that Mauger had fought like a champion, which added lustre to Sigurd's victory. However, in their eyes Ealdred was a pale-livered mare, a coward, and deserved no such mercy.

Still, I expected Asgot to churn like a resentful sea, but he did not. He simply nodded and sheathed his knife, flicking a hand to the Norsemen to release the big Wessexman. Black Floki shoved him back towards his countrymen and he went gladly.

'You're just going to let them go?' Olaf asked, staring incredulously at Sigurd. 'They're Christians! They'll scuttle off to some settlement inland, perhaps to the door of Karolus himself, and they'll bring an army of White Christ lunatics down on our heads.'

Sigurd shook his head wearily. 'No, Uncle, they won't. They have no lord now and we have row benches to fill.'

Olaf's face boiled red beneath the bushy beard. 'You'd have them aboard our dragons? You'd have them grip our oars?'

'They can still choose death, Uncle. I leave them that choice.' We all looked at each other like half-wit trolls. It seemed abhorrent that these men, who had been our enemies, would now be given the honour of a place at *Serpent*'s or *Fjord-Elk*'s oars. And yet Sigurd was right, we needed strong arms. Even five pairs was not really enough.

Grimacing, Sigurd walked over to the prisoners, the linen dressing on his left leg below the knee blooming bright red as he moved, until he was standing before the English.

'You can row for me, or you can die for him,' he said, nodding towards Asgot. 'Choose now.' His voice was pain-tired but hard as stone. Instinctively, the warriors looked to Ealdred, but Sigurd shook his head, the lank hair falling across his face.

'Do not ask him. He is nothing now. He decides less than a whipped mongrel and soon he will be worm food. The choice is yours alone. Row or die.'

The big straggle-haired warrior who had come so close to knowing himself inside and out glanced at the rest of us, then nodded, fixing eyes with Sigurd.

'We can still pray to the Lord?' he dared.

'The White Christ?' Sigurd asked, wincing because of some pain. The man nodded again, cringing slightly. Sigurd shrugged. 'It means nothing to me,' he said.

'Then we'll row,' the Wessexman stated without consulting any of the others, and Ealdred stared at his daughter like a man who feels the breeze from the oak tree about to land on his head but knows it is too late to move.

So, with Penda, there would now be six Englishmen at our oars – men who had been our enemies and who had sought our deaths.

And soon those six men would save our lives.

CHAPTER NINE

SIGURD TOOK TO HIS BED OF SKINS AND FURS FOR ANOTHER TWO days and we were lucky that there seemed to be no living souls within an eagle's view of our beach, though it did begin to rain and Olaf was hard pressed to keep Sigurd's wounds dry and free from rot. Cynethryth and Asgot would go off into the woods together, foraging for healing herbs, which I did not like one bit, but for the sake of Sigurd I swallowed that bad taste.

'Between them,' Olaf had said with raised eyebrows, nodding at Asgot and Cynethryth who were preparing some foul-looking poultice, 'they could bring a corpse back to life. I'd wager my nose on it.' He must have noticed my resentment at seeing Cynethryth and the godi together and he half grinned. 'Make a strange pair, don't they, lad? Like a dog and a cat sharing a fur by the hearth.'

'Warming by the same fire doesn't make the dog and the cat friends, Uncle,' I said glumly, at which Olaf chuckled and went off to see what was bubbling above the cookfire, leaving me to my brooding. I did not know then that the old godi was sinking his claws into Cynethryth and even if I had, what could I do whilst Sigurd needed them?

I used the time to train with the axe under Svein and Bram's guidance. Not the single-handed axe which many of us carried in our belts – a handy weapon in a shieldwall and equally useful for cutting firewood or breaking through your enemy's front door – but the two-handed, long-handled axe. It is a weapon ill-suited to the shieldwall because of the space you need to wield it and because it leaves your belly open to stabs. But if you reach your enemy with it he is a dead man. When you work with the great axe you soon gain a deeper respect for those who have mastered it. Fortunately, as a carpenter's apprentice, I was no stranger to gripping a good axe haft. Nevertheless, I was glad of all the rowing because it had piled muscles on my back and shoulders which you need for good axe work. I could not yet weave the thing through the air like Svein or Bram Bear or Olaf, but I had it across me that I would in time. I would make it dance and whisper, its polished head glinting in the sunlight. For now though it was enough that the training worked like a steerboard, turning my mind from Sigurd's wyrd and my hand in it.

On the third day Jarl Sigurd rose again and this time he rolled up the skins of his sickbed himself as though to put an end to the thing. He still looked weak and the wounds were far from healed, but Olaf said they were knitting well and Asgot admitted that Sigurd must still stand on the All-Father's good side to be walking so soon after such injuries, though he also added that he was a fool who bit into that coin and yelled silver, for Óðin was a shape-changer, which meant that his favour was a capricious, vaporous thing. 'It's easier to nail a fart to the door than to know the Spear-Shaker's mind,' he grumbled.

I was looping Bram's axe through the air, sweat coursing down my face, when from the corner of my eye I saw Sigurd watching me. So I tried to make the movement smoother, each circle flowing into the other like some skilled craftsman's design on a brooch or ship's prow, though I'd wager it looked more like a drunkard pissing patterns against a wall.

'Come here, Raven,' he said, and those three words laid a coil of iced rope in my belly.

'Here it comes,' I heard a Norseman mutter under his breath.

'It's been good knowing you, lad,' growled another.

'Tell him he still looks pretty,' Bram Bear rumbled behind his hand. 'It's your only chance.' For Mauger's shield rim had bitten into Sigurd's temple and the wound was pus-filled, puckered and sore-looking. Also, a shard of steel had sliced his cheek and Mauger's fingers had clawed the gash like an eagle's talon tearing into a fish and now there would be a large scar.

I gathered my courage, then walked the ten paces to my jarl. It felt like ten miles.

'Just the sight of the axe can turn your enemy argr,' he said, that word itself as terrible as an axe blow because it means unmanly. 'Here.' He held out a hand, the knuckles of which were scabbed with dark knots of blood. I gave him the axe and he nodded, gripping its throat in one hand and its shoulder in the other. Then he stepped back and, before I could advise him against it, looped the weapon through the air in twin circles, one flowing beautifully into the other, his face a grimace of concentration. He was barely off his deathbed and yet his skill made my attempts look like the flailing of a drowning man. I supposed that was why he was a jarl, I consoled myself, as he stopped the whirling axe head dead and handed it back to me, sickly sweat streaming through his dirty beard.

'It is a worthy weapon, the war axe.' He was breathing hard and I knew it had hurt him. Fresh pus yellow as cream leaked from the wound in his head. 'A magnificent thing. It will melt your enemy's guts and make him spray his own shoes with stinking fear. Train hard with it, Raven. Though if I were you I'd find a better teacher.'

Bram then made a gesture that you could not have mistaken even from the top of a mountain, and now it was Sigurd's turn to wink at me. The Bear rumbled like a distant rock fall and the jarl smiled wanly. There was a heartbeat's silence, which Bram heard loud and clear, and he walked off, leaving Sigurd and me alone by the tree line. Out to sea the sky was black. A storm was building somewhere beyond the horizon.

'Perhaps if I had used it against Mauger I would be nursing nothing more than a blister or two on my palms, hey.' Suddenly the silver ring on my arm was digging into my flesh. I yanked on it, trying to pull it off, but then Sigurd's hand was on mine and I looked into his fierce blue eyes and I could have cried.

'You did well, Raven,' he said.

'Lord?'

'Mauger was lucky to have you as his shield man.'

'But lord . . . I . . .'

'You did what I asked you to do,' he said, 'and you did it well.' He winced, a hand touching the gash in his temple. 'A little too well, I admit. But I cannot blame you for that, can I?'

'I thought you were going to cut off my balls,' I said, half smiling with the relief of it.

'If one of these wounds turns green, I still might,' he said, grimacing. 'Why do you think I asked you to bear Mauger's shields?'

I shrugged. 'The Norns themselves would struggle to make sense of your patterns, lord.' He raised an eyebrow at that.

'I asked you because I knew you would do it,' he said. 'I could have asked Floki or Bjorn or Bjarni. Any of them,' he said, nodding to the Norsemen, 'but do you think their hearts would have been in it? Do you think they would put themselves between my blade and a lump of cow shit like Mauger? Oh,

Floki . . . Floki would have waved the shield here and there, made it look good for a while, but he'd have let me kill Mauger the first real chance I got.' He ran a flat hand like a knife across the inside of his thigh. 'I wouldn't put it past him to have opened Mauger's vein when no one was looking.'

'That's what I should have done,' I said, remembering Mauger for the rotten toadspawn half-troll he was.

'No, Raven, you would not have done that. I knew you would not. Well, I hoped, anyway.' He took a step back, running his hands the length of his torso. 'Look at me, lad. I'm fine. A few new scratches to keep the others company and remind me why I should not play with my enemies like a cat with a mouse but be done with them swiftly.' Did he really believe he had controlled the fight with Mauger? To me it had seemed a desperate, terrible contest, fate seeming to favour each in turn like the shifting of the tide.

'The men saw me win the fight. And what a fight, hey! Worthy of a skald song, and a good skald too. The saga telling of it will warm our children's bones on freezing nights when they are old.' A cloud darted across his eyes then because he had had a son once but a horse's hoof had broken the little boy's head.

'I have never seen anything to match it,' I said. 'It was a fight to leave even the gods' jaws unhinged.'

Sigurd smiled proudly. 'But I won, Raven. I put their champion down, made him worm food, despite your best efforts. Who can now say Sigurd son of Harald the Hard has lost his luck?' He laughed then and I laughed with him.

Because not only was Sigurd as fierce as Thór, he was as cunning as Loki, too.

Later that morning, thunder rolled out of the west, bringing with it that musty-smelling air that always comes before heavy rain. We wrapped ourselves in skins newly greased with seal fat so that when the rain came it rolled in glistening beads off those skins like water from an otter's pelt. Torches were lit because thick, sullen, iron-grey cloud formed the roof of the world, turning the day unnaturally dark. One of the men complained that it was just like being back in the fjords and all he needed now was a woman barking in his ear and he would have believed he was home.

The Wolfpack had gathered. Rain soaked our hair and streamed from our beards and vanished into the sand, leaving a frothy scum on it. We gave the English skins too, for now that we had decided to take them with us they were worth more alive than dead from some fever or drowned by the pissing Frankish rain, as Bram put it. We stood in a half-circle around Asgot, Sigurd and Ealdred, because today was the day when the ealdorman would die. He looked a sorry figure. Gone was the arrogance that I had seen glint like steel shards in his eyes. Without grease, the long moustache he wore, a fashion then amongst the English, drooped limp and frayed like a length of soggy, ancient rope. His shoulders slumped pathetically, his hands were clenched and he had been stripped of any marks of rank including rings, a gold brooch and of course his fine sword, which Sigurd had given to Black Floki for his guarding of the jarl's silver hoard on the Wessex beach. Though Floki said he would sell the thing.

'A coward's hand has tainted it,' he said, spitting on the blade, 'and such a weapon can only bring ill-luck.'

When he realized what was happening, Father Egfrith began sniffing round Sigurd, begging him to spare Ealdred, despite the death looks old Asgot shot him. But the jarl took as much notice of the monk as you do of a wittering bird and this exasperated Egfrith until at last he stamped his foot into the sand and pointed to the sky.

'*Tu ne cede malis, sed contra audentior ito!*' he proclaimed, and this seemed to get Sigurd's attention. '*Tu ne cede malis, sed contra audentior ito!'* the monk repeated in his thin reedy voice, which recalled to my mind the sound children make by blowing along a wide blade of grass.

Sigurd's brow darkened and he turned to the monk, his hand falling to his sword's hilt. 'Are you spinning some Christ spell, little man?' he asked, his head tilted to one side.

The monk shrank back defensively. 'I was speaking in Latin, Sigurd, the tongue of the Romans and of all men of learning. I said you should not give in to evils but proceed ever more boldly against them.' Egfrith crossed himself.

'Ah,' Bjarni joined in, flapping his arms like a man falling from a cliff top, 'I thought you were having some seizure.' We laughed as Egfrith's weasel face burnt red with anger. Cynethryth stood between Penda and me, her hands clasped together, the fingers squirming like worms. I put an arm round her shoulder but she tensed and slipped loose of it, turning towards me and aiming those emerald eyes at mine.

'Don't let them kill my father, Raven,' she said suddenly, the words hitting me like pebbles on the forehead as the rain swept down our faces and the thunder of Thór's chariot rolled across the heavy grey sky. I glanced at Penda, who simply shrugged, showing his palms in a helpless gesture.

'But what can I do?' I said. Resolved now to the coming violence, Father Egfrith began commending the ealdorman's soul to his Christ's Heaven.

'Sigurd listens to you,' Cynethryth said, 'you are his talisman.' She stepped forward and took my hands in hers. Her skin felt cold and damp. 'You can make him spare Ealdred. I know you can.'

'But I thought you hated him,' I said. 'It is because of him that Weohstan is dead. Have you forgotten?' She winced at her brother's name and I bit my cheek because of course she had not forgotten.

'He is my father,' she said, daring me to counter that. And

how could I? 'He is the only family I have left. Even after what he has done, I cannot watch him die, Raven. You must understand that.'

'*Homo homini lupus*, my daughter,' Egfrith said to Cynethryth, shaking his tonsured head in sad resignation. 'Man is a wolf to man.'

'Keep up that tongue twisting, monk, and you'll join the Romans!' Bram growled in Norse, slapping the head of his axe.

'Courage, Lord Ealdred,' Egfrith said, ignoring Bram's threatening gesture and walking over to lay his wooden crucifix against Ealdred's forehead. I had seen the monk with a silver, jewel-studded cross before, but I guessed that now sat in pieces in the musty dark of a Norseman's journey chest. 'May the Lord forgive your sins and the Kingdom open its gates to receive your soul.' Ealdred's face was a twisted grimace, like a man preparing for pain. For shame his own men, those who should have protected him with their lives, could not watch, instead keeping their beards on their chests, though occasionally a man's eyes would flick up quick as an adder's tongue to taste the manner of their lord's death.

'Raven!' Cynethryth hissed. 'Do something.' My mind flapped like a caged bird. What could I do? And yet I must do something because Cynethryth was begging me, and for her I would have crossed Gjallarbrú, the bridge to the Underworld, and spat in the giant Módgud's eye.

'Sigurd, wait!' Those two words stunned me, then terrified me because men's eyes told me they had jumped from my own mouth like a pair of fleas from a fur. Old Asgot glared, riled by another interruption to his bloodletting, and Sigurd's brows knitted in annoyance. He could not deny his godi every time and he knew that the men expected sacrifices, needed them even, especially in a Christian land.

'What is it, Raven?' he asked.

'The gospel book, my lord,' I said, my mind grasping like a hand breaking the water's surface to clutch at a salmon. 'What will you do with it?' I felt the weight of the Fellowship's eyes upon me, crushing my chest and turning the breath in my belly into molten iron.

Sigurd scratched his beard. 'I don't know. We will decide that when this turd is no longer breathing the air meant for better men.' Sodden jeers fused with the low roof of grey cloud and Thór's iron-wheeled chariot rolled across the sky.

'Ealdred was going to sell it to the emperor of the Franks,' I said, cutting through the abuse being hurled at Ealdred, 'we know that much. Which means the book must be worth a fat hoard.' I gestured at the ealdorman. 'This one is sick with silver greed.'

'So?' Sigurd said, flicking out an impatient hand.

'So we sail up the river and we sell the book to this emperor,' I blurted, resisting the urge to glance at Cynethryth to weigh how well I was doing. There were rumbles amongst the Wolfpack, echoes of the thunder cracks in the west.

'We would be dead before our feet were dry,' Olaf scoffed, shaking his beard as though it was the worst idea since Týr put his hand in the mouth of the fettered wolf Fenrir. 'The emperor has no love of heathens, lad, haven't you heard?'

'We'd sprout Christian arrows thick as Bram's nose hairs,' Black Floki added, spitting vainly into the rain.

'Not if we had a Christian lord speaking for us. Negotiating for us,' I said, nodding at Ealdred. 'And a Christ monk, too. The fat hoard that would have been Ealdred's will be ours. Frankish silver for all the good men lost.'

After a moment's silence that was as heavy as a mountain, Svein the Red's beard was parted by a roguish smile. 'I've heard it said this king of the Franks is so rich that his balls are made of solid gold,' he said.

'And I have heard that he pisses holy water,' Olaf said, a

thick finger raised in warning, 'which will melt the skin right off a dirty heathen like you, Red.'

'So, we'll cut off his snake before we steal his balls,' Bram Bear blurted, raising a laugh which flowed to an excited murmur that spread through the Fellowship as the idea took wing in each man's mind.

'We could put crosses at the prows as they did,' Knut said, nodding at the Wessexmen.

'And what would our gods make of that, Knut?' Asgot spat, but no one heard him because their heads were filled with the rattle of coins and the clinking of treasure. I felt a smile creep on to my lips and silently thanked Loki, for surely it had been the Father of Cunning who had drawn his bow and shot the idea into my head. All around me the wolves were grinning, yellow fangs flashing amongst the gloom. And I knew that I had them.

CHAPTER TEN

SO, EALDRED WAS SAVED, AT LEAST FOR NOW. FAR FROM SEEMING
happy the ealdorman if anything looked disappointed,
dispirited and ashamed. Later, he would begin to scheme again,
to believe that there might be something to be gained through
guile and greed, but for now he was a shadow man. He had lost
his household warriors, his fortune and his son. His daughter
might have woven a new strand into his life's thread, which
had seemed about to be cut, but now she wanted nothing more
to do with him. Death, the only escape from shame, had been
denied him, had run from Ealdred like the rain dripping from
the blade that had promised deliverance, so that my hate for
him turned to pity. It is hard to hate a broken man, no matter
what he has done in the past.

I had expected Cynethryth to throw her arms around me, to
kiss me and thank me for speaking up and stealing Ealdred's
life from the grave. Perhaps she would even lead me to some
secluded place and those grateful lips would reward me in
soul-shuddering ways. I was still young enough to weave such
fancies.

But Cynethryth said nothing, did nothing, led me nowhere. I

supposed her mind still coiled over itself like two snakes fighting, one for Ealdred's death and the other for his life, and that was one hólmgang in which I wanted no part. And so I did not encroach on the space she put between us, but kept to myself and listened to the men's talk of Karolus, this emperor of the Franks.

Most captains would not have sailed in such weather, but Sigurd was not most captains and Knut and Olaf both agreed that the distant rumbles of thunder and flashes against the roof of the world were the last throes of a spent storm. Somewhere up there, Thór was slaying giants, but we would be safe enough so long as we stuck close to the shore. *Serpent*'s shallow hold was full to the brim with silver and amber and furs, deer antler and weapons, and so we took half of her cargo and placed it in *Fjord-Elk*'s belly, first putting a layer of skins over the smooth ballast stones we had taken from higher up the beach to replace the old ones which were covered with green slime and stank. Then we untethered the dragons from the mooring posts buried in the sand, put our shoulders against their rumps and shoved for all we were worth. We pushed and grunted and swore and the muscles in my thighs burnt as though my leg bones had been replaced with rods of red-hot iron, but the ships refused to move, which an ugly, long-faced Norseman named Hedin said stank to him like a bad omen. Bjorn, though, called Hedin a horse-faced bollock nose, grunting that it had less to do with omens and more to do with all the rain, which had soaked the beach so that the sand and grit now sucked the ships' hulls down hungrily. The keel and lowest two strakes were completely buried and in the end we had to break up the sucking silt with our spears and then dig the ships free with our hands, by which time the tide had retreated fully, meaning we had even further to push them.

The Wessexmen were put aboard *Serpent* because although they had rowed *Fjord-Elk* and might be more familiar with her, that ship's seasoned timbers had soaked up much Wessex blood and Sigurd thought it unwise to antagonize the warriors or stir them to some foolish action.

'There is nothing to be gained by reminding a man of his defeat and of the deaths of his friends,' the jarl said, 'not if you want him to row for you. Better to let them come to love *Serpent* as we do.'

'Aye, and besides, this way I will be able to keep my eye on them,' Olaf added crabbily as the Englishmen took to their new row benches, puffing from the labour of digging *Serpent* free and grimacing at their fingernails, which were bloody and broken. Luckily for all of us there was enough wind to enable us to hoist the sails and leave the oars stowed. It blew from the south-east and we were heading south, so we were prepared for slow progress, happy enough not to have to row. Those at the foreship handled the front of the sail, attaching the thick rope to the tacking boom to ensure that the edge of the sail was firmly held towards the bow and into the wind. This prevented *Serpent*'s great woollen wings being taken aback, leaving Olaf and Bram free to tack us with the bowline.

Everything aboard was soaked through and in just seven days had become covered with snot-like slime; our journey chests, the deck, the mast, the water barrels, the rigging and blocks, and the edges of the sail. All had to be scraped with blades, scrubbed with rough cloth and smeared with grease, for life aboard a ship is hard enough without sliding around in moss and filth. But it feels good to clean a longship, especially a dragon like *Serpent* or *Fjord-Elk*. You catch yourself murmuring, whispering to her tenderly. *There you go, let's get that dirt off you, that's better, isn't it? Yes, now we are all clean and beautiful again.* Because when you love a ship she will love you back. Even when the waves are mast-high or fat and swollen so that there is only a fingernail's length of free board above the water line, she will flex and ride and work for you, keeping your lungs full of air instead of brine.

I looked skyward, watching black marks push and jostle through the thick grey, then my eyes sifted them into gulls and swallows, like little arrow heads, and above them all three crows whose cawing cut through the mist and cloud every now and then.

Sigurd kept Ealdred at the stern with him and Knut the steersman, but the other Wessexmen were put just behind the mast so they could learn about the ship from watching the Norsemen work the sail. It took three men to constantly tighten the mast stays and this was a simple enough job, which Olaf had the Wessexmen doing before long. They did it well enough, too, and I swear their backs were pride-stiff as they worked.

'My father used to say that Englishmen sail as well as chickens fly,' Sigurd said in English for Ealdred's benefit, though I suspected these Wessexmen had it in them to prove Sigurd's father wrong. Sigurd suspected it too, for he caught my eye and nodded at the English, one eyebrow cocked and his lips pursed on the edge of amusement.

We tracked the coast slowly but steadily and at one point we sailed right into a dirty cloud of biting gnats. They got into our mouths and down our tunic necks and even bit some of us on our eyeballs, which we all agreed was a very low thing to do. We roared at Olaf and Knut to tack us out of that Hel, but even when they tried the movement of the wind across the sail was pitiful and so we had to endure it, cowering under furs and skins like frightened women. Afterwards, we laughed about it, for when Svein huddled beneath a white reindeer skin it looked as if a mountain of snow had dropped on the deck! We laughed and we teased each other and we scratched and when we saw three broad knörrs ploughing their own sea roads west and south we knew we had come to the mouth of the Sicauna. Sure enough we rounded a stubby peninsula upon which dozens of houses sat coughing black smoke into the grey sky. Once round that Olaf said we would see the river.

We were not close enough to land to see the people of that place, but they would certainly see *Serpent*'s and *Fjord-Elk*'s sails, even though the low line of their hulls would probably be obscured from view by waves.

'Christ alone knows what the Franks will make of us,' Penda said behind me.

'When *Serpent* came to my village, not even Griffin, the most experienced warrior, had ever seen or heard of nearly sixty men in brynjas,' I said, remembering the terror I had felt at the sight of so many armed men. 'Let alone each with his own sword, spear and axe. Let us hope these Franks have not either. It will be better if they are wary of us.'

'Oh, they'll be wary, lad, when they clap eyes on this murderous lot. I'd wager my best teeth on that. What happened to Griffin?'

Those words tugged at my guts. 'There was a fight. He killed one of them. Their shipwright,' I said, a distant, warm pride blooming for a heartbeat somewhere inside my soul, 'so they cut open his back, hacked the ribs to pieces, then pulled out his lungs.' I felt the twist of my own grimace. 'They call it the blood eagle.'

'I know what they call it, lad,' Penda said, 'blood-loving heathen bastards.'

Before we had set off, Bjorn and his brother Bjarni had hewn four of the mooring posts and lashed them together to make two crosses, and now Sigurd gave the order to stow the dragon heads and mount these Christ symbols instead. Asgot countered this abhorrence by untying a sack that had been squirming by his feet and pulling out a seal cow, whose throat he cut, letting its blood spatter into the cream whipped by *Serpent*'s bow. That foam churned pink and the godi held up the twitching animal for us all to see, then cast it over the side with a tangle of strange prayers.

It was certainly better than the mangy hare he had given to Njörd when we left the Wessex coast, and afterwards Bram joked that we should have eaten the seal meat first, then stuffed its skin with grass before chucking it overboard and hoping the gods were none the wiser.

'I'd wager old Njörd's belly never rumbles like mine,' Bram proclaimed, slapping his stomach, which was barrel-shaped yet solid.

'Thór's chariot does not rumble like your belly,' ashen-skinned Bothvar said, at which Bram Bear simply nodded and smiled proudly.

Now past the headland we were in the mouth of the great river and could see the green land closing in from either side beyond the wooden cross at *Serpent*'s prow – could feel it too. Hedin Long Face said the place looked like Fensfjord, where most of the Fellowship came from, but Olaf barked that that was hjem lengsel, homesickness, talking. Hedin considered this for a while during which you would have thought he had been asked to recall and recount the creation of the world in every detail. Finally, he admitted that Olaf had the right of it. The sea here was not as clear or deep, the land not as high and the air not as sweet as a Norwegian fjord. He even mumbled an apology to Frey the harvest god, who decides when the sun shall shine or the rain come down, for the insult.

We began to see boats of all sizes and shapes: broad merchant knörrs, poorly made pilgrim vessels with sails as tattered as the skeletons of old leaves, fishing skiffs, a levy vessel of twenty oars whose captain wisely pointed his prow away from us, and even a sleek dragon heading south, which must have been a raider, probably Danish according to Knut, for it was longer than *Serpent* and arrow thin. To me it did not look too seaworthy with that narrow hull. I could imagine a wave slamming against its side and rolling it like a log, but when I said as much to Penda he scratched his long scar and pointed out that it had got this far and so its makers must have known something of sea-craft.

'As a rule I'll not climb aboard any ship that needs bailing more than three times in two days,' Olaf said, 'but I wouldn't mind if these strakes leaked some more.' He was standing on the mast step, scouring the channel with his experienced eyes. 'I like to see you lambs back bent and bailing. In my father's day . . . and in mine . . . we rowed! Churned the sea till it was as thick as porridge. None of this sitting around waiting for the wind to blow us here and there.' This was met with a chorus of jeers from men who had heard Olaf hawk up the same bile a hundred times, but old Uncle took no notice. 'Soft as hot horse shit, you lot. Like all young men these days. Óðin knows what the world's coming to and I wager it makes his one eye weep.' Above his head *Serpent*'s faded red sail rippled and flapped, whilst around him men were beginning to prickle with excitement and nerves because we were coming to an unknown land whose people and spirits were likely to prove hostile, especially if they found out we were heathens. I became aware of the creaking of *Serpent*'s timbers and ropes and those sounds, those squeaks and moans seemed somehow human, like questions from a frightened child. *Are you sure we should be here? Is it safe? What if they hurt us like last time?* It was strange, but without the dragon Jörmungand at our prow, the Christ cross being fixed there instead, *Serpent* felt different, even vulnerable, and I was not alone in feeling that strange seidr-weight of being watched. All along the Frankish shore eyes bored into *Serpent* like so many keen-edged spoon augers and even though we had not mounted our shields along the rack and were not wearing our mail and helmets, it would not be long before the powerful lords of this kingdom came to sniff us out, for surely ships like ours were rare in those waters.

The levy knörr, which I had thought long gone, was in fact entering the estuary along the far shore, stalking us from a safe distance, biding its time like a carrion bird around feeding wolves. This in itself was not enough to worry us, but it did tell us that the Franks were wary of outsiders and that even these seaward frontiers were patrolled, despite being far from the centres of power. As Sigurd explained, this Karolus was after all king of lands far and wide, a self-proclaimed emperor in the old Roman way, and he had not won such power without caution, organization and, perhaps most worryingly as far as we were concerned, many spears at his command. And now that we had left the safety of the open sea behind and were entering the gullet, let alone the mouth, of the river, I could not melt the lump of ice-cold fear that had grown in my belly.

I watched Father Egfrith carry a rolled skin to *Serpent*'s bow, where Cynethryth stood awkwardly. Dutifully, Egfrith unrolled the skin and held it up as a screen and Cynethryth half smiled before disappearing to relieve herself in a bucket. Egfrith turned his face away and I felt a grudging gratitude towards the man for looking to Cynethryth's needs aboard this ship of rough men. Poor Cynethryth. It cannot have been an easy thing to live amongst us. She was after all the daughter of a lord of Wessex. Now she was in as much danger as the rest of us. Father Egfrith had enjoyed telling us that many of the Saxon people to the east, between the rivers Elbe and Ems, had been put to death under Karolus's laws because they had observed heathen ways rather than embracing the White Christ. Simply refusing to be pushed under the water by a Christ priest was enough, it seemed, to see your head and neck parted never to meet again. When I translated all this for the others, Bram's hairy eyebrows wove together.

'This Karolus does not sound like a Christ follower to me,' he said, biting a hunk of bread from the lump in his fist.

'Perhaps these Saxons stank like a sheep's arse,' Bjorn

suggested, 'and the king was tired of holding his nose, so he ordered his priests to wash them and when they refused . . .' He drew the edge of his hand across his neck.

'It's called baptism,' I said. 'A Christ priest pushes you under the water a heathen and when you come up you're a Christian.' This idea was clearly absurd to the Norsemen and I was met with sceptical expressions. I shrugged. 'Maybe there is more to it than that,' I said. 'But that much is true.'

'They think they can wash Óðin and Thór out of us with a little water?' Arnvid said, his face screwed up like a weasel's arsehole.

'I would like to see a Christ priest try to push my head under the water,' Svein the Red announced, smiling at Father Egfrith, who was watching us, trying to pick apart the threads of our words, or so it seemed to me.

'There isn't a river deep enough, Svein,' I said, meaning you could not wash the gods out of him any more than you could harpoon the moon and pull it out of the sky, and this simple statement seemed to settle it all.

I glanced at Ealdred, wondering if he would speak for us when the time came as I had hoped and told Sigurd he would. He did not have much choice of course, but then again he did not have much to lose either, other than his miserable life, and so we could not be sure. The other problem was that the Franks might not believe him anyway, which I thought likely looking at him hunched at *Serpent*'s stern like a ship's dog that has been beaten for shitting in a man's bed roll.

Olaf and Sigurd exchanged words, then Olaf turned to the rest of us, a grim smile cracking his bird's-nest beard.

'Put your combs away, you whoresons,' he called, 'it's about time you earned your keep.' Here, where salt water and fresh wove together, the estuary had narrowed, providing shelter against the sea winds so that there was no longer enough to make it worth keeping the sails up, especially with the river flowing against us. With a clatter of oars from both ships we made ready to row as Olaf, Black Floki and Bram lowered *Serpent*'s sail and then took to their own benches. Wind-heaped dunes rose on either bank so that it felt as though we were passing through a gateway, and upon those hillocks marram grass stood stiff as an angry hound's hackles. On either side, where the river's banks met the water, the tides had carved steps into the sand and above these I could make out, even from a distance, hundreds of dragonflies streaking madly, making the air shimmer strangely. Fat gulls squawked and dived to *Serpent*'s sternpost, hungry for the fish guts men throw overboard when they come in from the sea. A flock of swifts shot across our bow like a flight of arrows, veering suddenly as one over the brow of a sandbank. Then, as I rowed, my muscles bunching and spreading – knots of heat radiating their warmth through my body – we saw the first of them. They were sprouting one after another from the dune's summits, growing from the marram grass and standing stone still, like a great host of haugbui, the undead, risen from their howes. For luck I touched the amulet at my neck, the small carving of the All-Father's face, which had once belonged to Sigurd.

The beautiful, rhythmic sound of oars – ours and *Fjord-Elk*'s – dipping into the water in unison was as much a statement to the Christian god as it was to those who now watched us from the banks, their thoughts known only to themselves – though I'd wager they were fear-soaked, for Sigurd's wolves had come to Frankia.

CHAPTER ELEVEN

THERE WAS SOME ARGUMENT ABOARD AS TO WHETHER THE FRANKS' bows could land their arrows in our hulls if it turned out we weren't welcome, but in the end it was agreed that because we were a fair distance from the banks and moving well, the archers would have to judge expertly, aiming out in front of us. It would take rare skill or Thór's luck to make a killing shot.

'Let's hope in aiming for us they end up hitting those goat turds on *Fjord-Elk*,' Bjarni joked, thumbing over his shoulder, but few smiles reached men's eyes. For there were now so many Franks tracking us along the banks that regardless of the strength of their bows, we would be in real trouble if we made landfall and things went bad.

It is a bladder-loosening thing rowing up a river like a salmon into a withy trap. I was thinking as much when Penda cursed under his breath behind me.

'If these Franks have enough boats they could put them across the river behind us. Bung us up like mead in a flask,' he said.

'And we'd slice through them without even slowing,' I replied, though I did not believe it would be as easy as that. 'Sigurd is more sea-bold than any Frank,' I added and this I did believe, but Sigurd was also pale and pain-tired. Even now as we came to a new land he sat wrapped in a fur by Knut at the tiller and it was a hard thing seeing the jarl like that. Sweat glistened sickly on his face, which was carved with shadows. His hair, usually golden as Baldr's, lay flat and greasy against his head.

And so I looked back to the river road we followed. It twisted and turned, gnarly as a man's gut rope, but Knut worked the tiller skilfully, with Olaf calling from *Serpent*'s prow warnings of shoals and silt bars and the strange currents that they can cause. Uncle also kept a keen eye out for sunken vessels, for this was an ancient river and must have claimed many ships and only the locals would know where they sat.

The English at the oars were puffing like oxen and must have been glad that the pace Olaf had set was deliberately slow. Slow because we did not want the Franks to think we had come to raid, which they might if our oars churned their river, even though we were not wearing helmets. I smelt woodsmoke and heard dogs barking and looked over my shoulder to see that we were coming to a busy place. The sky was palled by the grey-brown smudge of hearth smoke, whilst gulls swarmed in shrieking clouds at the banks where men unloaded skiffs, mended nets, and worked on upturned hulls. There were a hundred Abbotsends – the Wessex village I had lived in for two years – which meant more people and more life than I had ever seen. The thought stirred my blood and quickened my heart as I watched those men at the river's edge stop their work to eye us warily. Beyond them, behind manmade earth ramparts that were protection against floodtides rather than raiders, it seemed to me, sat thatch-roofed dwellings, the straw blackened by years of smoke and made ragged by coastal weather. Then across the water from the land came a solemn clang, the sound decaying yet lingering faintly as another clang rang out. This was answered by the same sound but now from the opposite bank, so that it seemed two mighty blacksmiths competed to create a god's sword. The Norsemen listened with puzzled expressions.

'The sound of faith!' Father Egfrith yelped, his little eyes suddenly greedy and feverish. 'The chime of hope against the dark horizon,' he said, gripping the ship's sheer strake, for he was not worthy of an oar even though there were empty row benches.

'Óðin's hairy arse!' Bram exclaimed. 'Sounds like Völund's own hammer bashing the anvil.' Some of the men looked to the sky warily, or at Father Egfrith. Others searched the banks for the source of the rhythmic iron song. More than a few touched amulets or rings for luck.

'They're church bells, Bram,' I called, pulling my oar's blade through the sea, 'made of cast bronze if the church is wealthy enough. Hammered iron if not.'

'I would like to think that awful din is nothing more than a coincidence,' Bjorn said, looking straight ahead as he rowed. 'But my water tells me it might have something to do with us, hey.' I didn't have to see his face to know he was smiling.

'The Christians are pissing in their breeks, Sigurd,' Olaf called from *Serpent*'s prow where the wooden cross rode forth with a strange, quiet, empty arrogance. 'Even now, the little Christ slaves run around their churches, hiding their silver and gold and farting fear down their skirts.'

'You think they believe we're followers of the White Christ?' Sigurd called back, nodding towards the cross and coughing with the strain of shouting the length of *Serpent*.

'I think even the Christians are not so stupid,' Olaf yelled. And yet we hoped they were, as warriors were appearing amongst the crowds on the shore now, their shields clearly visible even from a distance, and these men began to trudge dutifully along the river's banks in the direction our prows pointed.

'Christ preserve us,' Egfrith muttered, and I saw Sigurd shifting uncomfortably, a black cloud across his brow.

'Here we go, Raven,' Penda said with some foreboding, untwisting his neck back round to stern. At first I thought he was referring to the levy knörr, which seemed to be cutting away from the far shore towards *Fjord-Elk* riding in our wake, but then I knew he was not.

'Plan, Sigurd?' Olaf yelled in English to fool the Franks in case they were in earshot, even though the name Sigurd would scupper that shallow cunning. I twisted but could not see above *Serpent*'s curved prow.

'Three boats, lad,' Penda said. 'Coming hard and fast.'

'Keep rowing!' Sigurd barked. 'Raven. Here, now!'

I pulled in my oar, sliding its blade through the slotted port, then laid it up with the spares across the oar trees before joining Sigurd, who grimaced in pain as he climbed unsteadily to his feet and gripped the taut back-stay.

'Find something for this goat's dick that will make him look important,' Sigurd said in English, thumbing at Ealdred who sat like a lump of shit in the hollow of *Serpent*'s stern. The ealdorman's frayed moustache twitched round a smile as tight as a nun's sheath as I turned and hurried to the hold, pulling up several loose planks to get to where the most precious or fragile cargo was stowed. I lifted the lid of a chest, pulled back a grease-stinking skin, and let my eyes drink in the sight of enough silver coin to pay for another *Serpent* or *Fjord-Elk*. But coin was no good to us now and I moved to the next chest and flung it open. Beneath that oiled skin was a treasure hoard any Norseman would trade his mother's teeth for. There were silver bowls, silver neck and wrist chains, finger rings, a dozen or more brooches set with amber, emeralds, and fine spirals of brass, several gold arm rings, silver torcs, silver Christ crosses – some set with jewels, some plain – the beaten-gold cover of a book long gone, and an assortment of ingots and silver fragments, many as long as my finger and as thick as my thumb. All bore nicks where previous owners had tested their quality and I supposed not a few of those late owners' bones were being nicked themselves now by raven's beaks or rat's teeth. To my eyes, though, the prize was a great, thick jarl torc that looked like a short length of silver rope. I could not resist lifting the thing from the hoard, just for a moment allowing my thumbs to trace the twisted cord, which was cold to the touch even on that warm day, and heavy enough to anchor a boat, or so it seemed to me. It was a torc fit for Thór, and I would have given anything to put it round my neck, to let its cool weight sink into me. But such an act would be even heavier with arrogance for I was not worthy of a thing even half as fine, and to wear a jarl's torc if you are not a jarl is likely to stir the wrath of the gods and hasten your own doom. So I replaced the torc gently, grabbing instead a round brooch of silver and bronze big enough to fill my open palm, and a wooden White Christ cross set with rubies and hanging on a leather thong.

'Play the part well, Englishman,' Sigurd growled at Ealdred, who glowered back as he pinned the brooch to his cloak and slipped the thong over his head so that the cross sat above his heart. 'You are an English lord and you have business with the emperor.' Sigurd nodded towards the largest of the Frankish ships, which had split from the other two and was approaching *Serpent* along her steerboard side. This ship was no dragon and nor were the others, but they were broad and packed with armed men, many of whom, we could see, carried war bows.

I joined Ealdred's household warriors at the mast step. 'If you men want to live, you'd better remember to be good Christians,' I said in English, gripping the sword hilt at my hip, and one of them, the big man who had been spared Asgot's knife, pulled a wooden cross from inside his tunic and laid it on the outside. This prompted two of the others to do the same and I nodded, hoping that this along with the crosses at our prows would be enough to fool the Franks.

With his hands to his mouth, one of the Franks in the lead ship shouted to us in a language that was one part English to two parts something else. The other ships held off, wary of getting too close to us or to *Fjord-Elk*, but staying near enough to join the fight with just a few strokes of the oars. The man shouted again. He wore an iron helmet and a blue cloak but I could not see his face other than its long moustache. We looked at each other with shrugs and head-shakes, then Father Egfrith grinned his weasel grin at me and crossed himself.

'*Alea iacta est*,' he said. 'The die is cast, Raven,' and with that he went to the steerboard side and spewed a stream of noise, which sounded like an infant's meaningless gabbling but which we now knew to be Latin, the ancient language of the Romans. '*Dominus vobiscum! Gloria in excelsis Deo, Dominus illuminatio mea!*' The little monk was full of the stuff. It tumbled out of him like droppings from a deer's arse.

'If he's betraying us I'll rip out his throat,' Black Floki growled between gritted teeth as he rowed. But Egfrith was smiling and waving his arms joyfully and I believed that far from betraying us as heathens he was enjoying selling the lie to the Franks that we were men of the White Christ come in peace to share the wonders of our faith.

When Egfrith had finished, Blue Cloak raised a hand, weaving an invisible cross in the air, then called back in the same slippery tongue, at which Egfrith turned back to Sigurd.

'His name is Fulcarius and he commands the emperor's shore guard. Says he and his men might as well nail their feet to the deck, as the Lord Christ's were nailed to the cross, for they spend every waking hour at sea.' Egfrith pointed downriver, back from where we had come. 'The threat of heathens lingers like a dark cloud, always on the horizon,' he said. I could have sworn the monk was chewing a smile. 'Only this morning they chased a ship full of Danes out into the channel before the devils could pillage some house of God or do murder to some poor soul.' I remembered the long thin dragon ship we had seen earlier and wondered if this Fulcarius knew that he had not chased those Danes far enough. Beyond the reach of this Frankish knörr, that slender dragon was no doubt stalking the shore for easier prey. Perhaps Fulcarius knew it and did not care. Or perhaps it ate at his heart to know that his handful of vessels were not enough to guard the whole coast. Still, there were probably others like Fulcarius, men charged with defending Frankia against raiders. As for Fulcarius himself, the man had swept down upon us sure enough, like a sharp-eyed owl dropping from a mead hall's rafters to snatch a creature from the floor rushes. And his ship was within bow-shot now, her oars slow and even as she passed by so that her captain could get a better look at us.

'Raise oars,' Sigurd said, tying back his hair and revealing his lean raw-boned face; 'let the dogs sniff around us.' Leaning on his ship's sheer strake, Fulcarius prattled on, no doubt asking more questions for which Egfrith seemed to have a stockpot full of answers, but I could see the Frank clearly now and his eyes and his men's were all over us like a nettle rash. They were backing oars, working against the currents to remain broadside to us. *Fjord-Elk* nestled in our port side three oar-lengths off, whilst the other three Frankish ships held some distance away, their decks bristling with spearmen and archers. A breeze from the north-west brought the acrid stink of Frankish sweat and grease to our noses, the latter telling us that at least one of the shore guard crews had recently weatherproofed their sail and cloaks with melted pig's fat. A cared-for ship usually speaks of a good crew.

We tried to appear calm, unthreatened and unthreatening, but I knew our men's eyes were beady as chickens' as they gripped their oars, hoping the lead knörr did not come any closer. Even if it stayed put, a swell might lift the boat high enough for her crew to see into our hull and if it did they would see the weapons and mail we had laid out at our feet. Luckily the water was flat, but that did not stop Knut and Sigurd scheming in low voices. I guessed they had already chosen an escape passage in case the emperor's men attacked. Having seen how the Norsemen fight at sea I was sure we could win even against four ships, but these Franks were not unprepared as Ealdred and his men had been, and chances were there would be heavy casualties. Even if we broke away and out-rowed the Franks there was a chance we would have to face more of them before we reached the open channel.

'Fulcarius says we look like Danes. He says these look like Danish ships, even with their homage to the holy Rood,' Father Egfrith said, pointing a thin finger at the cross at *Serpent*'s prow, 'but I have explained how Ealdorman Ealdred here, bravely and by the grace of God, fought and destroyed the heathens who came to plunder the kingdom of Wessex.' One of Ealdred's men swore loudly and began to pull in his oar. 'I have told him that our business is with the great emperor himself, the light and lord of Christendom,' Egfrith went on, as the Englishman's oar thumped and clattered on to the deck, 'may God protect him and keep him.' Egfrith could still have been speaking Latin as far as most of the Norsemen were concerned, but the agitated Englishman stood and, gripping the cross on his chest, faced the Franks like a storm.

'You dirty Frankish whoreson!' he yelled. 'Who are you to call us Danes? My sword still rings from crushing heathen skulls! Those scum came like hungry dogs to our land and we beat the bastards! Gave them each seven feet of earth, we did, and if you call us Danes again I'll swim over there and cut out your rancid tongue. Fucking Franks!'

The Norsemen tensed and some reached for helmets, thinking we had been betrayed, but the other Wessexmen on the steerboard side lifted their oar blades from the water and, with one hand, gripped the crosses hung around their necks, holding them up for the Franks to see. *Good lads*, I thought, hurrying across and throwing an arm over the Englishman's shoulder.

'Calm down, Leofmar,' I said, smiling. 'Fulcarius is just doing his duty and means no offence.' Egfrith glanced at me with raised eyebrows, then his eyes flashed shrewdly and he looked back to Fulcarius, who was talking to a fat man beside him. 'It is a bad thing to call a Wessexman a Dane, Fulcarius,' I called with a shrug of my shoulders. 'We Wessexmen are God-fearing but quick to anger. He is a fool who pokes a bull with a sharp stick.' The fat man spoke again to Fulcarius and I realized that that man spoke English and Ealdred realized it too.

'I have business with the emperor and very far to go, Fulcarius,' the ealdorman called, spitting on his fingers and smoothing the errant hairs of his moustache. Because he was not a big man, the silver cross on his chest stood out even more. 'If there is a tax to pay, let us be done with it, for we must be on our way.' Again Fulcarius talked with the fat man.

Beside me, Egfrith held out his palms helplessly, shaking his head and frowning. *'Auribus teneo lupum, Fulcarie!'* he crowed to the shore guard knörr. 'I hold a wolf by the ears!'

Fulcarius had chewed this meat enough and understood then that he risked starting a fight with a Christian lord of Wessex and his two ships of warriors. I guessed he decided he was not getting paid enough for that, for he spoke to the fat man, who smiled and nodded.

'Two pounds in silver coin is the tax for going upriver,' the fat man called. 'Three in hack silver if that is all you have.'

'Stupid Frank bastards,' Penda muttered under his breath as Olaf stifled a grin and Ealdred agreed to the price. It was no easy thing keeping the dragons leashed against the fast-flowing river, but the Norsemen worked the oars masterfully whilst the English amidships did the best they could.

'Fetch the coin, Raven,' Sigurd said. Then he made a show of dipping his head respectfully to Ealdred. 'How do we know we won't have to pay another tax ten oar-strokes further up the river?' he growled to the ealdorman through a smile. Ealdred nodded and asked Fulcarius, whilst I looked towards the river's banks. The people of the place were still eyeballing the exchange, those armed with spears and shields having gathered into a war band of a hundred or more. I was trying to count them when off *Serpent*'s stern a salmon leapt, a streak of silver that splashed into the water, which looked like beaten iron in the late afternoon light. Above us, low grey cloud mottled and bubbled, slowly encroaching on the last patches of blue so that soon the smoke from Frankish hearths would be trapped and would spread like a pungent blanket across the river.

'For another pound of silver Fulcarius is willing to give you a token,' the fat man called, 'a banner to tie to your back-stay to show that you sail upriver with the blessing of his highness the holy emperor's shore guard.' I saw his teeth. 'Of course, there are no guarantees.'

'What's an Englishman doing sailing with Franks?' Penda said distastefully, for it was clear from his accent that the fat man was no Frank.

'What is an Englishman doing sailing with Norsemen?' I accused him under my breath, at which Penda frowned and scratched the long scar on his face so that you might have thought I had asked him to count the grains of salt in the sea or the hairs in Bram's beard.

The deal was made and I stood amidships, holding three leather bags heavy with coin and hack silver whilst, a spear-throw away, Fulcarius barked commands at his crew. Those with arrows nocked or throwing-spears ready lowered their weapons, rolling and stretching the iron out of tense muscles. Those at the oars made ready to row.

'They're coming for the silver, Sigurd,' Olaf warned, brows

stitched together. He knew the English would see our war gear – brynjas, swords and helmets – in piles at our feet.

'Just keep that piss bucket away from *Serpent*, Uncle,' Sigurd said, watching the Frankish knörr like a hawk, his gaunt, bruised face slick with wound fever. Olaf nodded and took an oar from those stowed and Bram did likewise. At the bow of the knörr some Franks already gripped thick fender ropes and long staves to stop the ships crashing together in the currents. I could see Fulcarius clearly now and from the eager expression on his craggy, wind-burnt face I doubted he would notice even if Heimdall, warden of the gods, appeared then aboard *Serpent* and blew the Gjallarhorn to announce that Ragnarök was upon us. For Fulcarius's eyes were stuck like slug slime to the fortune in my hands. But one of the others would surely realize what we were, even if they waited until they had the silver before they let on.

In ten oar-strokes they would be upon us.

'All-Father, give me strength and luck,' I whispered, then I leant back and with all my strength hurled the first bag of silver high into the air and to my amazement it landed amongst Fulcarius's men, who were roaring in anger and disbelief.

'Have you lost your mind, Raven?' Olaf growled in Norse as the other Norsemen, equally appalled, swore and complained under their breath, but I was already pitching forward and the second bag was in the air and that one landed by the knörr's mast and must have split open, for there was a mad scramble amongst the crew. Fulcarius was all flailing arms, screaming at his men to keep their hands up where he could see them.

'Raven, you fucking fool,' I heard Penda say as I sent the last bag flying, but I misjudged this one, putting too much muscle into the throw given that the knörr was closer now, and that bag of silver would have splashed into the sea beyond her stern had one of the Franks not leapt brilliantly and caught it, toppling backwards into the river for his efforts. But this was proper Óðin-luck for us because the Franks began immediately to back oars, thrashing in their own wake to save the man, or more likely the silver, before it was lost. Fulcarius's ship was all seething madness and Ealdred, trying to justify what I had done, yelled across to them that some of our timber strakes were old and we could not risk a collision, though I doubted any of the Franks even heard him in their panic. Oars banged and snared and Frankish curses hammered the still air. Then, as Sigurd gave the order for us to pull off and Olaf called the rhythm in heys, wild yells of triumph rose from the shore guard knörr and as I grabbed my own oar and pushed it through the port to join the rest, I saw the half-drowned hero hauled over the side on to the deck. Through a momentary gap in the throng I saw the man standing panting but victorious, holding the bag of silver above his head like a champion and grinning as his fellows cheered wildly, their backs towards us as we churned the iron-grey river and left them behind.

CHAPTER TWELVE

SIGURD AND EALDRED BOTH SUSPECTED THE SCRAP OF BLUE CLOTH we tied to *Serpent*'s back-stay was not worth spit, even guessing that this Fulcarius had quickly cut the weft from his own cloak in order to wring more silver out of us. But even three pounds had been a small price to pay for avoiding a fight and for the freedom to sail upriver. That much silver was, as Bram put it, a fart in a storm next to the hoard we would get from the emperor for the gospel book. Lucky for me it had turned out well, but that did not stop some of the Norsemen shaking their beards at me disapprovingly for taking such a risk with so much hard-won silver.

Aslak in particular took a dim view of it. 'That much silver would get you a fine brynja and a good strong helmet,' he called from his journey chest on the port side, 'or even two or three big-titted thralls to warm your bed. And you nearly sent it to the seabed! Damned reckless I call it. Makes me think you've been swilling Bram's secret mead store.' *Some secret*, I thought. Everyone knew of the bulging mead skins Bram had stashed beneath two silver wolf pelts in *Serpent*'s hold, but only a brave man or a half-wit fool would wet his beard with that nectar without the Bear's consent. I wondered what that had made me when I had been dipping into that store to keep Penda's tongue wet so that he would keep quiet about my feelings for Cynethryth. None of that mattered now, I thought, leaning back with the stroke and looking over to Aslak, whose nose I had broken though you could not tell, much to my disappointment since he had also broken mine which has been crooked as a hare's hind leg ever since.

'It would have bought us Rán's favour, Aslak,' I said, 'which if you think of it is well worth having.' What *I* was thinking was that if I ever met the Frank who had caught the last bag and gagged on the Sicauna for his efforts I would buy him a mead horn as long as my leg to wash the slime from his throat.

'Rán's favour?' Bram bellowed. 'For three pounds of silver the old bitch would have climbed aboard and humped you dry as a dead man's fart!'

But Rán had not got her hands on our silver, Fulcarius had, and because of that we were now rowing deeper into Frankia, our faces catching the molten iron light of the sun which was sinking in the west far beyond *Serpent*'s stern. Those Franks who had kept up with us, trudging along the river's banks, began to disperse now, deciding that we were no threat, or at least guessing that we were not going to make landfall near their homes, meaning that we were someone else's problem now, and I felt relieved to shed some of the weight of all those eyes. The river here was wide and free-moving. There were few houses along the banks of this stretch, for it is no easy thing to launch a boat in fast-flowing water, or even to moor one there – one slip and your boat will make a bid for freedom faster than an Irish thrall slathered in goose fat, and you will never see it again. Up ahead, the river would snake again, taming the waters, and on that coil there would be more houses, wharfs and moorings. And no doubt more curious Franks.

The Wessexmen had played no small part in fooling Fulcarius

and his Franks. By brandishing their crosses they had done as much as they could, though one man in particular deserved our thanks and that was the man who had upbraided Fulcarius and threatened to swim over and cut out his tongue. His name was not Leofmar but Wiglaf. He was a thickset man with short, thinning black hair which he palmed forward so that a few strands stuck against his sweaty temples. His face was red, his nose long and pointed, and his chin round like a crab apple, and maybe he had not been helping us fool the Franks at all. Perhaps Wiglaf was truly riled at being called a heathen and a Dane and really would have jumped overboard to slice the tongue from Fulcarius's mouth. The man certainly looked shocked when Sigurd called him to Serpent's stern and gave him a gold finger ring pulled from his own left hand. We had taken anything of value from the Wessexmen after the channel fight, swords, knives, brynjas, belt buckles, brooches, rings and strap ends, leaving them with only the clothes they stood up in and the wooden crosses some of them wore, which we did not like touching if we could help it. By being rewarded now Wiglaf was taking the first step towards regaining his pride as a warrior, and though he accepted the jarl-gold dourly under the gaze of Ealdred and his countrymen, he must have felt the embers of hope stir in his chest. He might have been Ealdred's man and a Christian, but he was a fighter too and had seen Sigurd beat Mauger, who had been a formidable warrior. Wiglaf might have hated Sigurd but he must have admired him. Whatever, he put that gold ring on his finger and returned to his row bench, smoothly slotting the oar through its port and dipping the blade in time with the rest. His countrymen said nothing, but the big warrior Baldred, who had escaped Asgot's knife, nodded brusquely and that gesture was loud enough.

That night, as a chill dew seeped through our clothes and made everything aboard clammy to the touch, we moored in the shelter of a small holm in the middle of the river. Flat and muddy, it glistened by the light of the moon, which had cut through the clouds to curdle in long pennants and curls on the racing water. There was nothing on the holm to tie up to so both ships dropped their anchors and Olaf took the Wessexmen on to the mud to hammer in mooring stakes, and when they climbed back aboard they looked like walking turds with eyes. So they clung to ropes and washed in the river until they were clean and shivering, and all the while we laughed at poor old Uncle, who was a big, wet, white, naked growling monster. Then they hung their clothes over *Serpent*'s sheer strake to dry in the wind whilst they huddled in furs and Olaf asked us why it was that he, as the second oldest man aboard, was the one left to secure the ships whilst younger men sat around scratching their arses. It had been too dark to continue upriver but neither did Sigurd want to moor on the bank without knowing more about the river's temperament, the surrounding area, and the mood of the local Franks. Moored to this mire we could not go ashore, but the ships were protected and we were safe from the Franks. Tomorrow we would choose where to make proper landfall before it got too dark to see where we were going.

Cynethryth slept between me and Father Egfrith and when a stiff breeze began to whistle through the oar ports and over the sheer strake she shuffled up against me, the curve of her back inviting me to roll on to my side and envelop her. So I did, rearranging the skins so that they covered us both together, my right hand holding her hip and my right knee tucked snugly in the crook of hers. I slept breathing in the soothing scent of Cynethryth's golden hair and if Karolus himself had climbed aboard waving a sword alight with holy fire, I would not have moved a muscle.

The morning broke grey and damp and smelling of the weed and green slime that crept up the muddy holm and the river's banks. The Sicauna had summoned a mist that rose sluggishly from the water like an unwilling soul departing a body. Men

yawned and farted and stood along *Serpent* and *Fjord-Elk*'s
sheer strakes, their steaming piss splashing and spattering into
the river as they shook the sleep from their heads and rubbed
the dreams from their eyes. Hair was wild and beards were
crushed and we scratched and searched our clothes for fleas by
the weak dawn light. I put the back of my hand to my nose and
my stomach knotted itself because I could smell Cynethryth on
my skin.

Waking aboard a boat is a beautiful, unearthly thing. Yes,
you are always damp and sometimes your bones complain
about the ship's hard ribs and hull, and often you feel like
grass that's been trodden underfoot and you just want to
spring back up in the wind. But the seidr magic spans a boat's
deck like an unseen bridge to the spirit world. Men speak in
low voices and all sound is muted and even our futures are
silent, as though the Norns yet sleep or have not the light by
which to see the life patterns, the wyrds, they weave for us. As
for us mortals, the day is new and untarnished and we have
woken upon the back of a dragon and so we are free to roam
the sea road.

After a breakfast of cheese, dried seal meat and the last of
the bread, which was by now harder than seasoned oak, we
made ready to head upriver. Men tried to look busy, scheming
to get out of having to untie us from the stakes in the sucking
filth, but you could only take so long stowing furs, tying back
your hair and fetching oars from the oar trees. And this time
Olaf chose five Norsemen to help him, perhaps not wanting to
aggravate the Wessexmen again, though more likely because
we had laughed at him the day before, and I was unlucky
enough to be one of them. We slipped and fell and slithered
in the mud like new lambs in their mother's birth fluids, but
eventually we untethered the ships and when we had finished
we were covered in seven layers of shit. Cynethryth had
watched the whole sorry adventure from *Serpent*'s prow and

when I petulantly barked at Bjorn to throw me a rope so I could hang on to it and wash myself in the river she giggled and that made me even more cross. Then Bram hauled up the slime-covered anchor and we threaded the oars through their ports and dipped them into the calm water, setting off towards the sun, which, in its pale golden chariot, rolled slowly but inexorably into the sullen sky. And with it rose my spirits. The morning swim might have washed the scent of Cynethryth from my skin, but it had also washed the sourness out of me, and as my hair dried and the rowing warmed my muscles I could almost see the funny side. Still, I would remember not to laugh at Uncle again.

In our wake, *Fjord-Elk* sliced as smoothly as a hot blade through tallow, her oars dipping in flawless unison, more so than ours for the lack of inexperienced Englishmen at her benches. By the cross at her prow stood her captain, Bragi the Egg, named so because there was not a strand of hair to be found on the man from his head to the soles of his feet. Sigurd had made Bragi *Fjord-Elk*'s captain after her old captain, Glum, had betrayed him, and the Egg seemed to have the knack of it from what I could see. His brother Kjar was the new steersman, taking over from Glum's kinsman Thorgils, who had died with Glum and big Thorleik that night outside the shepherd's hut in the Welsh hills. I did not know Kjar well, but his pride at being made *Fjord-Elk*'s steersman was as blatant as a horse's hard-on, and this I thought was a good sign as I watched him standing at her stern, the tiller safe in his sure grip.

Even on a dull day like this the country through which we rowed was as colourful as the richest tapestry, and ever changing. We slid past bright limestone cliffs and valleys in which cattle grazed contentedly on lush green grass. We passed boundless fields of ripe yellow flax, yet even these eventually gave over to woodland of chestnut, beech, oak, walnut, fir and pine, amongst which pigs and boar rooted, their snouts muddy and their grunts carrying to us on the water. Deer could be glimpsed if you looked long and hard and Bothvar called out when he saw a huge silver wolf padding away from the river bank, though when we looked it was gone.

'Who's to stop us grabbing some of this emperor's meat?' Bram Bear offered to no one in particular. And no one had an answer for him, so a little later we tied up to a couple of willows on the bank and caught and butchered four pigs, an old boar, and three chickens which Black Floki found wandering free. Bjorn and Bjarni took skins and spears and built a smoking tent on the shore. Inside it above slow-burning oak and apple wood they hung the cuts of meat and then they joined the rest of us around a great open fire above which we turned the old boar and the three chickens which Cynethryth and Egfrith had plucked, stuffed with onions and rubbed with Wessex butter, coriander and salt. The smell of this made our mouths slippery and when Yrsa and Red-faced Hastein came round with bulging skins of mead, pouring the frothing liquid into horns and cups, I thought I must be in Valhöll.

'This land tastes good,' Bram mumbled through a mouthful of meat, wiping grease from his lips with the back of his hand. 'More food here than a man can eat.'

'And none of it guarded,' Svein the Red said, a huge grin splitting his glistening red beard as he tore off another hunk of meat. To the Fellowship meat and mead were as fine if not finer than gold and girls. 'These Franks are too generous,' Svein added, sucking his fingers. 'But no swineherds to batter. That takes the fun out of it.'

Black Floki sighed, shaking his head. 'Why do you think that is, you great lump of giant's snot?' he asked, raising his dark eyebrows at Svein.

Svein held a chicken leg up like war booty, then made a great show of biting into it. 'Their White Christ told them to feed the poor heathens?' he suggested, chewing with a great smile as the others chuckled. Even the Wessexmen, who could not under-stand what we were saying, seemed happy enough filling their faces. All except for Ealdred, of course, who ate with them but could not have seemed further away.

'This meat was not penned because whoever owns it believes no one will steal it,' Floki said casually. 'You are not in the north now, Red. I am thinking there are laws here, laws strong enough to keep these Franks blade-straight.' He pulled a piece of gristle from his mouth and examined it by the light of the fire. 'This Frank emperor holds his land and its people in a tight grip,' he said, flicking the gristle into the fire.

Svein shrugged, smacking his lips together contentedly as though he did not have a care, but Floki's words gave the rest of us something to chew on. Of course, he could have been wrong. Maybe the swineherd had fallen ill and could not tend the animals this day. Or perhaps the creatures we found had escaped from a nearby thorp. But somehow we smelled the truth in what Floki said. He was a brooding son of a she-wolf, but his nose had a talent for sniffing out a situation before others even knew which way the wind was blowing. Added to this, the shore guard ships that had swept upon us, and the towers we had seen along the coastal cliffs, all pointed to this Karolus being a man who knew how to bridle a horse and ride it too.

That night half of us slept aboard the ships and half slept onshore, and all slept with one eye open. The next day we set off again with full bellies and holds packed with delicious joints of smoked pork which would feed our muscles and keep our oars churning the coils of the Sicauna. Occasionally smaller craft heading downriver clung dangerously close to the muddy banks to stay out of our reach. One knörr, a new and unweathered vessel by its look and laden with three fat cows, a clutter of barrels and six crew, even ran aground trying to keep away from us. Her keel dug into the submerged bank, stopping the boat dead and flinging her crew forward. The Franks yelled at the frightened beasts which were stamping in terror, and the beasts lowed back at the Franks, and we slid past the chaos, leaving nothing behind but a wake of Norse and English laughter.

Others we passed without incident. We would wave and smile at whoever we saw and Father Egfrith would greet the boats' crews and yell his god's blessings as freely as if he were tossing them apples, and sometimes folk would wave back cautiously, but most frowned or shrugged because they feared us and could not understand the monk.

'My beautiful Latin,' Egfrith mourned through tight lips late that afternoon. Three old fishermen in a faering stared at us wide-eyed and slack-mouthed, none the wiser for the monk's swift sermon. 'The tongue of Pope Leo himself no less, God preserve His Holiness. Wasted on these clods,' Egfrith went on under his breath as we passed, still smiling and waving and blessing. 'Wasted like good wine on a Norseman. *Dominus illuminatio mea! Dominus vobiscum!*' he called after them. Then he shook his bald head. 'It may as well be the honking of a goose for all they know. Ignorant swine.' He looked at me for support but then rolled his eyes because he knew he would get none from me.

'You can't blame them for looking baffled, monk,' I called from my row bench, dragging the river past with my oar blade. 'They have never seen a talking weasel before.' Penda laughed and Egfrith glowered which made me laugh, but Cynethryth scourged me with a look so I tried my best to look chastened then, though my best was not very good.

By dusk the cloud had rolled away to the south and the blue sky began to darken, revealing stars which flashed and pulsed like embers from an ancient fire – some old god's death pyre. The moon hung impossibly bright. It poured cold silvery shadows across the river and fields on either side as we moored in some shallows amongst rushes where marsh hens and mallards guarded their nests with flapping wings and angry curruks, quorks and quacks. Gone was the brackish, tidal water of the estuarine reaches where freshwater and seawater fish live. Gone were the mudflats where geese and wading birds peck at water plants and shadflies, and gone were the rasping sand martins whom we had watched in the last few days leave their burrows to fly south for the coming winter. Here in the Sicauna's middle course the river flowed more gently, making the rowing easier, though we still hoped for a change in the wind that would enable us to stow the oars and hoist the sails. We would see tomorrow. For now we secured *Serpent* and *Fjord-Elk*, tying their bows to ancient gnarly root tangles laid bare in the bank by eternal coursing water, and sinking their anchors from the stern.

Those who had gone ashore the previous night remained on board this time. Sigurd had learnt a hard lesson on the English shore when Ealdred had attacked from land and sea with the use of fishing skiffs packed with men brandishing firebrands. From now on there would always be enough men aboard the ships to row them out of harm's way at a moment's notice. Those on shore could always run along the bank and meet the dragons further on, away from whatever threatened them. It was cunning craft and even though it meant half of us spending the night amongst hard oak ribs and sea chests, we did not mind. The fire scars that still pock-marked *Serpent* served as a painful reminder of how close we had come to losing her. We owed it to her now to keep her safe.

There was a faint orange glow in the sky to the south-east, which we took to mean there was a town there, or at least a village, beyond the bumpy silhouette of the woods further inland. Perhaps its people knew we were there and had lit fires to prevent our coming unseen amongst them. Or perhaps their fires were part of some celebration or rite, a marriage or a death. Either way we would not bother them if they did not bother us.

Ealdred and the Wessexmen were ashore, though the ealdorman was kept apart from the others as Sigurd wanted as much as possible, short of killing Ealdred, to break the bonds between his men and him. Penda and I nestled amongst skins at *Serpent*'s stern, playing tafl and drinking mead. Others aboard were sleeping already, making the most of rare space, or talking in low voices or doing tasks that the rowing had kept them from. Behind us, Cynethryth and Father Egfrith sat on the fighting platform and I had been thinking how quiet they were being when I realized they were fishing. The stone weights took their nettle-hemp lines spear-straight to the riverbed, yet for all their quiet patience the girl and the monk had caught not so much as a sprat.

'She thanked you properly yet for saving that bastard father of hers?' Penda asked, gesturing over my shoulder. With his spiked hair, scarred face and wild eyes Penda could not help but look savage, even on a clear, calm night like that and playing tafl. 'A little reward for young Raven, eh lad?' he said, eyebrows dancing. 'A dip in the honey pot?'

I shot him a sour look, appalled that Cynethryth might have overheard, but he just grinned his best imitation of a mischievous young boy.

'Keep your mind on the game and leave the fishing to them,' I muttered, sliding a scallop shell across to capture one of Penda's blue-black mussel shells. 'I'd wager even Svein could beat you, Penda.'

He scowled. 'You take so long to make every move I'm almost asleep when it comes to my turn. Playing you is about as much fun as watching trees grow,' he said sulkily.

'That's it, Cynethryth! Steady. Careful.' I turned to see Cynethryth hauling her line up swiftly and smoothly. 'Good girl, don't let him jump off the hook,' Father Egfrith said, hopping excitedly from foot to foot. Cynethryth's face was pure concentration, her eyes wide, teeth biting into her bottom lip.

'Whatever it is it's heavy,' Penda said, and I nodded, though neither of us thought to help. 'Probably a Frank's boot,' the Englishman added.

Then with a delighted yip Cynethryth turned, swinging the fish into *Serpent*, where it flapped and hammered against the deck. 'A pike!' Egfrith yelped, kneeling to grasp the grey-green mottled fish and disengage the hook. 'You must be careful of the teeth. Sharp as the Devil they are.' And he was right, the pike's teeth were wicked-looking things as it gulped in vain and spurted blood and shit over Egfrith.

'Gaddr,' Yrsa Pig-nose called with an approving nod from his journey chest.

'The English call it pike, Yrsa,' I said in Norse. Several other Norsemen had come over to share in the excitement and they were now arguing about how the sharp-headed gaddr compared in taste with the other river fish: roach, rudd, bream and perch.

'It's as long as my arm,' I said, impressed.

'It's almost as long as my prick,' Ingolf said, his smile more gaps than teeth.

'But much prettier,' Hastein barked, slapping Ingolf's back.

'Well done, girl, he'll make good eating,' Penda said, scratching his chin.

'I was beginning to think all the fish must be asleep down there, Cynethryth,' I teased as Egfrith hefted the fish by its gills as proudly as if he had caught it himself.

'Do you think I haven't caught a fish before, Raven?' Cynethryth said, her eyebrows arched in challenge.

'Of course not,' I replied, 'I just meant . . .'

'Go back to your game, little boys, and leave the work to us.' Egfrith grinned like a stoat and I could have smashed those

151

teeth through the back of his head but instead Penda and I moped back to our game and as I considered my next move, Cynethryth called, 'And Penda, you can squash those fleas jumping around in your breeks. Raven has had no reward from me.'

CHAPTER THIRTEEN

I WAS WOKEN BY CURSING. CYNETHRYTH STIRRED BESIDE ME and we both sat up in our furs to see what the commotion was about. I knuckled my eyes, relieved to hear that Ingolf's profanities were woven with other men's laughter. The gap-toothed Norseman was amidships, brushing his breeks with the backs of his hands, nodding his head furiously and using words that would make Thór blush. He had pissed all over his breeks. Well, he had pissed over *Serpent*'s sheer strake, but the wind had had its own ideas and now Ingolf was in fouled breeks and an even fouler mood.

'Thank Njörd for that,' Yrsa announced, stretching his arms and ripping a great morning fart.

'Thank Njörd that I pissed myself?' Ingolf asked incredulously, showing Yrsa the dark stain on his left thigh.

'No, you bonehead.' Yrsa cocked one eyebrow and tipped his head. 'Well, yes actually,' he offered. 'The wind has changed, you dirty swine. It's coming up from the south-west now.' He reached up and wrapped his knuckles on an oar stave amongst those lying across the oar trees. 'Which means these fuckers can stay where they are today.' He smiled through a wide yawn which made his eyes water. 'If I were you, Raven, I'd stay in my sack all day,' he said with a mischievous smile and one eye on Cynethryth.

'And if I were you, Yrsa, I'd tie myself to a rock and throw myself overboard,' I said, realizing it was no easy thing having a woman aboard a longship, especially a woman you are in love with. But Yrsa was right about the wind and the thought of not having to row put the men in a good mood as we prepared the morning meal. Cynethryth and Egfrith had between them caught two large pike and three perch and all these went into a broth with some horseradish leaves and the leftover bread that was now too hard to chew. With his bow Bjarni had taken two ducks amongst the reeds and these made another broth with some garlic and the bones of a hare, which Yrsa had saved from a previous meal. I did not know what those aboard *Fjord-Elk* were eating, but I did know that it smelt appalling and I was thankful for Cynethryth's fishing luck and Bjarni's skill with a bow. Mind you, I would have wagered those aboard *Fjord-Elk* were as glad as we were to be cooking aboard the ships for once, whatever was in their pot, for it was a rare day when Sigurd allowed a fire on the ballast.

'This water's mild as milk and you know why that is, lad?' Olaf had asked me the previous night as he dropped the anchor into the river and fed the slime-coated rope through his gnarled hands.

'Because it is shallow, Uncle?' I had guessed.

He shook his head. 'It's deep enough to drown a great lump of stone like you, lad,' he said, testing the knot on the mooring post on *Serpent*'s sheer strake. 'No. It's slow-running because its upper course is only eight spear-lengths above sea level, meaning it has not far to fall and so doesn't pick up much speed. Not like the rivers back home. They'll carry you down faster than Sleipnir and spit you into the sea and before you know where you are you're wiping seagull shit out of your eye.'

Because the river was calm, Sigurd had allowed those of us waking aboard the ships that morning to suspend our cooking pots above small fires lit on the slippery ballast stones, so long as we kept buckets of water nearby and sloshed the whole lot down afterwards. After breakfast we raised the sails and slipped our moorings, harnessing the breeze that had ruined the start of Ingolf's day. We pushed slowly up the Sicauna as the sun rose in the east, gilding the river and warming our faces, for we were not rowing and so sat towards the bows and the simple Christ crosses mounted there. We scrubbed our war gear, our brynjas, helmets and swords, removing the small rust spots that had begun to appear after days spent in the salt air. Men talked of their kinfolk back home and I listened mostly, for I had no kinfolk to talk of. Or if I did, I did not know who or where they were. Everything I knew or cared about now was sailing up that Frankish river into the heartland of an emperor. For my memory was like a dark, empty barrel because two years past some blow had cracked my mind and every experience and memory had leaked away. I had woken in old Ealhstan's house and he had fed me and worked me, but now he was gone and every day that I spent aboard *Serpent* the roots of my soul dug a little deeper into her hull. Though I could never explain it, I knew that my ancestors' saga stories were written in the intricate weave of her carved stem and stern posts and up Jörmungand's slender, reaching neck. I imagined that my father, if he still lived, was a lord of the sea like Sigurd. Had I been washed overboard in a storm along the Wessex coast to bash my head against the sea-worn rocks? Had I been part of another fellowship of raiders when an English cudgel had knocked me unconscious, to be left for dead? Perhaps I had woken long enough to wander senselessly before falling again near the village of Abbotsend. It was likely that I would never know and so I did not argue with my heart when it beat in time with Norse oars.

By noon we were rowing again, the wind on the sails being too feeble to overcome the Sicauna's inexorable wend to the sea. For the next three days we ploughed the river southwards, passing gaps in riverside copses of alder and willow through which fields of wheat and barley rolled like a golden ocean in the breeze. We never moored near any of the villages whose people eyeballed us from the banks and low hills as though we were green-skinned interlopers risen from their Hell.

'They must be muddled as Svein the Red counting his fingers and toes,' Knut had called from the tiller. 'Two heathen-built dragons with Christ crosses at their prows. Poor fuckers don't know whether to run or pray.' And we never stayed anywhere long enough for them to find out, instead rowing a great coil of slow water until the crosses at our prows faced the north-east. Two days later we came to Paris. I do not know what I had expected, but it was not what I found. We came into a great bowl where the Sicauna fattened and divided before passing either side of a low-lying island that was once, according to Egfrith, the home of a tribe of Gauls who fought Rome's greatest general, Julius Caesar.

'Your jarl would have liked Julius Caesar,' Egfrith had said with a barely disguised grimace. 'He worshipped pagan gods and slaughtered countless thousands.'

'I'd wager he didn't die a straw death,' Olaf had put in with an admiring smile.

'He did not have the time to die, Uncle,' I said, 'too busy killing Christians.'

Now Egfrith grinned, his little eyes glinting impishly. 'Julius Caesar's own friends stabbed him to death whilst he was discussing Roman laws,' he said.

Uncle had spat over *Serpent*'s sheer strake at that. 'No one likes laws,' he said.

On Sigurd's word Knut pushed the tiller forward so that we took the river's left-hand branch. It was wider than the right-hand channel, meaning we would have more water to manoeuvre in should we need to, and we all took in the sight of the place as we rowed with the beautiful, flawless rhythm we always kept when there were other sea-folk watching. The island's muddy banks sloped gently up from the river until they met a grassy manmade rampart upon which stood a spear-height palisade of smooth, pointed trunks. This defensive wall was broken at regular intervals by walkways of planks ascending the rampart from the water's edge right into the city. There were so many of them that I thought these Franks must be idle or foolish for choosing convenience over the integrity of their bulwark. It was a busy place. Dozens of skiffs, faerings and big-bellied knörrs were pulled up on to the mud and moored to sunken posts, their bows looking up expectantly at the city where their crews plied their trade. The day had been fair and bright before we had come within a bow-shot of Paris. Now the sky was a swirl of black, grey and yellow hearth smoke that lumbered slowly eastwards, almost too heavy for the breeze to shift.

Every now and then a section of white stone wall rose behind the palisade and there were even some crumbling bastions along its length, but there were not enough of these stone defences to be much use. Egfrith said it was the remains of the Roman wall that once protected Paris from Rome's enemies. It would be hard pressed to protect the city from a mangy dog now. Or us, I thought grimly, remembering the Wolfpack's burning of Abbotsend.

'Look at them. Like rats in a cesspit,' Bram said of the Franks who, having seen us, were now scrambling up the muddy walkways in panic.

'Looks like they are afraid of the Christ cross, monk,' I said to Egfrith, who was standing by Sigurd at the mast step.

'The crosses cannot disperse the fog of sin that cloaks these ships,' he replied flatly. 'You swine could put Christ's sandals on your feet and His robe on your backs but you would be no less savage underneath them. No less lost to the Almighty.' I hoped Sigurd might pick the monk up then and cast him overboard like a pail of piss, but the jarl seemed deaf to the weasel's mewing. In truth Sigurd was still weak, some of his wounds still staining the linen with foul-smelling yellow slime. He stooped slightly and was thinner than I had ever seen him.

'We'll moor there, Uncle,' he said, pointing to a spot free of boats where the bank was narrowest, only two spear-lengths wide before the manmade rampart rose. There were no mooring posts and I looked up to the palisade to see that there were no gates for three hundred paces in either direction. Sigurd had chosen the place because from that mooring we would see men coming along the bank from a long way off and have time to prepare.

'Cunning bastard,' I heard Penda mutter under his breath and we pulled hard for the last few strokes before slewing up on to the mud. Lightning quick we stowed our oars, grabbed our shields, helmets and spears and jumped from *Serpent*'s prow into the sucking mud. We did not bother with mail, for though we wanted to be ready should a fight come our way, brynjas would have announced, clearer than a war horn, that we had come to steal and kill. So we stood there in a loose cluster, eyes searching the ramparts and the banks. I cursed myself for having spent sailing time cleaning my worn old shoes, for now they were already misshapen clumps of leather and mud and my feet were wet as Rán's cunny.

Wiglaf and the Wessexmen took our own mooring posts and, with the butts of two axes, beat them into the mud before securing the ships with thick ropes. Sigurd hung for a moment from *Serpent*'s bow, then dropped awkwardly, slipping in the mud as he tried to rise, and I was not alone in pretending to be too interested in Paris to notice.

'Keep that lump of snot on a short rope,' he said to Black

Floki, who dropped on to the bank behind a miserable-looking Ealdred and shoved the ealdorman forward, grimacing. I had thought Floki's grimace was simply due to his revulsion for Ealdred but I soon understood it was something else. The comforting, sweet smell of the town's woodsmoke mingled with the robust stench of human shit and there was another reason why this part of the shore was deserted. Fifty paces north along the bank a slick, glistening trail of filth oozed down the rampart to be lapped at by the Sicauna. We were almost moored in a river of Frankish shit.

'Welcome to Paris,' Olaf said, hawking and spitting into the mud.

Giving my spear to Bjorn I squelched back over to *Serpent*, extending a hand to help Cynethryth down, but she dismissed the gesture with the flick of a hand and jumped, bare feet plunging into the mud. 'Maybe you should have helped your jarl,' she said.

'Cynethryth,' I hissed, and her lips pouted so that it was all I could do not to kiss her there and then. Instead, though, I turned because someone barked that the Franks were coming.

There were three of them – two soldiers and an official in knee-length boots, an oversized ermine cloak and a conical hat made from rat fur. You only had to see the man to know he was a self-important prick and I felt sorry for the armed men with him as they squelched towards us, sometimes sinking to the knee, trying to keep up with Big Boots.

A stream of incomprehensible words cut the stinking air. Then in heavily accented English, 'Who are you? What is your business here?' Big Boots's voice arrived long before he did. Sigurd said nothing until the man was within reach and staring at us balefully as his two men caught their breath and grimaced at the stench.

Sigurd looked at Ealdred, expecting the ealdorman to play his part as he had done before. But Ealdred said nothing, his long frayed moustache twitching as he scratched his chin, perhaps weighing up several possible outcomes. Cynethryth looked at her father.

'Who are you?' Big Boots asked again, looking at Ealdred now. Sigurd frowned and nodded at the ealdorman but Ealdred pursed his thin lips, and there was the hint of a smile there.

'I am Ealdorman Ealdred of the kingdom of Wessex in England,' he said at last, and I released the breath I had been holding. 'I have business with the emperor,' he went on haughtily, glancing up at the palisade with a sneer as though he was not in the least impressed by the look of the place.

'The emperor?' Big Boots almost laughed. 'You think the emperor lives here? In this reeking shit hole? The emperor only comes here when he wants more gold to build his churches,' he said without malice. 'And who can blame him for leaving again before his arse has warmed the imperial throne? His palace is in Aix-la-Chapelle. A very long walk north-east of here. Not that you will be walking anywhere until you've paid the landing tax,' he added, smirking at one of his men, whose teeth worried his bottom lip. Then Big Boots frowned, glancing at the longships and back to us – back to Sigurd. 'These men are heathens!' he said to Ealdred. 'I can smell it on them. They are heathen craft too,' he added, pointing at the ships, a crack defying his cocksure arrogance. His men glanced at each other nervously. 'You're no ealdorman,' he accused Ealdred, who merely shrugged and looked to Sigurd.

A bell was clanging inside the city now. I looked up at the smoke-bellied sky where loose mobs of jackdaws and rooks broke, several at a time, into the space above the valley to the south, then tumbled out of sight beyond the city's palisade. Big Boots is a dead man, I thought to myself.

'We are Christians,' Egfrith said assuredly, making the sign of the cross as though to ward off the evil of Big Boots's accusation.

'You are heathens!' Big Boots said, pointing a finger at Sigurd's face, which was the stupidest thing he could have done. Either side of him the soldiers were shifting uncomfortably, clutching their spears with white knuckles, their jaw muscles working silently. 'You are Danes,' Big Boots said, which was at least a change from heathens. 'I tell you I can smell it on you.' Egfrith shot Sigurd an *I told you so* look but Sigurd did not see because he was moving. In two plunging steps he was on the customs reeve, clutching the man's head and gouging his eyes. The soldiers turned and ran, leaving their screaming master to his fate. Sigurd pulled the man into his chest, turning at the hip, and gave a savage jerk, filling the air with a sharp cracking sound. Big Boots crumpled face first into the mire as the rest of us stood staring, apart from Black Floki, who was already running after the fleeing Franks.

'Go on then!' Olaf said to Bjorn and Bjarni, who looked at each other, then dropped their shields and set off, released to the chase like hounds through the mud.

'You are mad!' Egfrith yelped, signing the cross for real now. 'You are mad as beasts!'

Sigurd shrugged. 'We would not have got very far with that bladdermouth bawling like a stuck pig that we are Danes,' he said. 'Besides which, it's offensive. We are no more Danes than he is.'

'What do you guess they will think you are now?' Egfrith asked, shaking his head, his palms to the sky.

Sigurd sighed as though he was tired or bored. 'They cannot know what we are now, monk,' he said, which was at least true, though for how long who could say? I looked around. There was no one to be seen, which meant there was a chance that no one had seen what we had done. Black Floki and Bjorn were each dragging a mud-caked corpse back towards us, with all the ceremony of men lugging sacks of horse shit.

Ealdred was smirking and old Asgot grinned too, perhaps

because he thought Sigurd would give him the Wessexman now. The godi would in turn give Ealdred to the All-Father via his wicked sharp knife.

'Back to the ships,' Sigurd said. 'We don't know what we are dealing with here and we can't fight in this.' He frowned at the mud. There were no complaints as the Wolfpack worked the sucking, plunging mooring posts free and clambered back aboard.

'Let me stay,' I said, 'with the monk.' I surprised even myself with this request, but some part of my mind knew it made sense. 'We'll go into the city and ferret around. Dig up what we need to know.' Most of the Norsemen continued preparing to set off, but Sigurd and Olaf stared at me. Cynethryth was staring too.

'What if they saw us kill the reeve, Raven?' Olaf asked, nodding towards the city ramparts. All were aboard now but for those who would help the rowers by pushing the longships backwards before wading out and clambering up the boarding ropes.

'They didn't see, Uncle,' I said uncertainly. 'And even if they know something happened here, which they will when the reeve doesn't return, they will not lay it at the feet of a Christ monk.' Father Egfrith had to admit this was the truth when I told him in English. I think he was as eager as me to have a sniff around this city of the Franks. He nodded forlornly as though still stunned by the reeve's killing.

'I'll go with them, Sigurd,' Penda said, leaping from *Serpent*'s prow without waiting for Sigurd's permission. He slapped Egfrith on the back and grinned like a fiend.

The jarl looked at Olaf, who shrugged his broad shoulders and scratched his nest-like beard. 'We will go upriver,' Sigurd said, 'and find a quiet place. Be here at sunrise the day after tomorrow. We will come for you then.'

I glanced up at Cynethryth, instinctively touching the raven's feather which she had tied into my hair, and I thought I must be a fool for leaving her to go into a place of more people than I had ever seen – and all of them Christians.

'Look after Father Egfrith, Raven,' Cynethryth said with knitted brows. The skin of her cheeks, which had been snow-drop white, was now wind-burnt brown, but she was still the most beautiful thing I had ever laid eyes on.

'I'll keep an eye on him,' I said, wanting to say more.

'And I'll keep an eye on them both, lady,' Penda put in with a respectful nod.

'Take this, Raven.' Sigurd threw me a black scrip which chinked when I caught it. Then I realized it was not a scrip but a hat tied closed with a leather thong. It was the ratskin hat Big Boots had been wearing when Sigurd broke his neck, and now it was full of hack silver. Which was just as well, I thought, as *Serpent* and *Fjord-Elk* slipped back into the Sicauna, their crews backing oars skilfully. For I was in Paris.

CHAPTER FOURTEEN

THE THREE OF US TRUDGED SOUTH ALONG THE BANK, WATCHING the perimeter for signs of a commotion, which would tell us the Franks had seen what we had done to their reeve.

'They probably think we have done them a good turn,' Penda suggested. 'I don't suppose they like paying the bastard any more than we would.' Every step we took was accompanied by a squelch and a pop. 'If they'd seen anything we would have a levy on us by now,' the Wessexman added. 'I am guessing there's no inner rampart, fortunately. Otherwise we would have seen sentries peering over the wall.'

'Even if they did see your savage jarl wring that poor man's neck like a prize goose, they have no need to wade through this mire,' Egfrith said matter-of-factly. 'They can keep their boots clean; we're coming to them.' At that Penda and I looked at each other knowing that the monk was right. We could walk into that place and straight on to more spears than there are spines on a hedgehog.

A man and his son, both barefoot like Egfrith, had moored their skiff and were trudging up the bank carrying between them a reed basket piled high with bream and roach. I could tell they were father and son because the boy had the same livid purple stain across his cheek and forehead as the man. Silver tails flapped helplessly among the mountain of fish, though for all their rich catch the father and son looked as miserable as two monks with a pretty whore. Perhaps the marks on their faces stirred hatred or fear in others, as my blood-eye did. At least they will not starve, I thought as they passed in front of us, ignoring us and the blessing Father Egfrith gave them.

Up we went, stepping on the grass between the planks, for the planks themselves were treacherous with slick moss, and then we passed through the open gateway and for the second time that day my nose wished it were anywhere else. Out on the water smells do not hang around long enough to trouble you, not even one of Bram's farts, but in a place enclosed within a wall, the stink can water your eyes and make you wish you had rolled mint leaves stuffed in your nostrils. Human and animal shit, hearth smoke, cheese, spices, sweat, fish, damp wool, wet daub and straw, raw flesh, and the stale piss stench of the tannery, all created an overwhelming stink so thick you could chew it.

I suddenly realized why armed men had not poured from the place like water from a holed pail to avenge their reeve; they were far too busy doing a hundred other things to have noticed what was happening beyond the cesspit by the north wall.

The place was swarming with traders and craftsmen, fishermen and beggars and whores. A drunk with a pockmarked face stumbled past, falling against me and slurring something nasty as I shoved him off.

'You want me to hold that, lad?' Penda asked, nodding at the silver-filled hat in my left hand.

'It's safe with me, Penda,' I said defensively, nevertheless gripping the ratskin hat even tighter. There was enough silver in that hat to buy a decent sword and earn me a beating if I lost it.

'So many souls,' Egfrith sighed, as though he were somehow responsible for them all or else pitied whoever was. Wooden trestles groaned with goods of all kinds. There were fine furs of beaver, otter, marten, fox and bear. There was pottery, glass and metalwear, and items made of deer antler such as combs and knife and sword hilts. There were brooches and necklaces and rings of gold, silver and amber, and there were stalls of meat and vegetables, herbs and spices and sweet golden honey. I felt dizzy in this stinking cauldron of noise and commotion. Penda was already talking to a dark-haired whore whose red-painted cheeks and naked tits were intended to steer your mind from the fact that she seemed to have only one tooth. Clearly it worked on Penda, who held a tit in each hand, pursing his lips as though he were weighing grain against the merchant's price. Father Egfrith was too busy trying his Latin on a richly dressed horse trader to chastise the Wessexman.

'Where on Óðin's hairy arse do we start?' I said, scratching my short beard and looking for a path through the buzzing knots of mud-spattered folk.

'Did you leave your wits between your lass's legs, lad?' Penda asked, sending One Tooth on her way with a slap on the rump, at which she spat at him viciously and stomped off. 'Where do you think we should start, you bone-headed heathen son of a goat?' he grinned. 'In the tavern, of course! Bad enough that we can't speak the language of the place. Even worse we should have to try talking to these Franks with tongues stiff as dried herring.'

I looked at Egfrith, who had given up on the horse trader, expecting him to propose a more diligent course of action than Penda's.

'I agree with Penda,' he said brightly, raising his voice above the hubbub. 'A drop of wine will inspire us.'

'Wine, monk?' I said. I had heard of the stuff, of course,

but I had never wet my lips with it. Wine was a rich man's drink.

But Egfrith and Penda were already on the move. Folk instinctively stepped out of Penda's way, for he was every inch a warrior and a frightening sight, whilst the monk wriggled through the crowds like a weasel through a field of stiff green barley. So, clutching Sigurd's silver as though it were one of mighty Thór's precious iron gauntlets, I followed.

We fought our way through herds of pigs being driven to the butcher's block in preparation for winter. Fattened by the woodland mast of beechnuts, chestnuts, acorns, and other fruits of the forest, the hogs would make delicious eating, though to look at them swathed in filth, aggressive and wild-eyed, you would have thought they had just burst from the fetid pits of Hel.

Held down by three men, an old horse screamed as a fat woman sliced the artery in its neck, and nearby a pair of worn-out hounds quietly waited for death whilst their master sharpened his knife. It was that time of year, when a man must decide which of his animals will consume more fodder in the coming months than their remaining life can justify. Any old or ailing beasts would soon find themselves in the pot, and the tang of blood, stale and fresh, was just another ingredient of the fug.

We walked along an ancient, rotting gangway between densely wedged houses, some wattle-and-daub, others timber caulked with clay, and all leaking yellow-brown smoke through old thatch. A grey-haired warrior sat in the mud holding up a bowl containing three small silver coins. His left leg stopped at the knee where the breeks had been cut and tied off, and flies were swarming unopposed on a weeping sore on his neck. He looked a poor, wretched soul but for the tarnished silver warrior ring on his arm, which pride had not let him sell for food, though there was no pride left in his eyes. Penda produced a coin, stopping to drop it into the bowl, and the man grimaced, taking the coin and secreting it away leaving three in the bowl once more.

'Might have been something once,' Penda muttered, moving on as Egfrith signed the cross over the old soldier before hurrying after us. We followed the lane round to the right, passing a shoemaker, whom I told myself to visit later, and a hideously ugly woman selling an assortment of young girls. Far from looking terrified, these girls grabbed at us as we passed, trying to make us touch their fledgling breasts and crotches, and it was enough to make the bile rise in your throat.

'Holy Mary mother of Christ!' Father Egfrith screeched, throwing his hands into the air out of their reach, as though these children were the brides of Satan himself, which they might have been for all I knew, though they flinched from me when they saw my blood-eye. We hurried on, past a row of rowdy fishmongers, then sidestepped a pile of congealing puke and looked up to see a barrel hanging from the eaves of a squat timber building from which the sound of drunken men leaked with the meal-fire smoke. We went to rinse our hands in the rain barrel by the door, but the water was a suspicious colour and so we left it alone, instead ducking into the crowded dark place which stank of sweat, old mead and ale, and guttering mutton tallow candles. Penda's elbows carved us a ragged passage to a stout oak table behind which the tavern's owner, a tall, thin, beak-nosed man, greeted us with a curt nod and began filling three leather jacks with ale.

'Keep them coming, Frank,' Penda said as I handed the man a silver finger ring from the ratskin hat. He bit into it and nodded, satisfied, then grinned at me.

'I can fill them if you can empty them,' he said in heavily accented English, already turning to serve a rowdy knot of fishermen who stank of herring guts and were covered in glinting fish scales. Dark red joints of meat hung curing above the tavern owner's table, some missing flesh wedges where they had been carved to the bone.

Penda drank deeply, then dragged the back of his hand across his lips. 'Ah, that puts the fire out, boys,' he said, and he was right, it was good ale. 'Plenty of hops but not too much bog myrtle. As good an ale as you'll find.'

'And safer than drinking Bram's mead,' I said, stepping on a man's toes to let a pretty serving girl wriggle past.

'*Fils à putain!*' the man growled. I turned to face him and he frowned when he saw my red eye. Then he took one look at Penda and turned back round, continuing the conversation with his friends as though nothing had happened.

'I like it here, monk,' I said, amazed by the loud murmur of so many men all talking at once. It was a sound like the sea breaking and plunging amongst rocks. But Egfrith was already fighting his way back to the tavern owner, empty jack in hand.

'I think he likes it here too, Raven,' Penda said with a smirk. A few moments later the monk was back with a wine skin, looking serious. Cradling the skin as though it were his precious Christ child, he filled our jacks with the red liquid. When I tasted the stuff I wondered if I had in fact been killed on the beach by the reeve's men and was even now in Óðin's hall Valhöll drinking the Spear-Shaker's own drop. It was thin like water but had a strong, fruit taste which warmed my stomach, clouded my head, and put a stupid smile on my face. Before I knew it we were on our second skinful.

'Now I know why you churchmen are always celebrating the sacrament, Father,' Penda said. 'Cut off my hair and give me a skirt if it means drinking this all day. This, Raven, is the blood of Christ. Isn't that right, Father?'

I swallowed gingerly and stared at my wine, then stared at Egfrith, who nodded solemnly. 'The Lord Jesus on the night when He was betrayed took bread, and when He had given thanks, He broke it, and said, "This is my body which is for you. Do this in remembrance of me." In the same way also the cup, after supper, saying, "This cup is the new covenant in my blood. Do this, as often as you drink it, in remembrance of me." So it was written by Paul the Apostle,' Egfrith said, 'and so it is a great blessing to receive the Eucharist.' He frowned at me. 'You don't know this, Raven? There *is* a church in Abbotsend?'

'There was,' I said, 'but Wulfweard told me to stay away and that was fine by me.'

He shrugged and gulped another mouthful as though there really was a fire in his belly that needed dousing, but I had been put off and was now holding my jack at arm's length. 'No need to worry your twisted, black, heathen soul about it, Raven,' Egfrith said, filling his jack again. 'This wine has not been blessed. Not unless the tavern owner is one of the Lord's ministers, which is about as likely as you being born of a virgin. Which means that this is still just wine. Not a drop of Christ's blood in it.' He sniffed, saluting me with his jack before swilling some more.

But it was too late for me. I tipped the rest of mine into Penda's jack, the Wessexman smacking his lips together eagerly, and turned to shove my way to the serving table to fetch more ale. The White Christ must have been a giant with more blood in his veins than there is water in the oceans, I thought, if all his followers drank the stuff as vigorously as Father Egfrith.

Just before sunset there was a commotion when a Frankish official burst into the tavern with armed men at his back and began questioning the locals.

'Someone has killed Radulf the reeve,' Beaknose said, filling my jack again when I asked him what the excitement was about. He still seemed happy with the trade we had done and I wondered how much ale and wine a simple silver ring would buy. 'A fisherman found him and Bernart and Arthmael half buried in mud beyond the north wall. God knows what they were doing out there. Shame. Bernart was one of my best customers,' he said with a sad shake of his head.

'And some of that pork,' I said, pointing above his head. He fetched a joint down, whipped a knife from his belt and began deftly carving slices of the meat and putting them on a platter. 'Why would anyone kill the reeve?' I asked, my mouth watering at the sight of the meat. Beaknose shrugged.

'He was a nosy bastard,' he said simply, producing a great lump of cheese which he added to the platter, 'but a decent man all the same. Used to drink here most nights. All three of them.' He shrugged again, handing me the platter proudly. 'Still, no one likes paying taxes,' he said.

We pretended to be dead drunk when the official and his soldiers got as far as us. Or maybe we were dead drunk. Either way, the man realized he would get more sense from a cuckoo, and seeing that Egfrith was a monk he moved on into the press. As it turned out, another ingot of silver about half the size of my thumb bought us each a space on the floor at the rear of the tavern, fresh straw, as much ale as we could drink until sunrise, and the name of an English-speaking fisherman who might tell us what we needed to know. That name was Winigis and Beaknose said we could find the man at cock's crow by the jetty on the island's south-west side, where boats from across the river could moor free of the clinging mud of the banks.

Egfrith woke us at dawn. My head felt like an anvil being pounded by Völund's hammer and my mouth tasted like a dead dog's balls as I splashed fresh water over my face from the bucket Beaknose had left by my head the night before. Then, after a long, cool drink of ale I felt alive enough to follow Egfrith and Penda out of that stinking tavern and into the Paris dawn. In the east the sky was blood red. In the west it was still black as pitch. All across the city cocks were crowing excitedly, the sound frantic, desperate almost, as though the birds had never before seen the sun and were now fulfilling their life's duty with wilful pride. And yet tomorrow's dawn would break to the same strange song. 'If all I had to do was fuck and crow, I'd be good at both, too,' Penda said, holding the back of his head gingerly.

We walked through the streets thankful to find them all but empty, though the first traders were already setting up their stalls and carefully laying out their wares.

'I'll admit I have felt better,' Penda said as we lined up behind a hazel screen and pissed into a trench by the inner embankment which tunnelled beneath the mound and out of the city.

'You've looked better too,' I said, 'though not much.' A shiver ripped through me as the hot liquid left my body. Even Egfrith seemed jaded this morning, though he claimed that was down to the last skin of wine's having been bad. 'Or perhaps it was the cheese,' he suggested seriously.

'You're no Baldr the beautiful, either, lad,' Penda said, his neck bones cracking as he rolled his head. 'Whose idea was it anyway, to drink Paris drier than a nun's cunny like that?'

'Don't look at me,' I said, 'speak to the man with no shoes,' which reminded me to visit the shoemaker after our meeting with Winigis.

Egfrith let out a long squeaking fart that any Norseman would have been ashamed of. 'O Lord,' he chirruped, dropping the skirt of his habit to cover his little white legs once more.

'That was a prayer He could have done without, Egfrith,' Penda chuckled, pinching his nose.

We found Winigis the fisherman selling his morning catch of pike, perch, chubb and carp. The jetty was busy with boats coming and going and other fishermen were competing for trade with their own loud, repetitive cries. Nearby, apprentices knelt mending their masters' nets or stood in moored skiffs bailing rain and seawater from the vessels.

When Winigis saw us trudging along the bank towards him

he smiled broadly and spread his hands over his catch, which flapped in baskets on a crude trestle of three long planks on two old tree stumps set in the mud. He spoke too but we could not understand him and so Egfrith raised a hand in a gesture that told him to save his patter for other customers.

'We have been told that you speak English,' the monk said as Penda picked up a fat chubb and examined it. The man frowned.

'A little,' he said, pinching two fingers.

'Praise the Almighty,' Egfrith replied, throwing his arms heavenward dramatically. 'Then we have found the man we need.'

'Aix-la-Chapelle,' I said, checking that we were not being overheard. 'You know it?' Gulls shrieked above. The water, which moments earlier had looked black and cold, was now a distorted image of the brightening sky, its surface touched by gold, orange and red. A chill came off the moving water, making me huff into my cupped hands.

'I have been there. Once,' Winigis said guardedly. 'You have not come for my fish?' he asked, taking the chubb from Penda, who sniffed his hands and rubbed them on his breeks.

'No, we don't want your fish, Winigis. We want to go to Aix-la-Chapelle.'

'We have business with the emperor,' Egfrith said proudly.

Winigis shrugged. 'I do not see what that has to do with me. I am a fisherman. And you are obstructing my trade, so kindly move along,' he said, his eyes lingering on mine. Two women had come to judge Winigis's catch against that of the stall to the right, but Penda turned to them and gave them a smile that made them blanch and walk away. Winigis was beginning to get agitated. He took off his hat in frustration and, glancing at each of us in turn, decided to appeal to Egfrith. 'Please leave me alone,' he said. 'I am a simple man.'

'You have an apprentice? Or a thrall perhaps?' I asked. He

nodded, turning a palm to Egfrith as if to say so what? 'Then your boat will be safe until you return,' I said.

'Return? What are you talking about? And what is wrong with your eye?'

I smiled. 'You are going to take us to Aix-la-Chapelle, Winigis,' I said, 'and in return my lord gives you all that is in my hand.'

The man's pockmarked face was flushing red now, his cheeks beginning to flame with frustration. The other fishermen were selling well.

'I don't want whatever it is your lord is offering!' he snapped, glancing around now for help, perhaps looking for Radulf the reeve.

Then with my free hand I shoved a basket of fish off the trestle, spilling the glittering catch into the mud where some of the creatures flapped, perhaps thinking they were saved. Then I emptied the ratskin hat on to the planks. The hack silver, rings and brooches glimmered dully in the dawn light and Winigis the fisherman stood open-mouthed, his eyes wide as coins. 'Oh, I think you do,' I said, feeling the grin spread across my face.

CHAPTER FIFTEEN

FOR THE REST OF THE DAY WE WANDERED THE CITY, HAVING arranged to meet Winigis on the northern bank where his people's shit slid into the Sicauna. He had recoiled at our choice of meeting place, but the sight of all that silver weighed down his tongue so that he simply nodded, asking no more questions, and we left him picking fish from the mud.

We discovered that the island's eastern side was largely given over to the White Christ and Egfrith tried to convince us to visit the churches and monasteries there, but I would not and so he had to explore them alone. I still had the silver, so Penda would not leave my side. He had to come with me to the shoemaker's stall where I bought a pair of boots that came halfway up my shin and had soles of thick hide. In return I had to go with him back to the tavern to find a whore. Beaknose rustled up seven to choose from and Penda took a long time choosing, in the end settling for a big-boned, pale-skinned girl. I suspected he chose her because she had red hair like the girl from Wessex who filled his dreams. I settled for a skin of wine because the monk was not there to sour its taste with his talk of Christ's blood, and by the time it was half empty it could have been Christ's, Óðin's or my own blood for all I cared.

'Why don't you take one?' Beaknose had asked me, nodding at a sallow-skinned whore as he slammed a dish of steaming potage on the table before me. He seemed offended. 'Don't tell me you have a taste for boys. You do not look like a Greek,' he offered, scratching his pockmarked neck, 'but it can be arranged.'

'Raven has a skinny girl waiting for him,' Penda said, his voice muffled by the redhead's heavy breasts. 'She's pretty as the sun and a good girl, too. Not like these scraps of rancid mutton.' The redhead continued to coo over him, which I took to mean she understood no English.

'But this skinny girl is not here now,' Beaknose said, handing two cups of ale to a rough-looking pair of Franks armed with swords and long knives. 'There is no harm in poking a fire for warmth when you're away from your own hearth.'

'Poking fires is dangerous,' I said, blowing on a spoonful of potage and wondering what animal had gone into it, for the meat was an unusual ashen colour, though the dish smelled delicious. Beaknose shrugged and went about his business, leaving me to eat, drink, admire my new boots, and ignore Penda's fumblings in the straw behind me.

That night a waxing crescent moon silvered the Sicauna and the thatch roofs of Paris. The smoke seeping from those roofs glowed yellow and the deserted muddy streets and walkways which were not cast in shadow glistened. I was half asleep by the time Egfrith blew into the tavern, but that did not stop him gabbling on about the church of Geneviève and its most prized relic, an ancient bit of wood said to be a piece of the true Cross on which the White Christ died. Then he had gone to some monastery and prayed with the brothers there and done who knows what else, because I had pulled my cloak over my head to save my ears, though I could still hear his muffled chatter long into the night.

At dawn we found a woman selling freshly baked barley and wheat bread and we bought every loaf she had, filling three large sacks, a fourth being full of cured meat from Beaknose. Then I took off my new boots, tied them together and hung them round my neck before we made our way out of the north-west gate and across the mud where we found Winigis waiting. He wore a long kirtle of coarse wool and instead of a cloak a waxed skin fell to below his arse. In one hand he clutched his waxed leather hat and in the other a small oiled wool sack containing whatever else he had thought to bring for the journey. There the four of us waited, Penda reminiscing about his whore, Egfrith squeaking on about the churches of Paris, Winigis asking questions to which he got no answers, and I watching the misty river for sign of *Serpent* and *Fjord-Elk*.

We did not have to wait long. *Serpent* slid out of the mist as she had done when I had first seen her from the rocks of Abbotsend. Then she had put an iced knot of fear in my belly and frozen my limbs with terror, but now her swan-breasted hull was like a refreshing drink for my eyes, despite the Christ cross at her prow, and the rhythmic dip of her oars was a thrilling, soul-stirring sound. Olaf waved in greeting and Knut turned the ship to the shore, the oars quickening so that they looked like an eagle's beating wings as she came.

'Never thought I'd be happy to see such a thing,' Penda said, his left hand resting on the pommel of the sword at his hip.

'You are with them?' Winigis asked me, fear etched in his pock-scarred face. He glanced at Egfrith who half grimaced.

'She's called *Serpent*. And the other ship is called *Fjord-Elk*,' I said proudly, feeling my lips spread in a smile as Sigurd's second ship broke out of the vaporous murk.

'*Serpent*?' Winigis glanced back towards the city wall. 'It is not a very Christian name.' He licked his lips and his fingers worried at the hat he was clutching.

'Neither is *Fjord-Elk*,' I added, staring at *Serpent* as she slewed up on to the muddy shore, carving through the sludge as Olaf held on to the cross at her prow. 'And that's because those men are black-hearted heathens, Winigis,' I said as two ropes were thrown over the sheer strake for Egfrith and Winigis to clamber up. 'Well, most of them anyway.' The Frank took a step backwards, his eyes full of horror. I threw him the ratskin hat full of silver and he caught it wide-eyed and clutched it to his chest without even untying the thong to look inside it. 'Now get aboard, Winigis,' I said, and he looked to Father Egfrith who nodded and trudged forward. The Frank put on his hat, stuffed the silver into his oiled sack and followed Egfrith as Bjorn, Bjarni, Osk, Hedin and three of the Wessexmen jumped off to help Penda and me shove the dragon ship back into the river.

'So, lad, who is he?' Olaf asked, looking unimpressed by the frightened Frank standing at the mast step as I took my oar from the oar trees and fed it through the port beside my journey chest. Cynethryth smiled at me, her green eyes fresh as new grass in that place of mud and brown water. My chest tightened like a clenched fist.

'He's a fisherman, Uncle,' I said, falling into time with the other rowers so that our oar blades clove the Sicauna with the precision of a flock of birds in flight, 'and he is going to take us to Aix-la-Chapelle to see the emperor.'

'Is he now?' Olaf muttered under his breath as Sigurd began to question the Frank, his cloak wrapped tightly round his shoulders and clasped in one hand at his neck, despite the mild early autumn morning. 'And his reward is all of that silver Sigurd gave you? Every last shiny bit?' His eyebrows arched as he scratched his bushy beard.

'Apart from what we used to buy bread and meat, yes, Uncle,' I said, still looking at Cynethryth. 'All of it.'

'Then I suppose you found those handsome new boots, eh?' he said, and I smiled at Cynethryth and imagined what I would do with her if we ever got the chance to be alone together.

'Just sitting there unloved and footless,' I said, trying not to smile. 'Some of us are born lucky, Uncle.'

We rowed upriver watching the fortress island of Paris slide by our steerboard side. Along the shore on our port side men were felling trees, carving into the forest as teams of oxen dragged the trunks away, and Father Egfrith chirruped that that was just the beginning. In a few years that clearing would be crowded with dwellings and the sky above yellow with hearth smoke and church bells would join in song with those from new churches on the land south of the island. For Paris was a bastion of the true faith, he said, which would bloom like a rose as more of God's children flocked to the light, and soon the Christian west would meet the Christian east so that only at the fringes of the world would the darkness linger. 'At the fringes of the world and in your black hearts,' he said, instinctively touching the scar on his tonsured head etched by Glum's sword, 'though I will do my best to turn you away from Satan's path, so help me God.'

Most of the Norsemen could not understand him and tolerated his prattling, having grown accustomed to it. Even old Asgot the godi seemed less inclined to slit the monk's throat these days, though there were still those of us who half expected Egfrith to wake up dead one morning. But Asgot was still busy looking to Sigurd's recovery with offerings and poultices and potions and spells, for the day after we set off with Winigis Sigurd fell very sick. It was late in the afternoon on a dark, narrow stretch of the river shaded by dense forest of oak, chestnut and beech when Sigurd stumbled against *Serpent*'s mast and Bjarni said he saw the jarl's eyes roll back in his head before he crumpled to the mast step, his legs kicking and his mouth frothing like shaken mead.

'Keep rowing, you whoresons!' Olaf barked. 'I'll gut any man I see with an oar dripping!' For the river was narrow and so the current was strong against us. But I knew the real truth behind Olaf's anger. He did not want us to see Sigurd in that way. And he was afraid, too. So we rowed, and Olaf, Egfrith and Cynethryth made a shelter of skins on the stern fighting platform in which they laid our jarl like a dead warrior in his earthen barrow.

Even Egfrith prayed for him, pleading with his god to save him, for the jarl was the root through which the rest of the Norsemen's souls could be redeemed, and by saving the root Christ could save the tree. Asgot said we must moor and gather certain herbs and remedies. That night we made fast and men scoured the forest with torches for the things the godi needed. We did not care that we might bring danger upon ourselves.

By dawn we had found all but the waybroad, but Asgot sneered that without the waybroad Sigurd would die, so we went out again though we did not come across the plant. Exhausted and fearing the worst we watched the godi prepare his remedy. He took a handful of hammerwort, a handful of maythe, and two handfuls of wergulu and the roots of the water dock, though only those plants which men had found floating in pools and bogs. With these plants he put one eggshell full of clean honey and some clean butter and worked up a mixture which he then melted. When it set he melted it again and once more after that. He chanted an ancient spell over the blend before disappearing into the tent and I admit I did not know whether Sigurd was to drink the concoction or whether it was to be spread upon his wounds, though I hoped for his sake it was the latter.

'I think you should prepare yourself, Raven,' Cynethryth

said in a low voice that night as we settled down to sleep on thick furs amongst *Serpent*'s oak ribs.

'Prepare for what?' I asked, though I knew well enough what she meant. She stroked my face and smiled sadly and I looked out across the moon-glossed river. Bats tumbled and flickered above the reeds at the shadowy bank. Somewhere a vixen screamed, a distant sound above the low but infinite gush of the river. 'He will recover, Cynethryth,' I said after some time. 'Look at Black Floki.' The black-haired warrior was leaning by the fresh-water barrel forward of the hold, running his long knife against a whetstone. 'He looks well enough, doesn't he?'

'I don't understand,' Cynethryth said, taking the thongs from her golden plaits, which remained stiff, the hair too stubborn to unweave itself. 'What has Black Floki to do with it?' she asked, grimacing as she teased and tugged at the braids.

'When the Norns come for Sigurd they will also take Floki,' I said. 'It is their fate to cross Bifröst, the shimmering bridge, and walk through the gates of Asgard together. It may be mine too.'

'You cannot truly believe that?' There was no mockery in her voice, just sadness. 'You cannot believe that everything is already fixed. That we have no say in these things. That we are on a path we have no choice but to follow?'

'I believe it, because it is the truth,' I said, touching the Óðin amulet at my neck. 'And Sigurd will live.'

And whether it was Asgot's seidr, or Egfrith's prayers, or the meddling of the All-Father himself, I could not say, but Sigurd did live. For three days he lay in his barrow of linen and skins, his life spirit fighting a dark and desperate battle against death, and on the fourth day at sunrise he emerged to a scatter of murmurs from his men. His hair was no longer greasy and matted, but golden like the sun and shining. His skin no longer held death's pallor but was fresh and glowing, and his beard was woven into two thick plaits that looked strong enough to moor a dragonship. He did not slouch but stood tall and strong as an oak as he took three great lungfuls of dawn air, his eyes closed in the savouring as though he were breathing for the first time.

'Óðin's hand is in this,' Bram Bear rumbled, 'up to the elbow, mark my words, lads.' But none of us disagreed. I glanced at Black Floki who was grinning like a wolf.

'It is not possible,' said another man.

'Bugger me with Thór's hammer if he doesn't look stronger than ever, the soul-ripping son of thunder!' Olaf called. Then I caught Asgot sharing a fox look with Cynethryth and I knew that those two had been with Sigurd for much of the night. Had they rubbed the juice of raspberries or burnt clay powder into the jarl's cheeks to hide that death pallor? Had they smeared chalk beneath his eyes to conceal the dark circles? Perhaps.

'I'm so hungry I could eat a troll's breeks,' Sigurd announced, throwing his green cloak round his shoulders and pinning it with his silver wolf's-head brooch. 'What does a jarl have to do on this ship to get something to eat?' Men laughed and slapped each other's backs, throwing good-natured insults around, and I smiled. Our jarl was back. And we were going to be rich.

CHAPTER SIXTEEN

AFTER PARIS THE SICAUNA HAD SPLIT AND AT WINIGIS'S ADVICE WE had taken the left-hand tributary towards the rising sun. For seven days we rowed up a river which the Frank told us was called the Marne, a great coil like a man's guts that wound eastwards through a wide, empty valley. The days were shortening but the sun still had enough heat to warm our faces in the late afternoons when the ravenous wolf Sköll had chased it through the sky. 'One day,' Asgot had warned us, his face creased and bitter, 'when the doom of the gods is upon us all, Sköll will catch the sun. He will seize her like a hare in his jaws and swallow her.' Another wolf, Hati, he told us, would catch and swallow the moon and the world would be plunged into darkness. But none of this would matter, I thought. For at Ragnarök, the doom of the gods, those of us lucky enough to be chosen – the glorious dead – would be fighting alongside the gods in a desperate last battle against the frost giants, and from what I had learnt it was a battle we could not win and so what difference would it make if the world was dark?

Sometimes, one of the river's twists would put us before the wind and for those short periods we could hoist the sail and rest, stretching out our backs, arms and legs. But mostly we rowed against the river. It was hard going but it carved our bodies lean with taut muscle so that we were strong and dangerous as swords forged of iron and steel.

Cynethryth and Father Egfrith nearly always had lines in the water. They did not row, of course, and it seemed they wanted to do their part by keeping us rich in fresh fish, for which we were all grateful. The Marne teemed with salmon. They would gather in dark masses underwater and sometimes Cynethryth and Egfrith would abandon their lines in favour of nets which they cast from *Serpent*'s stern and hauled up full of flapping fish. Once they inadvertently caught an otter in the net. The creature had been hunting amongst a salmon shoal and when it came up, shiny chestnut brown and slick, tangled amongst the net and trying to bite through it, old Asgot laughed and danced around *Serpent*'s deck like a mad, drunken old fiend, the bones in his grey hair rattling.

'We're going to be richer than we ever dreamt,' he cackled, sure that the otter's misfortune was our good omen. 'Richer than kings. We will never have imagined such a hoard but it will be ours.' Cynethryth pitied the poor creature and wanted to set it free, but the godi simply sneered, snatching the net from her and beating the otter with a spear butt. Then when he bent to untangle it from the net it turned out that the fierce little creature was only half dead. It bit Asgot between his finger and thumb so that he yelped and blood dripped on to the deck and the rest of us laughed as he finished the hissing animal off with his knife.

'You whoresons can laugh,' Asgot spat, pointing an accusing finger at us, 'but this means there will surely be more death before we get our hands on a king's hoard. Some who laugh now will be beyond laughter soon enough.' And that was enough to silence us.

The days passed slowly on the river, which eventually

straightened itself out so that we began to sail south. Because the wind often came from the north, our sails could often outmatch the Marne's running and we could stow our oars. But sailing on a river is nothing like being at sea. It may be less dangerous than ploughing the unfettered ocean and Rán's rolling white-haired daughters, but I have never much cared for it. On a river you are confined, trapped like wine in a flask. As Cynethryth would have said about our heathen beliefs, you are on a path along which you have no choice but to go. I suppose you can turn your ship round if a river is wide enough. You can go back the way you came, but that course in itself feels stale, for you merely re-live what has already been. And being on a river in your enemy's land can be very dangerous indeed, as we would soon find out.

Sigurd was still not quite himself, though it was good to see him smiling with Olaf and standing at the tiller with Knut or at the bow with Winigis, learning from the guide which lord owned what land around us, and how we would have to pull *Serpent* and *Fjord-Elk* across three miles of dry ground before wetting their hulls in another river that would take us north. 'It can't be done,' Black Floki said, looking suspiciously at Winigis. A quiet, fearful man, Winigis stared out from beneath the rim of his hat, his hands gripping *Serpent*'s sheer strake.

'The Frank gives me his word that it can be done,' Sigurd replied simply, gesturing at Winigis. 'And since I told him I would rip his heart out of his arsehole if he was wrong, I am thinking we will soon be in Aix-la-Chapelle.'

Three days later, having passed several small vessels on their way to join the Sicauna, we came to the Marne's upper course where turbulent currents made the rowing difficult. The air was still thick with stoneflies and grey wagtails streaked about like tiny yellow-fledged arrows. The day after that the river narrowed and grew shallow between moss-covered boulders and stands of silver birch whose leaves fluttered in the breeze.

Peregrine falcons perched in branches, still as the dead, watching and waiting. Black dippers careered with insects in their beaks or dived into the water at the stream's edge to emerge with small fish. Here was where salmon and sea trout laid their eggs and we could go no further.

But Winigis made us go on, and we rowed gently, saying nothing, wincing whenever we felt *Serpent*'s keel scrape along the riverbed. 'The boats that come here are rarely this size,' Winigis had explained nervously to a frowning Sigurd as *Serpent* crunched against smooth river-worn pebbles. Then, round a bend, where the dangerously shallow water slowed to a trickle through which I could see sunlight glinting like gold ingots on the riverbed, we found the way to Aix-la-Chapelle.

'Everybody off!' Olaf called, nervous that our added weight was putting too much strain on the hull, which was now resting in the mud. We had nosed into a channel that had been dug into the bank and was only just wide enough to accommodate *Serpent*, and it was clearly the place where for years boats had been dragged from the water on to the land. This portage had been cut from the river's edge into the woods where it lay spear-straight and sun-dappled and muddied by countless journeys. The air was dank and smelt mossy and men's voices sounded small and intimate. Moss-furred tree stumps sat everywhere, the trunks long since taken, leaving only spindly birch, saplings, and misshapen ash and oak for the most part, though the forest thickened again a bow-shot in all directions.

We had only four hours of light left and so we would have to work fast. *Fjord-Elk* waited patiently a little further downstream in the deeper water, her oars stowed as Bragi the Egg and a group of his men took her mooring ropes round two jagged boulders. The rest of her crew came along the bank to help us with *Serpent*.

'*Fjord-Elk*'s crew will unload the ballast,' Sigurd said,

stirring a low groan from those men, 'and *Serpent*'s men will cut trees.' This received its own grumbles for we knew there was more to it than simply felling ash and oak. 'I want one good, smooth stake per man, smooth enough to roll, or else I'll use your damn legs.'

'What about those?' Ingolf asked hopefully, pointing to a great pile of slick stakes left by a crew who had brought their boat to this river and dumped the rollers for whoever might need them coming the other way. Sigurd drew his sword, walked over to the pile and hacked into one of the rollers. Just from the sound we knew the wood was rotten. Sigurd wiped the fragments of damp wood from his blade and sheathed it.

'Get cutting,' he said. And so we did.

We had to walk some distance to find good straight trees and I wondered what some crew making the same journey in ten years' time would do for then there would be no decent trees for miles around, but that was not our problem. We took our long axes and we chopped and when we had chopped we hewed. And when we had done that we smoothed them with hand-axes and sometimes our long knives, until we each had a pale stake twice our own height and good enough to drive into the ground to build a palisade. But we were building no wall. Instead, we would lay our stakes in the mud and then we would roll our ships over them.

That night I dreamt of cutting alder and elm for Ealhstan who had been my foster-father in Abbotsend. It was a peaceful dream and I had the feeling I was leading that dream by the hand, unlike most dreams, which lead you even if you don't wish to go. Then I was shaping the wood with the old man's adze, following the grain to make smooth planks, one after the other. I stood back to appraise my work but did not know what I had made. Dreams are strange like that. So I went closer and my heart thumped once as though it had been kicked. I had made a coffin. Slowly and afraid I lifted the lid and then in my dream I wept. For old Ealhstan lay in that coffin I had made, his fingers laced and his white hair long and his yellow eyes staring. *In somnis veritas*, I had heard Egfrith say once. In dreams there is truth. And in this at least the monk was right, for I had not saved my old friend and his death was my burden.

Next morning we hauled *Serpent* on to the land. Without her ballast she was surprisingly light, even with her cargo of silver and weapons, furs, amber, and other goods. When she was on dry land it was *Fjord-Elk*'s turn and Bragi and his steersman Kjar brought her to the portage where we unloaded her ballast, leaving two great piles of smooth stones which, no doubt, someone would find very useful afterwards. Since the day we had left Paris with Winigis aboard, Sigurd had made us put any guts from the fish we caught into a barrel. That barrel was now full of stinking gore and we were sick of the stench and the flies that buzzed around it even with its lid on. With a grim face Sigurd himself took fistfuls of the guts and smeared them on to the rollers we had spread out along the portage a little over twice the length of *Serpent*.

'Slippery as Ealdred and stinks just as bad,' Sigurd announced, smelling his bloody hand and holding it up for all to see, and even the Wessexmen laughed at that, apart from the ealdorman of course, who glowered at his former warriors. Those Wessexmen seemed little different from the rest of us now, though they prayed often and kept to themselves still. But they had given us not the least bit of trouble, perhaps hoping for a share in whatever hoard we would get our hands on when we sold the gospel book, which Father Egfrith guarded jealously in a small oiled sack over his shoulder despite none of us wanting anything to do with it, other than the silver it would bring.

We of *Serpent* lashed our ropes together to make two that, when their ends were held at the ship's prow, were each long enough to loop around the dragon ship, cradling the great curve of her stern. *Fjord-Elk*'s crew did the same and we took our places; some pushing from behind, some pulling on the ropes, others in pairs picking up the rollers after *Fjord-Elk* had run over them and hurrying to position them back on the track before *Serpent*. This last was the most exhausting work of all, I discovered, for we each took turns at every task and that one made my legs feel as though their insides were on fire. The best job was pushing from behind, as you could rest awhile, leaning against the hull whilst pretending to push. And in this way we set off north-east along the portage, our dragons – though their fierce heads were stowed and crosses sat at their prows – lumbering across the land in sad contrast to how lithely they swam the ocean and the rivers. Sure enough Sigurd's stinking fish guts helped the ships slide, but the stakes we had cut did not often roll as I had expected them to. Yet the hulls slid over them, the fish livers greased the way, and we trudged on.

It was slow going. A man can easily walk fifteen miles in a day. On a horse he'll make thirty. But hauling a dragon ship across mud, even if the ground is relatively flat, is arduous, backbreaking work and you will need hard men just to make five miles. A fine drizzle had begun that afternoon, turning into a relentless downpour by early evening that soaked us through leathers and cloaks and skin and muscle so that we were drenched to our bones and miserable with it. The portage track became a bog and our feet churned it worse still, making it even harder for *Fjord-Elk*'s crew, who moaned at us for our clumsy big feet when they were not gasping for breath or slipping and falling in the mud.

'Poor bastards,' Penda said as we leant into *Serpent*'s hull, our faces close enough to smell the tarred rope caulking and the pitch-soaked strakes.

'If you feel so sorry for them, why are you smiling?' I asked, grimacing and putting my shoulder into it as Olaf walked down the line to inspect *Fjord-Elk*'s progress.

'That's the way, Raven!' Olaf called. 'Put some spirit into it, lad! Or even better ask one of your friends up there . . .' he looked at a gap in the sodden trees through which the heavy, iron-grey sky could be seen, 'to get off their arse and help us along.'

'They'd be lighter without the Christ crosses, Uncle,' Bram rumbled, his face red with exertion as he hauled on a rope.

'Aye, and they'd be lighter without your secret mead hoard, Bram,' Olaf said, making us laugh despite the rain and the filth, though Bram looked horrified that Olaf should have revealed his greatest secret.

'Actually, Uncle, Bram's hoard is not so heavy these days,' I said, grinning.

'You greedy, red-eyed son of a goat-sucking whore!' Bram blurted, almost stumbling with the shock of discovering that we had all been at his stash.

It was early evening by the time we knew we had come to the end of the portage. The rain was lashing wildly and the wind was whipping through the forest, sending sodden leaves swirling and old branches crashing to the litter here and there. The eerie creak of boughs rubbing against each other in the wind was so loud that it seemed the forest itself was groaning, unsettled by our presence. We were close to the river but had not heard its gush above the hiss of the rain and when at last we did, we slapped each other's wet backs and shook the water from sodden hair and beards, for we knew we had earned a rest and some hot food. A camp was prepared and the cauldrons were fetched from the ships, and we took the spare sails to make a shelter amongst the lurching trees big enough for us all to sleep under cover. Some of us went to the river, where we found tree stumps, some new, some moss-covered, and great piles of rocks left there by previous crews, which we would use to replace the ballast we had left behind. Then after scouting the area we settled in for the night. Cynethryth and I shared two dry furs to keep warm and hoped that no boughs would crash down on us as we slept.

'This river joins another far to the north and that one will take us to Aix-la-Chapelle,' Winigis told Sigurd and Olaf next morning as we loaded up the ballast before sliding *Serpent* into the upper course of the river, which would be easy enough as the river here was wide and sufficiently deep. The rain had stopped in the small hours but the wind had yet to blow itself out and came in angry gusts every now and then.

'Will your emperor be waiting on the shore with an ale horn and a roasted boar?' Olaf asked, smacking his lips within his bird's nest of a beard which rippled in the wind.

'I expect he will be waiting,' Winigis said glumly, 'but with swords and spears and a thousand men. He'll be waiting to kill us.'

'But we are Christians,' Sigurd offered, gesturing at the cross on *Serpent*'s prow. The wind moaned through the trees and somewhere a branch, weakened in the night, creaked and crumped to the forest litter.

Winigis shook his head, taking off his hat to wring it out, still sodden from the previous day. 'They say the emperor is a clever man. He will know what you are. Now that I have shown you the way, perhaps I can go home,' he said, though there was no conviction in his voice, nor hope in his eyes.

Sigurd put an arm across the Frank's shoulder. 'We have come far together, Winigis,' he said, his teeth white and his eyes shining. 'I would not deny you the chance to see the emperor's great city one more time. Only accompany us to Aix-la-Chapelle, and you will be free to go your way whenever you wish.' Winigis looked to Father Egfrith but found no comfort in those weasel eyes.

'*Fiat voluntas Dei*,' Egfrith said with a shrug of his little shoulders. 'May God's will be done.' But I hoped Egfrith's god was attending to some far-away matter so that he had no will one way or another when it came to us, for they said that Emperor Karolus was the Christ god's sword, and that made us his enemy.

CHAPTER SEVENTEEN

THE RIVER, WHICH WINIGIS TOLD US WAS CALLED THE MASS, WAS with us this time, meaning that our oars could stay up in their trees. That was just as well with us, as we had spent much of the morning sweating our beards off loading both ships with ballast. Our sails were up, drying and slapping in the wind, wetting the men on their leeward sides with a fine spray, though they took no notice of it. We were all too busy looking up. Once we had left the relatively flat wooded country of the Mass's headwaters, the landscape had changed. Steep, sharp hills rose on both sides of us, following the river's course like the jagged spines of two enormous dragons. On those hills stands of dark green pine were scattered amongst beech, oak and ash whose leaves had begun to turn orange and brown, creating the overall impression of a patchwork of markings on those dragons' hides. Other than the odd wisp of smoke rising from the forest there was no sign of human life. The land was wild and huge and rich and ripe for the picking.

'Now this is like the fjords, hey!' Bram shouted from his journey chest where he was taking the opportunity to drink some of his mead before he woke up one day to find it gone. He wiped the foam from his beard with the back of his hand.

'But I want a nice cod,' Halfdan said, stirring murmurs of agreement. 'I'm sick of salmon. I've got salmon coming out of my ears.'

'You hear that, Cynethryth?' I said in English, 'Halfdan is sick of salmon and would like you to catch him a sea fish from this river.' Smiling, Olaf translated for Halfdan who suddenly looked embarrassed, his cheeks flushing red as he began to gabble in his defence.

'You can tell Halfdan that he is welcome to fish for himself but he'll need a very long line if he wants a cod,' Cynethryth said, eyeballing the Norseman like a hawk. 'And whilst he's at it perhaps he can catch me some new clothes too.' I translated this as the men laughed and Aslak reached over, cuffing Halfdan round the head for being a fool. Halfdan sulked then and I felt sorry for teasing him, but not too sorry, for we each got our turn at both ends of the tongue-whip. That is what it is like in a fellowship of warriors.

Each night half of us would go ashore and half would stay with the ships and those on dry land would hunt for hare, fox, deer or boar. They would train with their weapons, too, for we had not been in a fight for some time and we feared losing the edge that battle gives you and peace takes away. After five days on the Mass we passed a warship going upriver. It was a fine ship – not sleek and deathly quick like *Serpent* or *Fjord-Elk*, but broad and long enough to carry one hundred men to a fight, though there were no more than seventy aboard that day. Its oar banks were dipping fast and well, even though its sail was up and that sail was huge. It was of new white wool with an enormous red cross emblazoned on it. Egfrith, who had hurried to *Serpent*'s prow to bolster our ruse when Olaf had first spotted the Frank ship, now made the sign of the cross to her captain as she passed. The Franks aboard were tough, grizzled-looking men who glared at us despite Egfrith's bow sermon.

'One day I shall have a wolf's head on my sail,' Sigurd said jealously. 'On all the sails on all my ships. And I'll pay for it with this Christian king's silver.' The Frank ship had passed now, but the red cross was still visible from the sail's windward side as a huge pink stain. Then Sigurd said: 'There is power in that symbol,' scratching his throat and looking after the ship. 'I felt it.'

'Not enough power to see through our cunning, lord,' I said, which Sigurd accepted with a half-hearted nod. 'Your wolf's head will freeze men's blood and make them piss their breeks.' He chewed his lip, deep in thought.

'One day, Raven, you may have your own banner,' he said after a while. 'A black raven with great flapping wings.' He grinned. 'Such a thing would make me piss my breeks.'

I grinned at that too, perhaps because it was an impossible thought. For me to have my own banner I would have to be a jarl and there was more chance of Black Floki's shaving his head, putting on a Christ monk's skirt and spitting in Óðin's one eye.

We saw shepherds with their flocks on high-up meadows, and clusters of smoke-wreathed houses by the river's edge. We saw ruined dwellings of white stone like ancient skeletons bleached by the sun, and once we saw a church or monastery nestled on the western shore, which the Norsemen were tempted to visit. But all knew we were after a bigger fish than that and so Sigurd's wolves contented themselves with eyeing the place hungrily and imagining the cool silver and treasures within. Downriver, the pine-covered peaks softened and were eventually replaced by a boundless landscape of low rolling hills as far as the eye could see. Three days later we joined a tributary flowing east, and two days after that we took the river north, where we came to a settlement that seemed to us to straddle the river and we thought it must be Aix-la-Chapelle. But Winigis explained that we were between two towns, Tongeren on the west bank and Le Gi on the east. That stretch of river was bustling with ships of all shapes and sizes, so we lowered our sails and took to the oars to manoeuvre more easily amongst them. Merchants hollered greetings to one another and exchanged news of this place or that, their voices hard and flat above the seething river. Clouds of gulls shrieked and tumbled in the smoky air, excited by fishing skiffs coming and going. The thumping and chopping of wood carried across to us from the western bank where men were building a church. A group of solemn-looking monks were standing near the labourers and every now and then the mournful sound of their singing carried to us on the breeze, bringing a tear to Egfrith's eye.

'I don't blame you, monk,' I said. 'It's a sound to shrivel your balls and make your ears drop off.' But he ignored me, too intent on straining to hear the psalms as we rowed past. Vessels hurried to get out of our way, perhaps thinking we were the emperor's ships or perhaps simply because we looked dangerous, even with Christ crosses at our prows. But no one challenged us. We did not tempt the Norns by lingering and by midday we had passed another town, Maestricht, which Winigis told us had once boasted a great stone bridge built by the Romans to span the Mass in the time of Caesar Augustus. But that bridge was long gone, the last of its shaped stones now serving Christ as the foundations for his father's house in the centre of the city.

'This whole land stinks of the White Christ,' Black Floki had moaned when I had translated Winigis's explanation.

'We should burn it,' Svein the Red offered, pulling back in the stroke, his massive broad back expanding. The river was so wide here that the current had slowed to a crawl and the breeze had died to a whisper, so we rowed still. 'The Christ filth can't spread if we burn it from the place,' he added.

'There are not enough of us, Svein, you blood-loving oaf. And the trouble is you can't burn a stone building like you can a man's hall,' Olaf said, standing before us with his hands on his hips. 'But one day, lads, we'll come back. We'll come back and we'll take our fill. Until then let them worship their bloodless, weakling god. Let them grow soft like a rotting apple. Easier for us to squash them beneath our heel, hey!' The men cheered this and even Egfrith smiled, knowing no Norse and thinking we were just being high-spirited, and no one thought to enlighten him.

The next morning we entered a broad valley surrounded by wooded heights. The river here kinked and slowed. A wharf some five times the length of *Serpent* had been built into the eastern bank on great oak posts stained dark over a hundred years by the passing river.

'The river here is called the Wurm,' Winigis said to Sigurd, scratching at a pock scar on his cheek.

'A good name for a river,' Bjorn muttered.

Sigurd frowned. 'I thought we were still on the Mass.'

'We were on the Mass and now we're on the Wurm,' Winigis replied petulantly.

The wharf had been cut into the bank so that the boats moored against it were sheltered. At its upriver end a short jetty formed a breakwater that would further protect the moorings even from a current strengthened by heavy rain or swollen in springtime by snow melt. 'This is Aix-la-Chapelle,' Winigis said as Sigurd called to Knut to take us in to the wharf. There were boats all along the jetty, but a knörr laden with bolts of cloth was just untying and as soon as she cast off *Serpent* took her place. When we were moored up *Fjord-Elk* tied up to us hull against hull.

'Look,' Bram said, pointing further up the jetty where three short, narrow, high-prowed ships sat side by side. Their actual prow heads had been removed, but from what we could see, the carvings along the sheer strake appeared to be Norse.

'They could be the bairns of *Serpent* and *Fjord-Elk*,' I said with a grin, for they were half the length of our ships.

'I might take one back for the wife,' Bram replied, scratching his thick beard. 'She could row it into the fjord to fish.'

A crowd gathered on the jetty to see what we were. Father Egfrith greeted them all and made the sign of the cross in the air, though they understood him no more than we could understand them.

'Winigis, tell them that Ealdorman Ealdred of Wessex in England has come to pay his respects to their emperor,' Sigurd said, gesturing to Ealdred, who was cheerlessly polishing the silver and bronze brooch Sigurd had told him to wear. The wooden White Christ cross set with rubies hung over his chest and his cloak was of rich green cloth, its collar trimmed with white ermine fur. He had even shaved his face but for his moustache, which he had greased with seal fat so that the two thick, glistening whiskers drooped a thumb's length beneath his chin.

'Bastard looks like a lord again,' Penda said, hawking and spitting off the jetty.

'I hope he still remembers how to be one,' I said, realizing that some of the Franks were staring and whispering about my blood-eye.

'What in God's hairy arse are you sheep fuckers looking at?' Penda growled at them, at which they showed their palms and shook their heads and shuffled off. 'Better get that covered, lad,' he said and he was right, we did not need any extra attention. I took a clean strip of linen and tied it round my head, covering the eye.

'But that's the most handsome bit of you, Raven,' Cynethryth teased, a smile playing at the corners of her lips.

'That doesn't say much for the rest of him,' Penda said,

waggling a little finger and nodding at my crotch. I would have clouted him but Cynethryth did it for me, making Penda grin like some scar-faced fiend.

'Raven! Come here, my boy.' It was Egfrith. He was standing with Ealdred, Olaf and Sigurd by *Serpent*'s prow and he had that fox look in his little eyes. The rest of the men had secured the ships and were now filling the wharf, stretching in hauberks, arranging war gear and pissing off the jetty. 'Move yourself, lad, there's work to be done,' the monk called, clapping his hands. I went, and because Penda refused to miss out on any fun I might have, he went with me.

'Winigis says the emperor's palace is some miles east of here,' Sigurd said, nodding towards a distant stand of orange-leafed oak and elm at the end of the rich, grassy flood plain. Along the river bank there were several timber-built houses and to the west stood fields of stubble in which pheasants fed unmolested. Not liking the look of our mail, helmets, spears and axes, most of the locals had moved off, though some held their ground as though they were awaiting a chance to speak to Ealdred or Sigurd. 'We cannot lumber into this emperor's hall like a bear into a cave,' Sigurd went on in English. 'This Karolus will not deal with the likes of us. So Ealdred will go.' He looked at the ealdorman, whose face was blank, though his eyes were alive. 'Ealdred will go and he will tell this king about the Christ book. After what I have seen with my own eyes and from what Egfrith says it seems to me that Karolus will want the book. He will need it more than he needs food or ale or a woman in his bed. He will wonder how he has managed to live without it and he will give anything to have it. What we want is his silver, a hoard to make the dragon Fafnir jealous.' Olaf grinned at that. *But Fafnir's hoard was cursed*, I thought, though I said nothing. And what was more, the warrior who slew the dragon and stole his treasure died from the hoard's curse. And that warrior's name had been Sigurd. 'The monk and the girl will go too and between them they will convince Karolus that he can trust us enough to make an arrangement.'

'But you can't trust Ealdred,' I said in Norse, 'or the monk come to that. They will betray us, lord. They will bring the Christians down on us like before. You cannot trust them.'

'But I can trust you, Raven,' Sigurd replied in English, 'and you are going with them.' He turned to Ealdred now, the golden rope of his beard level with the ealdorman's eagle's-beak nose. 'Listen to me, Englishman,' he said in a voice that clutched my heart like an icy fist. 'You will make the emperor want the Christ book. If you fail, if you betray us . . .' there was a rasp as Sigurd drew his great sword and held it across his chest, 'I swear on my father's sword that I will come for you. Whatever hole you crawl into I will come for you and even death will not save you. I will come and I will cut slices of meat from you but I will not let you die. I will cut you and put fire to the wounds so that you cannot bleed to death and when you are out of your mind with pain and hunger and misery you will eat the rancid flesh I have taken from you and still you will not die. You will eat your own prick, scoff down your balls and your tongue, and then, Ealdred, I will let your daughter see you and if you still have a scrap of honour left in your rotten soul you will at last die of shame.'

I pitied Ealdred then, even after all he had done to us, because I knew Sigurd meant every cold word of it. I felt Penda behind me, felt him urging me on. 'Can I take Penda, lord?' I asked. 'Another Wessexman can only help to fool them into believing we are Christians.'

'He's right, Sigurd,' Olaf said. 'The Englishman is handy in a fight, too.'

Sigurd pursed his lips and then inclined his head. 'Black Floki goes too,' he said, calling the Norseman over. 'If this emperor becomes our enemy Floki will cut his throat.' Black Floki simply nodded as though it would be as simple as drawing breath.

So we made ready. The Franks who had been waiting to talk to Ealdred and Sigurd were traders on the sniff for coin and this had made them brave enough to stay when the others had slunk off. From one of them Sigurd bought seven horses on the understanding that the merchant would buy them back when the delegation returned. Another man sold Olaf four barrels of mead, two wheels of cheese and some fresh butter, promising to return that night with some women skilled in entertaining men with heavy balls who have been a long time at sea.

But for us there was just the wide flood plain and the muddy track which led to Aix-la-Chapelle. The afternoon threatened rain so we took oiled skins for the journey, rolling them and tying them to the horses' backs along with our brynjas and weapons and some food. Egfrith had grudgingly agreed to leave behind the gospel book of Saint Jerome, for we could not risk the emperor's simply taking it, or thieves robbing us. He secreted it away in *Serpent*'s hold and seemed somehow withered without it. We mounted amidst bellows of 'Óðin's luck!' 'Make us rich!' and 'Raven rides like a sack of rocks on a goat!'

Bjorn smiled like a young boy. 'Raven, tell the king of the Franks that Bjorn and Bjarni of Harald's Fjord want a brown-haired beauty and a barrel of wine each,' he said, and then his face hardened. 'If he brings them to us and pays his respects we might consider trading with him.'

With the sound of laughter in our ears we set off to meet an emperor.

CHAPTER EIGHTEEN

THE CLOUD WAS LOW AND GREY. A COOL NORTHERLY PUSHED THE heavy mass overhead, then on across the flood plain towards the southern horizon. Clouds of rooks tumbled out of the grey down to a ploughed field west of the oak woods, their toneless kaaing reaching us across the flat ground. To the east, tight knots of jackdaws approached a clump of alders already dark with roosting birds. I watched them jink sideways and up as though surmounting an invisible wall, then they seemed still for a heartbeat before dropping with perfect aim, each to a branch or twig amongst their brothers.

For the sake of appearances Sigurd had given Ealdred the best horse. After all, he was our lord now. It was a black stallion and spirited, the kind of horse that considers itself equal to, if not better than, the man on its back. I rode a broken old mare and the other beasts were not much better, which meant that Ealdred might have been tempted to make a break for it, despite Sigurd's threat. So Floki, Penda and I rode close to the ealdorman, close enough to count the fleas on his stallion's rump, and Floki had brought a pair of throwing axes with which he was a deadly aim. One kick of Ealdred's heels would see one of Floki's axes embedded between his shoulder blades.

'Aix-la-Chapelle used to be called Aquisgranum,' Egfrith chirped after a while, breaking the silence that had grown as each of us imagined the weave of our wyrds. 'In Roman times, of course. I think the name came from a Celtic god of water and health for it is said hot water erupts from the earth there and men bathe in these pools. Though I find it hard to believe the Celts went anywhere near them, whatever their heathen god's name, as they were a filthy people and still are. They say the emperor bathes in these hot springs every day. His skin must be as clean as his soul.'

'Maybe the emperor will let us wash our arses in his precious water, hey, horse?' Penda suggested, rubbing his chestnut palfrey's ears.

'And taint the blessed pools till Judgement Day?' Egfrith exclaimed. 'Karolus will not have you filthy beasts anywhere near the springs, as God is my witness. But perhaps Cynethryth and I will have the honour. Ealdred too as a Christian lord.'

'When your White Christ turns the water into wine, monk, then I'll be interested,' I said, dropping back a little to escape the man's prattle. But in this welcome calm a fresh and troubling matter bobbed up to the surface to trouble me. Why had Egfrith agreed to help us sell the gospel book of Saint Jerome? I had once heard him say that such a holy treasure was not to be bought or sold, even to the likes of the Emperor Karolus. Yet here he was coming along to help grease the trade. But I soon buried these thoughts deep in my mind's journey chest. My fathom rope was not long enough to test the motives of a man who served a god who let his only son be tortured and hung on a cross to die. For all I knew, Egfrith had curdled his own brains with prayers and nonsense and the White Christ's belly-warming blood.

Leaving the flood plain, the track wound through ancient

woods, at the heart of which stood countless giant ash trees, silent and eternal, and we looked up at them in awe because their highest branches seemed to disappear into the sky. They were the kind of trees that would defy Njörd's fiercest winds.

'They'd make good spears,' Penda said appreciatively. 'Straight as a shaft of sunlight.'

'Yggdrasil, the World-Tree, is such as those,' Black Floki said, 'but that is even more enormous. Its limbs hold up the nine worlds.' His eyes were dark and serious as I translated for the others. 'It was in that tree that Óðin All-Father hung himself for nine nights to gain wisdom. He was speared too. Here, I think.' Floki touched his right side halfway up his rib-cage. Even as I turned the words into English I saw the cloud settled on Egfrith's face, which proved too strong a temptation for me.

'Christ was hung on the tree of pain, wasn't he, monk?' I asked.

'Yes, young man, our Lord and saviour suffered on the cross for our sins.'

'And a soldier, a Roman I think, speared him as he hung there?'

'It is true,' Egfrith admitted, 'though perhaps that young soldier was trying to end the dear Lord's suffering.'

'And is it true that Christ cried out before he died?'

'He did,' Egfrith said with a solemn nod. Then he looked across at me, his eyes narrowing. 'But so would any man, I suppose.'

'True,' I admitted. 'Because Óðin cried out before he died. That must have been some sound. Then, of course, he came back to life. Did Christ come back to life, Father?' Cynethryth scorched me with a look.

'You know that He did,' Egfrith said indignantly.

'Floki says that Óðin also made an immense feast from some bread and a bucket full of fish,' I said. Floki had said no such thing but Egfrith did not know that. 'It seems to me that you Christians stole all your stories from Norse skalds.' Penda was grinning, but Ealdred's lip was curled as though someone had smeared dog shit beneath his nose.

'And it seems to me that you, Raven, are a dark and twisted young man who is closer to the bottomless pit than you realize,' Egfrith said, shaking his head sadly. 'And it is your people who steal their stories, not us.'

'Stop teasing Father Egfrith, Raven,' Cynethryth said. 'Take no notice of him, Father. Sometimes I wonder if there isn't a simple-minded child inside that big, dirty body.'

The monk was still frowning when we came to a clearing where the ash and oak had been taken years before. Stands of tall, straight silver birch burst from clumps of elder whose black berries the birds had eaten some weeks before. Cynethryth had taken the opportunity to relieve herself beyond a thicket of holly when Egfrith spotted a broken cart amongst a tangle of bracken and thorns. Perhaps once used to carry felled trees, it appeared to have lain there for years and looked a crude thing not worth repairing, which probably explained why the owner had left it to rot when its right wheel had broken.

'The Lord often finds a use for the meanest of His creations,' the monk said. Having dismounted, he was stuffing something into his sack but I ignored him because Ealdred needed to empty his bowels and it fell to me to go with him to make sure he did not run even if his bowels did.

We soon mounted and continued and even Winigis appeared excited when we broke from the woods and, by the blood-red light of dusk, saw the imperial city of Aix-la-Chapelle standing before us. We crossed an ancient boundary ditch, which was so shallow now that the biggest problem we had in crossing it was that the horses liked the look of the uncropped grass that grew in it and we had to kick our heels and cajole them up the far bank. Before us, three good bow-shots away, a stone wall the height of three men enclosed the city, cast in shadow now that the sun had slipped below the oak woods behind us. A fog lay across the pasture so that the grazing cattle appeared as legless shapes, and the tightly packed timber houses outside the city, which added their hearth smoke to the shifting cloud, leaked flamelight and looked snug and inviting. The fog even rolled up the city walls and curled back from their summit like spray from an ocean wave. Countless mud tracks led to and from the city gates along which shrouded shapes made their way, some leading animals to safety within the walls, for the mist would encourage wolves to come for their sheep, which the Franks' hounds must have known because they barked incessantly. The air smelled damp and green and the woodsmoke that wove amongst the fog smelled sweet and tempting.

'This place makes Paris look like a cesspit,' Penda said. The city stood on a slope and beyond the wall at the high northern end of that slope an enormous stone building dominated the view.

'Paris is a cesspit,' I said, trying to nettle Egfrith who seemed to think Paris was the light shining from his god's arsehole. 'Look at that place,' I said, gesturing at the long stone structure, which was the only building we could see clearly because of its position at the top of the hill. I asked Black Floki if on his travels he had ever seen its like. The Norseman shook his head, making his crow-black plaits dance.

'There is nothing like that anywhere in Norway,' he said. 'It could be Bilskírnir.'

'Lightning crack?' I said and he nodded solemnly.

'Bilskírnir is Thór's own hall.'

'Then we should be glad that it is not Bilskírnir, Floki,' I said, reining my mount around a glistening pile of sheep's droppings. 'I'd wager the Thunderer could not give so much as a fart for Egfrith's White Christ book.' Floki curled his lip and spat and we joined a track leading to a gateway in the city wall where two stone towers, often repaired by the look of them, loomed from the fog. A spearman at the top of one of the towers called down to someone inside the city and six soldiers armed with spears and swords and toughened leather armour came out to meet us.

'Peace be upon you, my sons,' Egfrith said, signing the cross in the air. Then he gestured to Ealdred, who looked down his long nose at the Franks. 'My lord Ealdred, Ealdorman of Wessex, has come from England to pay his respects to the great Emperor Karolus,' Egfrith said. 'These are Ealdred's men,' he flicked a hand at us, 'and this is Lady Cynethryth, the ealdorman's daughter.' A wolf howled somewhere out in the fog-shrouded land and the chilling sound was answered by the grating chorus of rooks and their flapping wings as they took to the darkening sky. A rhythmic squeaking announced another Frank, who appeared at the gate pushing a handcart.

'No weapons are allowed past these walls,' the soldier with the finest helmet and sword said, not in the least impressed by Ealdred's title. His language was not quite English but it was close enough for us to understand him. 'The emperor's palace is at the top of the hill, but he won't see the likes of you,' he went on as the newly arrived man took the weapons we offered him and dropped them carelessly on to his cart. Floki and Penda shared a grimace at seeing their swords being treated badly, but both held their tongues. 'They say the Pope himself has to wait halfway to Judgement Day to see the emperor,' the guard said, grinning with rotten teeth. Then he closed his hand into a fist. 'But then the Pope does not hold half the world by its balls.'

'Patience is a gift from God and I am certain His Holiness Pope Leo has been blessed with it by the cartload,' Egfrith said, nodding at the pile of weapons being wheeled away, which included the fine sword that Sigurd had given to Ealdred to make him look the part.

207

'Feels like I've lost a bloody arm,' Penda grumbled, and I knew how he felt.

'Bring this back when you leave and you'll get your blades,' the guard said, handing a small wooden disc to Ealdred.

'Ah, Saint Gregory of Tours,' Egfrith said, reading the engraving on the disc. 'Each disc must bear a different saint. How wonderful!' The guard shrugged.

'I'll look after that, my lord,' Penda said, taking the disc from Ealdred. With that the guards stood aside and we walked our mounts through the gate and into the city.

Aix-la-Chapelle did not stink of shit like Paris, but it had its own stench and it was the stench of White Christ worshippers. They were everywhere: monks, priests, bare-footed pilgrims with beards down to their knees and ashen-faced miserable-looking nuns. Even the cats and dogs skulked around the place with the sorry faces of creatures that know that their souls are damned till the arse end of time. Even Ealdred, who was a Christian, curled his lip at the sight of so many Christ followers. There were soldiers too, some of them wearing mail and all armed with spears and swords, but what made them stand out and marked them as the emperor's men were their clothes. They all wore impossibly white tunics of fine linen and bright red breeks embroidered with golden thread. From below the knee to the ankle they had wound scarlet linen wraps and their boots were of fine leather, the thongs tied in a crisscross fashion over the scarlet wraps. They had thick cloaks that reached to their boots and these were either blue or bright white depending, according to Egfrith, on the man's rank. Even their sword scabbards were covered with highly waxed white linen.

'Frisian cloaks,' Penda said enviously. 'They are the best you can get.'

'Aye, keep you warm in a Fimbulvetr,' Floki agreed when I told him what Penda had his eye on. Fimbul-winter would be three of the harshest, most ball-cracking winters rolled into one with no other seasons between them, and when that came we would know that Ragnarök was beginning.

I had never seen such a thing, men dressed to look the same. 'A clever way of making sure you don't kill your friends in a fight, hey, Floki,' I said in Norse.

'And a sure way of getting close enough to the emperor to cut his throat,' he said, one dark eyebrow arched. And he was right. All you would need was the clothes from one of these soldiers and you would be taken for an imperial guard.

'This is wonderful,' Cynethryth said and I hoped she did not mean the hordes of Christians but rather something I had not noticed, or perhaps the buildings around us, which were impressive I had to admit. Most of the houses were timber, but many were stone with thatch roofs or even thin fish scale type stones to keep out the rain, which Egfrith said were called tiles and were used in the old world even before the time of the Romans.

Merchants crowed about their goods, traders argued over prices, richly dressed women poked and sniffed at fruits and vegetables, meat sizzled on skillets, cauldrons bubbled, forges rang, horses neighed, children cried, and Christians prayed. The place was dizzying.

We said farewell to Winigis, who was itching to be off with the silver he had earned, and I thought the fisherman must have been happy enough with his catch. Then we gave the horses to a couple of muddy-faced stable boys and walked along the wide wooden gangway that cut through the middle of the city and led all the way to the great building at the top of the slope which must have been one hundred and fifty paces long. Smoke from a thousand hearth fires thickened the air and every sniff brought the half-taste of a different meal being pre-pared. Somewhere onions sizzled. Somewhere else mackerel, and above another hearth snails bubbled in garlic and butter.

'What makes you think the emperor will see us, monk?' I

asked, assuming that we were heading for the imperial palace. 'You heard what that guard said. We'll grow beards long enough to keep our feet warm standing at the door of the man's hall waiting for him to finish his prayers.'

'The heathen is right, Egfrith,' Ealdred said, taking in his surroundings as he walked. 'I'm an ealdorman, not John the Baptist.'

Egfrith's teeth flashed yellow and all that was missing were the rat's whiskers.

'We are not going to the palace,' he said above the sharp sound of stone being cut and the thump of rivets being struck, for everywhere buildings were being raised. It was as though a new city of stone was rising from the old one of wood.

'Then where, Father?' Penda asked, frowning.

But Egfrith did not say. I thought about twisting his head until he squawked, but then I was distracted by a stick-thin man around whom a crowd had gathered like flies around a dog's turd. The man seemed to be bleeding from the palms of his hands and from his bare feet. Some of those around him had dropped to their knees and others were making the sign of the cross, and the poor man himself seemed to be accepting his fate with an eerie calm.

'Father, did you see that man?' Cynethryth asked, tugging at the monk's sleeve, her green eyes wide.

'You must prepare yourself to see such things, my dear, even miracles, in the city where the golden prince of Christendom has set his banner,' Egfrith said without breaking stride. We marched up the hill through smoke so porridge-thick it stung my eyes and made us cough, all the while shrugging off blind beggars, ragged children, and hawkers thrusting their goods at us, though there were no whores, Penda noticed unhappily. Then suddenly there were no more houses. We had come to a wide space where the smoke was blown thin, revealing the most amazing sight I had ever seen. A long passageway built from a hundred smooth stone pillars stretched before us, its floor made of flat stones, all identical in size and shape. On one side of this passageway stood a great area of grass which looked as though no man nor beast had ever trodden on it. In the middle of that green space stood a huge stone dish that could have been a giant's drinking bowl, and an enchanted one at that, for water spurted continuously from its centre even though there was no stream or water nearby. Egfrith told us it was called a fountain, even though he had never seen one before. The water shooting into the air and cascading over the lip of the giant's bowl sparkled and looked clean and fresh and I instinctively touched the Óðin amulet that was tucked inside my tunic, for I did not understand how a stone dish could create water. Nor could I believe that no one seemed in the least concerned with collecting it. Other than a few monks sweeping along the colonnade and a group of men laying stones at the far edge of the grass the place was strangely quiet.

'Christian seidr,' Black Floki hissed at me in Norse. But I was no longer looking at the fountain. My eyes were full of a sight I have since conjured many times when imagining the buildings of Asgard in which the gods live. And yet the wonder now before me had been built by Christians, not gods.

'The church of the blessed Saint Mary!' Egfrith gasped, his arms outstretched. 'Will you just look at it!'

'The emperor must be richer than every English king and lord together,' Ealdred said, stroking his moustache thoughtfully.

'And you will have not one silver penny of it because you are a treacherous, snot-eating worm who murdered his own boy,' Penda snarled as we followed Egfrith towards a huge bronze door on the western side of the church. The monk was barely strong enough to push it open, but Cynethryth helped him. The mournful sound of Christ monks' singing oozed from the place as Ealdred and Penda followed Cynethryth inside.

'Come on, Floki,' I said, turning to the Norseman, whom I had sensed pull back as the great bronze door had begun to close behind Ealdred. But Floki shook his head, his dark brows woven together above his malevolent eyes.

'It is not for me, Raven,' he said. 'I will not go in there.' I could see that his hand was clutching the long knife beneath his tunic, which he had kept hidden from the city guards and now relied on to ward off the Christian magic of the place.

I nodded, knowing there would be no changing his mind, then I turned and walked into the lord of Christendom's sixteen-sided, treasure-filled church, my guts twisting and knotting because I was afraid.

CHAPTER NINETEEN

I HAD NEVER BEEN NEAR SUCH A PLACE, LET ALONE INSIDE ONE. None of us had. The vast interior shimmered with golden light from more guttering candles than there are stars in the sky. We stood in the middle of an enormous barrel-shaped stone building and I felt as though I were drowning. The voices of more monks than I knew existed swam around the wax-thickened air in dismal song. The sharp, chipping sound of stone being cut fought against the monks' cheerless moaning as groups of craftsmen worked away in nooks and high up on wooden supports that were themselves ingeniously made. And you could not help but look up. High up, so high that the back of my head pressed into my shoulders and swallowing was almost impossible. Above a long row of arched windows through which the last light of the setting sun filtered, there glittered a massive image of the White Christ.

'The Lord Christ is surrounded by all the worshipping denizens of Heaven who offer their crowns to Him for He is the King of Kings,' Egfrith said proudly.

It was not like any picture of the nailed god I had ever seen. This was not the usual weakling, tormented and sad and pathetic. This Christ was golden, his face strong and austere. This was a king's god and that told me much about this emperor of the Franks. 'It is the most beautiful thing I have ever seen,' Cynethryth whispered and I cringed to hear her say it, wondering how she could think this mosaic, as Egfrith called it, was more beautiful than *Serpent* or *Fjord-Elk*. Other mosaics ran along the lower walls too, Biblical scenes. They made me squirm, for I felt uncomfortable standing there, the study of so many dead men's eyes.

I had not even heard the approach of the monk who now stood before Egfrith. The man was tonsured like Egfrith and wore the brown habit, but unlike Egfrith he was fat and had several plump warts on his red-cheeked face. He glanced at Penda and me disapprovingly, for we did not need swords at our hips for him to know we were warriors, and then he and Egfrith gabbled at each other in Latin. It was clear that Egfrith was introducing Ealdred as a rich Christian lord, because the Frankish monk's eyes flickered greedily across the Englishman's face before coming back to Egfrith, who was opening the small sack strung over his shoulder. Then the Frank looked back to Penda and me as though he suddenly understood why a monk and an English lord and his daughter kept such rough company. A silver trickle of saliva leaked from the corner of his cracked lips as he watched Egfrith pull out a dark, fist-sized lump of wood which I suspected was a piece of the old cart with the broken wheel we had come across in the woods. I could not imagine what Egfrith was scheming or why this other monk was drooling like a dog with a fleshy bone at the sight of the worthless lump. The Frank's eyes swelled, almost jumping from their sockets, and then he waddled off, smoke and incense billowing in his wake.

'What are you playing at, Egfrith?' I hissed. Before he could reply, the Frank was back with another monk, a white-haired old man who carried himself with quiet authority. A breeze blew from somewhere so that what was left of the man's silver hair fluttered about his ears. Sharp blue eyes in a wrinkled face shone at Egfrith from under white brows as the two talked. Then, carefully and reverently, Egfrith handed this old man the lump of wood. Still dribbling, the fat monk made the sign of the cross and Egfrith nodded solemnly, turning everyone's focus on to Ealdred as though we should all be as grateful to the ealdorman as if it was down to him that we had been born with our balls in a bag. The fat monk sent two cowled figures scurrying off, their bare feet slapping the cold stone floor, then White Hair inclined his head to Ealdred, blinking slowly in recognition of the moment's import. The gloomy singing stopped now, the monks peering with curious pale faces at their silver-haired master who bore the lump of wood away with the care of a man carrying a polecat or some other creature that is liable to bite. Another monk, shielding a candle with his hand, introduced himself to Egfrith and before we knew what was happening we were following this young man back outside, where I found Black Floki throwing pebbles into the fountain. The Norseman joined us and we were led through the pillared passage, past a green holly bush shaped like a cross, to a short stone building with a newly thatched roof. Inside, the floor was laid with fresh reeds and two lines of straw-filled kips ran the length of the room. Apart from the general cleanliness, the place could not have been more at odds with the richness of Saint Mary's church.

'The abbot says we may sleep here tonight,' Egfrith said as the young monk floated around the place lighting candles made from tallow, not beeswax like those in the church. 'This is where important pilgrims and guests of the priory stay.'

'Then we are lucky to find it empty, Father,' Cynethryth said.

'I suspect luck has nothing to do with it, my dear,' Egfrith said, glancing at the young monk who was rearranging the straw and furs in one of the kips. Nearby, Penda tested his kips for comfort and I remembered the two monks who had scuttled off. Whatever Egfrith had done, it had put someone out on their arse for the night.

'If I have to ask you again, monk, I'll pull out your tongue and nail it to the wall,' I said. Egfrith's little face puckered at that mind picture.

'He gave the abbot a treasure, Raven,' Ealdred said, one eyebrow cocked.

'He gave him a rotten lump of wood from a broken cart,' I said. Ealdred grinned then and I wanted to smack those teeth through the back of his head.

Egfrith sniffed. 'To you and me, it was just a piece of old wood,' he said, 'but to the abbot and the monks of Saint Mary's Church and Priory it is a fragment of the True Cross on which Christ the Saviour died for our sins.'

It took a moment to sink in. 'They believe that steaming pile of vomit?' I asked, glancing at Penda who looked as appalled as I was astonished.

'Why would they not believe a lord of Wessex?' Egfrith said. 'It is not as though we tried to sell it to them. It was a gift and in return the monks will say prayers for Ealdred's soul. Because this city is Heaven-blessed those prayers will reach the Lord's ear on swifter wings than those spoken by monks in darker lands.'

'Pilgrims will come. They'll want to see the True Cross for themselves,' Penda muttered, scratching his scarred face, 'and the priory's chests will fill with silver.'

Cynethryth stared at Egfrith in disbelief, but the monk simply shrugged his little shoulders. 'I take no pleasure in the deceit,' he lied, 'but I have my reasons.' He closed his eyes and whispered something to his god, then opened them and looked at each of us in turn. 'Soon, perhaps even in the morning, you will all understand.'

He was right. Next morning we were fed and watered and Abbot Adalgarius told us to wait outside the west door of the church of Saint Mary at midday, for a man would meet us there. That was all he would say, though he did warn us not to be late. We waited and eventually a little man shuffled up to us. Old and shrivelled, his small face shadowed by a threadbare cowl, the man said his name was Ealhwine, which told us he was English before he had spoken twenty words.

'Though the Franks call me Alcuin,' he said, 'and I speak for my lord Charles, or Karolus if you prefer, emperor of the Romans.' I thought the Romans had been dust for hundreds of years but I said nothing, as Alcuin went on to introduce himself as the abbot of the monastery of Saint Martin of Tours, Master of the Palace School and chief adviser to the emperor himself. If Egfrith had not gripped Cynethryth's arm he would have fallen over.

'The Almighty is munificent indeed that He should let me meet the esteemed Alcuin of York,' Egfrith said. 'Your fame flies far and wide.' I stared at Egfrith and judged him to be telling the truth for a change.

Alcuin nodded wearily, his watery eyes lingering on me for a moment before looking back to Egfrith, who was introducing Ealdred and his daughter. 'A beautiful young woman,' Alcuin said, smiling at Cynethryth, 'the future of us all.' Then he turned back to Ealdred. 'My lord, you have given us a precious gift,' he said in a tired, raspy voice. 'Of all the portions of the True Cross scattered throughout Christendom, that which you have so kindly granted to us is surely the exemplar.' There was a knowing look in those eyes and it was clear that this Alcuin was no fool. 'Word of your charity has already reached the imperial ear. His gracious lord would like to thank you in person, if you will follow me to the palace?'

'It would be the highest honour,' Egfrith said, pressing his palms together and shaking his head in wonder. Ealdred bowed his head soberly, and I looked at Cynethryth who half smiled because at that moment we understood that Egfrith had been as cunning as Loki. We had been in Aix-la-Chapelle for less than a day and we were on our way to an audience with the emperor.

We walked up the slope towards the palace, which loomed like Thór's own hall Bilskírnir, passing many stone buildings that Alcuin explained were the homes of court officials and princes. We passed knots of imperial soldiers in their blue or white cloaks, some of them training with sword and spear, and a large group of children sitting silently before an old monk who was reading from a heavy-looking book. Black Floki poked a finger in my back, drawing my attention to what seemed to be a warrior on a horse, though both man and beast had been turned to stone by some powerful seidr. Before we could speak of it the palace doors were heaved open and we were surrounded by soldiers and herded inside. Two boys held brass bowls full of water in which we washed our hands and faces, and tapestries hung here and there creating many separate cells, each well lit with candles, in which men talked in low voices. In one, three monks hunched over books, scratching away on sheets of vellum. In another, a group of men grey with stone dust argued over a charcoal drawing of a building on a large cloth of white linen.

We followed Alcuin up a wooden staircase worn shiny and smooth, and emerged into a great hall dominated by two massive mead tables made of oak, dented and gouged by years of raucous feasting. Huge silver jugs inlaid with gold, cups and platters were set out along the length of the tables as though the gods themselves had been about to sit down to feast before some momentous event had called them away. Paintings of warriors in ancient armour covered the walls and beneath these heroes' blades their enemies – some dark-skinned or with

strange-shaped eyes and weapons which I had never seen before
– suffered and begged and died.

'This king likes to fight, I think,' Black Floki growled in
Norse and I tensed and shushed him because the last thing
we wanted was for these Christians to realize that there were
heathens amongst them.

At the end of the hall, behind a large square table of solid
silver, stood a throne carved from white stone and in that
throne sat the emperor himself, watching us as we shuffled
awkwardly into a line before him. Two hard-looking warriors
stood either side of the throne, their spear blades glinting
by the light of the candles mounted behind. The emperor's
hair was blond, his eyes were lively and his nose was long. He
wore his moustache long but had no beard and even seated
he was a tall man, solidly built and powerful. He emanated
another power too, as though an invisible mantle, woven
from all the deeds and triumphs and hardships of his long
life, cloaked him and would shrug off lesser men the way an
oiled skin shrugs off the rain. As for his clothes, they were the
simple garb of a wealthy merchant or thane: linen shirt and
breeks, a red woollen tunic fringed with silk, and shoes of soft
leather.

'*Karolus gratia Dei rex Francorum et Langobardorum ac
patricius Romanorum*,' Alcuin stated tiredly as though he had
spoken the words times beyond counting, and for his part the
emperor seemed equally bored by his own formal title. Then
Alcuin introduced Father Egfrith and Ealdorman Ealdred and
when he got to the part about Ealdred's bestowal of a piece
of the True Cross on the church of Saint Mary, the emperor's
intelligent eyes flashed and bored into the ealdorman like
augers.

Sweat cooled on my back and stung my eyes. My jaw ached
from clamping my teeth together, for I knew we walked a
knife's edge. All Ealdred had to do was expose us and seek

the emperor's protection and we would die there and then. But Black Floki knew this too, for he moved, almost imperceptibly, closer to Ealdred who half turned, sensing the Norseman's presence.

'You honour my church with such a gift,' the Emperor Karolus said in good English. 'We brothers of the faith have a duty to preserve such relics, Ealdred. You can be sure that precious vestige will rest safe here long after we of frail flesh are forgotten.' I had expected a mighty voice, the one that had roused thousands to fight beneath his banner and sent equal thousands to their deaths. But it was a voice no different from any man's. Ealdred dipped his head respectfully.

'I wonder,' began Alcuin, one wispy grey eyebrow arched suspiciously, 'perhaps, if something else brings you all the way from England to our great city. Something other than a good Christian's propriety and a worthy lord's beneficence.' I got the feeling that the old scholar was probably one of very few men of the emperor's court who would speak his mind whenever he felt compelled to do so, and Karolus clearly respected the man's intuition, for he sat back in his chair, bringing a ringed knuckle to his lips.

His eyes lingered on Cynethryth awhile, then were riveted once more to Ealdred. 'Is there something else which brings you here?' the emperor asked, sweeping his other hand through the fragrant air.

'My lord,' Ealdred began, flicking his eyes to Egfrith, who nodded, 'I have a book unequalled in consequence. It is a rare and most precious treasure, for it is the holy gospel book of Saint Jerome, lost for many generations but now, by the grace of Almighty God, recovered.'

'I have heard of this book,' Karolus said, leaning forward in his fur-cushioned throne. 'My old teacher spoke of it when I was a boy.'

'Jerome ranked first amongst the ancient exegetes,' Alcuin

said, frowning. 'His knowledge of the Good Word was consummate. How, Lord Ealdred, did you come into possession of this . . . work?'

Ealdred clasped his hands together solemnly. 'The book had fallen into the hands of an unworthy king, my enemy Coenwulf of Mercia. What worthy Christian could abide such an aberration?' he asked, extending his arms. 'I took it as my duty to rescue the book.' I almost believed Ealdred myself. The worm was slithering well. 'Since recovering the gospel I have been hoping to see it safe in the hands of a Christian lord who can keep it away from avaricious men.' Now Ealdred shook his head. 'But I am just an ealdorman. I am not a rich man, my king. I cannot keep such a treasure safe from the iniquitous for ever.'

'You want to sell it to me?' the emperor asked, flicking his fingers to a servant, who filled a silver cup with wine and handed it to his lord.

'It would ease my conscience to know the book was in your safe keeping, my lord,' Ealdred admitted, stroking his long moustache. 'The kings of England fight like dogs over scraps. Nothing is safe.'

'You have the book here?' Karolus asked, sipping the wine, his eyes never leaving Ealdred's. Beside him Alcuin was staring at me, one eye half closed but the other sharp as a rivet's point, and I felt the sudden need to empty my bowels. I was sure the old man could tell me for a heathen and I feared the accusation was crawling up his throat and was almost on his age-cracked lips.

'It is at the river wharf with my men who guard it,' Ealdred said. 'Forgive me, but I dared not bring it across the country. I am a stranger to this land and it is a fool who bears a sacrosanct treasure into the unknown.'

Karolus nodded. 'I see that beneficence, prudence, and . . .' he paused a moment, 'ambition,' he said, half smiling, 'dwells in your heart as surely as the Holy Trinity dwells at the heart of our faith.'

'Thank you, my lord.' Ealdred squirmed. 'You honour me and the people of the kingdom of Wessex.' His eyes flicked to Father Egfrith, then back to the emperor. 'The treasure is yours, my lord,' he said. 'For a fair price. After all, I have lost much in recovering it.'

Karolus leant back in his throne, still studying the Englishman before him. 'I have need to go to Paris,' he said, 'for I must inspect the work that has begun on my coastal defences. If it were not enough that I have to deal with the Saxons in the north, my shores are still plagued by the godless Danes, may the Lord scour them and their heathen kind from this world. On my way to Paris I'll find you at the wharf and I'll see your gospel book for myself. If it is the treasure you claim, we will do business. You will not find me an ungenerous man, Ealdred.' Ealdred fell to one knee and Egfrith hissed for us to do the same, which we did. 'Now leave me,' the emperor commanded, frowning as though suddenly struck by the aches and irritations of old age. I for one was eager to be gone from that place of enormous stone buildings and enchanted water before our ruse was uncovered. Father Egfrith was disappointed not to have had the opportunity to try the hot springs he had been telling us about, but the success of our undertaking more than made up for that – a success which owed much to the monk's own cunning. We took our horses and collected our arms, then left the city of Aix-la-Chapelle as the pale sun rolled westward across an autumn sky.

CHAPTER TWENTY

WHEN WE ARRIVED AT THE RIVER WHARF THERE WAS NO SIGN OF *Serpent* or *Fjord-Elk*, but we did find Hastein and Yrsa Pig-nose waiting for us. They were sitting on the jetty playing tafl by the light of a crackling, flame-filled brazier. Nearby a man was lying on his belly with a line in the water fishing for crabs whilst his hound lay beside him, its head on its paws. Other than these two the Norsemen were alone.

'We have moved further upriver,' Hastein said, pointing into the darkness beyond the shore houses and the black mass of oak and ash behind them.

'There's a town not three bow-shots from the water,' Yrsa added, grinning as he collected and pocketed the tafl shells whilst Hastein tightly rolled their furs. It seemed that the lure of trade and food and women and mischief had proved too strong for the Fellowship to ignore, despite our earlier caution.

'Then what are we waiting for?' Penda asked when I explained in English. 'They'll all be getting their ends wet by now. I don't want to be left with some sow who's so ugly she makes onions cry.'

'Penda!' Cynethryth snapped. 'You are a bad man.'

'I try, my lady,' he replied.

'Are we going to be rich, Raven?' Yrsa asked, happily digging snot from a nostril with his little finger and smiling.

'You are already rich, Yrsa,' I said, to which he nodded proudly, 'but yes, if the emperor doesn't kill us all we'll be richer yet.'

My heart leapt as it always did when I saw *Serpent*. She was tethered bow and stern to a high jetty with *Fjord-Elk* lashed to her steerboard side. I could see men aboard both ships and others on shore huddled under skin shelters round fires, though there was nothing of the raucousness I had expected. Instead the men were subdued, and I soon learnt it was because they were apprehensive and eager to discover how we had fared with the emperor of the Franks.

'This Karolus is no fool,' I said to Sigurd, regretting the words immediately, for of course Karolus was no fool. The man ruled an empire. 'Without the monk we wouldn't have got anywhere near him,' I admitted reluctantly.

Sigurd looked at Egfrith with a slight nod. 'So he will come?' he asked. The jarl leant against a rolled fur, flamelight and shadow playing across his gaunt face. Beside him Olaf was snoring; the sound, according to Black Floki, was like that of a reindeer at the rut. We had already told the jarl everything that had happened, but even he seemed sceptical that Karolus would actually come to us to judge what we had to sell.

'He is going to Paris, so he told us,' I said, 'and will meet us on his way.'

'Paris?' Sigurd said, as though surprised that an emperor should want to go to that stinking hole.

'To build defences against the Danes,' I said, smiling, though it was the smile of a helmsman feigning indifference in the face of a storm.

'You must keep your men on a tight leash, Sigurd,' Egfrith said, wincing. Behind us Svein and Bram were wrestling and some of the Norsemen were growling encouragement to one or the other. 'One way or another, once the emperor lays eyes on the gospel book he *will* have it,' the monk said. 'If all goes as I pray it will, I believe he will buy it and pay handsomely too. But if he discovers you are Norse . . .' he extended an ink-stained finger, 'then he will feel duty-bound to take the book from you.'

'Enough talk,' Sigurd said, giving a great yawn which seemed to offend the monk. 'Wake me if this emperor comes,' he said, pushing back his rolled fur and laying his head on it. 'But if you ruin a good dream I'll cut off your balls.' I went to the shelter Cynethryth had made. It was all very well for Sigurd to posture in that way – it was expected from a jarl after all – but he had not seen with his own eyes the stone world this king of the Franks was building. He had not met Karolus.

Two days later we woke at dawn to the barked warnings of our sentries. The emperor had come. We hurriedly put on our mail and helmets and gathered our war gear – not because we wanted to fight but rather because we wanted to make a good show of ourselves before these Franks. Warriors suffer from legendary pride and will do whatever they can to impress friends and foe alike. And we did look impressive. We were more than thirty, and all wore the finest brynjas and hefted spears, axes and swords. But if we thought we were impressive, that was before we clapped eyes on the Franks. They were awe-inspiring. We formed a shieldwall two men deep with *Serpent* and *Fjord-Elk* at our backs and men with bows at our flanks. Like that we waited and watched an army emerge out of the low dawn sun. Two shining columns of soldiers, each man wearing identical armour made of small iron plates like fish scales, poured across the landscape before us, their banners whipping in the wind.

'Frigg's tits! Somebody fetch my banner!' Sigurd roared, blinking at the incredible sight.

'It's all right, lad, don't twist your neck off,' Penda beside me said with a smirk, sensing my concern. 'She's at the rear with Egfrith.'

'What have we got ourselves into now?' Olaf said, thumping his helmet firmly down so that all you could see of his face was beard. 'There must be five hundred men there and every one of the pretty whoresons has a nice long spear to lean on.' A war horn blared and, with the clink of armour and the stamp of boots, the two columns melted and re-formed so that we now faced a shieldwall three men deep, longer than any of us had ever seen. Then that wall split neatly and a group of mounted men emerged, trotting their horses towards us.

'There he is,' Penda said, 'and doesn't he look just about the handsomest emperor you've ever seen.' Laughter came from the Wessexmen, which was good to hear from men in the front row of a shieldwall. Sigurd had done them a great honour by placing them there and they knew it. But they would also be the first to die and they knew that too.

Karolus raised a hand and his ranks held still as the stone horseman I had seen outside his palace. The hot breath of hundreds plumed in the morning air.

'He's not dressed for war,' Penda said, 'which is a good sign if you ask me.' The emperor wore a tunic fringed with silk and a fine red cloak fastened with a golden buckle, and apart from a gold-hilted sword in a jewel-encrusted scabbard he was unarmed.

'I suspect he has enough men to fight for him, Penda,' I said, gripping my spear with white fingers.

'Lord Ealdred!' Karolus yelled. Some of us turned but I could not see the ealdorman. We waited. The frantic *brrrrrruk* of a fleeing moorhen cut the silence and a black cloud of rooks spiralled up from a stand of elm, kaaing noisily.

'Here, lord,' Ealdred answered eventually, passing through the wall. Egfrith and Sigurd were with him, and though Sigurd should have perhaps stayed out of sight the restraint would have been too much for him. He stood behind Ealdred looking like Týr the god of battle, his hand resting on his father's sword.

'Go on, Raven,' Olaf said. 'Sigurd might need your tongue to dig him out when the Franks hear the Norse in him.' So I loped over to them, my brynja rattling conspicuously, and bowed my head to Karolus, though his eyes were fixed on Sigurd. Alcuin sat hunched on a palfrey on his lord's right, eyeing the shield-wall behind me.

'I have never seen such a show of arms, lord,' Ealdred said. 'Your army is magnificent.'

Karolus smiled, patting his black stallion's neck. Even his horse looked like a prince amongst horses. 'This is a mere breath of breeze compared to the storm I can summon when needs must. With a word I can bring ten thousand Christian warriors to any part of my empire. These days, thanks to God and to this sword,' he said, touching the gold pommel at his hip, 'I have few enemies who have the stomach or the spears to stand and fight me, though they are quick to attack the helpless. They kill and then run. Like a fox.'

On his right, Alcuin nodded tiredly. 'Deep bogs of evil spread where the springs of righteousness should give rise to streams of holiness,' he announced, staring at me with his old, worn eyes. I suddenly realized I was not wearing the linen strip over my blood-eye. 'There are signs that our world is in its last days.'

'Which makes more pressing the need for us to vanquish the enemies of Christ,' Karolus said.

'Or convert them, lord,' Father Egfrith amended with a raised finger and an almost imperceptible sideways glance at Sigurd.

I suddenly felt sick, for my mind had unravelled the knot that had hidden Egfrith's reason for helping to sell the book. I had long known the little weasel had it in his mind to convert

227

Sigurd, but now I feared my jarl might have agreed in return for Egfrith's help.

'The book,' Karolus demanded. 'I will see it for myself.'

'You have enough silver, king of the Franks?' Sigurd challenged in his thick accent, his eyes wolflike below his helmet's rim. 'Or have you spent it all on blue cloaks and fish scale armour for men who would make better farmers?'

My guts twisted. The emperor glared at Sigurd. Egfrith's face paled white as death and I thought we would all die in a great rush of Frankish steel. But then Karolus smiled, the lines round his eyes carved from a hundred thousand such smiles.

'And who are you?' he asked Sigurd, who stepped in front of Ealdred.

'I am Sigurd, son of Harald,' he said. 'Some call me Sigurd the Lucky.'

'You are a Dane?' Karolus's smile twisted into a grimace.

'I am no Dane,' Sigurd said.

'Do you serve Ealdorman Ealdred?' the emperor asked, nodding at Ealdred.

Sigurd spat and wiped his lips with the back of his hand.

'No, I did not think so,' Karolus said. 'And they are your men, aren't they? And your ships moored there?'

'They are mine,' Sigurd said.

'You are heathens then?' Karolus challenged. That question rode the back of threat.

'This monk has it in his mind to wade me into a river and push my head under the water,' Sigurd said, gesturing to Egfrith. 'It seems to become a Christian you need to be half drowned.'

'And you have agreed to be baptized?' Karolus said, suspicion making slits of his big eyes.

'I have not decided yet,' Sigurd replied. 'Perhaps.'

'The book, my lord emperor,' Egfrith spluttered, offering the gospel book to Karolus, who flicked a hand directing the monk to give it instead to Alcuin. The old man began immediately to pore over the thing, his face as creased as oak bark as the emperor's eyes bored into Sigurd's.

'It is genuine, my lord,' Alcuin said eventually, shaking his head so that I could not say whether he was simply amazed to have such a thing in his hands or horrified that the treasure had until now been in ours. 'This book is impossibly important,' he murmured, at which Karolus shot him a sour look. Alcuin might have been a deep thinker in some ways, but he was a poor trader to drive up the price like that. Sensing rather than seeing the emperor's glare, the old man raised a hand acknowledging his carelessness, though to me he seemed much too interested in the gospel book to care.

'Then I will have the book, Sigurd,' Karolus said and with those words the worm Ealdred saw to the saving of his slippery skin.

'My lord emperor, save me from these men!' he blurted, wriggling past Sigurd and falling to his knees before Karolus. 'I am a Christian lord and these heathens have kept me prisoner these last weeks. My daughter too.'

'Bastard,' I heard Penda snarl.

There was a tinge of distaste in the way Karolus looked at Ealdred, but as the burning light of Christendom he could not ignore such a plea.

'You have my protection, Lord Ealdred,' he said, gesturing for the Englishman to get to his feet. 'Where is your daughter?'

Ealdred turned and pointed to the shieldwall and the Norsemen glared at him with promises of death. 'She is back there, sire. Amongst the heathens. She is called Cynethryth.'

Karolus nodded. 'Come forward, Cynethryth!' he bellowed and there it was, the voice of an emperor. There was the clump and clatter of shields and the rattling of mail as Sigurd's shieldwall parted to allow Cynethryth through.

'Lord Karolus, this worm is mine,' Sigurd snarled, but even Sigurd looked small before this great host of Franks.

The emperor gestured for Alcuin to give the book back to Father Egfrith and the monk nodded respectfully as he stepped back with that Christian treasure in his hand. 'You will have your silver, Norseman,' Karolus said casually with a flick of the wrist. 'Come here, girl.'

Cynethryth came over to us and inclined her head to the emperor, her golden hair plaited so that she could not have looked more Norse, though Bram would have rumbled that her hips were too narrow.

'You are safe now, daughter,' Karolus said, and even though he was old his eyes lit up at her beauty. 'Your captivity is over and you are free.'

Cynethryth's eyes flicked to me. 'My lord,' she said in a sure voice, 'I am no prisoner and chose to sail with these men. They may be heathens, sire, but they are honourable men.' Then she pointed to Ealdred. 'He is the one with no faith and if I were you I would not trust him any more than I would trust a fox.'

At that Ealdred snarled and stepped forward, backhanding Cynethryth viciously so that she staggered backwards, her eyes huge and full of shocked fury. Then she screamed and from her belt drew her eating knife and flew at Ealdred, fast as a hawk, and plunged the blade into his eye. Now Ealdred screamed.

I leapt, pulling Cynethryth back, which was not easy for she was frenzied. My mind was reeling at what had just happened as Karolus roared orders that built a wall of warriors with raised shields between them and us. Ealdred writhed on the ground, his hands slipping on the blood-covered hilt so that he was unable to draw Cynethryth's knife from his eye.

'The girl is bewitched!' the emperor said, his eyes wide, though not as wide as Alcuin's beside him. The old man looked about to fall from his palfrey. 'You she-devil! These godless men have defiled your soul.' Then his expression changed from one of shock to inquisitiveness and he asked something of Alcuin, though it was in the Frankish tongue and so we could not know what it was. 'But we will break that spell,' the emperor said then, 'with the Lord's help. Step away from her, boy, or you will both die where you stand.'

I held Cynethryth tightly.

'Do as he says, Raven,' Sigurd said.

'But lord . . .'

'Now, Raven,' Sigurd demanded, and so I released Cynethryth who simply stood there watching Ealdred who was flapping like a fish, his screams replaced by a strange gurgling sound. Except for Egfrith who was kneeling by him praying, no one moved to help the ealdorman, perhaps because it was obvious that there was no saving him now.

'You will come with me, Cynethryth,' Karolus said, 'and, God willing, you will be . . .' he paused, 'healed,' he finished and his stallion screeched and tossed its head as though in warning.

'Cynethryth stays with us,' I said, swallowing hard and feeling a tremor in the arm holding my spear.

Karolus looked down his long nose at me and his eyes seemed to catch fire.

'You,' he accused me, 'are the thing that has twisted this poor girl's soul. Satan has marked you as one of his own.' He gestured at my blood-eye. 'I knew it the first time I saw you. But the dark one holds no sway here, boy, and you will hold your fetid tongue if you want to keep it.'

'I am afraid of no man,' I said, raising my bearded chin. In truth I was so afraid I could have pissed down my own leg in front of them all. I glanced at Sigurd, who I could have sworn had the faintest of smiles playing on his lips, for there was a part of Sigurd that loved chaos.

'There is no need to let high spirits lead us into foolishness,' Alcuin said, calming his palfrey with a flick of the reins. 'We have more important matters to attend to.' He looked down at Ealdred and made the sign of the cross for the ealdorman was quite clearly dead, the small knife, which must have pierced his brain, still jutting from his right eye.

Karolus sucked a breath deep into his large stomach and closed his eyes and when he opened them the fire was gone. 'As always, my dear Albinus, you are the rein on my temper.' He smiled at Alcuin, then looked back to Sigurd. 'I will have three barrels of silver brought to you before the full moon.'

'Five barrels,' Sigurd said, scratching his chin, apparently unaware that we were in no position to negotiate.

The emperor frowned. 'For five barrels I could build another palace,' he said, shaking his fair, greying head.

'Five barrels and I'll let this Christ monk wash me in your river,' Sigurd said loud enough for all to hear, and I turned to see Black Floki pull a face that could sour milk. He understands some English then, I thought. Olaf too was all beard and grimace, and the Wessexmen glowered because their erstwhile lord had not spoken for them. But Karolus must have thought he now had a deal worth making, for he simply nodded to Alcuin.

'You will have your silver, Sigurd the Lucky,' the emperor said, pulling his horse around. 'Bring the girl,' he commanded two of his men, who nodded, each taking one of Cynethryth's arms. Then he and Alcuin walked their mounts back to the great, shining army. 'And may Christ grant you the strength to see your purpose through, Father Egfrith!' he called. And Cynethryth did not look back at me as they led her away.

Ealdred was dead at last, which was no bad thing. His death had been coming a long time, though none would have guessed it would come at the hands of his daughter. Still, I felt sick. I felt sick because Sigurd had agreed to be baptized as a Christian, but most of all I felt sick because Cynethryth was gone. Though, other than Penda who cared for Cynethryth because he had loved her brother, none of the others seemed anything other than cheerful. We had met with the great Christian emperor and survived. Even more surprisingly, the man was going to give us more silver than we had ever dreamt of, and Norsemen dream in silver. The way they saw it, things could not have been better and most of them did not even seem to mind that Sigurd would be baptized.

'It will make no difference,' Bram Bear rumbled, chewing some dried seal blubber. 'Sigurd is a wolf and will always be a wolf. Dunking his head in another man's river won't make a gnat's arse of difference.' He grinned, his lips smacking noisily. 'But this emperor believes it will, and that's why we're going to be rich, lad.'

There were some, including Asgot, Black Floki and Olaf, who did not like that idea at all. Still, we were alive and would soon be rich, so even they could live with it for now. Men were left with the boats and the rest of us made for the nearest town, which was called Vaals. I much preferred it to Aix-la-Chapelle, because it was made of wood, not cold stone, and it was full of normal people and not Christ slaves. It was the first time in a long while that the Norsemen had had the chance to spend some of their well-earned silver and it was not long before we were all roaring drunk. As for the Frankish whores, they came out at night and could not give a spit that we were heathens. Smelling money, they were over us like flies on raw meat. I could only think of Cynethryth, but the others had no such thoughts to belt their breeks up. I stood drinking with Asgot, who claimed he was too old for ploughing, whilst all around the Norsemen humped for all they were worth. I swear I could hear bones rattling. Svein the Red had two women, one in each arm, their bare breasts glistening in the torchlight, and Sigurd was sitting at the back of the tavern with a black-haired beauty's head in his lap. Even Hedin, who with his long face was so ugly that men said even the tide wouldn't bring him in, was at it. The sight of his white arse flying up and down like a washerwoman's elbow was almost enough to sour the ale in my cup.

'He's watching us,' Asgot creaked, his yellow eyes following a spider which was descending from a rafter on its invisible string.

'The spider?' I slurred.

'The emperor, you brainless fool,' Asgot hissed.

'The emperor has gone to Paris, old man,' I said, wishing I had not been left alone with the twisted old godi. It was hard to be near him and not remember how he had killed Ealhstan. I had killed one man, Ugly Einar, for his part, but I had not touched Asgot.

'He has more eyes than a hound has fleas,' he rasped. And I saw that the old cunny was right. There were men in the tavern who were clearly charged with keeping an eye on us. It seemed they did not even mind us knowing, for when I locked eyes with one of them, a young man with short black hair, I saw undisguised disgust in his face. But these spies seemed content to let us spend our money, and the Norsemen were too busy humping to care.

Later that night Bjarni staggered over to me, spilling a river of mead as he dragged a small Frank behind him.

'This man is going to tattoo us,' Bjarni said, his head seeming too heavy for his neck and lolling in circles. 'He assures me he is very good.' The Frank nodded uncertainly, searching Norse faces for one that looked less like those strange see-through creatures that float in on the tide. He could not find one and so he looked back at me and I looked at Bjarni.

'What tattoo?' I asked, not liking the idea at all because I was not in the mood for pain.

Bjarni's eyes rolled and he staggered back, rocking on his heels. 'Something that reminds us who we are.' He frowned.

'And what we are. We travel so far from home I don't want to forget.'

'I don't think there is any fear of that, Bjarni,' I said. 'We are wolves.' And with that his blue eyes blazed and his teeth flashed and I suddenly knew what mark this little Frank was going to carve into our skin.

CHAPTER TWENTY-ONE

THE FRANK DID A HANDSOME JOB WITH HIS SMALL, WICKED SHARP knife and a bowl of fine wood ash, so that when the others saw the blue-black wolf heads carved into our shoulders they sought him out and he must have been rich by the end of it. Sigurd was the last and we all stood round and watched the snarling wolf slowly appear in his white skin. When it was done there was a cheer to lift the rafters of the Blacksmith's Dog alehouse and we all got so drunk that we slept the whole of the next day and only roused ourselves when it was time to start drinking again. Sigurd was still not himself, but it seemed he was getting stronger and he suffered less and less from the fevers that had left him soaking and weak. That he had survived so many wounds was proof to us all that the All-Father still favoured him, though he looked different. Once golden and shining, he was now battle-battered as a shield. There was a puckered scar in his temple from Mauger's shield rim, which you could see when his hair was tied back, and there was an ugly scar in his right cheek. Beneath his eyes were dark rings and his cheekbones pressed sharply against the skin. These marks changed Sigurd in some deeper way, making him seem more like other men, men of flesh, blood and bone. And yet now he looked even more dangerous. To look at him you might think his byname, Sigurd the Lucky, was better left in the past. Now he looked more like Sigurd the Terrifying.

The moon swelled and waned and there was no sign of Karolus's silver. His spies watched us still, but we had grown used to them and made ourselves at home in Vaals. We drank and organized wrestling contests between us and the Wessexmen, and generally made a nuisance of ourselves, until it became clear that even the alehouse owners were growing tired of us, for their regular customers left any place we entered, the way cats slink off when hounds pad into a hall. Only the whores seemed to possess an endless patience for us, and if anything the Norsemen tired of them. There were so many other things to buy in that town when their peckers needed a rest, from brooches, buckles and tanned leather to cloaks and fine Frankish blades which proved irresistible to some. But I was miserable. All I could think about was Cynethryth. My stomach ached and my throat felt as though an invisible hand squeezed it from the moment I woke until the moment I fell asleep, and even then I dreamt of her.

It was not until the moon curled like a sliver of shaved wood that the emperor made good on our arrangement. A man found Sigurd in the Blacksmith's Dog and told him that the silver would be at the wharf in two days, along with some churchmen who would come to witness the jarl's baptism. I was horrified, but Sigurd merely shrugged and poured himself some more ale.

'I was getting fond of my own stink, Raven,' he said with a resigned shrug, 'but in two days' time I will bathe and afterwards I will be rich enough to buy myself a kingdom in the north.' He leant forward and filled my cup with ale from his own. 'I know you are no trader, but even you must smell the ripeness of this deal.'

'I don't trust these Christians, lord,' I said petulantly, glancing at Father Egfrith who had two of the Wessexmen on their knees praying forgiveness for 'yielding to the temptations of the flesh' as he put it, or crushing some Frankish fur as I saw it. Behind the monk two braided whores jiggled their tits at him and one of the Wessexmen closed his eyes, the other biting his lip as they desperately tried to appear contrite.

'What if their spells work some hold on you?' I asked. 'What if becoming a Christian puts you in thrall to the Christ god?'

'Pah!' Sigurd batted the questions away and sat back in his fur-lined chair. 'Words and water, Raven. That is what we shall get from these Christians two days from now. And silver,' he added, smiling, 'if their prattle does not bore us to death first. You worry too much for a young wolf.' I scowled at him and he chuckled. 'Sometimes the sword needs a little grease to pull free of the scabbard. You understand me? When we have the silver we will go. We will raise *Serpent*'s sail and leave these Franks to their old king, and they should pray to their god to keep him alive, for I am thinking that when he dies this land will itself become a ripe deal for whoever wants a slice of it. Too many rivers,' he said almost to himself. 'Too easy.' Then he held my eye a moment and my thoughts tumbled out of my head and lay at his feet like rune stones, the way they always did under that canny blue gaze. 'Monk!' he called. 'Come here!' Father Egfrith hurriedly made the sign of the cross over the kneeling Wessexmen and scuttled over to us, his weasel face pinched.

'You still intend to go through with the baptism, Sigurd?' he asked, shooting me a suspicious glance as though he feared I had talked Sigurd out of it.

Sigurd nodded, scratching his chin. 'I will stand in your river, Egfrith,' he said, cocking one eyebrow, 'but before I do, you will go to the place where they have taken Cynethryth.' He pulled a ring of twisted silver from his finger and gave it to the monk. 'You will give her this, from Raven, but you will not tell her that the boy whines after her like a puppy taken from its mother.' Sigurd winked at me and I felt my cheeks flush. Egfrith smiled too and nodded, putting the ring into the scrip at his waist before disappearing into the noisy crowd. 'Now, lad, have some fun for the love of Thór,' Sigurd barked. 'For days you've been wearing a face that would make blind bairns cry.' I tried to smile. 'Bram!' he yelled at the hulking figure by the serving table, 'find something pretty for Raven to play with.'

Two days later at dawn the emperor's silver arrived. It came with a hundred warriors in their fish scale armour and the blue cloaks of the imperial guard. The emperor's adviser, Alcuin, came too, and with him a gaggle of churchmen, who I would later learn were Borgon, bishop of Aix-la-Chapelle, an archdeacon, an abbot and a prior. These men were grim-faced, though they could not hide their unease at seeing us battle-arrayed before our ships, mail polished, blades clean and sharp, and our wall of brightly painted shields with their dented bosses boasting of old fights. Egfrith was with them. The monk looked strangely uncomfortable among his own kind, making me wonder if he had spent too long in the company of heathens. I was desperate to hear of Cynethryth, but Egfrith was busy discussing Christian things with the churchmen and I could not catch his eye as Alcuin ordered the contents of five barrels to be tipped out on to a great sheet of linen laid on the grass. There was a gasp and then a murmur like the sea from Norse, English and Frank alike as more silver than you could ever imagine spilled noisily, glistening and fluid, on to the linen. The sight snatched your breath away and left you jaw-slack. There were solid silver bars, jarl torcs, arm rings, buckles, brooches, rings and cloak pins. There were silver cups and bowls, ingots, ornaments and hack silver, all impossibly bright and washed in the pink dawn light. It was a god's hoard.

At a word from Sigurd, Olaf walked forward with the gospel

book of Saint Jerome, holding it at arm's length, and gave it – gladly, it seemed to me – to Alcuin, who could not prevent a smile from creasing the corners of his old eyes. I for another was glad to see the back of that book over which so much blood had been spilt.

'You looked like you were giving that old man a turd, Uncle,' Bram chuckled when Olaf had come back and retaken his place in the shieldwall.

'This emperor has won many fights to lay his hands on so much booty,' Olaf said, ignoring him, and I suddenly imagined that the white buildings I had seen around Karolus's palace were made from the ground-up bones of his defeated enemies.

'How much more must he have if he is giving us this much for some good-for-nothing book?' Bjarni asked, shaking his head behind the shieldwall.

'Not just for a book, Bjarni,' Olaf reminded him bitterly, 'but for Sigurd's bending his knee to the Christ,' and as if in answer Bishop Borgon yelled a stream of Latin, a powerful voice bursting from his stick-thin body. As one, the entire Frankish army fell to their knees with a clatter of mail and arms, except for one warrior. This man stood at Borgon's right shoulder, gripping a huge spear in one hand and a short axe in the other. He was clean-shaven but for the plaited beard that hung from his chin like a length of black rope. It seemed he was exempt from prayers so that he might keep his dark eyes on his master, and I thought that any man who spurned a shield in favour of an extra blade must be as dangerous as a two-headed bear with a hangover.

'Here we go,' Bram rumbled somewhere in the shieldwall. 'Someone wake me up when it's all over.'

'The All-Father must be yanking his white beard off if he's watching this,' Hastein moaned, for Sigurd was apparently satisfied with the hoard which blanketed the ground in a thousand tales of glory and wanderlust, war, plunder and death. The jarl was standing before the churchmen like a wolf amongst sheep.

'Raven, bring me a horn of Bram's mead!' Sigurd yelled in Norse, raising a few laughs from our line and a muttered curse from Bram, who came to me, pulling a mead skin from the inside of his tunic and pouring the liquid into the horn I held out for him.

'It's warm, Bram,' I said with a grimace, wondering how long the skin had been secreted against Bram's hairy belly.

'It's the only safe place around you thieving swine,' he protested. I took the mead to Sigurd who drank it down in one go, dragging his hand across his mouth and eyeing Borgon's bodyguard. I noticed beads of sweat along the scar in his temple and I realized he was more nervous than he would have us believe. For he knew it was no small thing to fold your knees to the White Christ. He must have wondered if Óðin All-Father was watching with his one eye and if so what was in the Far-Wanderer's mind.

The dawn sky was lightening to a cold bright blue in which rooks squabbled and several kestrels hovered against the wind, looking for voles in the long grass.

'There, Sigurd, amongst the reeds, we shall be protected from the current,' Father Egfrith chirped, pointing downriver of *Serpent* and *Fjord-Elk*. The churchmen's robes whipped in a sudden gust and from a good bow-shot away, even above the river's murmur, I heard the noise of the nearby beechwood in the wind: leaf striking leaf, branch grinding against branch.

'So the heathen understands English, Father Egfrith?' one of the churchmen said, looking at Sigurd the way a man looks at a horse he is considering buying. Egfrith nodded.

'A savage tongue,' a short, pockmarked priest said through a twisted smile because they were using that tongue themselves, 'but the fact that it speaks at all,' he went on, nodding towards Sigurd, 'should mean that the beast will be easier to tame than that bitch the emperor gave Abbess Berta.' Egfrith's eyes flicked to me like a lizard's tongue, then back to Sigurd. 'I hear she has not uttered a word,' the short Christ slave added, signing the cross.

'Come, Sigurd,' Egfrith said, 'it is time you discovered the true path and the joy of joining the Shepherd's flock.' Was it really going to happen? Was Sigurd going to turn his back on his gods in favour of the White Christ? My stomach lurched at the prospect.

'Will the others take the ablutions, Egfrith?' the richest-looking Christ slave asked, eyeing the Fellowship, who watched with mistrustful eyes, their bearded faces hard as rocks.

Egfrith seemed about to reply when Sigurd rumbled: 'Some of them would rather grind your bones into porridge, priest,' making the man wince. From somewhere I heard old Asgot mumbling his strange prayers to the Norse gods as though he sought to unpick whatever seidr spell the Christians were about to weave on his jarl. Perhaps Egfrith's god was rubbing his hands together at the sight, knowing that where Sigurd led other Norsemen were bound to follow.

'Clothes off, Sigurd,' Egfrith said with a strained smile. Sigurd nodded to Olaf, who sent Bjorn from the shieldwall to take the jarl's cloak and sword. I helped him wriggle out of his brynja, which Bjorn then rolled and slung over his shoulder. Then Sigurd pulled off his tunic, revealing chest and shoulders that were as taut as *Serpent*'s back-stay and carved with the deathly white scars that mark every warrior like so many runes etched in a living tree, each one telling its tale.

'If he tries to drown me, Raven, kill him,' Sigurd said with a smile, nodding at Egfrith, who had stripped down to his undergown and whose body looked like a child's next to Sigurd. Another gust of wind blew Sigurd's golden hair across his face and for a moment he looked up at the blue sky, which was white at the edges. A black smoke-twist of jackdaws stretched across the cold emptiness, the creatures revelling in the gusts, and their unruly *jak-jak-jak-jak* sounded to me like a warning. Then Sigurd strode into the soft, mossy earth at the river's edge, sinking up to his knees amongst the reeds, and Egfrith followed him, shuddering as the dark water closed around his waist.

'What of Cynethryth? I called to Egfrith through the gusts, but he seemed not to hear me as he took another unsteady step. 'How is she, Egfrith?'

'Later, Raven,' the monk snapped, his breath short as the cold water squeezed his heart and lungs. 'Do not interrupt the Lord's work.'

'Screw the lord's work, tell me now,' I barked.

'Hold your tongue, heathen!' the pockmarked priest blurted, and I turned to him, a terrible heat rising in my belly. 'Do not obstruct the will of God!' he yelped, his eyes little holes of malice.

Bishop Borgon put a hand on the shorter man's shoulder. 'Peace, Arno,' he soothed, then prattled to him in the Frankish tongue, but he pointed at me and I heard the name Cynethryth and then the word *diabolus* which I knew from Egfrith meant devil. The hollow-cheeked bishop pulled his silk-trimmed cloak around his thin frame as the pockmarked priest tilted his head and eyeballed me, so that my hackles were stiff as frozen grass.

'Then it is no wonder Abbess Berta is struggling to unburden the bitch of Satan's seed,' he said in English just for me. 'I shall take my own hazel switch to the girl. Beat the filth out of her myself, by the Lord's grace.'

I flew at him. In a heartbeat the priest's throat was in my fist and I was squeezing so that only the gristle of his gullet stopped my fingers and thumb from touching.

'No, Raven!' I heard Father Egfrith yell amongst the clamour of other voices, but my belly was full of rage and I was snarling

243

like a beast and shaking the priest like a hound with a hare. Then something struck the side of my head and I dropped to my knees, flashes of white light ripping through my head. The great hulking figure of Borgon's bodyguard loomed over me. I fumbled for my knife and slashed into his thigh below the fish scale brynja. He roared and slammed the butt of his spear against my helmet, dropping me again. It felt as though the sky had caved in and all was swimming pain and swirling blue cloaks as the emperor's men came. A blade scythed towards my face but another met it with a loud ring and Bjorn was there. He chopped a Frank's face in half, spattering me with blood as I tried to rise. Another Frank hacked into Bjorn's back and he yelled in fury and turned, taking his hilt in two hands and ramming his sword deep into the man's chest. Hands gripped me and I could not break free but was forced back down to my knees. Through a blur as though I was underwater I saw Sigurd slipping and falling as he struggled out of the river. Behind him Egfrith thrashed madly.

'Thór!' Bjorn roared as Frankish blades ripped into his brynja, carving the flesh beneath so that blood and broken iron rings mixed in a slick gore.

'Bjorn!' I screamed. As quick as a breath he grinned at me and then Bishop Borgon's man swung his short axe, taking off Bjorn's head, which landed in the long grass, the blond plaits somehow still perfect.

'Hold! Hold!' Sigurd yelled to the Wolfpack, for the shield-wall had broken and men were running to help Bjorn. 'Get back and hold, damn you!' Sigurd yelled, the cords in his neck straining, because without the shieldwall we were all as dead as Bjorn and the jarl knew it.

'The silver! To me!' Olaf yelled and a knot of warriors ran with him and stood over the hoard, shields locked and spears facing the Franks, who seemed unsure what to do next.

'Enough! No more!' Alcuin cried, repeating the order in the

Frankish tongue. A knife, gripped by one of the men holding me, began to bite into my throat. 'In the name of the emperor, sheathe your blades,' Alcuin implored. He might have been old and frail but the blue cloaks listened to him. 'My children,' he said to them, 'we did not come here to fight these men. Let us not spill blood on the feast day of Saint Crispin and his brother Saint Crispinian. Let us all be brothers today!'

'That devil tried to kill a priest of God!' Borgon protested, saliva flying from his old mouth as he gestured at the pockmarked worm whom I had not strangled quickly enough. The little turd was holding his neck and wheezing, spittle at the corners of his lips, as the other Christ slaves sought to comfort him. The main bulk of the Fellowship stood in a solid wall with their backs to the wharf and *Serpent* and *Fjord-Elk*, but Olaf and some fifteen men, including, I noticed, some of the Wessexmen, were horribly vulnerable where they stood before that glittering hoard. The Franks could close round them like a river round a monk's skinny body. Yet I knew Olaf and the others would all die trying to protect that silver. I remembered then that Óðin means 'frenzy', and I suddenly knew he had been watching it all, maybe even had a hand in that chaos, moving us like tafl pieces and laughing as the blood flew.

Egfrith stood shivering in his dripping undergown behind Sigurd, who had found his sword and now came to me, pointing the blade at the knot of men who still held me down.

'Let him go or I will kill you where you stand,' the jarl growled and the men looked to Alcuin, their grip on me tightening, though the knife drew back from my throat. Borgon's giant, his leg blood-slick, stepped towards Sigurd – without limping, I noticed – his spear and axe raised to strike, but then the bishop shouted something and the Frank stopped dead as all eyes looked to Alcuin. The old man nodded his grey head and the Franks stepped back, allowing me to get to my feet, my head still ringing and my sight fogged. Sigurd nodded at Alcuin, then went over to where Bjorn's head lay in the grass. Carefully, he picked it up, the once blue eyes now grey and staring, and walked the five paces to the Norseman's body, placing the head on the bloody stump of Bjorn's neck, making his corpse whole. 'The hoard is mine,' Sigurd declared to the mass of Frankish soldiers. 'It is the blood-price for this man, who was called Bjorn.'

'All that silver for one man?' Borgon asked, his old, ink-stained palms outstretched.

'He was worth it and more,' Sigurd said, holding Bjarni's eye a moment. Bjorn's brother was in the shieldwall between Svein and Aslak and his handsome face was drawn with the agony of seeing his brother killed. 'Take your men and leave this place, Alcuin,' Sigurd warned, 'before it is too late. A man who puts his hand in a wolf's mouth cannot be surprised when he is eating his next meal one-handed.'

Alcuin watched as some Frankish soldiers dragged away the two men Bjorn had killed before he himself had fallen, a great prize for Óðin's death maidens. Then Alcuin's watery eyes stared at Sigurd and he seemed to tremble slightly though not through fear. 'We will leave, heathen,' he said, 'but do not mistake reason for weakness. You are lucky you are facing me today and not the emperor, for he would see this field blood-slick before noon. He would cut you down himself. I am old and tired of men killing each other. One day you too may tire of it, though I fear you will never grow old, Sigurd son of Harald.' He pointed to the longships. 'Take to your ships and leave. Take the silver, too.' He grimaced. 'It is the price of peace. Now go while you can.' He gestured to a soldier with a crested helmet who roared orders at which the Franks flowed like water into two columns of eight abreast. Then at another command they turned their backs on us, stamping their boots so that I felt the ground tremble.

Bishop Borgon looked horrified, as though he could not

believe they were just going to walk away from all that silver and, worse, the hurt done to his priest and through that the insult done to him. And yet it was clear that Alcuin, though no soldier, held the reins of this army in the emperor's absence. Borgon's giant stared balefully at me and I stared back with my blood-eye, promising him pain I could not inflict.

'Father Egfrith, come with us,' Borgon snapped, beckoning the monk with sharp gestures. 'You have tried your best and cannot do more. Some men are beyond salvation. Even the gates of Heaven are closed to such as these.'

The Wessexman Wiglaf gave Egfrith a cloak, which he wrapped round himself and clutched at his neck. 'Thank you, my lord bishop, but I will stay,' he said, adding: 'by your grace,' with a slight bow. 'My course is set and even the fiercest wind will not turn me from it. *Deus vult.*' He sniffed loudly.

Borgon looked surprised. 'God wills it?' His thin lips curled. 'Then may He grant you the patience of Job,' he said, then turned and with his bodyguard and the other churchmen joined Alcuin as the blue-cloaked columns began to march.

'How's your head, lad?' Penda asked as the shieldwall broke and men pissed their nerves away and drank long and deep from mead skins.

'At least it's still on his shoulders,' Svein said, looking at Bjarni who was kneeling by his brother's corpse. 'Óðin gains a great warrior today.'

'Bjorn saved my life,' I said.

Svein swung the great bearded war axe on to his shoulder. 'It was a good death,' he said, walking off to help the others pile the silver back into their barrels.

'Egfrith, what of Cynethryth?' I asked. 'If you had told me before, Bjorn would still be alive.' In truth I knew Bjorn was dead because of me, because I had let the pockmarked Frankish priest feed a fire in my soul. But Egfrith did not deny the accusation. Instead his little eyes were full of pity, which I liked even less.

'I would have told you after the baptism, Raven,' he said, 'on my word I would have told you everything, but Christ was calling Sigurd and I must not be deaf to the Lord.' He glowered. 'Thanks to you your jarl's soul remains in darkness.'

'Spit it out, monk,' I snapped, touching the egg-sized lump on the left side of my head, and Egfrith sighed, closing his eyes a moment.

'Very well,' he said with a nod. 'Cynethryth is confined to the convent at Aix-la-Chapelle. Abbess Berta has her beaten,' he grimaced, 'and worse, I suspect. For she believes the girl's soul has been defiled.'

'By me,' I said, anger rising inside me again.

'Because she has lived with heathens outside the Lord's shadow,' Egfrith said, touching my arm. 'I pleaded for her, Raven. It broke my heart to see what they had done to her. But the abbess is a powerful woman and I am just a monk. She even accused me of being tainted by heathen sin.' He shook his head sadly. 'I am sorry. I know you care for the girl in your own way.'

'Do not be sorry for me, monk,' I snarled. 'Save your pity for that foul bitch abbess and any other who has laid a hand on Cynethryth.'

A gust plucked at my cloak and Egfrith shivered, shaking his head glumly before walking away. And I stood with Bjorn's blood cold and sticky across my face, my soul seething in its dark place.

CHAPTER TWENTY-TWO

―――――――

THAT NIGHT WE BURNT BJORN'S CORPSE ON A GREAT PYRE AND THE slick flames taunted the darkness beside the river where we camped. We dared not leave our ships or the hoard and go into the town, but neither were we going to skulk away from Alcuin's threat like a whipped hound. The next day I went into the beechwoods with Bjarni and we found a boulder with one flat side and on to that rock Bjarni inscribed a rune pattern which spoke of his brother. It took the whole day and half of the next day too, but when he had finished the carving it was beautiful. A serpent coiled in the rock and inside the beast's length was written, *Bjarni son of Anundr carved this stone in memory of Bjorn, who sailed with Sigurd and cut down his enemies. We will meet again in Óðin's hall, my brother.* Into the carving we rubbed red clay dug from near the river and when we were done, the other Norsemen thought it was a very fine rune stone and drank themselves senseless in memory of the sword-brother they had lost.

'Bjorn's name will live for ever,' Sigurd said, slapping Bjarni's shoulder. 'Old Anundr would be proud to see this stone so far from your home.'

'He was a good brother,' Bjarni said with a nod, emptying the drinking horn down his throat, and for me that stone was a powerful seidr thing, for it would whisper Bjorn's tale until the end of the world. I still think of it sometimes, standing in that beechwood half swallowed by thickets, its red runes still as clear as the day Bjarni carved them with his chisel those many years ago.

We were rich. We were richer than any of us had ever believed possible and when we loaded the barrels of silver on to *Serpent* she creaked in complaint and sat a little lower against the wharf. We had honoured Bjorn and now it seemed many thought it was time to take the sea road north again before the winter came. We had certainly done enough to ensure that the name of the Wolfpack would be spoken around hearths by old men who had once sailed their own dragons to far-off lands, and by young men eager to test themselves and taste their own glory. Asgot was as happy as a fiend. That night, during a feast of roasted meats, he pointed at me from the far side of the fire, cackling and spilling glistening juices into his beard.

'You are a blade with two edges, Raven,' he said, his knowing yellow eyes like rivets in my soul. 'The All-Father wields you like a sword and when he does, men die. Good men. But because of you our jarl did not give himself to the nailed god.' There were murmurs of agreement. He raised a drinking horn to me and I looked over at Sigurd.

'Asgot is right, Raven,' Sigurd said simply. 'The All-Father did not want me washing in the Christians' river.' He smiled at Egfrith. 'Or perhaps, monk, your nailed god did not want a wolf in his sheep pen.' Egfrith sat slumped and defeated and it was clear that he was bitterly disappointed to have come so close, yet failed to ensnare a great jarl in his White Christ net. 'I thought it would not matter,' Sigurd said, 'but I was wrong.'

'Bjorn died because of me,' I said gloomily, drinking deep of my mead horn.

'And now my brother drinks in Valhöll!' Bjarni yelled, rais-ing a chorus of 'hey's. 'Do not pity him, Raven. Would that we all had such deaths.'

'We have a hoard the like of which has never been seen in the north,' Olaf said. 'It will blaze for years and light the long winter months. It will keep our old bones warm.' He raised his horn to the Fellowship. 'And our jarl has seen the sense of telling the Christ god to go and fuck himself.' He smiled such a smile as I had not seen from him since before his son Erik was killed at Ealdred's hall. 'It is a good day,' he said, banging his drinking horn against Svein's. But it was not a good day from where I sat. A good friend was dead because of me, gone to the afterlife too soon. And then there was Cynethryth. The Franks were beating her because they thought I was a devil who had entrapped her soul by some foul seidr.

'Don't drown yourself, lad,' said a voice. I dragged the back of my hand across my mouth, turning my foggy head to see Penda leaning on a rolled skin, watching me in a way that told me he had been at it a while. He slid his long knife over a whetstone. 'I want you with a clear head in the morning,' he said, spitting on the stone. 'We have scheming to do.' I looked at him, my head spinning and too sick with misery to poke around for his meaning. 'You hear me, lad?' he said, pointing the knife at me, then testing its edge against his thumbnail. 'No more mead. I want you sober.'

'Why?' I asked dolefully.

'Because tomorrow night we're going to get Cynethryth,' he said. I felt my mead-slick lips pull back from my teeth.

The plan was simple. Too simple, it seemed to me. Father Egfrith had come up with it next morning, which had surprised me because I thought he was still too sour about Sigurd's failed baptism to help us free Cynethryth. But when he heard Penda and me talking about breaking Cynethryth out of the convent, his weasel eyes came alive.

'Cynethryth is a good girl,' he said, rubbing the stubble on his cheeks and frowning. 'I have grown fond of her. What she did to Ealdred . . . well, that was unfortunate.' He shook his head sadly. 'She must seek the Lord's forgiveness for that terrible sin. But she has suffered too. I believe Christ weeps for the poor child and how cruelly the Franks are ministering to her. There are other, kinder ways to tend to Cynethryth's soul. As for Abbess Berta, she is a curdled old crone. Forgive me, Father,' he muttered, signing the cross over his chest. 'She is misguided. I do not agree with her methods and I do not believe our Heavenly Father does either. Therefore I cannot stand idle whilst the poor child suffers.'

And so Egfrith was to take some of the silver, go to the monastery of Aix-la-Chapelle and there buy from the cellarer two large, cowled habits and then meet Penda and myself at nightfall by the boundary ditch between the forest and the city.

'I'll pay the cellarer well enough to see he will not ask questions,' Egfrith said confidently. Then he looked at Penda and me dubiously. 'So long as you keep your mouths shut and your cowls up, we should be able to enter the convent and steal young Cynethryth away.'

'We can do that, monk,' I said, glancing at Penda, who smiled mischievously. 'Just get us in and we will do the rest.'

'You'll be poking a wasps' nest with a big stick,' Olaf warned, cuffing a trickle of mead from his beard. The sun was rising fast, shining through the misty eastern woods so that the lichened ash trunks seemed on fire. Pigeons cooed softly, their patient song clashing with the noisy trilling of robins, wrens and chaffinches. 'The Franks will spit teeth when they find out,' Uncle added, 'and that spindling bishop would have fought us last time if that old goat Alcuin had not been there to keep the Franks' swords in their scabbards.'

'Uncle is right, Raven,' Sigurd said, 'so you must be quick.

We will be at our benches and have the ships ready to leave. But if they catch you in the city you will be on your own.'

'I understand,' I said. Penda nodded agreement.

'Let me take some men and go with them,' Svein the Red asked, his broad forehead wrinkled with worry. 'We can wait for Raven in the trees, but at least we can be close in case there is a fight.'

'We only have six decent horses, Svein, and none of them would move faster than an ox with you on its back.' Svein harrumphed sulkily.

'I will go,' Black Floki offered, his mouth grim-set. 'Halldor too.' Halldor was Floki's cousin. A man obsessed with his weapons, Halldor had given them all names and you could be sure that his blades were the sharpest of any in the Wolfpack. He nodded simply at his cousin's suggestion and Floki held Sigurd's eye. 'We will wait for them as Svein said, out of sight amongst the trees. But our spears will be ready in case the Franks come after them.'

'If we can we will spirit the girl away without the nuns knowing anything about it,' Egfrith said hopefully. Sigurd nodded, but his eyes betrayed doubt.

'Thank you, Floki,' I said, 'and you, Halldor. Light a torch so that we can find you when we have Cynethryth. But do not leave the trees. If we are caught it is our concern. I don't want the Franks seeing Sigurd's hand in it.'

Floki scowled. 'Just try not to bring a herd of the blue cloaks with you,' he said.

The five of us set off on horseback. At dusk we came to the edge of the forest from where we could see Aix-la-Chapelle and there we waited below a rookery suspended high up in a stand of ash and watched Father Egfrith ride on, his horse flicking its tail at the clouds of flies that followed.

When the monk returned he was puffed up and his weasel

face glowed with pride, though I could not blame him, for he had managed to get hold of two new habits of brown wool.

'Well done, Father,' Penda said with a grin as he disappeared into the scratchy garb, his spiky head soon emerging so that with his scarred face he did not look like any monk you have ever seen.

Black Floki spat disapprovingly, but Halldor laughed. 'You two make good Christ slaves,' he said, plucking the wool at our shoulders where the habits were far too tight. 'The Christ brides will bolt their door on the inside and make you poke the cobwebs from their cunnies until Ragnarök.'

'If there is a good-looking one amongst them I might,' Penda said, earning a scolding look from Egfrith.

'*Cucullus non facit monachum*,' Egfrith muttered, cocking an eyebrow. 'The hood does not make the monk.'

We left our mail behind because the habits were tight as it was and because the iron rings might be heard rattling beneath, but we wore our swords and long knives and hoped that their hilts would not be visible against the wool. Then, because we were humble monks, we left our horses with Floki and Halldor and set off on foot, passing the old boundary ditch and gazing up at the city walls which loomed before us, reflecting the last of the sun. Even from a distance as we walked amongst the clutters of smoke-wreathed dwellings, I could hear the birds in the rookery far behind, their parched, leathery rasping sounding like a tavern full of drunken men.

'It doesn't get any less impressive, does it?' Penda said, the tilt of his cowl betraying the focus of his unseen eyes. The city wall dominated the landscape, its stone construction mocking the timber-built houses without, mocking even us men who were, after all, mere flesh and mortal. For they would stand long after our names had dissolved like smoke in a gale. Like Bjorn's rune stone, I thought.

'It is a monument to civilization in a barbarous world,

Penda,' Egfrith said, casting a blessing at a woman who was milking a goat by the path. The woman dipped her head gratefully.

'This civilization you speak of beats young women who have done no wrong, monk,' I growled, touching the All-Father amulet at my neck. Egfrith wanted to say that Cynethryth had been wrong to kill Ealdred, but he thought better of it and held his tongue.

The imperial guards manning the gate did not ask questions this time, for they were used to monks and their vows of silence, but one of them did pull his head back and look Penda and me up and down. I wondered if I could get to my sword before they ran me through with their spears. I doubted it. But then Egfrith took out his small wooden cross and touched it to the guard's forehead and spouted a stream of Latin, which turned the man's suspicion to confusion. He nodded stiffly to Egfrith and waved us on, muttering under his breath to the other man, who seemed amused and relieved to have escaped the monk's attention.

'Benedictine brothers do not tend to have shoulders that could take a yoke,' Egfrith muttered once we were inside the walls. I could see his point. The rowing and the training had made me as broad as the other Norsemen, broader even than some of them, and I wondered if my real father, whoever he had been, had had big shoulders and strong arms from ploughing the whale road. And though I felt horribly conspicuous in a Christ slave's habit, it seemed that to the folk of Aix-la-Chapelle I was invisible. The merchants and the children and the whores let us alone so that we walked the gangplanks above the mud, following the wall westward and avoiding the seething heart of the city. Hearth smoke stung my eyes. Delicious smells made my mouth water one moment, only for some foul stench to bring a lump to my throat the next, and I was glad of the cowl because it felt like a refuge from the chaos around us, giving my thoughts room to breathe. And my thoughts were of Cynethryth.

The city was in shadow when we came to the Convent of Saint Godeberta. The pasture beyond the western wall would still be flush with twilight, but the city walls defied the setting sun so that imperial soldiers were going round lighting fires in braziers atop iron poles. These flames gave instant life to stuttering shadows and attracted moths by the hundred, whilst cockroaches and rats scurried for the darkness beneath the bulwarks.

The convent had walls of its own, though the whitewashed stone was crumbling in places and it could be climbed easily enough as a last resort, though I did not relish that prospect. There were too many guards walking the streets and we would not last long in monks' habits instead of brynjas.

'Remember,' Egfrith warned after thumping three times on the gate, 'keep your mouths shut and your heads down.' After a while Egfrith thumped again, harder this time, and soon there was a commotion from inside, followed by the drawing of a bolt. A face appeared at a shutter, the eyes suspicious if not angry, followed by a stinging rattle of Frankish, which I could not make head or tail of. Calmly, Egfrith replied in Latin and the eyes widened. 'You are the English monk,' the nun accused. Then she giggled and I was surprised to hear that sound from a Christ bride. 'You are the one who tried to baptize the heathen jarl and nearly drowned,' she said, her English so good she might have come from Wessex.

'I did not nearly drown,' Egfrith insisted irritably. 'I assure you, sister, I swim like a fish. Now are you going to let me in?'

Within the dark space of her wimple the nun's eyes narrowed again. 'What business have you here with the sisters at this late hour? It is compline, Father Egfrith, the sisters are at prayer.'

'I am well aware of the hour, sister, but I have been sent by Bishop Borgon, who believes I may be of some help to the Reverend Mother.'

'Help?' the nun said suspiciously. 'Help with what?'

'I really do not see it as any business of yours, sister, but since you seem to share a pig's bent for rooting around I will indulge you with this acorn. The girl Cynethryth. I am told she is not . . . cooperative.'

The nun frowned. 'That one's lost as a coin dropped in a tavern,' she said. 'Abbess Berta says she has spent so long with the heathens that the good Father has turned His back on her. She struck the abbess.' Her eyes betrayed a hint of amusement at that. 'Can you imagine that, Father? But the sisters made her pay for it.' I was about to break down the door when I felt Penda's hand grip my arm.

'And yet despite the sisters' efforts I hear the girl is still full of wickedness,' Egfrith said, shaking his head sadly.

'We pray for her soul, Father Egfrith,' the nun said.

Egfrith wagged a finger before her eyes. '*Facta, non verba*,' he said. 'Sometimes what is needed is actions, not words, my dear child.' He swept a little arm back. 'I have brought brothers Leofmar and Gytha who, as you can see, possess the strength to challenge Satan for the poor girl's soul. Bishop Borgon believes they will be more . . .' he paused, 'persuasive than the good sisters, who are after all but sweet and gentle creatures. Now, please let us in so that we may begin our work.'

The nun peered at Penda and me through the slit as a trickle of sweat ran down my back. Then she unbolted the gate, which creaked with complaint to be opened at such a late hour. We walked into a courtyard of grass upon which shadows danced, born of flaming torches that seethed quietly. Round the edge of the grass ran a covered walkway of polished oak in which faces and crosses had been carved with great skill. Somewhere the nuns were praying, their voices deadened by stone walls, and I fixed the sound to a small church on the east side of the courtyard. Other buildings of varying sizes surrounded the grass, some of wood but most of stone, which the nun who had let us in took pleasure in naming as we passed each one: the kitchen, the buttery, the refectory, the library, the chapter house, barns, bakeries and store houses. There was a peacefulness about the place that weighed heavily on me, making my chest tight as a full mead skin. I could feel the White Christ breathing down the neck of that coarse monk's robe.

'Beyond the workshop on the far side we have vegetable gardens, grain fields, and even an orchard,' she announced proudly.

'A safe harbour in a world of sin, sister,' Egfrith said with a solemn smile.

'You will have to wait in the guest house until Abbess Berta has finished compline,' the nun said, addressing Egfrith but staring at me. I kept my hands clasped, my head bowed and my mouth shut. Then the woman showed us to a stone building with a thatch roof, opening the door and ushering us inside as though she was suddenly afraid of the other nuns seeing us. 'I will have wine brought and maybe some bread if you and the brothers are hungry.'

'Thank you, sister,' Egfrith said, 'and God bless you, child.'

The nun swept away and Penda shut the door behind her, leaving us alone in that place in which the heavy darkness was illuminated by sweet-smelling beeswax candles. I could also smell freshly baked bread and the faint aroma of fennel.

'Stirs the juices being here,' Penda said, scratching the long scar on his face, 'being walled up with all these women.'

'Where is Cynethryth, Egfrith?' I asked, instinctively touching my sword's hilt through the thick wool of my habit.

He sniffed loudly. 'I believe they will have her in a cell in the dorter,' he said, 'but we need to move now, before compline ends and the sisters go to their beds.' His eyes were wide and sweat was beading on his bald pate. 'Are you both ready?' I looked at Penda, who nodded, then the Wessexman opened the door and we stepped into the flamelit cloister to find Cynethryth.

CHAPTER TWENTY-THREE

EGFRITH LED US ALONG THE WOODEN CLOISTER, OUR FOOTSTEPS thumping and clumsy, it seemed to me, in this place of White Christ brides. But there was no sign of the nuns as we passed the rancid-smelling latrine and then the infirmary from which leaked a low moaning mingled with the soft cooing of another woman. Swallows arrowed across the shadowed courtyard and bats flitted between the wooden arches of the cloister, snatching moths from the air.

'Here,' Egfrith hissed. My heart was hammering and my mouth was as dry as smoke at the thought of seeing Cynethryth. The dorter building was next to the stone church and we could clearly hear the nuns in prayer now, which meant we still had some time. Egfrith lifted the latch and we went inside. I felt myself grimace as the wooden staircase creaked underfoot, but we soon came to another door, which Egfrith pushed open gently, stepping into a narrow corridor in which Penda and I had to stoop. Off to both sides were doors open to small cells. Each contained a bed and stool and nothing more but for a few personal effects such as wooden crosses, wimples and habits. At the end of the corridor another staircase led down into darkness, but before that on the right was another cell, whose door was shut.

'I'll wager she's in there,' Egfrith said, pointing. 'It is locked,' he confirmed a moment later. 'Cynethryth,' he called softly against the thick oak. 'Cynethryth, my girl, are you there?' We put our ears to the door but heard nothing.

'Maybe they are keeping her in one of the other buildings,' Penda suggested. Just then we heard a door open out of sight at the bottom of the stairs.

'We must go,' Egfrith rasped.

'But you think she's in there?' I asked.

'I don't know where else they would put her,' he hissed, 'but we have no time.'

I pushed him aside and leant back and with all my strength I kicked the door so that either the lock or my leg had to break. Luckily for me it was the lock. The splintering crack brought several gasps from up ahead, but we were inside and there was Cynethryth. She was tied to a bed and gagged, her bare arms and legs scraped raw by the coarse ropes. 'Holy mother, you poor, poor creature,' Egfrith whined as I took my knife and cut through the bonds. Cynethryth was almost unrecognizable. Her hair was a matted clump, her eyes were black holes and the skin of her face was stretched thin and looked brittle as old parchment. She did not seem to recognize me.

'You're safe, my peregrine,' I whispered in her ear, lifting her into my arms.

'What in the name of the Blessed Virgin is going on?' a voice boomed and we turned to see a woman who could only be Abbess Berta herself standing in the doorway. By Óðin she was a big bitch. Behind her stood several nuns, whose eyes were plump with shock. 'Father Egfrith? What do you think you are doing?' Berta thundered.

'I am taking this poor girl away from here, Reverend Mother,' Egfrith snapped.

'But she is in danger, Father! Her soul is black and we are trying to wrest it from the Dark One.' As big as any Norseman, she blocked the doorway, gripping its frame, her craggy, death-white face trembling with rage.

'You are a cruel old hag!' Egfrith declared, pointing a bony finger at this woman who was thrice his size. 'We're leaving.' Some of the nuns were clattering back down the stairs, probably going for help, so we had no more time to waste.

'Give her to me, lad,' Penda said, 'and do what needs doing.' He shrugged. 'I'm a Christian.'

I put Cynethryth in Penda's arms and then I strode over and punched Abbess Berta in the jaw, dropping her like a sack of stones.

'Raven!' Egfrith exclaimed. The nuns screamed and fought each other to get away from us, bouncing along the corridor, and we followed them down the stairs and out into the night where I took my knife and cut slits up the front and back of our habits. Then we ran, our legs free now, straight across the grass courtyard for the main gate. Once through that we were out and clumping along the gangplanks skirting the city below the convent walls. As yet there was no sign that we were being followed. Aix-la-Chapelle was quiet but not deserted. Drunken men stumbled through the streets, jeering at by-passers and whores. Small groups of imperial soldiers patrolled, their scale armour reflecting the crackling flames of braziers. Dogs fought for scraps in the mud, unseen cats shrieked in the shadows, roof thatch rustled with mice, and we ran.

When we saw the towers of the west gate we stopped and I took Cynethryth from Penda who was puffing like a carthorse. 'There are too many guards,' I said, eyeing the blue cloaks. There were two in each tower and eight more standing by the barred gates, talking and laughing. 'They will ask too many questions.'

'Can she walk?' Penda asked, looking doubtfully at Cynethryth. I looked into her eyes, which were heavy, their lids falling closed for long stretches. She had not said a word.

I shook my head. 'She's exhausted, Penda,' I said.

'Then we'll have to take the chance,' he said, making for the gate.

'Wait!' Egfrith said. 'There.' He pointed to a leatherworker's shop – a timber lean-to whose thatch roof sloped up to meet the city's west wall. It was a little higher than the lean-tos on either side and the reach to the top of the wall was less than a spear's length. We pushed over the leatherworker's rain barrel and upended it against the eaves, then Penda clambered up on to the thatch and I passed Cynethryth up to him, which was easy because the poor girl weighed no more than a sack of flour. Then Penda left Cynethryth at the apex against the wall whilst he leapt for a handhold and missed. On the second attempt he cursed like Thór. His right foot had crashed through the thatch and now came a surprised cry from inside the dwelling. The Wessexman yanked his foot out just as the door clattered open and I looked down from the barrel to see a big man standing there in nothing but his linen breeks, his hair and moustache as wild as his eyes. He grabbed Egfrith round the neck and began to strangle him. I leapt down and when he saw me he tossed Egfrith aside and came.

'Help Penda!' I yelled at Egfrith, who was coughing and spluttering. The Frank swung a fist but I blocked it with my forearm and stepped inside, ramming my forehead into his face. He staggered backwards, blood spurting from his nose, and I ran up and swung my boot into his groin so that his eyes almost burst with pain as he toppled sideways and curled up in the mud like a dying dog, teeth gritted. Another yell tore the night and I heard boots stamping along gangplanks.

'They're coming, Raven!' Penda shouted. I jumped up and together Egfrith and I lifted Cynethryth up to Penda, who was straddling the city wall, his spiky hair silhouetted against the dark blue night sky.

'Reach up to Penda, Cynethryth,' I said, and she said nothing and I thought she had not heard me, but then she stretched her wasted arms up and with a great heave Penda hauled her on to the wall. Soldiers were shouting and I did not know if they were angry because we had climbed on to the leatherworker's roof or because they had learnt about our raid on the convent. But I knew they would kill me for hitting that cow Abbess Berta and so I was up that wall like a cat up the side of a butter churn. 'I'll go first, Penda,' I said, easing myself over the wall and then taking Penda's hands so that, lying flat, he could lower me as far as possible to shorten the fall. It was still a drop of some ten feet, but the ground was wet and soft and the fall did no damage. I was about to tell Cynethryth not to worry, that I would catch her, when she jumped, and somehow I caught her, wincing at the impact of her thin bones and hoping none had broken.

'Now you, Father,' Penda said, as an arrow whipped close to his head. The next thing I knew he and Father Egfrith were down and I had Cynethryth in my arms and we were running between the close-packed houses then out across the moon-silvered pasture. Up ahead the woods were a dark mass and somewhere amongst those trees Black Floki and Halldor were waiting with horses. If we got to the trees we would be safe.

Behind us the gates of Aix-la-Chapelle clunked open and the next sound I heard chilled my soul and turned my bowels to ice. It was the sound of galloping hooves on damp earth. I did not dare turn and look but pumped my legs harder. In my arms Cynethryth bounced horribly. The Franks were yelling and it sounded as though there were a hundred of them.

'Wait. Penda, you must take Cynethryth,' I said, stopping and crouching with Cynethryth in the dewy grass. The others squatted too and the whites of their eyes shone ferally. My chest heaved. Every breath was a tortured rasp.

'I'll not leave you, lad,' Penda said with a shake of his head. I looked at Egfrith.

'Then you will have to take her,' I said, to which the monk nodded without a heartbeat's hesitation. 'Get to the trees, monk. Whatever happens.'

'But I see no torches,' Egfrith said, looking to the tree line.

'That's because they know we are being followed,' I said. 'Black Floki will find you. Now go. We will keep them off you.' I do not know where the monk found the strength, but he took Cynethryth in his little arms and ran, his white legs and the girl's pale face reflecting the moonlight as he carried her off.

Penda and I drew our swords and threw back our cowls. I grinned at him in the moonlight. Then I roared the name Óðin Spear-Shaker, jarl of the gods, and we ran towards the horses and the men carrying flames.

The riders heard us, for they yanked their reins round, the animals screeching with the thrill of it, and then galloped towards us, fish scale armour and helmets glinting. I wanted to look back to see if Egfrith had made it to the woods, but the first rider was on me. He swung his sword, but I leapt back and it flew wide. Then another rode in and his couched spear snared in the sleeve of my habit so that he had to let go as his mount took him past. I picked up the spear and turned as another Frank was upon me. One-handed, I thrust the spear into his left shoulder, then spun, scything my sword through the air, just missing a man's back as he galloped by. Penda had taken two riders down and I saw him hack off a dismounted Frank's arm at the shoulder before I turned to face two others whose intention was to ride either side of me, leaving their spears in my chest as they passed. Dozens of Franks had cleared the houses west of the city walls and were running across the pastureland towards us, their cloaks flying behind them. An arrow snagged in the flapping wool between my legs and I cursed because I was not wearing my brynja and I knew it would only be moments before Frankish steel tore my flesh.

Then the flat of a sword clanged against the back of my head, sending me stumbling, but I still gripped my sword. I tried to raise it as a rider came straight at me, but the beast ploughed into me, knocking me halfway to the next world. I lay in the grass for what seemed like an age, looking up at the stars, unable to move. I felt the dew softly falling on my face and saw bats whirling above me. Then the blue cloaks were there, dragging me on to legs that I could have sworn did not belong to me.

'You still breathing, lad?' It was Penda. The Franks were all over him but still they seemed afraid of what he might do to them, as three men lay broken in the dew-laced grass. 'Looks like the bastards want us alive, so we might as well kill a couple more if we can,' he barked, almost smiling despite the arms binding him. The Wessexman was as vicious a man as I had ever known. He could kill without even trying. As for me, I had not managed to kill a single Frank, though one was nursing a bruised shoulder, and I gained a new respect for their fish scale armour. The mounted soldiers were ranging across the pasture now, their firebrands streaking through the night like lightning bolts from the heavens as they searched for Cynethryth. 'See her safe, Floki,' I murmured, aware that my hair was sticky with blood.

The fact that we were still alive meant that either someone thought they could get a good price for us at the slave market, or else someone – maybe the Abbess herself – intended to show us the error of our ways. Or perhaps both. If I could have chosen then, I would have slapped the manacles on myself rather than face Abbess Berta again after what I had done to her. Later, I would change my mind, preferring anything that big bitch could have thrown at me.

They took us back to the city but not to the convent and not to the palace either. Instead, they led us through the north side of Aix-la-Chapelle, through streets that were filthy and whose gangplanks the oozing mud had reclaimed long ago. The houses here were cluttered and pitiful, little more than shelters draped with rotting skins and blankets. Even the whores were nowhere to be seen. I saw the naked body of a newborn bairn half buried in the sludge, and a threadbare dog chewing at the rotting ribcage of another. This was a part of the great Christian city Father Egfrith had not told us about, and the place made my flesh crawl. I felt an overwhelming longing to be aboard *Serpent* with the salt wind whipping my hair. But I was a prisoner now and could expect only death, which would almost have been a blessing, for I suspected that Frank's sword must have cracked my skull like a hazel nut. My head was a sickening tangle of pain and dizziness, leaving me unable to do anything but go where the booted feet and spear butts pushed me.

We passed a small wooden church outside which a great wooden cross had been set in the earth. Next to that cross several men were sleeping on freshly laid straw, each swaddled in a faded blue cloak. Then the sprawl of hovels thinned and I soon smelt why. A two-foot wide reeking ditch ran from the south of the city and out under the north wall. It was a sluggish stream of shit and most of it came from the better half of the city, some perhaps even from the imperial arse itself. Around this fetid trench the shelters seemed as though they would soon dissolve into the mire, with no living thing having the slightest care.

We crossed this ditch and eventually came to a palisade of sharpened stakes. Our captors banged on the gate and we were taken inside. A longhouse sat in the middle of the compound, its windows covered with thick skins. Next to it were smaller buildings, also of wood, but well made, their thatch still golden, sound protection from cold and rain. As for the longhouse, it would have been impressive in its day. It was easily eighty feet long with a hefty skeleton of thick beams and great sloping roof, which covered an area sufficient to graze twenty goats. But the thatch was patchy and rotten, the daub walls were crumbling, and I guessed the house had stood here long before the emperor's buildings of smooth white stone rose up on the hill.

'Maybe they've prepared a feast for us, Raven,' Penda suggested, earning a smack around the head with the butt of a spear. Our captors spoke with the enclosure's guards, warning them that we were not monks and that they should be wary of us. I thought this should have been obvious enough given not only our build and the state we were in, but also the blue-cloaked corpses flung across three horses who now nuzzled the few sprouts of grass poking through the mud. The Franks shoved us towards the longhouse. A soldier unbarred the door whilst another opened it, and a smell I shall never forget hit me like a hammer blow. It was the rank, putrid stench of death, and Penda and I were cast into its maw. The longhouse was a prison. And it was full of stinking, starving, dying men. Most did not even move to see what we were, but some white eyes stared out of the darkness, watching as the Franks shoved through a tangle of shifting bodies, creating a meagre space into which they slotted us, stirring moans from the closest inmates. They foraged in the stinking darkness, emerging with a length of chain on to which they shackled us with wrist manacles, and I soon realized that this chain coiled through the whole noxious place like a great iron serpent, enfettering a hundred or more souls. Having no wish to remain with the dead and dying, the guards scrambled free, their cloaks held to their faces, and in moments the door clunked shut behind them.

'Some feast, Penda,' I said, testing the iron bindings.

Unfortunately for us they were the newest thing in the whole rotten place and would probably hold Fenrir himself.

'It could be worse, lad,' the Wessexman said.

'How by Thór's hairy balls could it be worse?' I moaned, trying not to breathe because of the stink.

'They could have chained you to that fart-faced old cow the abbess,' he said, and despite my pounding head and the shackles I laughed, because Penda was right.

'Is something funny, English?' a thickly accented voice rasped somewhere in the darkness. And that accent had the deep cold of the fjord about it.

'What is it to you?' Penda growled back.

'We are laughing because I punched a Christ bride, which is the most Týr-brave thing I've ever done because she was bigger than me,' I said in Norse. A few dry chuckles broke the tension.

'Who are you?' the Norseman asked cautiously. I shifted, trying to find the man, but then the men between us shuffled and bent low to give us a view of each other. He must be an important man in this death place, I thought. He sat two spear-lengths away to my right and despite the clinging darkness I made out the gaunt angles of his face.

'I am Raven of the Fellowship of Sigurd the Lucky,' I said, 'and this is my sword-brother Penda of Wessex.'

'Hrafn?' he said, the Norse for raven. 'A Norseman travelling with an Englishman?' The man spoke Norse but his accent was unfamiliar.

'And who are you?' I asked.

'I am Steinn, son of Inge,' he said. 'We are Danes.'

'So the dragons at the wharf are yours?'

'Not mine,' Steinn said. 'They belong to Yngve, our jarl.'

'Where is Yngve?' I asked, glancing at the shadow-cloaked faces around me.

'He is over there,' Steinn said with a rattle of chains as he pointed to a corner of the longhouse. I strained to see in the blackness, past dark huddled forms, then made out the outline of a big man leaning against the rotting daub wall. 'You can probably smell him. He has been dead for nine days,' Steinn said. 'The wound fever finished him eventually.'

I translated for Penda, who I knew would be rankling by now at not knowing what was being said. 'The men here, Steinn, they are all from your Fellowship?' I asked.

'Those that still breathe,' he said. 'This land has been our curse. We should never have come here.'

'Your jarl was a fool to fight this Christian emperor,' I said, which caused some men around me to bristle and grunt threateningly.

'We came to trade,' Steinn said, which was probably a lie. 'Our mistake was to trust these Franks.' *Your mistake was to fight them*, I thought, *and now your jarl is worm food and your Fellowship rots in the darkness*. But that looked like my fate now, too. I imagined the three Spinners sitting somewhere looking at the tapestry they had woven for me and laughing. 'Did you fight them?' Steinn asked. 'Where is your jarl and the others?'

'The Franks caught us breaking into their convent,' I said, knowing what these Danes would assume that meant. But I saw no reason to explain it all. 'The others are safe. They are with our dragons at the wharf.'

'Will they come for you?' Steinn asked. I let that question hang for a long while in the thick darkness, thinking this Dane would have the patience to wait, seeing as his name meant 'stone'.

'Perhaps,' I said.

CHAPTER TWENTY-FOUR

OVER THE NEXT THREE DAYS TWO MORE DANES DIED OF WOUND rot or thirst. The Franks would sometimes open the door and throw in water skins and scraps of food, but some of the Danes were by now too weak even to chew the scraps from a bone. For these there was no hope, so those who still clung to life took whatever they could get their hands on, devouring it like dogs, their pride long forgotten. There was very little talking, for no one wanted to waste their strength, and besides, what was there to talk about? There was nothing to do but wait for the slow, miserable death that was coming. After that I lost track of time. The days and nights were just one long nothingness of stomach-twisting hunger pains. At first we were so thirsty that it became almost unbearable, but as we became weaker we hardly noticed the thirst, which Penda suggested must be a very bad sign. My skin dried and cracked like the daub walls of our prison and my lips split so that I always had the taste of blood on my swollen tongue. We had to shit and piss where we sat, but there was not so much of that because our shrivelled bowels were empty. And still no one came for us. Once I was woken by the clink and rattle of the chain as one of the Danes strangled his friend, giving him the small mercy of a quick death. We all listened in the darkness, clenching our teeth at the Dane's last struggles, until eventually it was over and the killer's heavy breathing turned to sobbing. I am sure I cried too, with pity and anger and shame, though my eyes had no tears to give. These Danes had been like the Wolfpack once: free and full of boasting and life. Now they were nothing, and I cursed myself for being taken alive when I should have died with a sword in my hand.

Some time after the strangling I was drifting in and out of consciousness when I slowly became aware of a ruckus in the enclosure outside. Soon after, the door was unbarred and daylight flooded in, blinding me completely so that I had to turn my head away. The Franks were bringing in another prisoner and I wanted to shout to him, to tell him he would be better off fighting now with all his strength and dying under their blades than letting them put those manacles on his wrists. But I said nothing. I was too exhausted to do anything other than watch as the poor soul was shoved into the stench-ridden place. Flies buzzed everywhere now, feeding off the rotting Danes, and you could hear the soft, sticky sound of maggots writhing in flesh. Sometimes you could even hear rats gnawing on bone, and when you know it is the bone of a man it is a sound to freeze your blood. Then the Franks were gone and pitch darkness claimed the longhouse once more. My eyes had begun to close again when a voice I knew brought me back.

'Is this the way you welcome me to your shit hole longhouse, Raven? Óðin's teeth, I've smelled sweeter things come out of Svein's arse!'

'Bram?' I said.

'So you *are* in here, lad. Well, that's something. Who are these other reeking pigs' bladders?'

'They are Danes,' I croaked feebly, feeling the blood in my

veins again at hearing the Bear's gruff voice. 'What happened, Bram?' I kicked Penda awake and the Wessexman groaned.

'What happened is that the blue cloaks set on me and threw me in here with you,' Bram said.

'You fought them?' I asked.

'Fought them? Has your little brain got wood-rot, lad? If I had fought them I wouldn't be in this rancid pit, would I? I'd have smashed their pus-filled heads in. No, lad, I had to let them beat me. Sigurd's orders. Sigurd's plan. Had to start a little fight in some fleapit tavern in Aixla . . .'

'Aix-la-Chapelle,' I helped him.

'Aye,' Bram said, 'had to break a few noses and eventually the blue cloaks came and . . . well . . . here I am. Not very homely, is it? Lacks a woman's touch, that's what Borghild would say.'

Just knowing that Bram was with us and that he was still strong and had recently been with the others raised my spirits, though not as much as the words 'Sigurd' and 'plan' did. But we could not take any chances and so I hoped Steinn was as resilient as his name suggested.

'Steinn,' I called. 'Steinn, are you still with us?' There were a few murmurs. 'Steinn, are you a man to give up?'

'I'm here, Raven of Sigurd's Fellowship,' the dry voice rasped. 'What do you want with me?'

'I need your men to help me, Steinn. I need to move closer to my friend Bram. Tell your Danes to move with me.'

'They are not my men. They are Yngve's men. Let them die in peace.'

'Yngve is a rotting lump of worm food,' I said. He did not reply to this. 'Steinn, your men do not want to die in here. This was not in their minds when they packed their journey chests and set out on the whale road. There is no glory in this death. There is no Valhöll.' I let those last words sink in, for they were heavy words. 'You Danes. Do you want to see your ships again? See your women again? I can get you out of this stinking hole. I can give you back your lives.' Men were stirring now. Chains were clinking and tongues that had whispered their death prayers now ripped free of dry, sore-encrusted palates.

'If you really can get us out of here we are yours,' Steinn said in the darkness. 'Men of Trelleborg. Find your strength again. Help this Norseman. Yngve was a great warrior, no man can say otherwise. But Yngve led us to death. This Hrafn says he can lead us back to life, so help him, you sons of whores.' Men groaned and grunted like beasts, moving half-dead limbs and dragging the corpses of those beside them so that I could inch closer to Bram. Penda and I still had some strength and we did what we could. In the end we all collapsed in our new places amongst other men's shit and congealed blood.

'You smell worse than a troll's armpit, Raven,' Bram muttered, his teeth glinting in the darkness.

'And so will you before long,' I grumbled. 'How is you getting flung in here going to get us out? Are you sure you didn't just wake up drunk in some whore's lap after breaking a priest's head?'

'Me?' He sounded surprised. 'I told you, lad, Sigurd planned it. And it's low cunning, Raven,' he growled with a grin. 'Loki-low cunning.' The whites of Penda's eyes shone as he watched us. Bram had been stripped of his brynja and cloak and, wearing only his tunic, breeks and boots, did not appear to be in much of a position to break us out. Then he lifted his manacled hands to his head, to one of his thick plaits, and pulled the thong from it. But the plait was stiff, so he began to tease the braids loose and as he did so his smile widened even more. From that plait he pulled a piece of steel the length of a finger. The thing was clearly missing its small wooden haft and the frame meant to hold the serrated blade under tension, but even in the darkness I knew immediately what it was. It was a hacksaw, its tiny teeth no bigger than a mackerel's but wickedly sharp and steel strong.

'It would take you a year to cut through a lump of cheese with that,' Penda croaked, but Bram did not understand the Englishman and nor was he listening. He was sawing. Hours passed. The teeth of the blade were so fine that they made little noise as Bram patiently worked on the thin iron of his manacles. Even so, it helped that one of the Danes was groaning constantly with wound fever now, which was accompanied by enough coughing and spluttering in that place of death to cloak the work. It seemed that Bram's coming and Steinn's words had stirred the last embers left in these Danes' souls so that they realized they were not dead yet and might still see another dawn. But gods it was slow work. Only half its original length and lacking the tension frame and haft, the saw was barely useful and soon Bram's thick fingers were slick with blood, though he did not slow, but let the blood cool the blade to prevent its breaking.

He was almost through when the door of the longhouse creaked open and five Franks came in, each holding a spitting firebrand. Usually they threw slops at us, collected the empty water skins and retreated as quickly as they could, retching as they went. But this time they came further into the place than usual, poking men with their spears to check who was alive and who was dead. Perhaps they had more prisoners to chain up and would take the corpses away to make space. Or perhaps it was a routine check. Either way two of them were now barely a sword-length away from where we huddled in the foul, flame-licked shadows, and if they noticed that Bram had cut through his manacles we would be dead. The Norseman hunched over, trying to hide his hands, but one of the Franks seemed suspicious and put the blade of his spear into Bram's beard to lift his chin. This is it, I thought. Bram is dead.

Just then there was a shout and the soldier turned. A Dane hammered his arms against the back of another guard's legs so that the Frank buckled and then the Dane was on him, smashing his face with his manacled wrists. The Franks tried to help their comrade but the Danes grabbed and clawed at them like animals so that the blue cloaks struck out left and right, trying to carve paths to their friend. Then one of them broke through the throng and yelled, plunging his spear into the Dane's shoulder. The other Franks fought their way through and joined in sticking the Dane over and over as their bleeding comrade crawled free to gather his firebrand and spear. His eyes were wide with fear and shock and his face glistened with blood. Then it was over and the brave Dane who had saved us from being discovered was nothing but a lump of raw, hacked flesh. In the retreating flamelight as the Franks left the longhouse I saw the mutilated mess of his back and under my breath I asked Óðin to take the Danish warrior into Valhöll. Because it was Steinn.

Bram went back to work as though nothing had happened and it was not long before he had cut through his irons. Then he began on mine. I told him to do Penda's first, as Penda was a much better fighter than me, but Bram would not listen.

'I'll not cut an Englishman free before a Norseman,' he said in his gruff voice, though it made little difference anyway, because he was not even halfway through mine when the little hacksaw snapped. His curse roused the half-conscious Danes around us.

'What now?' Penda asked, to which I shrugged and Bram leant back against the wall, his face sweat-glistening. At least he was free of the great chain, but he could not do much alone.

'Why didn't the idiot bring the other half of the saw in his other plait?' Penda grumbled. 'Or even up his arse come to that?'

'Tell that ugly English whoreson if he gives me that look again I'll twist off his head and bounce it off the roof beams,' Bram growled, talking to me but looking at Penda.

'So what is the rest of Sigurd's plan, Bram?' I asked, thinking that having these two at each other's throat was the last thing we needed.

Bram chewed his bottom lip and scratched his head. 'He didn't tell me, lad,' he said. 'But I'd wager my beard he knows.'

CHAPTER TWENTY-FIVE

WHEN THE FRANKS HAD LAST COME IN IT HAD BEEN LIGHT OUTSIDE. We waited a while and, guessing that night had fallen, Bram began slowly and carefully to dig into the rotten wall of the longhouse using what was left of the little saw. Eventually a small but delicious gush of fresh air told us he had broken through and the Norseman soon confirmed it, saying he could see braziers burning and soldiers moving around the compound. The hole was small enough not to be noticed by the Franks but large enough to give us at least some awareness of what was going on in the world beyond those wretched walls. Then we waited, hoping that Sigurd would come, but fearing his coming too, for it must surely ignite a full-on battle with the Franks, which he could not possibly win.

With the loss of Steinn the Danes were beaten again and a desperately heavy atmosphere pervaded that hall, which stank of the utter loss of hope. But we three stirred when an age later there were shouts in the enclosure beyond.

'What is it, Bram?' I muttered, lifting my heavy head.

'I can't see,' he said. 'Wait. Smoke. Coming from the west, I think.'

'What else?' I asked feverishly.

'Nothing, lad. Just smoke,' he said. 'But the Franks don't sound very happy about it.' We waited. And waited. The clamour of voices began to rise as panic started to spread its dark wings. Now and then a blue cloak flashed past Bram's spy hole, but eventually he turned to us, his eyes shining in the puncturing shaft of light. 'I have to move now,' he said. 'Let's hope I can get through this,' he tapped the rotting daub wall, 'before the Franks stick me. With Thór's luck they will be too busy shitting their breeks to notice.'

I wanted to tell Bram to wait a little longer, to give Sigurd, if it was Sigurd, more time. But I knew this might be our only chance and so I nodded, feeling helpless chained up to a hundred dead or half-dead men. Bram was on his feet, and being Bram had decided to kick his way out for better or worse, rather than burrow away with the broken hacksaw. 'I'll have those chains off you soon enough, Raven,' he said. 'You too, Englishman,' he added in Norse to which Penda nodded. Then, with all the power in his oak-strong legs, he slammed his booted foot against the daub, which split and crumbled like cheese. Again and again Bram kicked and we thought he must have alerted every Frank within a mile, but eventually he had made a hole big enough to crawl through. Then in a heartbeat he was gone.

I could smell smoke now, not hearth smoke but the acrid smoke of damp, ancient thatch burning. I had smelled that same smell when Sigurd had burnt my village and now as then it knotted a coil of fear in my gut.

'Fuck, we don't need that,' Penda murmured and I looked up to see a pall of smoke swirling beneath the old roof.

'Why would they burn this?' I said, instinctively testing the iron manacles for the thousandth time. 'They know we are in here.' Panic was welling in my gut at the thought of being burnt alive.

Then Bram was back, gripping two Frankish hand axes, one of which was bloody.

'Are you coming or not?' he asked with a grin, then crawled back inside. I held my hands still against the floor so that he could chop through the rest of the shackle to finish what we had started with the hacksaw, for the shackles were made of soft iron and the axe blade was edged with good Frankish steel. Even so, he ruined the axe cutting through Penda's manacles. But we were free.

'Now them,' I said, pointing to the men who were watching us, the whites of their eyes pathetic and plaintive as worn-legged hounds.

'They are Danes,' Bram said.

'I gave them my word, Bram,' I said, taking the good axe from him. We did not have the time or the tools to break all of their irons, so I waded into the middle of the hall and the Danes shuffled out of the way to give me the room I needed. Then I took what was roughly the middle of the length of chain that passed through every man's bound arms and I cut it. Penda and Bram helped me to haul the chains out from the dead and the living, until the Danes were free. Their hands were still in irons but those that had the strength could now at least escape that place of death. 'Get to the river if you can,' I told the Danes who were rising on unsteady legs, wide-eyed like men who had just dug their way out of their own grave barrows. They looked unlikely to make it beyond the palisade, let alone the day's walk to the river. 'Your ships are moored at the wharf. We will help you if we can.'

'Raven,' Bram growled, and so I turned and nodded and followed him out into the light. At first glance the stockade looked deserted. Two blue cloaks lay dead by the front of the longhouse; the Bear's work, I knew. But then two young guards came round the corner of the hall and their eyes nearly popped with the shock of seeing us free. They seemed unsure whether to attack or run, but then a ragged knot of Danes flew at them, heedless of the Franks' spears and ravenous for revenge. In a heartbeat the Franks had disappeared beneath the Danes, who were like rabid wolves gouging and tearing and snarling.

'Bastards are hungry,' Penda muttered as we left the Danes to it and broke into the three small huts, in the last of which we found our swords and some spears, shields and helmets. The air was thick with yellow smoke, most of which was drifting in from the west. The thatch of the western eaves of our former prison had sprouted a hungry flame and there were many men who, had they not been looking to their own survival, would have enjoyed watching that place burn to the ground. We ran for the main gate, which had been left open, and then we were in the mud-slick thoroughfares of the poor quarter of Aix-la-Chapelle. The thatch of one or two shabby dwellings smouldered dangerously, but most had no thatch to burn, which would be their saving.

'There's something to be said for living by a river of shit,' Penda said, then he looked to the west. Black smoke billowed into the blue sky, most of it seeming to come from the houses outside the western gate, but plenty of houses were burning inside the city too. The local Franks were standing around, staring like us, though when they saw the Danes spilling from the rotting longhouse many of them crossed themselves and hurried off. Dozens of imperial soldiers were running towards the smoke, including no doubt those who had been posted in the longhouse enclosure, which was why we had not been challenged.

'I told you Sigurd had a scheme,' Bram announced proudly as we set off at a loping stride towards the flames, gripping our Frankish spears and shields. I was weak from hunger and the running made my head swim, but Penda must have been just as frail and if he could run then so could I. When we reached the west side of the city the place was seething chaos. Men and women were flinging pails of water into their thatch, hoping to prevent a leaping flame or falling cinder doing to their homes what they had done to so many. Imperial soldiers were amongst the traders and craftsmen, helping where they could, their captains trying to bring some order to the desperate work. But the Wolfpack was nowhere to be seen and we could not understand how they were burning the place.

'Maybe this has nothing to do with Sigurd,' Penda suggested as we ran through the tumult, hoping the soldiers would not notice a bear-like man who could not have looked more like a heathen, and two monks in ragged habits carrying arms. Yet not a single blue cloak challenged us. Beyond the city walls the wind was whipping enormous sheets of flame through the tightly packed timber houses and those gluttonous flames roared like the ocean. The burning wood popped and cracked in violent anger. Then we were clear and I turned, coughing horribly, and saw the first of the threadbare Danes spilling through the houses and out into the pastureland like so many tortured souls.

'Look!' Penda yelled, pointing at a smoky streak whirring through the air. 'That's no fire arrow.' Then the thing tumbled from the sky, leaving a wisp of dissolving smoke against the blue. We ran over to it and to my disbelief I saw that it was a little bird. Then we saw others lying here and there, smoulder-ing amongst the grass. I picked the dead creature up by its feet and the three of us stared, breathless, stunned and coughing. Someone had tied shavings of fur to the bird's back and that fur was charred but still glowing with an ember because it had been smeared with wax and set alight.

'They must have used nets, or Óðin knows what, to catch so many,' I said, nodding towards the forest beyond the boundary ditch. It must have taken hundreds of birds to do what they had done. But Sigurd had known the birds would wing back to their roosts under the eaves of the Franks' houses, and now those houses were burning.

'No one will believe this,' Penda said, shaking his head. 'I don't believe it myself.' Now a quarter of the city was ablaze and the emperor's soldiers were too busy trying to save the rest of it to care that we had escaped.

'Come on,' Bram said as I tossed the poor creature aside. 'They'll come for us soon.' We ran towards the sound of rooks high up in the ash on the edge of the woods, where we knew Sigurd would be waiting.

CHAPTER TWENTY-SIX

SIGURD, BLACK FLOKI AND TWENTY OTHERS WERE WAITING AMONGST the ash. They were dressed for battle and their beards split with smiles when we met them.

'I was wrong when I said you two make good Christ slaves,' Halldor laughed, finding our wretched state funnier than he should have done.

'Hungry, lad?' Sigurd said, pulling a loaf of bread from a sack and handing it to me. I ripped a hunk off and gave the rest to Penda. There was a glint in the jarl's eyes that I had not seen since before the hólmgang, which I put down to joy at seeing his scheme weaving itself into a wondrous pattern. 'You stink worse than a troll's fart,' he said, taking a step back and laughing.

'It seems hard to believe,' I said, 'but the Franks did not invite us to bathe in the hot pools we have heard talk of. The spiteful cunnies.' I was suddenly aware of the fleas biting my skin and crawling beneath the filth-stained habit. I glanced round for Cynethryth, hoping she would not see me looking so foul, but of course she was not there, for this was a war band.

'They won't be wasting water on bathing now, Raven,' Sigurd said, 'not with their arses on fire.' Satisfied, he planted his spear butt into the forest litter and turned to leave, but then he stopped, seeing that some of his men had been alerted by the snap and crack of twigs. We made ready to fight.

'It's all right,' I called, 'they are Danes. They escaped with us.' The first of the Danes stumbled through the trees towards us, their gaunt faces gripped by fear. They looked like hunted animals and did not know whether to come nearer or bolt off into the woods. 'They helped us, Sigurd,' I said. 'And their jarl is dead and rotting.' Sigurd seemed to consider the skeletal, long-bearded Danes in their rags, and the Norsemen looked to their jarl, awaiting his order. 'They will follow you, lord,' I said, 'and they are brave. They must be hard men to have survived in that place.'

'Follow me?' Sigurd said, scratching his golden beard. 'They can barely walk, Raven. These Danes could not follow a stream.' More Danes were joining their comrades so that there were now at least twenty, almost all gasping or doubled over with exhaustion, their hands still manacled. Sigurd picked up the food sack, took a step towards the Danes and hurled the sack to the nearest man. Then he turned and his men turned with him. 'They can come, Raven,' he said. 'But if they are not at the wharf by dawn we leave them to the Franks.' And with that we set off with long strides, leaving the Danes to struggle after us.

It was night time when we reached the wharf. I could wait no longer, and asked after Cynethryth. It turned out that Black Floki and Halldor had been watching for us from the woods when they had seen the mounted blue cloaks with their firebrands ranging across the pasture. There were too many Franks for them to break cover, so they had waited and eventually they had found Egfrith lying exhausted beside a fallen elm, Cynethryth beside him. Knowing they could do nothing for Penda and me, Floki and his cousin had brought the monk and the girl back to the ships.

Egfrith was tending to Cynethryth now in a makeshift shelter before *Serpent*'s hold, for, Olaf told me gently, it seemed that the girl's mind was in a dark place and the monk was trying to tempt it back to the light.

'I will go to her, Uncle,' I said, still trembling from the exertion.

Olaf put a big hand on my shoulder. 'Give her some peace, Raven,' he said. 'Let the monk see to her. She doesn't need the likes of us sniffing around. Get some rest, lad.' I nodded because I did not have the strength to argue. Penda and I and even Bram were dog-tired, and after changing back into our own clothes we collapsed on to furs with handfuls of meat and skins of ale. Sentries were posted and *Serpent* and *Fjord-Elk* were made ready in case the Franks attacked, though the orange glow in the sky to the east told us that they still had other worries.

Sigurd was wrong about the Danes being unable to walk. Somehow, throughout the night and into the dawn, sixty or more of them made it to the wharf. They came as though the river itself had summoned them, as though their wretched souls heard in the gushing water a promise of life and freedom for which they had clawed their way back out of Hel. When the Norsemen saw the strength of will that must have driven these men to reach us, they broke into our supplies and fed and clothed them as best they could and helped them cut off the manacles.

'I wonder how many did not make it,' I said to Penda, thinking of the Danes who even now lay stiffening in the woods between us and Aix-la-Chapelle, wound sickness or starvation having killed them in the dark as surely as any Frankish blade.

'You and Sigurd have given them back their lives,' Penda said, rubbing his wrists where the irons had left their mark.

'If not for Sigurd we would be rotting, too,' I said, thinking of the jarl's incredible cunning in using the little birds to burn the town. It was surely the most ingenious plan ever conceived, though it could have been no easy thing to catch so many birds and tie bits of fur to them.

With dawn came rain, which was bad for us and good for the Franks. A brown pall still hung in the east, mingling with the low grey cloud that slid in from the north to douse the day. The thatch fires would probably be out, but new embers would be growing in the hearts of the Franks and these would soon ignite into the fires of revenge.

Many of the craft moored at the wharf had gone now, their captains uneasy berthing next to so many warriors, even though the Norsemen and the Wessexmen had let them and their crews go about their business. But now, at Sigurd's order, Svein the Red was hacking into the cross at *Serpent*'s prow with his great axe and this was enough to see the last Frankish boats slip their moorings and slide downriver. The Danes were busy preparing their own ships, which, though no *Serpent* or *Fjord-Elk*, were well made and seaworthy, their graceful lines and the carvings on their prows marking them as heathen-made. A man named Rolf seemed to be the nearest thing to their leader and he was doing a good enough job overseeing the checks to ballast, rudder, caulking and sail lines, so that despite their sorry state the Danes might be ready in time.

Penda and I had drunk so much ale and mead, trying to wet our bones, that we were falling down drunk when Kalf and Osten ran from the woods, their slung shields bouncing against their backs and their spears held low. We gathered round to hear their news.

'We've pissed in a bear's cave, lord,' Kalf said to Sigurd. 'The blue cloaks are getting ready to fight. And not just them; the people have armed, too. I am thinking they are not happy that we burnt their houses.'

'That piss-thin Christ slave is leading them,' Osten said, meaning Bishop Borgon, 'and he's even waving a sword around.'

'Pah!' Olaf said. 'I'd wager the bony bastard'll cut his own leg off before he gets here.' Borgon had been itching to fight us since the day Sigurd was supposed to be baptized and now he had his chance. Sigurd glanced at *Serpent*, perhaps thinking of the immense treasure hoard resting in her belly.

'Then now is a good time to leave,' he said. 'Make ready to cast off, Uncle.'

Now that we had really made enemies of the Franks, the only way for us was north, away from their heartlands and the snaking rivers along which they could ambush us a hundred times over. North meant downriver, and on any other day that would mean we could raise the sails, catching whatever wind there was and riding the current. But there was no wind to speak of and there had not been much rain, which meant that the river was sluggish and we would have to row or risk being caught by the Christians. Rowing drunk is not easy. Assuming you do not fall off your bench you really have to concentrate to stay with the rhythm, making sure your blade bites the water and doesn't just knock the spume off the surface. But at least Penda and I were drunk enough not to know how weak we still were, which was just as well, and I think we matched the others stroke for stroke.

In our wake the three Dane ships were moving well too, their shorter oars dipping smoothly, which was impressive given the state of the men who worked them. Rolf knew to push his men hard enough to keep close astern of *Serpent* and *Fjord-Elk*, riding the water we had broken, and because there were three of them they took turns to slipstream us. Luckily for them *Serpent* and *Fjord-Elk* were heavy with silver and arms and rich wares, so that we sat lower in the water than normal and were much slower. It would be unlucky for us, though.

'Your skinny-arsed Danes are rowing well, Raven,' Knut shouted from the steerboard. 'But ploughing a river downstream is not the same thing as ploughing the sea.' His lips were curled in the smile that always rested on his face whenever his guiding hands gripped the tiller which they had worn smooth.

'I hope they get the chance to prove themselves, Knut,' I replied, for none of us knew how far it was to the open sea or what we would find along the way. As for myself, beyond that I knew even less. We had fought great battles, made powerful enemies and woven schemes that Loki would be proud of. As warriors we had earned glory so that the name of Sigurd's Fellowship would carry far, the tales of our deeds weaving around men's hearth fires like sweet smoke to be inhaled by young and old. Our dragons' bellies were so full of silver that we were all rich men now and Sigurd would likely become a king of his people, though he might have to kill a king first. For once out in the open sea the jarl would surely turn our prows north toward the fjordlands. Eventually I would set foot on the rocks these Norsemen talked of so fondly, and I truly believed that when I did the fog in my mind would clear and I would remember. I would know why old Ealhstan had found a heathen knife hanging round my neck. I would know that the fjordlands were my home. For why else had I obsessed with the oaks in the forest near Abbotsend if it was not some seidr memory of searching for the straight limbs from which to make the keel of a dragon ship like *Serpent*? Why did my heart beat with the rhythm of a sword against the back of a shield? Why did my breath measure against the plunge of spruce oars into cold water?

'That was quick,' Svein the Red on the steerboard side said, pulling back in the stroke with his inexhaustible strength. We looked over to see mounted imperial soldiers appear in the hackles of marram grass along the ridge of the east bank. There were five of them, scouts most likely, because they appeared lightly armed. Then, as quickly as they had appeared, the blue cloaks galloped off north in the direction our prows were pointing.

'That won't be the last we see of them,' Penda said.

'Let me see some sweat, lads!' Olaf yelled, for we all knew we were now in a race against the Franks, our oars against their horses, with the river as fickle as a god, favouring us on its straighter courses and the Franks with every bend. We lost ourselves in the rowing, letting bone, sinew and flesh loose in the relentless cadence that is as natural to a Norseman as breathing. But the pace was hard enough to dry my throat, make my heart hammer against my chest, and draw streams of greasy mead-sweat down my face. A quick glance back told me that the Danes were falling behind despite the extra weight in our holds, and I whispered a prayer to Thór that they might find the strength to keep up. For we had given them some poor spears and a couple of hunting bows but little else, and if the Franks caught them it would be a slaughter.

The craft we saw on the river that morning were ploughed nose first into the reeds, their captains having desperately sought to get out of our way. Their crews watched us with awe and fear as we pushed past, grunting in rhythm, our oars beating like wings. Then we began to see folk along the east bank, not soldiers but ordinary Franks, farmers and craftsmen and even women, and this was a bad sign. It meant that the riders had already passed through their villages, alerting them to our flight, and these folk had come to the river to watch. Knowing that we could not risk stopping, some of the Franks loosed arrows that clattered on to the deck or looped over us.

'Bastards,' Penda grumbled when an arrow thwacked into the hull beside him. It was just as well we had mounted our shields along the sheer strake, for these afforded at least those on the steerboard side some protection. The sun was as high as it was going to get when Knut warned Sigurd, who was himself rowing with the rest of us, that two Frankish war ships were preparing to launch from a jetty up ahead.

'This will be a close thing, Sigurd,' the steersman warned. 'They're proper craft, of that I'm sure, but we might get past before they can cast off.' He grimaced. 'The beardless sheep fuckers are excited enough by the look of it.' But Sigurd did not want to risk being caught with every man at the oars and so, even though it would slow us, he ordered us to form a fighting group.

'Svein, Floki, Bram, Aslak, Bjarni, Raven, to the prow,' he commanded, drawing his oar back through its port, 'and you, Penda, you might as well come, seeing as you row like an English girl.' We eight stowed our oars and grabbed spears and shields and hurried to *Serpent*'s prow and I saw that Bragi the Egg was forming his own fighting group aboard *Fjord-Elk*. 'Now row, you whoresons!' Sigurd yelled to those still at their benches, 'row as though your fathers were here!' The first Frank ship had cast off, its oars chopping sharply to take it out into the river. The channel beyond its bow would soon be too narrow for us and the Danes after us to pass through.

'Bishop Borgon is aboard,' Egfrith said, pointing at the banner of red silk flying at the ship's stern.

'Harder, you sons of thunder!' our jarl roared, 'your ancestors watch you now from the high end of Óðin's hall. The All-Father rot your guts if you bring shame on them.' At these words the men roared with effort, with the pain of near bursting lungs, for every man knew that if we got snared up in this river more Franks would come and we might never get out.

But the second ship had launched now and we were not going to make it. I thumped my helmet down and we formed a small Svinfylking, the Swine Array wedge, with Jörmungand at the point, the beast's head having been restored to its rightful place. I thought I saw Bishop Borgon, his thin arm raised as he shook a sword rather than a White Christ cross at the cloud-slung sky.

'Get those shields up,' Bram growled as the first arrows clattered into us and fell on the deck or deflected overboard. Normally we would get close enough to smell what our enemy had eaten for breakfast. Then we would throw grappling hooks and haul the ships together, fighting across the decks as we would on land. Not this time. An arrow thudded into Black Floki's shield and the Norseman turned the shield in. With his sword he chopped the shaft off, leaving the iron head still embedded.

'Half-cocked whoresons are eager to meet their god,' Floki murmured, spitting over the side.

'Brace yourselves,' Sigurd bellowed, then Knut yelled for those on the steerboard side to pull in their oars and *Serpent* veered to port, heeling wildly. But it was not enough, and her prow thumped into the Frank ship's forward port side. The sound of splintering wood tore the air. A roar went up and we threw ourselves to the steerboard side to meet the enemy, hurling our spears if the chance came but mostly keeping our shields up. For the Frank ship with its deeper draught sat high in the water so that they had the advantage of looking down on us. The men on our steerboard side were up now, defending themselves from arrows shot from deathly close range, but those on the port side were still at their benches, gripping their oars, unable to join us for fear of tipping *Serpent*. A Frank leant forward, yelling orders to his fellows further along, and quick as lightning I rammed my spear into his gullet, twisting it fiercely before yanking the blade free. An arrow tonked off my helmet and Svein the Red swung his great axe into a man's shoulder, hooking him, then wrenching him over the sheer strake so that he fell between the ships, smashing his face on our hull before disappearing beneath *Serpent*'s belly. Sigurd cast his spear, which took a fat Frank in his fleshy neck, and the man screamed like a woman, clutching the haft as he fell back from view. Arrows thudded all around, sprouting from *Serpent*'s deck and men's shields, and some even stuck in brynjas or were fouled in cloaks. I heard another great thump and knew that *Fjord-Elk* had passed portside and struck the second Frank ship. But a river doesn't stop flowing just because men want to kill each other, and we were moving clumsily, sideways with the current, both vessels slowly but inevitably turning their bows downriver. Kalf staggered back, an arrow in his shoulder and his face a grimace of pain, and Halldor's face was sliced open so that the flesh of his cheek with its bristling beard hung free, revealing the jawbone as his eyes widened in horror.

'Uncle, get this shit bucket off us!' Sigurd yelled, slamming his sword against a Frank shield. Then I saw Cynethryth at *Serpent*'s stern and the short Englishman Wiglaf pleading with her to stay behind his shield. But the girl was pointing eastwards and when Wiglaf saw what had caught her eye his face said it all. At least three, but maybe more, smaller Frankish vessels full of armed men had cast off from the jetty and would soon pour arrows and spears into us from the steerboard side.

A spear streaked from the enemy throng and bounced off my shield boss. Then Olaf and Bram Bear were amongst us, hefting oars which they rammed against the enemy hull, leaning, heaving with all their might, trying to push the Frank ship away. Grabbing oars Bothvar and Yrsa joined them, so now instead of fighting some of us covered those men with our shields because they were horribly exposed. Asgot, Ulf and Gunnar were hurling the poorer-made spears we had collected, trying to keep the Franks' heads down, but neither we nor the enemy had thrown grappling hooks, which made me think these Franks were not so sure they wanted to be tied to us any more than we wanted to be tied to them.

The Danes had caught up now and began trading arrows

and spears with the smaller Frankish boats, which was good for us, but Rolf was wise enough to keep his prows pointing downriver to avoid getting ensnared amongst the Franks. There was water now between *Serpent* and the enemy ship and Olaf spurred his party to one final, enormous effort, bawling at them to shove off from the Frank ship which, he yelled, had been made by the blind half-wit sons of a one-armed troll. Bram and the others needed no encouragement, and with the increased distance between the ships half the men on the port side grabbed their oars and took to their benches whilst the rest of us each chose a man to cover with our shield. Then the oars were in the water and we were moving, arrows and some spears still clattering around us.

'Raven!' someone yelled. 'Raven!' And I looked round to see the giant, Bishop Borgon's bodyguard, ploughing his way through the Franks to get to the stern where men still fought, the ships being as yet no more than an arm's length apart.

'What does that big bastard want?' a Wessexman named Ulfbert said, sheathing his sword and grabbing a spear which he hurled towards the giant Frank, just missing his face. Then Borgon's man was standing on the sheer strake, Norse arrows whipping past him, and even though the gap between the vessels had widened he seemed about to jump for it.

'Overgrown arse maggot must be crazy,' Penda said, wide-eyed.

'I am here, you big dung heap!' I yelled, standing up on the mast step and thumping my sword against my shield. 'Here, you boar-faced troll fucker!'

The Frank saw me and a grin spread across his face even as a Norse arrow bounced off the iron scales at his shoulder. Instinctively, the Norsemen at *Serpent*'s stern stepped back, creating space before the tiller, their shields raised still, though the missiles had thinned now. Then the giant bent his powerful legs and threw out his arms and leapt, landing with a thump aboard *Serpent*. It was an impressive jump given his size and all his war gear and it was a sign of respect that the Norsemen had allowed him to make it when they could have lined the deck and bounced him to the dark depths.

'He's mine!' Svein the Red bellowed, striding towards the Frank, who spared his former ship not a single glance as our oarsmen at last put some water between us. The Franks lined their ship's sheer strake, staring at us from beneath their helmets, their swords and spears still in their hands. Then orders were screamed and they took to their own row benches, thrusting their oars into the river to take up the chase.

'No, Svein,' I spat, gripping Bjarni's shoulder for he too had stepped forward to fight the man who had taken his brother's head. 'This fight is mine.' *Fjord-Elk* was free, I saw, the ship she had been fighting backing oars now, not wanting to get caught between two dragon ships, and this allowed the Danes to slip past so that we were now the trailing vessel. The giant grinned at me, beckoning me forward with the short axe in his left hand.

Svein frowned at me and I knew he wanted to command me to stay out of his way whilst he introduced the Frank to his two-handed, long-handled axe. Instead the Norseman bit his tongue so as not to make me seem less in the Frank's eyes, though his own eyes protested loudly enough. 'This big lump of troll snot has already felt my blade bite his flesh,' I said. 'Now I'm going to spill his rancid guts and throw them to the fish.' I hefted my shield and strode towards the Frank, my guts twisting with fear. I suddenly needed to relieve myself and could have filled a bucket. This warrior who carried no shield was enormous, as big as Svein, and he moved with the confidence of a man who kills without breaking stride. Furthermore, by jumping aboard *Serpent* he must have known he had spun his own doom, meaning he was either fearless, stupid, or crazy, none of which helped me much.

'Take him, Raven!' someone called from his row bench behind me.

'Gut the whoreson!' shouted another, amidst a rolling thunder of encouragement as Norse and English arms pulled the oars.

I glanced at Sigurd, who grimaced but nodded, perhaps knowing that I had to face this man to make up for the death of Bjorn who had given his life for mine. That was why Bjarni had stepped back too, however much he hungered to kill the Frank himself. This was my fight and everyone knew it. But I could not have been more afraid if I had been lashed to a boulder and thrown overboard.

Black Floki, Svein, Bjarni, Penda, Olaf, Sigurd, and Knut at the tiller were the only men not rowing now. As a sign of respect for the Frank's bravery they sheathed their swords and gathered by the rearmost row benches, which were unmanned at present, though Bjarni placed himself and his shield in front of Knut to protect the steersman who was busy with the tiller. The Frank ships were holding off our bow, their captains, and Bishop Borgon I shouldn't wonder, keen to watch the coming fight, though I imagined Borgon was spitting teeth at his man's foolhardy action. Even if the giant killed me, the bishop must have known he needed to find a new bodyguard.

'Cut him a new arsehole, Raven,' Black Floki snarled.

'Rip the ugly dungheap's balls off, lad,' Olaf said, scratching his bird's-nest beard.

I whispered to Óðin to be with me and I kissed my shield's rim. Then, setting my jaw and swallowing the lump of fear in my throat, I stepped forward.

CHAPTER TWENTY-SEVEN

THE FRANK HAD A FACE THAT LOOKED AS THOUGH IT HAD BEEN carved from a rock and I knew how Beowulf must have felt when he faced the monster Grendal. I remembered Black Floki telling me that when fighting a man much bigger than you you should go for his legs. 'Cut the fucker's legs,' he had said, 'and it's as easy as chopping down a tree.' *But trees don't fight back*, I thought to myself now, wondering how I could get to this Frank's legs without being speared or chopped in half by his wicked-looking axe.

'God be with you, lad,' Father Egfrith called, making me grimace, for I wanted Óðin with me, or brave Týr Lord of Battle, not Egfrith's puny god of peace.

'Come, little man,' the Frank said in English through black teeth. I stepped forward and his spear streaked for my face but I got my shield up in time and it struck with incredible force for a one-handed thrust. There was little room to manoeuvre, meaning I could not lead him around to leg-tire him. That spear came again and again but each time I managed to stop it with my shield, which was desperate work. But the Frank was smiling still as though it was no more than a game. His

297

arrogance bit deeper when he reversed the spear, using its butt to hammer my shield and even scything the shaft through the air like a harvester, slamming into me from the right and left, sweeping for my head and legs. I swung wildly, trying to hack into the shaft but hitting nothing but air. He struck my right shoulder a blow that numbed the whole of my sword arm and it was all I could do to keep my fingers curled round the weapon's grip as I stepped back, watching for his next move.

The next strike put a dent in my shield boss and the one after that glanced my left eye, gouging the flesh and making it stream. A finger's width to the right and the spear's butt would have crushed my eye socket. Then the Frank was too slow pulling the shaft back and I scythed my sword into it, knocking it aside, but he stepped inside and swung the short axe. I flung my shield up to meet it. There was a terrible crack as it cleaved into the limewood and stuck fast, the blade jutting through a hair's length from my forearm.

The Frank grunted and tried to yank the blade out, but my arm was in the straps and the axe head was stuck. With a roar the giant almost lifted me off *Serpent*'s deck, my bones rattling as he tried to wrench the axe free, then in frustration he hurled me, shield, axe and all, against *Serpent*'s hull. I landed with a clatter, the wind knocked out of me. The shield was too unwieldy with the axe in it, so I slipped my arm from the straps and clambered to my feet, aware that I had not so far given much of an account of myself in front of my jarl. My friends were still yelling encouragement, their faces red with fury and blood-hunger, for they bristled to tear into this huge Frank who was surely going to finish me now.

'Kill him, Raven,' Sigurd said, a steel-hard edge to his voice, his blue eyes burning into me. 'Kill him now.'

I felt Cynethryth watching too and suddenly I knew I would rather die there and then on the end of the Frank's spear than be beaten around the deck like a flea-bitten dog for all to see.

298

'Your mother must have screwed a bull to spawn you,' I said to the Frank, removing my helmet and laying it on the deck. My left eye was streaming, making it difficult to see, and blood ran into my beard. My hair was lank with sweat and my saliva as thick as frogspawn. 'I have never seen such an ugly beast,' I went on, grinning at the Frank. 'I saw your father grazing in a field yesterday and he was even more ugly than you.' I did not know if the Frank could understand me, but he knew I was insulting him all the same and his lip curled as his grip tightened on the spear. 'My friend Svein will enjoy using your skull to drink from,' I said, unpinning the brooch at my right shoulder and letting my cloak fall to the deck. Then I threw my sword at the Frank's feet and the Norsemen groaned or yelled at me, but I just stood there, the breeze sending Cynethryth's raven feather floating in front of my face as *Serpent*'s oarsmen pulled her down the river.

The Frank's face twisted with disgust and loathing, his long moustache quivering and his eyes ripe with shock as he realized I had cheated him out of his saga story. The truth that he had made that jump, knowing he wove his own death, only to face not a warrior but a gutless worm who would not fight him was too much for such a man.

'Fight him, lad!' Olaf yelled.

'This is shame, Raven,' Svein growled in warning. 'Fight him.'

I threw my arms wide, inviting that great spear, and I felt Sigurd's eyes boring into me. Then the Frank screamed a curse and lunged and I twisted to the right and the blade scraped the mail along my ribs and I flew at him, smashing my right fist into the left side of his unprotected throat. He staggered back, then clubbed me with the spear, sending me reeling.

'Hit him again!' Olaf shouted. 'Hurry!'

But I did not hit him again. I stood in front of Black Floki, watching the Frank and waiting.

'Fight him!' Svein bellowed.

Then the Frank's eyes rolled and his huge body began to convulse. Spittle flew from his mouth. He raised a fluttering hand to his neck in confusion and disbelief and his fingers found something there.

'Thór's hairy arse,' Svein said, shaking his red head.

'A Loki trick if I ever saw one,' Olaf agreed, seeing the brooch pin more than half buried in the Frank's neck. The giant yanked the pin from his flesh and a fountain of dark blood came with it, pumping out then in a rhythm twice that of *Serpent*'s oars hitting the water. But still the Frank somehow kept his feet.

'Finish him, Raven,' Sigurd commanded.

'Here,' Floki said, handing me his wicked long knife. I nodded, taking the knife, then walked up to the Frank, who was now leaning against the sheer strake, still unaccepting of his end.

'I am Raven,' I said, and he spat in my face. Then I stuck the knife up into his guts, beneath the iron fish scales of his armour, and I sawed the deadly sharp blade across and heard a gush of escaping air from below. Hot guts poured over my hand and thumped on to the deck, and I smelled his shit and piss. 'I am your death,' I said, looking into the Frank's eyes as the light in them faded. Then, even though it would mean losing his fine arms, I pushed him over the side. His glistening purple gut rope followed and he splashed into the river, his white face staring up at the sky.

'I'll clean it,' I said to Floki, gesturing at his knife.

'Do it well,' he said with a grim nod, fetching down his oar from the oar tree and going to his bench. The rest of us took our oars and joined the others rowing, for the Franks were coming hard again now, lashed by Bishop Borgon's tongue no doubt, and we had no wish to tangle with them again. Kalf was already rowing, even with the arrow still in his shoulder, but Halldor was lying by the mast step, his brynja sheeted in blood and his face half hanging off. Cynric, one of the Wessexmen, lay trembling beside him, his throat ripped open by a Frankish spear, and others had gashed faces and wounds to their upper bodies; the sight of them all was a harsh reminder of the danger posed by the emperor's high-sided ship.

It did not take us long to catch up with the three Dane ships and we looked across at their crews, their thin arms all bone and sinew at the oars, their straggly hair and unkempt beards giving them the desperate look of starved animals. But they were rowing well and I felt proud of them, for I had shared a little of their suffering and knew what they had been through in that rotten longhouse that was now smoke on some breeze and a pile of cooling ashes. I was rowing well too, the trembling that had filled me draining away with each stroke and being replaced by sheer exhilaration that filled my stomach like hot iron. For I had survived a fight that should have been my doom. I had faced a great and brave warrior and sent him to the afterlife and I silently thanked the All-Father and Loki, too, knowing that it must have been one of those gods who gave me the low cunning idea of using the brooch pin as a weapon.

'I'm disappointed in you, Raven,' Svein the Red called from the port side, his huge arms making light work of the rowing.

'That overgrown troll would have squashed me if I'd fought him fairly,' I said in my own defence, to some murmurs of agreement.

'Ja, I know that,' Svein replied, 'but I thought you were going to give me his head so I could drink from his skull. Olaf said that's what you told the Frank.' The Norsemen laughed even with the Frank ships ploughing downriver after us.

'I'm sorry, my friend. I'll get you another one,' I said. 'Bigger.'

'Any bigger and we could stick oars through the eye holes and row the thing,' Olaf said. 'Now shut your mead holes and row.'

The river narrowed and for a while its willow-lined banks were less than half a bow-shot apart as we pushed hard on *Fjord-Elk*'s stern, riding this breathless gush, our oars dragging the churning, spumy water past. Ulf and Gunnar behind him lifted their oars and began to wriggle out of their brynjas and I thought to do the same, for it was hard work rowing in mail. Besides, I did not think the Frank ships would catch us in this stretch of river even if we all stopped rowing. But Olaf, still rowing himself, yelled at them to get their blades back in the water.

'No one takes off his brynja until I say he can,' he added. 'What do you think those riders were doing whilst we were butting heads with that tub back there? They were riding, weren't they, Ulf, you witless wonder! And by now they'll have told half the captains of Frankia to slip their moorings and prepare us a warm welcome.'

So we rowed, sweating in leather and heavy mail, and it was not long before Olaf was proved right. Hearth smoke, brown against the grey sky, told us we were nearing a large village or town, even before we saw the long jetty with its breakwater protecting twenty or more craft from the current. Three of those craft belonged to the emperor from the looks of their fighting platforms and near identical builds, and two of them were already brimming with spearmen as we approached. Olaf, Bram, Svein and Penda took their oars to *Serpent*'s bow in order to fend them off, though luckily this time we slipped past, a few arrows thumping against the hull. However, it was clear they saw *Serpent* and *Fjord-Elk* as the richest prizes for they turned their bows downriver and joined the chase, ignoring the three smaller Dane ships in their wake who were now stuck between them and the five Frank vessels behind them. Townsfolk lined the quay, cheering the emperor's soldiers and clamouring for our doom.

We were getting tired. The third imperial ship had cast off

now and these three new enemies were fresh to their oars, which made up for their vessels' being slower than ours, even with our holds crammed with heavy silver. None of us spoke, each man lost in his own pain, shoulders and arms burning, chest as tight as *Serpent*'s halyard. We ploughed the coils of the river, mindless of the occasional arrows shot from both banks, which clattered amongst us or lodged in the deck and hull, and I summoned Cynethryth's face to my mind, because I had not seen her properly for days, now she stayed in the shelter by the hold.

'Bastards are like dogs . . . that don't know when to stop chasing their own tails,' Penda muttered through gritted teeth some hours later. His was the bench in front of mine and the deck around that bench was dark with sweat.

'Bishop Borgon knows . . . how much of his emperor's silver . . . sits in our hold,' I replied, gasping for breath. 'He'll chase us . . . off the edge of the world.'

By dusk it was clear that before chasing us off the edge of the world the Franks intended to drive us out to the open sea, which could not have been too far away by then, because gulls wailed somewhere above in the orange sky and the fields on either side had given way to marshland and mudflats where geese bickered and birds waded. The water had become brackish too and the rowing had become a little easier, as though the river here was tidal in our favour, being sucked out to the estuary.

The river curved round to the west and we passed a ruined, scorch-marked fortress on the south bank, which reminded us that we were not these Franks' only enemies. Then to our surprise our pursuers fell back, even letting the Danes pass with only a flurry of arrows to sting them as they went. I was amazed that the Danes were still rowing and could only think that their sleek ships were even more well made than they appeared, cutting through the water like arrows through the air.

'They've had enough!' Gunnar shouted, raising coarse cheers from parched Norse and English throats. We eased off the oars, our rhythm slowing to half speed as we dared to hope that we had at last escaped Bishop Borgon and the blue cloaks. My screaming heart began to slow and I took the chance to drink from the water skin by my feet. Then we came round the next bend, where the river narrowed again, and saw two small fortifications facing each other from either bank. They were squat wooden buildings built atop foundations of worked stone sunk deep into the flood plain, and both were crowned with a rampart and palisade. Men with bows were scuttling up ladders on to these ramparts, their captains' yells percussive across the water between the slap and plunge of our oars.

'Get ready for rain, lads,' Olaf warned, meaning that we could expect a shower of arrows. Then we heard a thunderous, bone-crushing sound, a grinding noise the like of which I had never heard before. Facing *Serpent*'s stern I could not twist round fully to see what was making it, but I could see Knut's face, which was enough to sink my heart.

'Sigurd!' Knut yelled. 'You need to see this.' Many of us lifted our oars and turned to look. The forts were open on their river sides, which had seemed strange until now. Now, with utter horror, I realized what those buildings were for and I saw the source of that terrible noise that sounded like an iron dragon grinding its teeth. Emerging from the water on both banks was a huge chain, rusty and dripping and forged of links as big as your fist. Inside the forts men turned great windlasses, drawing in the chain so that it would soon stretch taut across the river. When it did we would be trapped.

'Row hard, men!' Sigurd shouted, hurrying back to his row bench and gripping his oar. 'Harder than you have ever rowed!'

'But Sigurd, there's no time!' Olaf exclaimed. 'That chain will be up. It'll crush us to kindling.'

'Hold your tongue and row, Uncle,' Sigurd yelled, pulling with his enormous strength. 'And be ready when I give the word!' And though I agreed with Uncle and didn't think I was the only one, I worked my oar as though Óðin himself was choosing men to fill the benches on his own dragon ship, because Sigurd was my jarl and I believed the gods loved him. The blood pounded in my head. My world closed in around me, but through the mind-fog I heard Sigurd bawling orders from his bench and I readied myself. I heard arrows too, whopping into the water beyond *Serpent*'s prow, and I knew it would be any moment now.

'Move!' Sigurd bellowed. I pulled in my oar, letting it clatter to the deck, then grunting with effort I picked up my row bench, my sea chest full of silver and arms, and together with the others I half ran, half stumbled in my brynja to *Serpent*'s stern, into the press of men, as arrows thwacked off the hull and bounced off our mail. *Serpent*'s bow lifted, Jörmungand leaping into the twilight sky. The terrible thumping scrape of the chain against *Serpent*'s belly filled the world. Those nearest the mast step were flung towards us, spilling their heavy chests. Then, as soon as the momentum was spent, Sigurd roared again and we lumbered forward, tripping on discarded oars and thumping into each other, hurrying to the bow as *Serpent*'s stern now surged up and she slid down off the chain.

'Thór's teeth, we did it,' Olaf said, wide-eyed. No sooner were we over than we looked back to watch *Fjord-Elk* follow our lead and we winced to see her prow leap and hear the scrape of the chain across her hull. But she made it too and we cheered Bragi the Egg and his crew. Now it was the Danes' turn.

'They're small and light enough,' Penda said hopefully as we returned to our places, puffing like bellows.

'But they don't have the weight on board to lift the bows

over,' I said, putting my oar back through its port and waiting for Olaf to order the first stroke.

'Those skinny-arsed lads have done it!' Bram Bear cheered.

'Not bad for Danes,' round-faced Hastein offered with a grin. And then the second Dane ship was over and we all cheered again and yelled insults at the Franks watching from the riverbanks. But then we were silenced by a splintering crack that ripped across the water like the voice of doom. The third Dane ship had looked to be over but lacked the momentum to slide all the way down and had come to rest with the chain beneath its hull, just rearward of the mast. That crack was the ship's back breaking and the cries from the men on board told us that they were all done for.

'Poor bastards,' Wiglaf said, shaking his head. The Dane ship was in two pieces now and both were spilling screaming men into the fast-flowing river.

'Why don't they go back for them?' Yrsa Pig-nose asked. 'Why don't the others go back?'

'That's why,' Osk replied, pointing to the chain leading into one of the forts. It was slack again now, meaning that the Franks were sinking the chain so that their own ships could pass. Meanwhile, another Frank ship was launching from the bank, meaning we now had a whole fleet after us.

'Hey!' Olaf called and we plunged the oars into the river and began to row again. Sigurd pulled on his oar, his back bulging and his sweat-soaked golden hair stuck to his brynja. That chain should have stopped us. Then the Franks would have killed us. But Sigurd had come up with an outrageous plan and it had worked, and I shook my head at the sheer brazen impudence of it. I have since heard men talk of our escape that day and attribute it to themselves or others. Some of these are lies woven by men who talk a good saga tale – men who have heard of Sigurd's Fellowship and steal their stories the way rats steal scraps from a king's table. But maybe some other men *have* tried the same thing, and maybe many of them even now lie with the crabs.

The smaller Frankish boats stopped only to spear the drowning Danes and that was terrible to see, for those brave men deserved better deaths than that after what they had been through. But all we could do was row, which by now was backbreakingly hard. We were exhausted and Sigurd must have been tempted to fight the Franks whilst we still had enough strength to lift our swords. But he also knew that our enemies would surround us, hurling their missiles from all sides, and it would be a desperately hard fight. So we rowed, the sun having rolled into the west and now sinking fast. Even as the light drained from the world and the first stars glinted through tears in the high clouds, we rowed. And we prayed we would make it to the sea.

CHAPTER TWENTY-EIGHT

THAT NIGHT WAS DARK ENOUGH TO BRING WITH IT THE RISK OF running aground on a sandbank or rock, but light enough for Knut to be able to keep *Serpent* near the middle of the river where the danger was less. At any other time I would have happily exchanged places with him, working the tiller instead of breaking my back at the oar, but not that night. He could keep it and good luck to him, I thought, watching his face, which was as tight as a cat's arsehole, his brow heavy with the great burden of steering us down that gloom-filled course towards the sea.

We were in a daze, rowing as though the rhythm was as deep a part of us as our heartbeat or our breathing. We did not talk, having no strength for words, but simply pulled the oars, muscle and bone imitating the movement our eyes saw in the body in front. You would not have thought it possible to go on like that, but it was possible. What's more, the Franks were still coming too. With our oars' up stroke we could hear theirs chopping the river somewhere in the darkness behind us.

Dawn brought mist. It rose from the water and curled out along the marsh and mudflats above which lapwings streaked and dragonflies hung, blurs of colour against the reedy grass. We were half dead at our benches. *Serpent* was a ship of draugr men, the corpse-pale undead hauling our oars as relentlessly as the coming of Ragnarök. But whereas the gods' doom still lay in the fog of the future, ours would be upon us before the sun was fully risen.

'What's to be done, Sigurd?' Olaf rumbled, the big Norseman a spent force at his oar, his neck barely able to keep his head on straight. 'The whoresons'll soon be on us like fleas on a dog.' He was right. The two biggest Frank ships had been gaining all night and now they were almost close enough for a strong man to sink a spear into *Serpent*'s mast. As for the Danes, there was no sign of them and I thought they must have given up or been overcome in the night. Perhaps they had simply died of bone-tiredness at their benches, their death ships even now nosed into the reeds and waiting silently for the ravens.

'We'll fight the whoresons,' Bram Bear called, his words dry as old wheat husks. But how could we fight? We could barely lift our eyes let alone our war gear. Even with my leather gambeson beneath my brynja, the mail had rubbed my shoulders raw, and as for my legs, I was not even sure they would carry me if I stood.

Being lighter, *Fjord-Elk* was up ahead and though I was sure she would come back to help us fight the Franks, it would only be a matter of time before the other imperial vessels turned up to join the fray. Our situation was desperate and Sigurd's silence sent those roots of doom creeping even deeper into our souls.

'We fight,' the jarl said eventually, stirring a smattering of agreement.

'I'd rather die in a fight than at the fucking oars,' Black Floki said, and no one disagreed.

'Wait, Sigurd,' I shouted, 'there is another way.' There was a dragging silence but for the dip and creak of the oars, so that

I began to wonder if I had spoken aloud or merely thought to. Then Sigurd told me to join him at the prow, so I stowed my oar, relieved to find that my legs still worked, though they were full of knots and cramps. Men raised their heads as I passed and the hard pride in their eyes was cut with hope that weighed on me heavy as a wet wool blanket. I glanced back and saw the prow and the first beating oars of the lead Frank ship emerging from the mist. I ducked as an arrow streaked past and felt ashamed when I turned back to Sigurd, who had not even flinched.

'Well, Raven,' he said, braiding his hair for battle, his scarred face haggard and his blue eyes doused of their usual fire, 'what Loki scheme are you weaving?'

I almost shook my head and turned round, for I was sure Sigurd would not go for my plan. I was not even certain I wouldn't rather take my place in the shieldwall and face the Franks than go through with what had weevilled into my mind. But, though Sigurd was preparing to fight, his eyes held the same fragile hope that I had seen in the others, as though he half dared to believe that I knew of a way to see his Fellowship escape an ill-fated end. So I told Sigurd my scheme. And his face crumbled like dry snow.

'Forget I said it. We could fight instead, lord,' I said. 'If we hit them hard, bleed them quickly, they might turn tail before their friends get here.'

Sigurd put a hand on my shoulder and shook his head. 'It is a fine scheme, Raven, a Loki scheme if there ever was one. Thank you.' He moved past me towards the hold. 'Now help me, lad.'

We pulled the oiled skins back to reveal *Serpent*'s hoard. In the middle stood the five barrels of silver Alcuin had paid for the peace we had soon sent up in flames. Around those barrels were all of our other treasures too, from cloaks, brooches and torcs to antler, amber and whetstones. With Sigurd I began pulling these things out and laying them on the deck as the men at the oars forward of the hold looked on dubiously. Then we began to pull up the planks that lay across the floor timbers to keep the cargo safe from the seawater that inevitably seeped up into the ballast. Sigurd called Bjarni over and had him help me lash these planks together and when we had finished we had four small rafts, each big enough for a man to lie on with his arms outstretched, though his arms from the elbows down would get wet. We laid thick furs across these rafts and then we hefted the barrels from their safe place and tipped their glittering treasure across those furs so that the coins and hack silver were half buried amongst the long reindeer hair.

Some of the men moaned and complained, at last realizing what was happening, and word spread from man to man. But Sigurd ignored them because like me he could see a knot of Franks at the prow of their ship making ready with ropes and grappling hooks.

'We must hurry, lord,' I said, hefting a pair of solid silver candlesticks and laying them across the carpet of coins on one of the rafts, at which Bjarni groaned mournfully.

'Svein, help us,' Sigurd said, and the big Norseman stowed his oar and came over, sweeping his sweat-soaked red hair back from his face.

'Thór's balls, this is a black thing, Sigurd,' he griped, taking one side of a raft with Bjarni as Sigurd and I lifted the other side. Then he shot me a sour look which I ignored, grimacing at the enormous weight of the thing as we carried it to the side and rested it for a moment on the sheer strake.

'Good men died for that,' Orm grumbled, leaning back in the endless rhythm.

'And so will you if you don't hold your damn tongue,' Olaf barked. Then we lowered the raft over the side and dropped it the last of the way and the river half swallowed it so that one of the candlesticks rolled off and shot like silver lightning into the dark depths. But to our relief the raft was buoyant and did not tip but rode the current like a leaf in a stream, the old sodden reindeer pelt dark and slick as otter skin.

'Now the others,' Sigurd said. One by one we lowered the rafts, setting our great hoard, our hard-won treasure, adrift. Almost immediately our speed increased, the loss of weight raising *Serpent* so that there was less of her in the water for the oars to have to pull along. But that was only part of my plan and Sigurd and I rushed to the stern to see if the other part would work too. I was appalled to see that Bishop Borgon's ship was still coming and I was about to beg my jarl's forgiveness when Sigurd began to shake. I thought he was about to rupture, to turn on me spewing rage like Ragnarök for losing his hoard. But then a great peal of laughter burst from him, rolling like thunder.

'Óðin passed the mead horn round when you were whelped, Raven,' he said, then pointed beyond the bishop's ship. 'Can that red eye of yours see that?'

Then I felt my own wolf smile crack my dry lips as the second Frank ship burst from the mist, its prow nosing towards the north bank where one of the treasure rafts lay fast, tangled amongst the roots of a half drowned willow. Another of the rafts was stuck in the muddy shallows further along, whilst the other two bounced along our wake.

Yells carried to us from both Frank ships as the silver-greed took hold on the trailing ship, sinking its needful teeth into men's souls.

'You see!' Sigurd yelled. 'These Christ slaves are not so different from other men after all. They would rather fish silver from the river than fight Óðin's wolves.' And then, perhaps because Bishop Borgon knew he could not fight us alone, or perhaps because the glint of treasure shone in his eye as brightly as it did in lower men's, the lead ship's oars slowed their beat, her steersman turning her bow towards another of the dawn-gilded rafts. We rowed hard still, until the sun was out of the east and the Franks were somewhere far behind us, weighing their hoard, we wagered, and slapping each other's backs for having chased the heathens from their lands. Then, as though the gods had run out of torments for us and were themselves in want of a rest, Njörd sent a decent breeze from the south-east, which combined with the westward snake of the river was enough to let us haul up the sail and stow the river-worn oars.

Serpent's sea-stained, faded red sail snapped and bellied, spraying clouds of dry salt over those forward of her as men struggled wearily out of brynjas and laid furs by their journey chests. Having dipped into his bag of herbs and gathered some clean linen, Asgot was trying to put Halldor's face back together while the Norseman sat clutching a Thór's hammer in each white fist and made a low thrum in the back of his throat, one knee bouncing incessantly. Olaf drew the arrow from Kalf's shoulder and Kalf roared something about Hel's huge reeking cunny before he passed out, blood streaming down his white-scarred chest and belly into his breeks. The Wessexman Cynric, whose throat had been ripped out by a Frank spear, was a stiff white corpse now, staring up at the circling gulls, his beard full of blood. His friends wrapped him in two cloaks and tied the ends, determined to bury him in the Christian way as soon as we made landfall, though Olaf warned them that Cynric would be thrown over for the fish the moment he began to stink. Other men saw to their own hurts and time would tell whether the wound rot would claim any of them. Sigurd himself took the tiller, sending Knut with his face as haggard as an old crone's off to rest. Black Floki kept watch from the prow and but for a couple of others we all curled up and slept like dead men. I had never been so exhausted and I did not dream as such, but rather my spirit-self pulsed, weaving in the deep soul-darkness some monotonous, never-ending pattern as though it yet rowed.

Eventually I woke to the screech of gulls and the smell of food, a mouth-watering broth that bubbled in a great iron pot suspended above the ballast, sternside of the hold. Arnvid's smiling face was wreathed in steam as he stirred, and I sat up, squinting through crusty eyes at those who sat drinking mead and talking in low voices, and those still asleep. Then I became aware of another sound above the creak of timbers, the spit of the cookfire and the cry of seabirds. That sound was the vast murmur of the open sea and I struggled up like an old man, gripping the sheer strake, and my stomach rolled over itself because we were no longer in that cursed river but had made it out to the unfettered ocean.

'You looked dead, lad,' Penda said, 'and no one had a mind to rouse your mean-tempered shade for fear of being killed with a brooch pin.' He grinned, scratching the short bristles on his neck, then he chuckled and I glowered groggily, a heartbeat later joining him.

'Where are we?' I asked.

'River spat us out there,' he said, pointing to the mouth of the river where fresh water and salt water churned and hissed, sheltered by a rocky prominence whose summit was stained white with ancient bird shit. We were moored in the lee of an island and *Fjord-Elk* bobbed beside us, anchored and boulder-tied to stop our hulls bashing against the rocks. I was amazed that I had slept through the berthing and told Penda as much, but he shrugged, running a hand through his tufty hair, and suggested with no little sarcasm that perhaps great cunning exhausted a man as much if not more than fighting did.

I ignored that. 'No sign of the blue cloaks then?' I asked, imagining the Franks greedily grasping for that floating silver like old men at whores' tits.

Penda shook his head. 'But that lot made it out by some miracle,' he said, thumbing over his shoulder. I looked round to see the two surviving Dane ships moored in a cove off our port side, their crews little more than shrouded shapes as they slept still, perhaps dreaming of the freedom they had won.

'Frigg's tits,' I said, shaking my head. 'I thought we had seen the last of them. They must have slipped past when the Franks were scratching their silver itch.'

'I like to think that Bishop Borgon and his men killed each other over it,' Penda said, pursing his lips. 'That much silver would set brothers at each other's throats.' One eyebrow rolled like a caterpillar. 'Or it could be that one of your gods fished the Danes up and dropped them gently in that cove. Who knows? But they're here now and they have you to thank for it,' he finished moodily.

'Getting over that chain was Sigurd's cunning, not mine,' I said, wanting to get past the subject of losing our treasure as we had got past that chain until I knew how it sat with everyone. Penda half acknowledged this with a nod. 'How's Halldor?' I pressed on.

He grimaced. 'He's going to make bairns cry wherever he goes,' he said. 'The poor swine'll be even uglier than you, lad, but he'll live, I think. Same goes for Kalf, so long as the wound fever doesn't get him. Leaked enough blood to float a knörr, that one, and lived. The wound should have washed clean with any luck. Christ, I'm hungry.'

'Me too,' I said, my stomach grumbling in complaint, then I nodded to the smoke-shrouded cauldron above the ballast stones. 'Sigurd's open-handed tonight, allowing a fire aboard. And the mead skins are not putting up much of a fight by the look of it.'

'Your jarl is trying to swill down the lump that's sticking in everyone's throat at losing a silver hoard like that,' he said, and there it was, bobbing to the surface again like a dead fish full of air. 'It's enough to make any man belly-sick,' he went on, shaking his head. Then he must have felt the cool shade of my black look, for he shrugged casually. 'But a hoard is no good to the dead.'

'No, Penda, it's not,' I said, the words hot and sharp as hammer scale. 'And I hope the others have the half-sense to see it that way too.'

'Them?' he said dubiously. 'They're Norsemen, lad,' he crowed as though that was all the answer I needed.

We did not think it the wisest idea to linger at the mouth of the river where the emperor's ships were likely to pass sooner or later, and so the next day we let the wind push us west to a cluster of low islands tufted with long grass and ringed with birch trees. Having studied the journey patterns of a pair of cormorants, *Fjord-Elk*'s captain, Bragi, had known we would find the skerries after a short sail, and he was right. So we moored up, us and the Danes, because Sigurd announced we were to hold a ting, a gathering, that dusk in which men could speak their minds openly. The mood was iron heavy and dark as Hel's arsehole. I had not seen the Fellowship hold a ting before and Bjarni told me they never had for as long as he had been oath-tied to Sigurd.

'Sigurd has always spoken for us all and that has been good enough for me,' he said, sitting on a rock whittling a stick to a sharp point the way his brother Bjorn often did. Bjorn never had Bjarni's skill for intricate work and could never have carved a rune stone like the one his brother had raised in his honour. But now Bjarni seemed to take comfort in the crude work his brother had enjoyed. 'Sigurd has invited that skinny-arsed slash of piss to join the ting and speak for his own,' he said, nodding towards Rolf, the man who seemed to lead the Danes now. 'It's bad enough they've got their beaks in our food. You should have seen them with their heads together. Looked like scheming to me.'

'Next they'll be sluicing their gills with our mead,' Bram moaned from behind a tree where he was squatting. 'Danish goat fuckers,' he said, finishing with a thunderous, rolling fart.

'At least they won't get their hands on our silver, seeing as it's now either sitting with the catfish on the riverbed or lining the Franks' journey chests,' Kjar griped, shooting me a look from those close-set eyes of his that would pierce a fine brynja. And I thought to put it to *Fjord-Elk*'s steersman that he would almost certainly be reeking of the corpse-stink by now if we had not sacrificed the silver. But I knew there was no point and so I skulked off, muttering to myself that I had known hounds with more in their heads than some of these whoresons.

I cursed the island for being so small when I climbed up a yellow moss-mottled rock to get a view of the sun sinking in the west and came across Father Egfrith on his knees in the grass talking to his nailed god. He turned and arched his brows as though his prayers had been answered sooner than he had expected. 'Ah, Raven my boy,' he said with a sniff, 'I'm glad to see you.'

'No wonder your god loves thralls and whores, monk,' I said spitefully, pushing my tongue against the inside of my cheek crudely. 'They're always on their knees too.'

He frowned and climbed to his feet, sweeping downy hawks-beard seeds from his habit. 'Keep your filthy appetites of the flesh to yourself, young Raven, and we shall talk man to man.' But I did not want to talk to him and so I turned to make my miserable way back down to the ships. 'Wait, lad,' Egfrith said. 'I want to tell you something.' Thinking I had nothing better to do I decided I might at least stay a while, if only to fling a few more insults the monk's way. Then I wondered if he meant to talk of Cynethryth, whom I had still not spoken to since the night we had broken her out of the convent. And even then she had not seemed to know me. So I walked back over to Egfrith and looked out across the agitated slate-grey sea. Low evening light dappled the water with silver, taunting me for what we had lost, and the salt-dried wind whipped my braids against my face. 'Your idea saved us all,' he said.

I hid my surprise behind a cold face. 'You are the only one who thinks so,' I said, 'apart from maybe Sigurd, though I am thinking even he regrets it now.'

'They are simple men, Raven, which is why they make easy prey for peddlers of superstition and iniquity. Why they close their eyes to the true path.' He shook his weasel head. 'Hounds have sharper wits than most of them.' He smiled then. 'But they know the truth of it, lad, I am sure of it.'

'Careful, monk,' I warned him, 'I am one of those *simple men.*'

'Ah, but you see, I don't think you are, boy,' he said, raising an accusing finger, 'which is why you are a particularly interesting challenge to me. Your jarl too, come to that. If I can prise you and Sigurd from Asgot's clutches then there is hope for the rest.'

'Asgot?' I spat. 'I have no love for that flea-bitten old wolf.' I thought I saw the lightning bolt of a smile flash behind his eyes at that.

'Because he killed your friend the carpenter,' Egfrith said with a thoughtful nod.

'Because he's a twisted hemlock root and has no honour,' I said. The monk seemed to consider this, the greying tufts of his hair shivering like duck down in the breeze around the terrible livid scar left by Glum's sword. The sword which now sat at my hip. *Fjord-Elk*'s last captain had carved a chunk of flesh from Egfrith's head – bone too perhaps – but somehow the monk had lived to torment us all like a biting horsefly.

'The ting is happening soon,' I said, taking in a great lungful of the chill air and thinking that winter would soon be upon us. Then I turned and walked away.

'I came up here to pray for her,' the monk said. 'She is lost, Raven. She is lost and Asgot will find her.'

I did not turn round, but kept walking across the rock, through bristling patches of grass and down through clumps of sea kale. And the monk's words, *She is lost, Raven*, repeated in my head like waves against the shore, or spruce oars churning a Frankish river.

CHAPTER TWENTY-NINE

I FOUND CYNETHRYTH SITTING ALONE IN THE WIND-SHADOW OF A large rock on the east side of the island. Beside her a small fire crackled and gave off an acrid filthy yellow smoke that caught in my throat. Burning hair. She had cut off her hair and thrown it into the flames where it blackened and withered and stank.

'How do you feel, Cynethryth?' I said gently, sitting down beside her. She was looking out past the half-submerged rocks where the currents converged, throwing the water up in spumy gouts that never made the same pattern twice, towards one of the much larger islands we had sailed past. We had not moored there for such a place was likely to be inhabited and thus patrolled by the emperor's war ships. I asked again, thinking that her mind must be elsewhere. I turned to her and she to me, and my flesh shivered then so that to my shame I had to look away. Her eyes, once green as spring buds, were hard and dim as old ice, and the skin of her face stretched tight over the bones, giving her even more of that wildness, that peregrine look, than before. 'What did they do to you, Cynethryth?' I asked, watching the burnt threads of her hair pulse red and black in the flames. I felt those eyes penetrate me like a biting north wind. Somewhere a carrion crow croaked three times, its rough voice grating against the sea-bashed rocks.

'Never ask me that, Raven,' she said. 'Never ask me for I shall never speak of it.'

I was chewing my lip. Hard. 'One day I will kill them,' I said clumsily, feeling like a boy stealing a man's words.

This poor motherless girl. Ealdred had poisoned her life with betrayal and the killing of her brother Weohstan and now he was dead by her hand. Then the Christ slaves had beaten her and done Óðin knows what other unspoken things so that now the girl's soul seemed still locked in some foul place, preyed upon by vicious memories that clung like ferrets on a rabbit's neck. I cursed myself for ever having saved Ealdred from Asgot's knife, though I had only done it for Cynethryth.

'Have you eaten?' I asked, wanting to touch her but lacking the courage.

'I'll eat when I'm hungry,' she snapped, her glower deflecting me like a shield. 'I'm sorry,' she said, the words empty as chaff. 'Please leave me, Raven.' She forced a smile that did not crack those ice eyes. 'I will come to you when I am ready.'

I stared into the flames awhile, searching for words that were as elusive as the smoke drifting up towards the dark clouds floating westward after the sun, their bellies black as pitch. I used my knife to shift the unburnt ends of the sticks into the flames, then stood as a ragged skein of geese cut south-west, screeching like a loose wheel on Thór's chariot. 'The ting will have begun,' I said. 'Are you coming?' But Cynethryth was somewhere inside those flames and I might as well have been the other side of Bifröst the shimmering bridge. So I left her and made my way back to the moorings, glad to be away from the stench of burning hair.

'Hold on to your coins, lads,' Bram Bear said, feigning panic and clutching the leather scrip at his belt when I came amongst them. 'Young Raven will have them off you and in some fish's belly before you know you're silver-light.' Some of the men laughed, but others frowned at being reminded, not that they could have forgotten.

'I'm steersman on the wrong fucking ship,' Kjar jeered. 'I should have jumped aboard one of Raven's silver rafts and taken it back to Norway.'

'You could not find your way back to Norway,' Olaf said, stirring more taunting and laughter and carving a scowl in Kjar's hound-narrow face. I looked over at Rolf, who now wore a good cloak over his rags, a gift from Sigurd to bolster his pride now that he was amongst the legendary sword and axe men of Norway. He had the look of an honest man did Rolf, if not a war leader or even much of a warrior. He had cut his red hair and beard short, as had all the Danes after washing off the filth of that Frankish prison, and now he stood saying nothing but watching much, which a wise man is wont to do amongst strangers. The rest of the Danes, some thirty-six men in all, sat a little distance off amongst the birch, moss, and grass hackles further up from the water, watching us with parched, sunken eyes, like dogs waiting beside the mead bench to be fed.

I looked around me. 'There's no watch,' I said to Penda. Every bearded face, every hard sword-Norse and Wessexman had gathered there in that hollow on the flat rock, where men's voices were made louder so that you ought to be sure what you wanted to say before you said it.

'Uncle told me that Sigurd wants every man to have his say,' Penda replied, his eyebrows arched. 'A rare thing in a lord. I'll wager he regrets it afterwards.'

'All but a few of these men are oath-tied to Sigurd,' I said, 'and must follow him back to Frankia should he choose to return there.'

'Oaths can wear thin as the sole of your shoe, lad,' Penda said with a grimace as Olaf called for tongues to be still.

'Jarl Sigurd son of Harald will speak first,' Olaf announced, fiercely eyeing the hard men around him, challenging them to dispute their jarl's authority. 'Those of you who have words in your bellies and edges to sharpen will get your chance. The Dane will get his chance, too, and you'll let him speak or you'll have me to deal with.' Then Olaf stepped back and nodded to Sigurd, who nodded back.

Sigurd stepped into that circle of warriors and stood for a while, his left hand resting on his sword's pommel and his right clenched behind his back. He eyed his men, those he had fought beside, with whom he had killed and bled, and they eyed him back, proud men all.

'When we left our fjords in the north we were empty like a sail on a still day. We had nothing but our own boasting which filled my hall like farts and made our women hoist their brows and shake their heads, for they thought our words men's bluster, nothing more. We had all been boys listening to our fathers' and grandfathers' tales of times when Norsemen were hard as seasoned oak and Týr-brave. Like me you tired of white-haired men's saga tales and thirsted for your own.' Men grunted and nodded at this. 'Patiently, we filled our boasts with sweat, building *Serpent* and *Fjord-Elk* whilst our women worked their fingers to the knuckles weaving their sails. We raided in the north and burnt many halls until we could afford ringmail and fine swords and helmets. Then we ploughed the whale road and I knew that the Norns had been as tireless as our womenfolk, for our story began to grow as we killed our enemies and filled our journey chests.' There were more affirming ayes and murmurs.

'We lost good men, too,' Ulf said, and men nodded and touched their amulets and sword hilts for luck.

'Too many, Ulf,' Sigurd agreed, holding the man's eye until Ulf withered beneath that gaze and looked away. 'Now you are pride-hurt. The shame comes off you like a stink,' Sigurd said with a grimace. 'But know this. If we had not set our hoard adrift on that ill-lucked river we would have had a hard fight of it. There would be many empty benches and oars left in their trees.' I felt eyes on me but I kept my own on Sigurd. 'But that means nothing to you who stand before me, for a man rarely counts himself amongst the dead, some not even when they are stiff in the ground.' Some chuckles at that. 'We have lost the hoard that would have seen us return home with a greater saga story than our fathers ever told, and I know this is a hard thing to swallow. It sticks in my throat more than any man's and I will fight the one who says otherwise.' No one said otherwise. 'Oh, we have some silver and good bone and enough trinkets to please our womenfolk. Frigg knows they would strut around the market like hens, flapping their wings and clucking to get noticed. But it is not enough for us. Our fame-thirst clamours for more than cold silver and gold torcs. If we skulk back to our hearths now and let our swords and brynjas rust the gods will turn their backs on us and it has all been for nothing. I am no farmer. I am a sword-Norse and my saga tale has many twists yet, like the world serpent devouring his own tail. This is why I will not be going home.' With that Sigurd stepped back, showing that it was the turn of others to wag their tongues.

'I have lost good friends,' Halfdan said, scratching his beard nervously. 'And it seems to me that they died for nothing seeing as *Serpent*'s belly is empty but for the stuff you would find at any decent market.' Some rumbles – though whether for or against I couldn't tell. 'I would go home to my woman and bairns while I still can. Maybe farming is not so bad. Valhöll can wait for me.'

'The All-Father's favour blows in and out like the wind,' Asgot said. 'If you don't know this by now you are a fool.'

'You a farmer, Halfdan?' Black Floki spat. 'You couldn't grow a hard-on.' Men laughed at that, but Sigurd held up a hand and they held their tongues. These men had fought for Sigurd in the kingdoms of Mercia and Wessex. They had bloodied the valleys of Wales and bent their backs to Sigurd's oars, and they sensed the weight of the moment.

'I understand, Halfdan,' Sigurd said with a nod.

'But we are oath-tied, lord,' Arnvid said. 'No man here would break that bond.'

'Most of you are oath-tied to me,' Sigurd agreed, looking into men's eyes as though through them he could see their hearts, and maybe he could. 'But as from today that old oath is dead. I release you all from it. Those who wish to go home are free to go.'

Men's jaws unhinged and those who had been drinking mead stopped, dragging their hands across their beards in stunned silence. Sigurd's blue eyes remained calm but his heart must have been hammering as ours were.

'If there are many who want to return, they can take *Fjord-Elk* and their fair share of the silver and booty we have won,' he said, 'for there would not be enough strong arms left to take both ships where I am going.'

Every man's eyes were riveted to the jarl at those words.

'Where is that?' Bragi the Egg asked, dark-browed.

'Miklagard,' Sigurd said, glancing at Rolf the Dane. There were murmurs at that word and I could tell that some men had heard of the place.

'Miklagard?' Bram said, his hairy brows woven together.

'It means the great city, Bear,' Olaf said.

'I know what it means, Uncle,' Bram growled, 'but where in Óðin's hairy arse is it?'

Sigurd nodded to Rolf and the Dane stepped forward, half starved and vulnerable as a goat amongst wolves. 'It is far away in the east,' Rolf said, looking at Bram but speaking to all. 'In Grikaland. Some call it the Golden City for even the buildings are made of gold and the streams run with molten silver.'

'Then the folk of Miklagard must be thirsty,' Bothvar said,

scratching his balls as men laughed to relieve the tension, for the air itself was taut as a full sail.

'I have seen coins from this city and they shine like Freyja's eyes,' Knut put in, straight-faced as a woman washing her man's breeks. 'And an emperor rules there whom the people worship as a god.'

'Not another fucking emperor!' Yrsa Pig-nose complained, shaking his head.

'You know the way to this city?' Bram challenged the Dane.

'I do not,' he admitted, raising a chorus of jeers and moans. 'But there is a man amongst us whose brother claimed to have been there.'

'And where is this brother?' Pig-nose asked, craning his neck to search amongst the Danes. 'I expect he's the one in the golden brynja with the silver cock and giant rubies for balls.'

'He is dead,' Rolf said simply. 'He died with many others in Frankia.' He glanced at me, for I had known the horror of that stinking hall where men lay in their own filth and rats and insects chewed on their pride. 'But perhaps his brother can show us the way, for Trygve spoke of his journey before he died.'

Bram shook his shaggy head, his face, battered as an old shield, gloom-shadowed. 'We are not the Fellowship we were,' he said. 'Too many have gone.' Some uttered in agreement.

'My Danes will join Sigurd,' Rolf said. 'We do not want to return to our women with empty sea chests.' I could barely believe my ears and I was not alone. When had Sigurd and Rolf cooked this up? Then I remembered Bjarni saying he'd seen them together. *Looked like scheming to me*, he had said.

'Your Danes are half dead!' Bram accused Rolf. 'You are lucky Sigurd has allowed you to join this ting, for you are nothing.'

Sigurd let the insult stand and watched Rolf to judge his response.

The Dane, swordless and stupid, squared up to Bram, which showed he had pride at least, if not brains.

'We rowed as hard as you did and with empty bellies,' he said. 'Our hearts are as strong as yours and our limbs will catch up given meat and mead.'

It was well said and men nodded as much. Even Bram had nothing more than a 'pah!' for him before he turned back to Sigurd.

'I am with you, Sigurd, you know that,' he said. 'And if the sea road keeps my ears out of reach of Borghild's biting tongue then I am happy. I'll row you to this Miklagard even if the houses are made of mud and the rivers run with piss. But even better if there is silver at the end of it. I'll not have Danes pilfer fame meant for me.'

'Those who come with me will swear a new oath. The Fellowship will be re-forged,' Sigurd said. 'We will raid and we will fill our journey chests. We will carve our wyrd in the land, raising rune stones to mark where we have been. One already stands in a forest in Frankia and I doubt those beardless Christians will forget about us in a hurry.' He grinned his wolf grin then and I noticed that Bram was half smiling too, and I wondered if he and Sigurd had arranged for him to voice those doubts so that other men would feel that their own misgivings had been led out, all the while with Sigurd holding the reins. I would not put it past a man with Sigurd's low cunning.

'I am with you, lord,' Svein the Red boomed, thumping his spear's butt into the earth with a little too much show.

'You know me, Sigurd,' Olaf said with a shrug of his broad shoulders. 'I go where the wind takes me and where there is no wind I will row. You'll have my oath.' Sigurd nodded curtly, as though it was only natural that men such as these would follow him even to the world's edge.

'I am not going home until I have filled Bjorn's journey chest as well as my own,' Bjarni said.

Then the others declared their loyalty, each man out-boasting the next and claiming riches he had not yet clapped eyes on, so that even those who had had half a mind on going home forgot all about it and even Halfdan laughed at his earlier talk of farming. Old Asgot went off to scatter the runes and Black Floki simply nodded at Sigurd, his eyes dark and edged with malice, and Sigurd nodded back, for that was all that was needed between those two.

'I go where you go, lord,' I said when Sigurd looked at me.

'Of course you do, Raven,' he said, 'for we have a saga tale to weave and we are joined, you and I.'

So I joined the others greasing their tongues with mead so that they might glide across the words of the oath we would give, and perhaps so that the speaking of them might weigh a little less, for an oath is a soul-heavy thing. And then I walked to the west side of the island to watch the sun slide into the grey sea, holding my breath in case I could hear the far-off hiss of fire quenching itself, like a red-hot sword plunged into a barrel. And in Valhöll the gods laughed.

EPILOGUE

IT'S ALL RIGHT, GUNNKEL, YOU CAN BLINK NOW. WASH THOSE MILKY opals of yours before they dry and shrivel like an old man's breeks snake. Take a breath, Arnor, and whilst you're at it have one for me, would you? It has been a rare ride, hey! You all look rough as oak bark and wild as trolls – as if you've ridden the back of this night in Thór's own chariot pulled by the goats Tanngnjóst and Tanngrísnir and them with their tails on fire! But I suppose it's only natural you should sit there like that: mead holes catching flies, eyes round as pennies and hair on end like hedgehogs. For it is some saga tale and don't I know it. Most of you, I'd wager, have never been past your own privies. There are rocks that have travelled further. There are snails that have seen more of the world than you hearth lovers. Ah, don't give me that sour milk face, Hallfred. I heard you only found Hildr's honey pot because she drew you a map, isn't that right, Hildr?

So, you now have your teeth in the tale and a taste for those old days. And yet the feast is still to come. As you see, I am no young Baldr, wet behind the ears and boasting my first bristles. I have lived a very long time and you have only just jumped aboard. We are barely off the jetty and into the fjord. The mooring ropes have yet to snake out their kinks and the anchor is still weed-slimed. Listen to me trying to spit it all out before it's too late! You would have thought age and patience were kinsmen, but I have found them to keep company less as the years roll by. Come again tomorrow night, but only if you have the stomach for it, for the next chunk of my tale will take some swallowing. Like the ox-head Thór used to bait his hook when he went fishing for Jörmungand. As for today, if the chill in my bones is anything to go by we will have snow before dark. We'll be breaking ice on rain barrels and bringing our animals inside. Perhaps it will be the beginning of Fimbulvetr, which will mean many kin-slayings and battles and all sorts of degradation, the chaos that begins Ragnarök. If that is so I will be ready. You think I'm a hoary old wolf who has outlived his wyrd, but you know my sword is still wicked sharp. Only a fool lets his blade dull or waits to watch the rust spots appear before cleaning it.

Tomorrow night then. If we are not all snow-tombed by then. And bring me some of that wine you've got stashed away, Olrun. Even I will need to take the edge off that tale's telling.

ABOUT THE AUTHOR

Having Viking ancestors himself, **Giles Kristian** believes that the story of Raven has always been in his blood – waiting, like the Norsemen, for the right time to burst upon the world.

Inspired by both his family history and his storytelling heroes, Bernard Cornwell and Conn Iggulden, Giles began writing a thrilling tale of an English boy's coming of age amongst a band of marauding warriors from across the grey sea. This novel, *Raven: Blood Eye*, was published to great acclaim, including a wonderful accolade from Bernard Cornwell.

Giles currently lives in Leicestershire where he writes full-time, though he enjoys nothing better than working in his family cottage that overlooks the mist-shrouded Norwegian fjords.

To find out more about Giles and his writing, visit his website: www.gileskristian.com